SEVEN HILL CITY

SEVEN HILL CITY

something like a novel

b. thompson stroud

iUniverse, Inc.
New York Lincoln Shanghai

Seven Hill City

iUniverse, Inc.

For information address:
iUniverse, Inc.
2021 Pine Lake Road, Suite 100
Lincoln, NE 68512
www.iuniverse.com

ISBN: 0-595-27850-7

Printed in the United States of America

For Zuckerman's Famous Pig.

For Hayao, Jesus, Akira,
and the men who shaped me.

For the woman who always told me
I was her favorite.

For me.

"*You are the object of the affectionate solicitude of your mother and father. Then you have been born a Christian. When you reflect that the great majority of men are born in heathen lands in dense ignorance and superstition it is something to be thankful for that you have the light that giveth life.*"

—Samuel White, prosperous piano manufacturer.

"*I feel most ministers who claim they've heard God's voice are eating too much pizza before they go to bed at night, and it's really an intestinal disorder, not a revelation*"

—Rev. Jerry Falwell, Lynchburg, VA

Contents

The Bible, the Holy one, says that when the "End" finally stops being near and gets here, it will be in a city of seven hills. If illustrated Christian literature has taught me nothing else, it has taught me that Satan will grow his hair out and fill out his facial hair to pass himself off as Christ. He and his angels will settle down in a rebuilt temple to rule for three and a half years, and the world will eat it up. Then, out of the blue, the real Jesus will do a double take, say "wha wha what?" and we'll all be doomed. All of the Christians meeting the criteria will ascend to Heaven and the ones who haven't painted the walls and set up the beds for Jesus in their hearts will be left behind.

The problem with this is that history associates four ancient world capitals as having "seven hills:" Byzantium, Babylon, Jerusalem, and Rome. In one of the more morbid and defeatist coincidences of humanity, all of the founders of these cities searched out locations in valleys and between rivers where they could glance up from their hut or ziggurat or and be surrounded by the world influence and fame that comes along with being host of our eternal damnation. Even today the major Christian landmarks of the world rest silently between seven hills. Twelve year old Jesus taught in a temple in Jerusalem. The Pope lives in his own tiny country in the middle of Rome. A statue of Jesus stands watch above Rio De Janeiro.

Four hours south of Washington, D.C, there is a city called Lynchburg. Sixty-five thousand people. They shop in stores and live on normal streets. They can see Jerry Falwell, minister and Speaker of the House for Christianity, walking in the mall. They wave to him, and most of the time he waves back. We went to the same high school, he and I, he in the forties and I in the nineties. In the grand scheme of legendary towns Lynchburg is a dot, a flesh colored-dot that can only be seen if you look closely. Unless you've lived there or can be told, you can never understand how we feel, waiting for something to happen, knowing that when Jesus really does show up, fake Jesus or no, we will see him first. Lynchburg is not a normal city. There is a man in town who has been hiccupping for sixty-four years. In 1958 a factory exploded and covered downtown in six inches of popcorn. Lynchburg is home to a NASA "turning station," home of rocket engines that are fired when Earth's rotational speed needs changing.

God lives in the heart of every born again Christian, but God lives in my hometown.

September

CHAPTER 1

Staring down at the little reflective puddle of water at the bottom of the toilet I can see her face, which is weird because I don't really have any identity problems. Tenth grade Spanish class gave birth to this ritual, when a girl with flippy hair and breasts carved by old Greek men in sandals responded to my childish affections with a resounding, "I don't date white guys." If she's still the same her eyes are almost blue but are more yellow and her teeth smell of smoke. Her skin reminds me of this porcelain, actually. I begin to daydream about the one I was compensating for; the girl in the graveyard with the big eyes and ratty white hair; the inconsequential girl that inspires poets to become melodramatic and shoot themselves. I wipe some of the vomit from my chin and smile.

They don't have bathroom stalls in graveyards, which I think is a crucial mistake. If I stand by his coffin long enough I start to feel the rumbling in my stomach and wonder if the ritual would help bring him back. That's great logic, thinking that by jamming my index finger into the back of my throat my friend will have somehow miraculously not blown his brains out of his ears. Working in logic like this, and understanding that it is complete bullshit, is one of the joys of being twenty-two years old. I get to stare back at moments in my life like tenth grade Spanish class and rationalize my stupidity until it sounds poetic enough to start a novel with. I get to stare into holes in the ground and see my friends lying there and not blow my own brains out of my own ears. I have small ears, too, which would make that extra difficult.

My shoulders are broad and my morale is low, which makes me perfect for the job of pall bearer. When I graduated from high school I thought I'd be dating supermodels and using millions of dollars from various movie studios to blow myself on the silver screen. The idea of wearing an ill-fitting sport jacket and hauling my dead friends up slippery hills never crossed my mind. Sometimes during Spanish class Curtis and I would laugh about how our lives would eventually be so much better than this one day. Between verb conjugations we would cast meek glances at `the girls we didn't have the nerve to talk to; between sentence diagrams he would pass notes about Tasha Mills, the girl of lowered privilege who sat, feet on the seat, two chairs in front. Curtis was tall and lean with cropped blonde hair and a square jaw, the ideal man in the eyes of society and popular culture. In his mother's eyes he was a place to pound her fist, a ways and means for income when the pot money ran out. In Tasha's eyes he was an awkward mess who deserved many things before he deserved the warmth between her supple thighs. In my eyes he was a great friend who never really thought highly enough of himself and hung out with losers like me, chubby kids with greasy hair and acne problems. Curtis couldn't ever see himself through his own eyes, so he put a gun between them and poof, there he went. An interesting postscript to this creative association is that I'm the one who carried him up the hill and put him in the hole in the ground. I keep wondering about the whole worms stereotype, but I learned in biology class once that earthworms have five hearts, so Curtis should be okay.

It's easy to imagine his eyes rolling back in his head because I saw him do it so many times during lunch, when I'd launch into one of my delusional rants about how I was going to get up enough nerve to ask Aranea Cavatica out on a date. "Date" might be pushing it, I'm pretty messed up when I get giddy. I probably went on and on about holding her hand, skipping through meadows with her, and riding unicorns around. Curtis would always bark out some pessimistic anecdote about how Tasha didn't know he was alive and I'd just ignore him and go on daydreaming. Those daydreams were great because I was tall and lean like I am now and I could sweep her off of her feet to the pulsating rhythm of a hit soundtrack. She got out of band in the middle of our lunch period and would walk by my table on her way to Latin. This gave me the break I was looking for, my chance at pheromone romance if you will. I would always watch her until she made eye contact with me, and then I'd lower my head and fondle my spork around in the square pizza as she walked on by. I would regret those days if it weren't for all the wonderful lunch geometry experiences.

Sometimes after lunch my nerves would begin to twitch so I'd race off to the boys bathroom for some of that ritual expunging, but I'd get second thoughts when I'd get there and find all of the woodshop kids smoking. I'd look at the stalls, then I'd look at their mullets, and then I'd turn around and stumble away. High school bathrooms have nasty floors that leave suspicious marks on your knees, plus I didn't want those kids to know that I had the girl eating disorder.

I'd go home and the popular culture icons I held, and at times still hold, so highly would betray me. On channel four, Arnold suspects that Kimberly has an eating disorder when his slender sister is secretly gorging himself, but not gaining any weight. Arnold seeks Mr. Drummond's help in confronting Kimberly with her problem, and the family comes together to help her fight the eating disorder, bulimia. Happy ending. Flipping to channel eleven Blossom suspects that Six is bulimic. Happy ending. Flip. Mrs. Garrett helps Sue Ann come to grips with her self-esteem before a big date. Flip, flip. D.J. is working out too hard and not eating, and Uncle Jessie is concerned. Flip, flip, flip. Happy, happy, happy. After a while I just hurl the remote across the room and sit there on the couch helpless, partially because I realized that my problems were rotting me from the inside and partially because I had to walk all the way across the room to pick up the remote. According to television everybody had an eating disorder, but I was the only one I could see squeezing tears out of the corners of my eyes because dinner was coming up too hard.

"She's really special," said Melissa VanOverloop, my friend and bizarre admirer from Aranea's sixth period Art class. Melissa would sit across the table from Aranea and stare at her through her milkshake-thick lenses and bemoan her existence. Melissa would go about drawing fairies with giant eyes and colored-pencil wings while Aranea created masterpieces; grand paintings of impossible landscapes, calligraphy poems of unnatural significance, portraits of John Lennon. Melissa's hair looked like a tattered rug. Aranea's hair looked like a thousand balloon ribbons, flat strands cascading downward into perfect ringlets, colored like water with a twist of lemon. "I think she has a lot to offer," Melissa would say, before lowering her head and fumbling away from me.

"That girl is a freak," said the jocks with sloping foreheads and felt letters on their breasts. This species includes the blue-eyed-messy-haired Alpha Males who would comment on how her teeth are just a little too big for her mouth, and how she's got one freckle in the center of her chin. "It's weird," they'd say, clutching trophies and trophy girlfriends, "you two would be perfect for each other." They'd laugh and punch me in the arm,. then walk away playfully grabbing tight butts in tighter jeans as I walk away wishing I could've given them a dragon uppercut for insulting her. But I didn't. Sometimes I still wonder if it was the hair gel seeping into their brains that caused them to have such a bent sense of taste. The girls they stared at, or, more accurately, the butts of the girls they stared at, all looked the same, from close or far away. They all had names like "Kristy" and "Katie" and "Jennifer."

Mr. Woodford, fourth period Latin teacher and editor of the Brookville Bee-Line magazine, described her as a "fine girl" and a "great student," and advised me to write less about her and more about the junior varsity girls volleyball team who went eight and six despite losing their equipment manager and two starting players to Mono. "The ability of Coach Brown to keep the Lady Bees' spirits high is a testament to her twelve years as athletic director!" When he wasn't looking I'd backspace over that and type "Aranea Cavatica's arms are so long that her elbows rest comfortably at her waist. Her neck is long, her eyes are big and green, and her upper lip is the same size as her bottom lip. There is an unbearable earnestness to her beauty, and it bothers me." Woodford kicked the plastic wastebasket clear across the computer lab when he caught me and ordered me to get back to work. I'd backspace again, but I didn't mind, because I couldn't think of any description that does her justice anyway.

None of those people are at this funeral, which cements the idea that even in my flashbacks I am all alone. Melissa moved to California to meet and fornicate with her Internet boyfriend a few months ago, the jocks are off to college and busy date raping, and Woodford is kicking trashcans across rooms full of people I'll never meet. They've all gone off to the recesses of my memory and I couldn't care less. I look around to see if she is here, because she is always here. Every moment of consequence we've shared since the first time I stared into the reflection of her eyes and saw myself has taken place at one of these gatherings. I want to take a few moments to contemplate how morbid the idea of falling in love with a girl who keeps showing up at all of your funerals is, but I'm caught off guard by how I feel in love with her via the moisture in her eye sockets and forget all about it.

Maybe it was less about the moisture and more about her kindness; how she walked a good two hundred yards away from a funeral service to hug me when she didn't even know me. Her cheeks were stained with how sorry she felt for me. My grandfather had a stroke while testifying on the joys of God's love and fell into the lectern. He sat in a wheelchair in a pool of his own refuse for six months. He couldn't speak for four months and couldn't hear for three. God loved him enough to take him away after that and my family was left in a depressed funk of confusion and questions of faith. My family, who loved my grandfather dearly and pulled me arms first into Christianity from birth, sat silently around the hole in the ground watching him go down and talking about how sad they all were while I sat on a wet, grassy hill and cried. My Dad hugged my Mom. Grandmother sobbed into her Bible. Aranea Cavatica wrapped her frail little arms around me and held her hands together over my heart until I felt better.

The little girl looked as if she was cut from somewhere else and pasted onto the funeral procession. The tears in my eyes greedily refused to give up their spots in the weeping process and I could not see her until she had enveloped me, unkempt and lopsided curls draping my shoulders and neck. Her fingers laced timidly to keep my heart from breaking my chest. The first words she ever said to me are lost in the recesses of my mind, because I was too surprised to listen closely and too busy trying to figure out who she was to want to listen at all. After a few moments the hug began to seep in, and my heart slowed. I remember trying to ask her who she was, and where she came from. The words were flawed and confusing to my tongue, so they were birthed prematurely and died in the oxygen tent.

"It's okay, you don't know me," is what she said. "I fell out of the sky," she laughed. "I landed on a pile of grass and now my butt is wet." She was ten years old and I was twelve. The sky was off-white and I've never forgotten it.

The summer sky was gray and scarred as black as tar across the clouds the next time we were there, huddled together in the wet grass a hundred yards from my grandmothers tombstone. Gloria was buried on a Sunday. I was seventeen and working my way out of the spandex waistline. It was raining that morning. My Grandmother was the most unbelievably wonderful stereotype of what the perfect grandmother should be; making homemade Christmas cards for me every year with her last ten dollar bill crammed inside, making cornbread and coleslaw on Sunday afternoons, teaching me about Saul's redemption and how to be the kind of person I should be on Sunday mornings. She had broad shoulders that shriveled and folded into cold and purples the further I drifted from her. When Aranea's shoulders rested on mine I lowered my chin to her slender forearms and noticed that she had my Granny's touch; delicate and forceful at the same time. I forgot to ask her what her name was, or ask her where she lived. Her hair was prettier then, longer and combed with hints of a faded yellow dancing along the edges. I was happy that her beauty was becoming real. She hugged me harder that time because she knew what I was going through, or because she didn't want to slip and get grass stains on her pants. Either way I was glad that she was there holding on.

I had not seen her in five years, and even now the moments between the burials seem like seconds. Four weeks later during a warm, eleventh-grade

September I began to feel the imprints of her elbows on my shoulder and smile even when she wasn't there, which was always. Moments would stammer up to me while sleeping and drive their icy fingers deep into my brain, awakening me with the same kind of picayune pondering associated with mainstream teenage angst. I wondered who she was, why she was there, why she hugged me, what the word "picayune" meant and why I hadn't studied for the vocabulary test. Then one day, scratching my forehead with the eraser of my pencil, I glanced and through the glass noticed her pushing a giant cart full of televisions down the hallway. It was her. She was here. She was outside pushing televisions and I was here surrounded by cheerleaders and steroid monkeys and had no way to dramatically press my face to the glass and scream her name. Then I scratched my head again and realized that I'd never actually gotten her name. I thought about how small-minded I'd been. I always managed to pass the vocab tests in the strangest ways.

I made a decision then and there to find her and let her know how much I appreciated the limited amount of the her that I knew. I rushed out of English class and into the hallways looking for her, bounding up on my toes to peer over the heads of the countless unimportant students not allowed in my romantic ecosystem. She was gone and I sat down Indian-style in my biome and waited for her. Two years and seventy-two square pizza-sporkings later I was still waiting, partially because of my dismal failure at nominal puberty, and partially because I was a geek with a girl disease. I counted the days because they were counting down towards my graduation and I'd lose her all over again. I counted the sporkings out of hapless teenage desperation.

I had the photograph from the ceremonies stuck to my computer monitor until the little piece of scotch tape got little hairs all over it and started looking like a Band-Aid. Curtis and I are suddenly transformed into masculine super-stars adorned in gaudy burgundy and gold robes, displaying laminated substitutes for our diplomas-on-order. She is there too, like she never is, two fingers raised for victory. The part of me that isn't a complete idiot assumed she was there to film the festivities for the yearbook video or to support friends. The other part of me saw her as the divine explanation to why I'd been forced through such a ridiculously unimportant high school term: "The Big Payoff." Graduation was my moment to shove the space where the Presidential gold seal would go on my diploma when it arrived in everyone's face and wave the banner of accomplishment whether four-hundred thousand other kids waved it along with me or not. For once I did what everyone else in the world did. I sat around and was bored out of my mind until they decided I was good enough for the stamp and the paper. There I was, the winner. The champion. Watching her walk away with a smile on her face through my tears was the greatest moment in my entire life. If I hadn't seen the grotesque bulging belly of the girl from my Spanish class waddling towards a blue-collar sports car to embrace the Hispanic food server who filled her with the miracle of life, I would've cried forever. It made me want to throw up, but I laughed instead.

Two events lead to my admission to college—my application essay, which consisted solely of a poem announcing the heinous revenge I would plot on the school and it's alumni if I weren't admitted and was forced to be homeless for the rest of my life, and the "one word I would use to best describe myself:" Compensation. The dean of admissions thought it was a revelation and threw the papers on his desk high into the air. I sat in the same tweed clothes I'd worn to my grandmother's funeral and stared as he jotted down notes onto loose-leaf paper about my potential, my "creative blessings," and how I'd be wasting myself in Law School. For the next seventeen months he would randomly show up at my dorm door with papers in hand, giving me the scoop on where all the in-crowd English majors were getting together and how grand of a learning experience it would be for me, the compensator. He'd find me in boxers, Indian-style on the futon watching professional wrestling and eating salt-and-vinegar potato chips. I'd stare towards the doorway and he'd go into rapture, mumbling to himself about the brilliant way that miracles happen every day. He'd trot away into his infinite faith and I wouldn't even get up to shut the door.

I spent most of the months with a film major with horrible taste in movies named Auburn. Auburn hid behind dark sunglasses pushed up harshly against the bridge of her freckled nose and waited out the duration of classes. We spent most of our nights sitting Indian-style on the picnic table outside of the girls dorm, discussing nature themes in Miyazaki films. Sometimes I helped her bleach and gel the tufts of red hair into clumps and spikes of platinum. One humid night, lying beside her in a hammock, watching the sweat trickle down her shoulder and roll onto my chest, she told me about her life. Her life actually began as "Elizabeth Bear Bryant." While the nurses attended to her mother, a wealthy industrialist who donated millions in revenue to her alma mater the University of Alabama, Elizabeth's father, a struggling blues musician in his late thirties with faults of boredom and being white, assured the receptionist that the papers were checked and all was in order. A few days later while little Bethy Bear slept silently in her crib, gunshots were undertaken. Mrs. Bryant awakened the next morning to find her husband slumped over in the pantry, the barrel of a hunting rifle propping his head up and poking out like a mouse from the back of his neck. Taped to his chest was a copy of his only daughter's birth certificate, with the words "fuck you Doris" scribbled across the top in crayon. Doris screamed in horror as the words on the line read "Auburn Bryant." The ultimate insult.

I turned compensation into an art form in these times; my indemnities were dressed and hung in the same galleries as genuine accomplishments, which were arriving fewer and leaving farther between. Instead of sitting around eating potato chips all the time I decided to really make a go at education and sign up for an afternoon foreign language course. Instead of an afternoon foreign language course I chose to rub my nose along the Japanese words "shin chuu" inked down Auburn's back, taking in each freckle and tasting the brackish beads of moisture that burned down her spine in the sweltering Virginia autumn. Instead of falling in love with her, I began writing about Aranea and all the things I knew about her, where she was going to school now, and what her family was like. Instead of telling Auburn how I felt, I watched her softly smile herself to sleep and spent the evenings sitting on her couch eating potato chips.

I found out that the only thing I cared about were the fractured memories of a girl I didn't even know. I took out my frustrations on the library restroom floor, grinding my kneecaps against the tiles as I purged myself of the guilt. As my mind expanded body deteriorated, leaving me confused as to why I was here and what I was doing. I always made sure to cry into the mirror and tell myself how stupid it is to vomit just because you feel bad after it was done, and how all the cool kids would cut themselves or get pregnant to get attention. Sometimes I'd stand there for hours staring into my own face, watching the blood vessels swell and strain against the ashy gray of my eyes. Then some janitor would wander in to wash his hands and I'd scuttle away so he wouldn't know I had the girl eating disorder. I have to commend him, though, the floors were spotless.

I kissed the steel ring curving up over Auburn's crimson bottom lip and promised her that I would keep in touch across the thirty minute drive between school and home. Seventeen months after learning that I would be given a twenty-seven thousand dollar a year scholarship to a thirty-thousand dollar a year school, I frowned at bill for three-thousand dollars and sadly made my way back home. I took a menial task job at a grocery store to support myself but never found a coworker to discuss nature themes with. Jobs like these allow a person to see the full scope of humanity; to notice teenage mothers buying powdered formula and smacking their crying children under the big "baby needs" sign in aisle nine. I shrugged my shoulders and went back to writing little notes about Aranea on the backsides of discarded receipts.

The best part about an early life collegiate failure is the chance to reconnect with the people you left behind in the first place. I learned that the girl from my Spanish class no longer had flippy hair or Spartan breasts thanks to her rapid-fire child birthing, and was the assistant manager at the local fast food chicken restaurant. I was happy to hear that Tasha Mills had finally given Curtis a chance, and how they lived together in his mom's trailer. I spent a Sunday afternoon at the movies with them I saw his vacant smile and nodded through his hushed acceptance. I saw the stretch marks on Tasha's hips when her shirt would ride up too high. I knew what had happened, everyone did. I made a date for old times sake to watch Monday night wrestling with my best friend for the first time in almost two years the following day, nine PM sharp.

I wore my old wrestling mask and waited on the couch for him to show up. He never called me back and suddenly he's in a hole. I missed Thursday night wrestling to attend his wake, where his family members stood around being hugged until they could figure out which one was to blame. I clumsily passed by old schoolmates and nodded and waved, but I can only remember images. I remember how his hair was combed back instead of forward, how he always wore it. I remember how they buried him in a T-shirt I'd never seen and thought about how he was never going to see how all the angles were going to turn out on wrestling. I don't really feel bad for him. The shows haven't been very good lately.

Once I was out of random thoughts to compensate for Providence's inability to put the right words in my mouth I couldn't take it anymore. I shoved my way through the mystery Aunts and Uncles making their appearance and pushed open the doors of the funeral home in that smooth way that angry people do, pushing too hard and slamming your shoulder into the glass and generally looking uncool. I'd seen it too many times before, men driven to courageous acts of violence by extreme loss, driving their cars at breakneck speeds and breaking their necks wherever necks are meant to be broken. This was my time, my apex of fury, my unrelenting expression of brokenhearted rage that would echo through the ages, at least until my own wake when my own family would stand around looking for somebody to blame. Ah, there's the rub! Kick the tires and light the fires! I would roll backwards in my own grave until the Earth started rotating against it's axis and send everybody flying into the sun. I stomped through the puddles into the bleeding ink of night looking for my own person to blame until Providence put the right words into her mouth, when I left it alone.

"Brooks?"

I stopped in the middle of a puddle and considered not for a moment the condition of my shoes. I turned and through the dimly lit parking lot saw her standing there ten feet away from me in a long brown jacket with furry edges. It looked like a frock. It was completely uncool, like me, and I smiled.

"Hey," she waved.

"Hey," I said, without waving. I'm suddenly looking around for square pizza to spork.

"Are you…I mean, are," she began, before taking a few steps towards me and whispering, "I…made you a present." She stretched her arm out across the distance that seemed like a thousand centimeters and raised her hand towards my chest, clutching a tiny piece of paper between her index and middle fingers.

Unable to speak I took the paper from her and unfolded it slowly. Inside, in perfect calligraphy, read the words: "I'm sorry." I felt my stomach fold and jerk as I let out a heavy breath of air and felt the tears slide into the crevices of my eyes. Before I could move she lunged towards me and wrapped her arms tightly around my chest, resting her head against my chest and not saying a word. I wanted to touch her but my hands wouldn't do it and just stayed floating in the air an inch from her shoulders as she hugged me. My body began to jerk and she held on, because she is always there, holding on. I closed my eyes.

When they open I'm still standing here by the hole, wishing he'd just shown up to watch the wrestling and not shot himself. My entire life has been built on a steady theme of compensation but for some reason I never imagined having to compensate for this. He is gone and will never come back, no matter how good wrestling gets. Tasha Mills will have moved on and found a new boyfriend before the season is over and I, with all of the blessings I've received, can't seem to stop looking into graves and seeing the only people I've ever met that didn't deserve to be there. I imagine his eyes rolling back in his head and my nerves begin to twitch and I wonder why there aren't any bathrooms in this graveyard.

"Brooks?" She is here ten feet behind me before I even know she is there and it all begins again.

"Hey," I say, turning and waving.

"Hey," she says, without waving.

CHAPTER 2

I steadied the camera on Curtis, his lean frame balanced precariously on the wooden rail extending up to my Grandmother's front porch. "Ladies and Gentlemen, in my twenty-five years in the business I have never seen what we are about to see! 'The Man From the Streets' is gonna fly!"

I bellowed the words as though I was witnessing a miracle. Curtis pounded his fists against his loose-fitting black tank-top, adjusted the Los Angeles Raiders ski cap that qualified him as "street" enough to be a man from them, and took flight. With God's own grace, comparable to a bird hit with a baseball, Curtis somersaulted forward and landed a solid foot from Chinese Gordon, a friend of ours from the housing project up the road positioned strategically on the sun-bleached mattress. Curtis managed to extend an arm out and catch Chinese in the sternum with the back of his wrist, which prompted the Chinaman, portraying the masked rudo Desperado Joe Gomez, to bounce around in agony like he'd just been shot. "Good God! Good God look at the carnage! Gomez has been broken in half!"

Chinese Gordon is one of those unique souls you only read about in brilliant short stories; a peach-fuzzed Central Virginia white boy who showed every single ounce of the three-hundred pounds his body could support underneath a stitched-together wrestling mask and his older brother's hand-me-down soccer shorts. He got the name from an eighth-grade history project video taped in his basement on the Crimean War. We also dubbed his older brother "Neptune" for his incomparable performance in the backyard sprinklers during our "Homer's Odyssey" project. His sister's name was Cecilia.

Curtis shook out the cobwebs and prepared for the finish of the match. Journalists these days often place a spotlight on backyard wrestlers—kids with nothing to lose who put their bodies and lives on the line to violently emulate their television heroes. I've seen people leap off rooftops, bash each other over the head with light bulbs, and scar their friends with whatever is lying around wrapped in barbed wire. Our video taped broadcasts set out to honor the more ridiculous side of professional wrestling. The action consisted mostly of random banter and silly in-jokes peppered with the most fake looking forearm shots and knee drops allowed by natural physics. The characters were unforgettable, ranging from our Middle Eastern tag team champions "The Belly Dancers" (Curtis and myself with towels wrapped around our heads) to Chinese Gordon's portrayal of "The Lumberjack," hailing from "deepest, darkest Canada." I think the worst thing that ever happened was when a schoolboy roll-up attempt ended with Chinese sitting down on top of my head. My hair smelled like damp soil for a week.

The Desperado struggled to his feet and was met with a big boot to the stomach and a DDT for the 1-2-3 in the center of the mattress. "Another successful title defense for 'The Man From the Streets,' unbelievable, just un-bee-lievable," I shouted, as Curtis grabbed the standard men's belt with a piece of cardboard duct-taped to the center and resumed his perch on the wooden rail. He held the spoil high into the afternoon sun as the crowd, fourteen year old Brooks White covering his mouth and going "aaaaaaah," went wild.

"One Friday afternoon we were told to bring in something that reminded us of childhood, it was a group exercise to help us learn about ourselves, or something. Anyway, I brought in a stack of crayon drawings of unicorns and mermaids swimming in lagoons, and letters that I'd written to myself when I was teeny tiny. Everybody snored through my ramblings and tangents and then Curtis came up with these tapes of you and your friends wrestling in the front yard, and everybody just went bonkers. I think the biggest reaction was for when Gil Gordon ripped his shirt off. The girls in the class shrieked and the boys started chanting along, we should've charged admission to class. It was darn near a cultural event." Aranea inches closer to me as she raises her arms high into the air and brings them down bent to her waist. "What was that thing he used to do to you all the time that really made you mad? The thing where he'd drop you on your head and you'd end up throwing the camera at him?"

"You mean you actually paid attention to that stuff?" Standing there like an open wound I begin shuffling my feet in the grass, forming pyramids of dirt to save time for the ants, if there are any. "If I'd known women would be watching I would've kept my shirt on."

She smiles brightly and pushes me in the shoulder. "Of course I was paying attention." Aranea speaks softly and affectionately about the class, telling me stories about the community college, and how she and Curtis had bonded not because of the common link to me, but because they were the only ones who seemed like they wanted to be there. Somewhere in her tangent I lose track of her words. I laugh to myself so delicately that the breath never leaves my throat. "Besides," she continues on topic, "what are you supposed to do when Chinese is in his underwear and yelling things in Japanese?"

I mutter under my breath trying to escape the horrible reality of being caught and enjoyed during countless moments of embarrassing childhood brain damage. "It..., the move, it was called the Tiger Driver '91. He's supposed to kinda pick me up and drop me on my head really, but I didn't actually want him to do it."

"Ninety-one? There are ninety other 'Tiger Drivers?' Do any involve actual tigers, or driving?"

"Nah," I shrug. "A guy in a tiger mask invented it, so it's tiger, and your head gets driven into the mat, so that's driver. 1991 was the year he debuted it. Chinese's brother got him a Best of Japan tape and I guess the urge to Tiger Drive me overpowered his natural urge to not want to hurt me."

"A guy in a tiger mask?" she asks.

"You wouldn't believe me if I told you his name."

"I promise I'll believe you."

"His name was Tiger Mask."

"Ha ha!" she shouts, making a point to enunciate each "ha." "I don't believe you. And the Japanese yelling? Does Tiger Mask yell?"

"That was Chinese imitating the announcers on the tape. They always name the moves in English but they, you know, speak Japanese, so 'tiger driver' comes out sounding like 'tie-gar du-rive-ar-uh.'"

She crosses her eyes and belts out "tiegaruh driveruh" at the top of her lungs, loud enough for some members of the congregation still murmuring around Curtis's hole in the ground to glance over in confusion. This of course is followed by uproarious laughter from the prettiest girl there and an emotion somewhere between divine joy and a smacking of the head from myself.

"Yeah, we were pretty retarded back then," I say, resting my palms on a headstone. The bones just beneath the skin are drawing lines on the back of my hand, and no matter how hard I press I can't free the soul trapped here, nor can I accept my own. "I guess everybody was, though. It's the public education system." Aranea purses her lips and squints her eyes like my Grandmother and for a moment I lose track of my own thoughts.

"Curtis really meant a lot to you, didn't he?"

I respond silently.

"I'm sorry." Her fingers reach out for mine but don't find them.

"God," I utter with cracked voice through a throat full of stupid memories of front-flips off of rails. "I played Nintendo with him last Saturday. We were supposed to watch wrestling together on Monday, and he never..." I pause, shaking my head and grinding the tips of my fingers into the stone. "I haven't been back long and we were supposed to watch wrestling on Monday and he never called me, and I thought 'well it's another one of those times,' like when we were, like when we were kids, you know? Like sometimes he'd be convinced that he needed better friends or..." I struggle for the words and end up stammering with burning teardrops slipping into the corners of my mouth. "It's like he waited for me to come back. It's like he...it's like he wanted to say goodbye to me, and that's just so melodramatic and obvious, and I..."

The green in her eyes swirls and focuses on the area just behind mine. A moment passes supported only by the sound of his mother and some people I've never met crying, and I wonder, for only that one moment, why I'm a hundred yards away from that feeling, commenting on the pigmentation in the eye of a figment of my imagination born from the admiration of a little girl who has always been just randomly there.

"Here, look at this," she says, pulling up the sleeve of her secondhand store coat. She's grown a bit since my faith first left me. Her arms are still a little too long for her body and remind me of string cheese stretching out from the confines of the tight novelty T-shirt wrapped around her body. The shirt is blue and the trim is white. The inside of her arm looks like milk and the shirt says "radiant" in block letters. She swings her arm up towards me and flips her hand out, revealing a pair of inch-long scars in the shape of a cross on her right palm. "My stigmata. You know how I got this?"

"You've been chosen by God to spread the faith and bring good will towards others?"

"Nope. I should be so lucky." She grins and rests her tongue between her teeth. "Curtis was showing me what a 'dragon screw leg whip' was. By the time I realized I was being hurled across the room by my leg I stuck my hand out to break the fall, and took a glass on the table and two coasters down with me. Cut my hands all to pieces, and this is what stayed." She raises two fingers and rests them just an inch away from the tip of my nose. "And ever since then I've been completely insane."

I cross my eyes towards her fingers. "You're insane?"

She bites down softly on her bottom lip and raises an eyebrow. "When was the last time you were forced to be that symbolic? I'm getting the urge to write epic poetry about myself." Aranea Cavatica has yet to say a word to me outside of this collection of tombs and somehow it fits. It's like when you set the clock and lay back in bed, and the only thing you can think about is "did I set the clock correctly?" So you sit back up and check, and then twenty minutes later you roll over and check it again. It fits, but it shouldn't. She brushes her excess of hair behind an ear adorned with silver jewelry and stares back towards his casket, slowly being lowered down. A few stragglers stick around to drop roses they probably bought at the grocery store down into the hole. She turns back to me and squints her nose. "I hate the tent they put over people when they're being buried. It's like they're having a big furniture sale or something."

"Technically I think they are. The casket cost his family about thirty-nine hundred dollars, and those folding chairs are at probably twelve-fifty or so a piece, so at what, thirty folding chairs that's three seventy-five right there."

"Yikes, I hope they get to take the folding chairs home as souvenirs at least."

"Souvenirs?" Suddenly my mind races and I prop my butt up against the tombstone to steady myself, and begin untying my shoe. The shoe comes flying off, and the sock becomes just another victim of inspiration and abstract thought. She puts her hands together behind her back and bends down, confused, for a closer look.

"You're doing…what exactly?"

"Showing you something," is my answer. I lean back on the tombstone and hoist the size thirteen into the air like it's the arc of the covenant. A safe and sanitary distance from her eyes rests my pale ankle. Extending across the center of my foot is a raised scar. Her eyes widen as she turns to look at me.

"Your stigmata?" she laughs.

"Yup. Wanna know how I got it?"

"Your subconscious caused you to inflict the wounds on yourself, and then later you forgot and claimed that it was a miracle to all the news people? And then you saw some statues bleed?"

"Nope." I smile and fold my legs, wiping some unsightly lint from the bottom of my foot. "I was going to body-slam Curtis into one of the bushes outside my Granny's house and I stepped on the mattress in the wrong place and one of the springs tore up and went all the way through my foot."

"Ouch."

"Yeah, right before I went for the slam I screamed something about how 'this was it' for the Man From The Streets and how nothing could save him, and then I went and stabbed myself and dropped him on the grass."

"Divine intervention, eh?"

"I guess so. I never did try to slam him into the bushes again, and every time I put on my shoes I get that image of him lying on the grass, laughing at me while I jumped around with a bloody foot screaming like a girl. Because of this scar, no matter what happens, I'll never need a folding chair to remember him by. So yeah, I guess to answer your question I have at one point or another been forced to be pretty symbolic."

Her pigmentation shifts and light reflects in the recesses of her eyes and for the first time since I read "Curtis Dean Bunch" in the obituary page I start to feel like myself again. She looks at her hand and then softly places her scars to mine.

"Aww, it's like we're soul mates. Soul mates via unsupervised wrestling."

I smile. "Is there any other kind?"

From a hundred yards away I catch a glimpse of Curtis's mother Crystal wandering towards me, her hand raised, clutching a tissue, and waving. She is famous in my home circle as the "Mom With the Most Last Names." Crystal Marie Ware Bunch Scott Robertson Scott, five last names stretched out across four failed marriages in her forty-four years of tumultuous life. She obtained no nominal amount of physical beauty or mental attribute during those years, choosing to spend most of her time smoking discount cigarettes violently down to the filters and collecting and displaying novelty owl-related merchandise on her trailer walls. She smelled like her home, dank and musky, a combination of stale smoke and mildew. It was not her fault, however, because she was not the reason for her situation in life and she was not the reason that every man who'd ever been inside of her trembling warmth eventually turned to violence. During sleep-overs Curtis and I would listen for crashes and try to guess which household appliance or ornamentation she'd been punched into. On days when he wasn't mad at her Curtis would wear his badge of only son on his sleeve, taking the punches for her and reciprocating them. The boyfriends and husbands would recoil from the attacks, stumble through the doorway and we'd never see them again, until their long lost brother from a different mother would show up and the show would begin again. Even today her face is bruised.

"Thank you so much, Brooks, thank you, you did such a good job, you looked so handsome I really appreciate it." Crystal sometimes goes into new sentences before finishing the ones she has just started. Aranea takes a few steps back, folds her arms, and looks off towards the quickly grayed clouds as Crystal wraps her arms around my waist and begins to sob. "Why did he do it Brooks why did he do it to me whyyy did he do it to meeee" and all I can think about is the scar on my foot and the way it felt against that touch. Crystal continues to hug me as I think about the size of my waist, and how when Curtis and I were best friends my waist was so much larger, and how she always seemed so much taller, and how the dust from her hair is getting all over my dress clothes. Simultaneously I contemplate the unimaginable anguish of a mother losing her only son just two decades into having him and see images of her striking him down for protecting her. I don't want her to touch me and I begin to hug her and miss him.

After her snot slides down her nose and onto my borrowed suit jacket she turns from me and frowns toward Aranea, who doesn't hesitate for a moment and goes straight into compassionate hug/butterfly back patting. Moments of "why did he do it to me why did he do it whyyy" pass and I feel sort of selfish for not "thinking of her in her time of trouble." I want her to shut up and stop making excuses and remember all of the times when she smacked him and threatened him and burned him with cigarettes. I want her to stop touching Aranea Cavatica. I don't want Crystal to receive the same gentle caress that I just got, because she doesn't deserve it. I want to say my good-byes to Curtis and leave her blubbering carcass to rot in that run down trailer down the street from me. Aranea pulls away from the hug but not far enough to lose contact. Crystal is pulled down by the weight of her frown but can not pull away from the eye contact, and I see her try to form words and make noises but fail.

"Curtis loved you, no matter what you did." Crystal begins to murmur but the sounds aren't given life, buried there beside Curtis, clutching to his cold body, underneath the blowing breeze of Aranea's gossamer words. "He's fine. I promise you, he's fine," she smiles. "I checked for you."

I stop for a moment. I see The Man From the Streets in my head again, standing triumphantly on a rickety oak railing with the belt I wore with my church clothes swinging in the air and I realize for the first time that Crystal Marie Ware Bunch Scott blah blah never got to see him the way I saw him. To her he was a baby clutching to her breast. To her, he was a scared little kid in a Turtle Ninja T-shirt who was too scared to let the doctor prick his finger with a needle. To her he was more than he was but an extension of her and how she felt bad every time her brain wasn't smart enough to control her actions. She never meant it, I know she didn't. She just didn't know any other way. In one inconsequential moment from an uneventful childhood the World Heavy-weight Champion turns to look at me and I completely break down.

"To all my fans out there, to all you Man From the Street-ites, I just want you to know that I am totally invincible and can never be defeated!" Curtis flexed his thin arms as Chinese Gordon snickered at him from somewhere off camera. "This Sunday I will meet my arch-nemesis, the overrated and totally uncool Jack Mask, Jr., the Tijuana Superstar. He will surely feel my fury!" The champ bared his fists and spun around, only to trip over one of his own socks and fall backwards into a bush. "Oh crap!" In the bottom right corner of the screen the low battery alert flickers and dies, and the screen goes to static. The tape is over, and he's gone.

Thunder breaks in the distance and the hole is full of dirt, and Crystal is gone. Sitting on the hood of my white 1978 Toyota Corolla with the big rust stains on the side I stare at the tiny dark circles on the pavement where the rain is beginning to hit. It always ends up raining on days like this and it's barely even lunchtime. In a few minutes she will be gone as well, fading back into imagined obscurity until the next time I'm forced into a suit and tie and told to carry one of those damned boxes up some other hill. I've cried all I can cry and now am overtaken with empty sobs, the dry heave of the melancholy. Where does this go from here? Why does this go from here?

Clunky black shoes cover the increasing number of raindrops and suddenly she's standing there before me again, a look of discontent in her eyes and a giant umbrella that looks like a panda bear propped up just above her head. "Hey," she mutters. "Are you going to be okay?"

Before I can answer she bends down and positions her nose so close to mine that light can barely pass between them. I'm thankful that her goofy umbrella with googly eyes is keeping the oncoming rain out of my hair. "Yes. You're completely okay. You know why?"

"Wait, why does your umbrella look like a panda?"

She smiles. "The panda-like qualities of my umbrella aren't what we're talk-ing about here. We're talking about you and your state of okay-ness."

"Actually it's pretty funny looking. I mean, who thought up the concept of a big umbrella with googly eyes and…"

"Hey!" she shouts, and hops onto the car hood with me. With my eleven-hundred and ninety pounds denting it her slight form and exaggerated hop don't even register. "The panda umbrella is cool, yes, but more than that you're going to be completely and utterly full of okay." Her fingers glide along my chin and push down to open my mouth slightly. My eyes lazily dart towards her and my eyebrows raise. "This is the part where you say 'oooookaaaay whyyy.'" She lets out what could be considered a giggle but is more like a snort and I'm forced to comply.

"Ooookaaaay whyyyyy?" I say as she squeezes my cheeks to form the words.

"Because you've got a guardian angel looking out for you."

I jerk my head away from her tender grasp and roll my eyes. "Please. What's he gonna do, teach me the true meaning of Christmas? I don't…"

"No," she interrupts. "There's a lot more to it than that. Can't you just take my word for it? Like you said, I've been chosen by God to spread the faith and bring good will towards others." She flashes her palm across my eyes again. The cross is burned into my brain. "I'm fully prepared to make all of your statues bleed."

I raise my leg and hold it out into the rain, watching balloons of water pop and burst on my dress pants and drain onto my ankle. "Those poor statues."

"Exactly." She presses her hands against the car and hoists herself back up onto her feet, into the increasingly damp street. The rain is picking up now, and feels like shards of ice hurled at the back of my neck. I'm starting to miss the big stupid panda bear. "I'm not qualified to write your biography or anything, but it looks like you've gotten all the bad stuff in your life out of the way early so it's nothing but daisies and waterslides from here on out." She reaches out and takes hold of my hand, squeezing it softly one last time. "We'll make it through together, okay?"

I respond enough to let her know "okay" and she nods. A few seconds later I stop feeling the rainfall on my nape and try to figure it all out in my head. Thirteen years of my adolescence I spent on a hard red bench listening to old men I barely knew talk about God's saving grace and forgiveness, and thirteen years I sat in a folding chair listening to my Grandmother speak of meekness and understanding. I used to look so hard but I didn't see it, and I still don't. Where is all the love? Where are all the saviors riding white horses around in the sky? If I walk into the James River are the waters going to part? I feel like I'm one of Christ's ex-girlfriend's records that accidentally got left in his collection when they broke up. There's a big fracture down my center and I keep skipping. Doomed to repeat the same line for eternity.

About five minutes into my internal metaphor I realize that she's a hundred yards away from me and I'm sitting on my car hood being rained on. Desperately I spring to my feet and shout for her, swinging my arms around in the air as if independent from my body.

"Aranea! Hey! Where are you going? Don't do...why does...you're only here when..." Her clunky shoes stop in the street and the panda bear swivels to reveal her smiling face staring back at me. "Don't worry," she yells back. "Whenever you need me, just think about that guardian angel." With that, she continues on her way.

I stand in the downpour babbling without words through an open mouth until she tops a hill and disappears. I raise my arms to my side in a complete act of desperation. Without a sound I angrily swing open the Corolla's door and slam myself inside. A few more moments come and go like raindrops and, without any better way to express my inabilities, rest my slightly oversized forehead on the steering wheel. Another series of moments I can't forget and she's gone again. Same as it ever was.

Knock knock.

I open my eyes and turn my head to see her, panda bear hoisted in a protective stance, smiling that amazing smile through my driver's side window. I roll the glass about halfway down as drops of moisture collect and dribble in onto the arm rest. Her grin penetrates my defenses and catches hold of my brain stem, shaking my gray matter around until she makes me smile too.

"Hey. I was just kidding. That would've been pretty lame." Without any background music but the sound of precipitation she reaches through and drops a folded piece of paper onto my lap. She flashes me the peace sign with ringed fingers. Clumsily I fumble with the paper, folded the way that a middle school girl with a set of markers develops a black belt in, as I watch her feet kick up puddles of condensation as she runs. Exasperated, I glance down at the words.

❧

"Dear Aranea Six Years From Now,

Hi! How are you? I am doing great (but since your me you hopefully already know that!). If you have not changed your name by now I'm gonna time travel to the future and kick your butt!

This is a letter I have to write for class for a time capsule so that when I graduate I can remember what it is like to be 12. I do not think I will be much different than I am now so I made a list of things I hope to have done and here they are:

1) I hope you have moved out of Illinois and have moved somewhere wicked awesome like New York City or Paris or at least somewhere near a lot of waterslides because waterslides are really fun!!

2) I hope you are in school and learning about all kinds of neat things and that daddy has gotten a better job and doesn't have to keep moving around. If you read this tell him that one day he will win the lottery and not have to dig holes anymore! But I hope he has already.

3) I hope you have found somebody who takes care of you and is not mean to you, and who doesn't make fun of your teeth or your hair. I hope you are still eating a lot.

4) Do not give up! Your dreams will come true if you just believe in yourself and hang in there. The cat hanging from the branch would not lie to you even if that poster was made in the 70s like I have heard.

Keep God's love in your heart and a smile on your face and everything will be okay. You have a guardian angel looking out for you so do not mess it up. I do not know how much Jesus pays them so make it worth there time.

Yours till Niagara falls,
Aranea C. Cavatica

Her name is written extravagantly in number two pencil, adorned with a collection of ladybugs and what appear to be daisies. I smile and realize so many things at once that I can't really remember anything at all. I turn to look at her and feel the right words building up in my throat. She isn't there. In her place, written in perfect calligraphy with a finger on the condensation of my window, are numbers.

CHAPTER 3

"Accidents will happen
We only hit and run
He used to be your victim
Now you're not the only one."

"So, I'm wondering if, like, I should start being more open with my feelings and tell people when something really affects me." The sound of Elvis Costello drowns out the squeaking of the futon. The mattress has slid down to my lower back so that my shoulders are resting against the cold, metal bars.

"Mm, yes, I think that's a good idea. I think you should always be incredibly open," she says, digging her royal blue fingernails into the tense white chest beneath her. "Complete dehiscence."

"But what happens if I'm open and I don't get the reaction I want?" I ask, clenching my hands and watching a drop of sweat drip from her chin onto my abdomen. "What happens if someone I care about doesn't feel the same way and ends up laughing in my face? That'd crush me, I've got this whole allegory about biomes and everything."

She arches her back and presses her palms violently against my ribcage, smiling so that the stainless steel ring curving up over her bottom lip rests against her bottom teeth. "The sacrifice of personal existence is necessary to secure the preservation of the species, hon. Your struggle is not a unique one."

My eyes close and I turn my head away as my fingers consider the sharp edge of her hip, trembling out of habit more than consequence. "I've just seen so much…so much pain already in my life, I would hope I could avoid the pain I brought upon myself. Sometimes the desperation is so much that I want to do something I'll regret, just so I'll have something different to worry about later."

In rhythmic motion she runs a hand through her scorched-white hair, matted with sweat, and asks, "Am I not helping?"

"You're helping," I say, gasping, "I just don't know why I keep on living if I can't live well."

"Mm," she mumbles. She grabs my hair and presses her index finger between my eyes aggressively. "Then why don't you just kill yourself?"

"I tried. Once when I was thirteen we were playing kickball in gym class, and when it was my turn up to 'bat' I kicked with all my might and my shoe just went flying off." I kick my leg out for dramatic license, causing her to lose her balance and fall, her chest heaving against mine. "I hit the pitcher, this big black Jehovah's witness kid, right in the side of the face. After class he and his friends backed me into a corner and took turns throwing a Trapper Keeper at my head, because they knew I wouldn't do anything. I was just the scared, fat, little white kid."

All movement stops, as her eyes become sincere for the first time on record. "You've always been forced to mire in the refuse of humanity, I suppose. I'm sorry, for what it's worth."

"Yeah, well, I went home that day and tried to stick my head in the oven. But there was a roast in there."

※   ※   ※

"You may never be attracted to the likes of me,
But accidents will happen and I'll be around,
And maybe there'll be no one else but me around..."

When I was fifteen I had an insurmountable faith in the idea that my personal anguish would, eventually, reap incomparable rewards. I never imagined that I would be spending an afternoon crouched over a shoe box in the living room of Aranea Cavatica. I can hear her in the kitchen on the telephone, asking the local bird sanctuary what to do when a cardinal cannons itself into one of your windows. I'd finally gotten up the nerve to visit and found the bizarre scenario, complete with a Frank Sinatra soundtrack playing lightly in the background.

Her house isn't as I would've pictured it. It isn't even a house, it's half of a duplex, a one floor, two-bedroom domicile that could pass for an antique store. The living room had everything you wouldn't imagine in a beautiful girl's home; A plaid couch with a heavy throw rug pulled over to hide the tears, old black and white photos in thick wooden frames, shag carpet. Out of the corner of my eye I spot one of her baby pictures. Aranea is easily recognizable even as a small child. She sits, with one awkward ponytail on the side of her head, an absent-toothed grin in front of a giant trash can on her front steps, different front steps. She is clutching a baby doll.

"Here, I warmed these in the stove," she says, walking in and handing me some warm cloth, "they should be good enough for the bedding."

"So it just flew right into your kitchen window?"

"Pretty much." She sighs softly and gives me a pained look. "I was actually going to make you a grilled cheese sandwich since you were so nice to me on the phone. I figured hey, that's what civilized people do these days, right? So like right before I harnessed my culinary chi I looked up and the poor thing just collided, it's not even fully grown yet, it was horrible."

She drops to her knees and scoops the tiny bird into her hands as I stuff the cardboard box with the linen. I hold it steady as she places the motionless cardinal in the upper right corner, pulling some of the heated cloth down over it like a bed sheet. All the while I'm looking at the side of her face, watching the concentration in her eyes, noticing that her hair is pulled back into a perfect French braid with little accessory ringlets floundering out from the sides. She is in pain and she is perfect.

"There," she says triumphantly with tears in the corners of her eyes, "now they tell me we just have to wait and hope for the best."

"If you're worried about the grilled cheese sandwich, it's okay. I appreciate the offer. It would've been delicious, though."

"Yeah," she smiles, "stupid bird had to go and disrupt my picnic luncheon. I hope it doesn't die though, that would disrupt many picnic luncheons." Her voice lightens and she turns towards me, sitting there on the floor as we waste the perfectly good couch. "My Dad once told me a story about how he found a family of birds buried beneath some of the dirt he was trying to clear, and how he decided to just up and change locations instead of disrespecting them, you know?" She squints her eyes and I am a child again. "My Dad's a great guy, I'll have to introduce you sometime."

Trying valiantly to insert small talk where slack-jawed babbling is normally produced I manage only a, "So what does your Dad do for a living?"

"He digs graves," is her response.

❀   ❀   ❀

"And it's the damage that we do
And never know
It's the words that we don't say
That scare me so."

"If you were in a grave I would be sad, yes, but it's just another aspect of existence." Auburn is stretched out on the futon wearing my hockey jersey and her old junior varsity volleyball shorts. She rolls onto her back and uses her toe to turn the stereo up, half to enjoy her favorite part in the song and half to drown out my response. "Forgive me for not jumping in front of a train at the thought of it."

I'm sitting Indian-style on the harsh carpet of her dorm room beside the scene of the crime, positioned with my back to her so I can stare into the mirror on the back of the door and bemoan to the various parts of my functioning brain about how horrible I look without my shirt on. "I think I'm just ready for something more in my life, something more than the grocery store, you know?"

She gasps melodramatically. "Something more than the grocery store? Do we dare dream the impossible?" She reaches past my shoulder to grab the container of Play-Doh on the floor. "I've always wondered what was out there, you know, past the Play-Doh and the casual sex."

"Stop it, I'm serious."

"I can tell, you're using man voice."

"Yes, I'm using man voice. Situations like these call for man-voice. It's one of the perks of actually being a man." I stretch out to grab the blanket, thrown across the room earlier in the festivities, and pull it over my stomach. "I've been thinking about it a lot lately, and I'm finally ready to get my act together. I need to get a second job so I can go back to school, or start writing that book I wanted to write, I have this great beginning in mind about a poem about my Spanish class…"

"Look," she says, finally realizing that the song isn't drowning me out. "What exactly are you looking for in life, and what elaborate plan do you have to achieve those goals?" She rolls the putty into a perfect ball and pokes her fingernail into it.

"I...don't really have a plan. But I think I'm in love, you know? And that's a start, at least."

"Love," she curses under her breath. "What a grave mental disease." She stares at the little clump of Play-Doh on her fingernails and draws a connection so high above my head that she doesn't even say it. "I hate to break it to you, love, but I'm not exactly the housewife type."

"I wasn't talking about you." I pull the cover up over my shoulders.

She goes on with her mannerisms without a sound. The room is silent as Elvis finishes his song. After a few moments I feel the coldness of her ring and the heat of her breath on the back of my ear.

"Good," she whispers, kissing the back of my neck.

Auburn hops to her feet and trots towards her door, barefoot, stopping only to ask me what I want from the cafeteria.

🍁   🍁   🍁

"Forevermore may never start, you may ignore my hopeful heart,
And chances are not the one to make you fall,
But accidents will happen after all."

The words across the screen say "The Natural Beauty of Illinois!" and the music makes me feel like dancing, in an elevator. "Illinois is a land of diverse landscapes and terrain, and to the nature lover," booms the announcer, "offers an abundance of wildlife and scenic beauty!" Stock footage of cardinals nesting and violets swaying in the wind cause even the most industrious industrialist to break into tears.

"When it comes to road trips, getting there is definitely half the fun! Along with the famed Route 66, Illinois has five National Scenic Byways that not only put you on the path to fun, but also offer plenty of natural beauty, fascinating history, incredible things to do and cozy restaurants and hotels." The loving parents on screen pat their precocious little blonde offspring on the back of his head and usher him into mini-van loaded with what I can only assume to be wholesome good times. "When you're planning your road trip, don't miss out on these outstanding Illinois highways and byways!"

The climax involves a park ranger ushering a group of kids who, excited to learn, stare up in awe at the majestic oak. "Right here in Illinois, we've got an incredible number of great state parks to explore and enjoy this summer! Two-hundred sixty-two, to be exact. You'll find places for picnics beside quiet rivers.

You'll discover white-water for kayaking, rock faces for climbing and eagles in their native habitat." These are all, of course, illustrated for those who can't follow along. "You can experience some of the best fly fishing in the entire Midwest. All right here, right now in Illinois."

Aranea scoots up excitedly on the couch to point the remote towards the television and, in hunt and peck fashion, cranks the volume. "All right, here we go," she says. "Get ready." I look on anxiously.

The words "Call today for your free brochure!" line the bottom of the screen as we're whisked away to a beautiful church, where five stunning teenage ivory figures with crystal blue eyes and tar black hair smile graciously for our viewing pleasure. All at once, in perfect pitch, with perfect posture, they give us the crucial information we've been waiting for since birth:

"Illinois! The fun starts here!"

Aranea plops backwards against the back of the big, brown polyester couch with a huff and shoots me a dissatisfied glance.

"Ladies and Gentlemen," she says, opening her hand and directing my attention towards the television, "the World Famous Cavatica Sisters." She's wearing plaid cloth pants that hug her thighs and a tank top with a pig on it. Halfheartedly she motions from left to right, "Artemis, Ashley, Aeris, Adelle, and Alexander. The first one was born nine years into my parents' marriage and another hit sequel followed every summer."

"You have a sister named 'Alexander?'"

Aranea clasps her hands together to feign whimsy. "Every time one of them would come out of Mom the doctors and nurses would gasp, and exclaim things like 'oh my, what a beautiful baby,' or, 'I've never seen a baby so beautiful!'" She wipes her fingers across her brow and sticks her tongue out. "Of course they all had full heads of hair and they all smiled at my parents even though babies aren't supposed to smile, but isn't it remarkable that they all smiled! Isn't it just the magical world of wonder! They're all truly miracles given to us by God, and we'd be shortchanging Him if we didn't name them something beautiful." She shrugs. "My Dad always wanted a boy to name after Alexander the Great. After the fifth time I guess he just said 'to heck with it.'"

"That's pretty weird," I mutter, "is she okay with that?"

"Oh, sure," she nods, "every time she got egotistical she'd bring it up. Then I'd tell her she was really named after the guy from 'Family Ties.'"

Laughing under my breath I glance towards the television, taking in the paused image of the five attempts it took to perfect a daughter. "So where are you in the commercial?"

She pauses. "I'm not in the commercial."

"Why not?"

"Well, uh, I guess you could say I never participated as much as they did. They got really famous locally for singing in church, they would travel around to all the local churches and sing. They've been doing that since I was probably four years old, I just never had the inclination to sing with them." She closes her eyes and lowers her head only slightly. "Don't get me wrong, though, I like to sing, and they're all really great singers. I just…"

"Just what?"

"I'm…I'm just the runt, it was never really my place to be with them in the first place." Her voice fades from a light aria to almost a whisper as she continues. "I was never entirely on purpose, which proves that you can be a World Famous Cavatica Sister without actually being a World Famous Cavatica Sister."

Silently I sit and listen to her speak. Hearing her talk about her family and her life gives me a powerful sense of nostalgia until I realize that I'd never heard the stories before. It's like a deep longing for something you never had, like teenagers hanging out in a fifties-themed restaurant. When she talks her eyes convey a thousand emotions, at least three or four hundred I haven't begun to feel yet. In moments of utter satisfaction I find myself spacing out, trying to figure out what great deed I did to earn this time with her, until I'm staring at the pig on her shirt like a zombie. Then I realize that she probably thinks I'm looking at her chest and resume eye contact, difficult as it is.

"My Mom was forty-two when she had me. I was unplanned and they didn't want me, but my family doesn't believe in abortion or anything so I was just sort of an obligation. Burden begins at conception." She reaches up and tugs at a loose strand of hair floating in front of her nose. "I was all wrong. I had green eyes instead of blue, and my hair was solid white, no color at all. The doctor said something about how I might be albino, and it scared everyone. I thought my Mom was going to write all over me in red pen. My Dad thought I was a miracle, a natural miracle, that's how I got my name. It means 'spider's web' in Latin. In some Latin dictionaries. Latin is so hard to figure out though, in some other dictionary it probably means 'aural turd.'"

"Want to know something pretty sad?" I say, smiling from ear to ear as my cheeks burn from pale white to a growing pink.

Her eyebrows raise as she looks me over before retorting, "sure."

"I already knew what your name meant. When I found out I went to the same school as you and found out that was your name, I got my friend Melissa to ask her Latin teacher what it meant." Suddenly my frontal lobe starts to work and my motor skills kick in, so I can stick one foot in my mouth and kick my own butt with the other one. "Not that that isn't…entirely creepy."

"No, no it's not," she reaffirms, patting the back of my hand. "Okay, actually it kinda is," she says, laughing, "but it's still sweet. My sisters all stayed in Illinois when my Dad lost his job, so I became the default only child. They are all married now and have beautiful children, and sing at fairgrounds and picnics on the weekends. I was the only one young enough to be uprooted and shoveled off. I've learned to love Lynchburg since then. It's so delightfully unnerving. It's like my Shire."

With her hand on the back of mine the right words are suddenly thrust into my brain, compliments of overnight delivery from Providence, and I fight to get them to my mouth before I forget and end up saying something about grilled cheese sandwiches again.

"Hey, Aranea, I wanted to thank you for…" And out of nowhere the tiny cardinal, resting beneath the cloth in the shoebox, begins to chirp.

"Do you hear that?" she asks. My response is silence, because the words don't arrive and are stamped return-to-sender.

Aranea awkwardly throws her legs into the air and hops off of the couch, leaning down to scoop up the shoebox and examine its contents. She turns to me and blinds me with a smile so that her bottom lip almost covers the freckle on her chin. I assume correctly that the patient is well on his way to making a full recovery. Without a sound she eases the shoebox into her kitchen, and, leaning over the couch, I can see her open the window and slide the box onto the windowsill, lid open, so that the cardinal could make his own way out. I turn back and face the television again, staring at the image frozen in time, as Sinatra croons softly in the background.

CHAPTER 4

The personal check has a fetus in the upper left hand corner surrounded by a thick font reading "Abortion is Murder!" Slowly I glance at the old lady, trying to figure out her angle in this. I notice her husband, complete with "Choose Life!" foam/mesh combination hat resting atop his grayed and spotted head, wandering around toward the cigarettes and the sticker machine. He is waiting to die, or waiting for his wife. She grins through pearled spectacles as I circle her phone number and run the check through the scanner, summoning the dark power of the supermarket register, supplying the proper change, and sending her on her merry way. She grabs her husband by the arm as she exits, pulling him from the precarious balance his rickety knees had previously provided. As I insert the slip of paper into the register's bowels I notice a stamp that reads "38 Million Murdered Babies—The American Holocaust!" inked there beneath her signature. I never stop to voice my opinion on the matter, but I have to say that I admire all the exclamation points.

Scotty, the pierced bagger from the high school down the street, reassures me.

"Yeah, one time I saw a bumper sticker that said, like, 'unborn babies have no laws to protect them, but dolphins do,' and I was like, 'wow, that's really meaningful,' and then I felt sorry for all the dolphins, cause they had to have laws to protect them.'"

Scotty was hired to replace the mentally challenged girl who worked nights when she left to pursue a job with more career advancement opportunities. He only works on Thursday afternoons. As the story goes, Scotty was stuffing chewing tobacco into his pullover and, in a stroke of luck, wandered into the position. His eyes have a permanent glaze and his frontal lobe is laced with menthol, but you can't deny his warped initiative.

"Oh, and this one time, right, there was this bumper sticker, right, that said 'racist people suck' and the 'suck' was in huge red letters, and that was on the same car I think."

"Yeah," I reply, "but I bet a really clever racist could blow that guy's mind." We stand there silently for a moment, before the next customer, an oafish teenage mother, presents her "MVP Savings Card" and asks the same questions that every other person who exists asks.

"Are those buy one get one free? I thought they were buy one get one free. The sign says they're buy one get one free. Them's buy one get one free, ain't they?"

"Indeed them is," is often my retort, but it never gets out because the customer is still busy thinking up new ways to ask me whether or not they are buy-one-get-one-free. I stare directly at her bushy eyebrows as she digs feverishly through her change purse to find the coupon that will save her thirty-five cents with the purchase of two of something she doesn't need. As the moments stretch out into hours and then into decades my eyes are drawn to her children, ages roughly five and maybe three, bouncing up and down in the bed of her shopping cart. The boy has a steady stream of what we in the business call "throw up" trickling down his chin and my mind wanders back to the time when I could've fit into one of those carts. I always shopped in the "husky" department, so I can barely remember those times. I do, however, remember the songs.

"Doon doon doon doon, doon doon doon doon." The congregation of the First Assembly of God watched their children and their children's bewildered friends swing their arms and stomp their feet in time. Dozens of eyes were fixated on an overweight woman in a paper pirate hat, armed with a microphone in one hand and the flapping head of a humanoid puppet in the other, leading them in a chorus that rocked the very foundation of Heaven. "I may never MARCH in the infantry…"

The entire room begins to pantomime riding a horse. This is accomplished by holding two clenched fists together and bobbing them up and down in front of one's crotch. "…RIDE in the cavalry…" Index fingers began flying into the air and waving violently back and forth. "…SHOOT the artillery!" Parents smile and, under the watchful eye of the blood of the lamb, I'm sure at least some of these kids went on to mow down their drama teachers in high school.

Like a flock of majestic birds our wingspans stretch out until we're karate chopping our neighbor in the chin. "…I may never ZOOM over the enemy, but I'm in the Lord's Army!"

"All together now!"

"I'm in the Lord's Army, yes sir! I'm in the Lord's Army! I may never MARCH in the infantry, RIDE in the cavalry, SHOOT the artillery! I may never ZOOM over the enemy but I'm in the Lord's Army!" In that one beautiful moment the entire life's teachings of Jesus Christ were compressed and expressed neatly in a twenty-second song about wanting to kill people. "YES SIR!"

Being there at your church and watching your family clap along isn't the worst thing that could happen to a kid growing up Christian, it's actually quite fun. The worst thing that could happen would be if they were your bewildered friends marching along. The looks on their faces alone could brand you for life. My friends thought my family was insane. I was more interested in accosting the stupid kids who sang "ride with the Calvary."

Those puppets were reason enough to attend the First Assembly of God "Children's Crusade," the annual summer get-together where you got to hear what people with their hands up the asses of imaginary people think about forgiveness and the like. I spent most of the time thinking about how I was going to sneak into the back rooms in the fellowship hall after the show and do wrestling moves on all the puppets. These intimate moments helped shape my fragile little world, and to be honest with you I can't remember my first day of school or the names of my goldfish, but I can remember the time my guidance counselor told me that her dad was a "Methodist" and I asked her if that meant he worked on one part of the body over and over until he could get the submission.

This time in my life was when I began to understand my own luck, and embrace it as one of those wacky character traits that would define me to those who learned to love me. I spent an entire Tuesday afternoon missing all of my favorite television shows to memorize all one-hundred fifty-five words of Ecclesiastes 3:1-8 so my team (the boys) would win a giant candy bar. I took one for the team and recited the verse perfectly to the pastor, who congratulated me and informed me that I was the only boy to have memorized the verse in total, that the girls were the winners of the giant candy bar, and that I should give them a big hand. I didn't show up on Thursday out of protest. The memory verse was 1 Thessalonians 5:17—"Pray without ceasing." I used my allowance to buy a bag of fun-sized candy bars and a bundle of rubber bands, and cut my losses.

Growing up in Lynchburg, Virginia, the bright shiny buckle on the Bible belt, a young man learns to confide in the wisdom of puppets. "Excuse me," one of them says to me, poking its head from behind an oversized cardboard reproduction of a mailbox. "Excuse me!"

"Excuse me!" says the single mother, who wants to get her free milk and her free cheese and her carton of smokes and get out of the grocery store with her children's' lives intact.

"Oh...sorry," I say as I shove the goods down the counter for Scotty to bag. "Your total tonight comes to...fifteen dollars and seventeen cents." As the words go through the motions and sluggishly wander out of my mouth she is already closely inspecting the receipt to find out what I did wrong. She signs her name on the printout and exits abruptly, dragging her cart by the corner as the little boy smacks the little girl repeatedly in the head. I normally wouldn't condone such violence or sexism, but I'm just glad they escaped the American Holocaust.

"Wow, she sure was grumpy!" says my next customer, a fresh looking middle-aged man in a pink polo shirt. His sunglasses are resting atop his mighty forehead, holding back the silver pompadour. He has friendly eyes and a friendly smile, and, like a sailor uses a whore, I used him for mid-shift grocery store conversation.

"Yeah, I don't know what the deal was. But if that's the worst thing that ever happens to me I'm blessed, I guess." I run his diet shakes and yogurt-in-a-squeeze-tube across the scanner and slide them down to Scotty as I talk. "I tell you, the people in this town never cease to amaze me. Every time I think I've experienced the full range of customer relation mishaps somebody shows up and reminds me how menial this job really is."

"I know what you mean," boasts the man, "you wonder if these people have the love of Christ in them at all. Tell me, where do you go to church?" He peers at me, mouth agape, waiting for my answer. I just know he's got a pamphlet ready somewhere in his khaki pants to whip out for me if I don't say something fast. Before I can answer with a lumpish hush Scotty cuts in, his eyes glowing as though someone has finally flipped the "on" switch.

"I go to Timberlake Christian," he says.

"Oh, really? I go to Thomas Road."

"Oh," Scotty says.

"Yes!" assures the customer, "I heard a great sermon last Sunday evening about how immigrants, not Americans, must learn to adapt in this new, patriotic America. It was really moving, you should try to get a copy of it if you can."

"Oh I will, definitely," says Scotty, who has transformed from dullard to disciple in an instant. "We did a scripture reading from first Corinthians, totally amazing. It really gave me an understanding on how open-minded the church has become lately."

"I agree!" exclaims my conversation whore, casually throwing around those exclamation points. Money is exchanged for goods and services, and with a hearty handshake that sort of creeps me out, the man collects his bags, wishes some sort of blessing on Scotty, and meanders out to his utility vehicle. In one swift motion I flip off my register light and maneuver a wheeled cart full of discount American flags into my line, blocking it off.

"Scotty, you never told me you went to church."

"What, you don't?" is his reply. "I go to a lot of different churches, with my friends and all. There are some fine women at church, know what I'm sayin'?" He pulls an embroidered stocking cap over his shaved head and heads out for a smoke break. I follow him out of curiosity. He leans against the brick wall of the store beneath the sign so the rain won't put his cigarettes out. I hop onto the guardrail across from him with complete disregard for the dryness of my pants. "There's this one girl, right? and she's got like a huge rack, right? and I totally wanna hit that," he informs me.

"So you just go to church to pick up women, then?" I ask, as I hop down and swat at the puddle forming on my butt.

"Nah dude, 'course not. It's like, it's where we all go, it's like a hang out and we get to praise and all that. I'm all about the praising, no doubt." He flicks a half-smoked cigarette at a wet bird puttering around on the concrete, causing it to fly away. "The women are just tight as hell, that's all."

"I wouldn't have ever pictured you as the church type, no offense."

"What else am I supposed to do in this town?" is his reply, and I can't think of anything witty to say to it. "Besides," he continues, "it's what you're supposed to do. It's all, righteous or whatever."

I didn't say anything because I knew he was right. The sound of my family screaming and crying alongside what I suppose was my grandfather hitting his head on the corner of a lectern on the way down has been haunting me since it happened. My grandmother was my Sunday school teacher every weekend for the first thirteen years of my life. She was the woman who taught me about equality, and about selflessness, and about love. That day I saw her rushing up and down a crowded hallway. I saw her crying. I watched some men I didn't know carrying her husband of forty years away on a stretcher and I watched the colors of the sky twisting around. I didn't go back the next Sunday and I haven't been back since. The First Assembly of God was shut down due to housing costs and what was left of my family relocated to a bigger, whiter church across town. Even then I couldn't pick myself up and set my faith down into one of those folding chairs to hear the same sermon I'd heard better before. Then my grandmother died, and in a way my faith died with her. I imagine it's there with her, in the box, in the hole, waiting down there for me until I get there. I close my eyes for a moment and wonder if I could find a shovel strong enough to dig for it.

Suddenly the splash of water awakens me from my daydream and I turn to see a mammoth silver sports utility vehicle barreling towards me. It stops, and the man with the glasses on his forehead hops down and strides towards me. I look him directly in his glasses.

"Ho ho ho! I almost forgot to give you this!" he joyfully shouts, as he hands me a little packet with a rainbow across the cover, proclaiming the "Real Facts of Life!" that lie within. He shakes hands with Scotty, who seems to enjoy it. After a few superfluous waves he climbs back into his assault vehicle and rockets away, splashing water just inches from my shoes. I look down at my shoes, and then towards Scotty. Then I realize that my religious rediscovery metaphor came dangerously close to grave robbing and ball the pamphlet up in my hands. I fake, and then shoot for the three. The paper hits the top of the trash can and bounces out into the street. I shrug, and make my way back into the grocery store.

Before I can get another thought in I am home, pressing my face against the hard curve of the toilet seat. I'm downstairs in the half-bath so my parents won't hear me. Forcing yourself to vomit is a habit born out of a desire to control; to push the mush that used to be food out of your stomach, to expunge all the hatred of the days events. After a few weeks you sort of get used to it, and it comes easily. Tonight my throat is burning because it isn't coming easily, and the sick yellow paste keeps rising up over my index finger and down my tongue so I taste nothing but bitterness and warmth. To fail at something only you can control is one of the worst feelings imaginable.

As I begin to cry I hear a knock on the bathroom door, locked just inches from my head. I wipe my hand across the bathroom floor mat and wipe the red tears from the corners of my eyes. From the other side of the door I can hear my mother ask, "Are you okay?"

"Uh, yeah," I lie as I open the door and discreetly avoid eye contact. My Mom is the antithesis of me; a dark-skinned, rail-thin, raven-haired woman with nothing in her eyes but good intentions. The last thing I want to see in moments like these are good intentions. "What's up?" I flippantly bark.

"You've got a phone call," she says, running her fingers down my arm and over moisture on the back of my hand. She squeezes the hand to let me know that she knows, and that it is okay, even though it is completely not okay. "It's a girl," she tells me, and sadly wanders back upstairs.

There is an unwritten rule in my home that a girl on the phone for Brooks means one of two things: One, that someone has called in sick to work and my manager is calling on "Old Reluctantly Faithful" to fill the spot, or, two, Auburn Bryant is having some kind of family crisis and needs positive reinforcement. It's become a fun exercise to "talk her down" from her rampages. It gives me a moment to focus on something other than my own petty problems and help someone out. She starts by screaming about wanting to drop out of college to become a vagrant in the streets of Paris, sleeping on a bench beneath the Eiffel Tower and sketching nude models on the weekends. I condescendingly pity her. This makes her mad. Then she starts firing off faux-intellectual quotes from important literary influences and swears to never speak to me again, until she realizes, like she does each and every single time, that I've taken her mind off of her problems. Then we have sex, because neither of us feels very good.

"Helloooo?" My voice is low and full of expectations, because I've been at work all day and there is only one other type of phone call.

"Hey, it's Aranea. What's up, homeslice?"

My mind, trembling on the vine, is suddenly raped by the violence of existing for a third type of phone call. "Uh, hey," is my standard, intelligent contribution to any memorable discourse. "I didn't even think you knew my phone number, I..."

"Oh, I didn't," she interrupts. "I tried to look you up in the phone book, and about halfway in I remembered that I had no idea what your Mom or Dad's name was, so I started to call all thirty-four 'White' listings until I found you. Did you know there's a guy named Barry White who lives a few blocks down from you? But he's a construction worker. Really let me down."

"I...didn't know that."

"Yeah, he's got a wife named Betty, too, which is pretty freaky."

"What, are you soliciting people now?"

She laughs on the other end of the phone and that horrible taste starts to leave my mouth. "No, but you're the eleventh White family listed. After five or six I got bored and started making conversation."

"Good deal." I begin to notice wonderful little details about my living room that I'd never noticed before, like how the wood railing on the couch matches the wood on the picture frames.

"So hey, yeah, I actually called you for a reason. I wanted to know if you wanted to maybe…you know, do something this weekend?"

Suddenly I'm Pablo Picasso, deftly adding the third eye to a portrait of his lady love. "Yeah, absolutely, I'd love to, what did you have in mind?"

"Well I thought you might like to come to church with me on Sunday." Suddenly I'm sitting on an ugly couch and I'm me again. "We're having a lunch afterwards and I'm bringing grilled cheese sandwiches specifically for you. They're going to be delicious, how could you possibly say no?"

"I…I don't know, I…"

"Oh, gosh, I'm sorry," she says. "You probably want to go to your own church, which I'm totally fine with."

"No, it's not that, I just…" I wait for her to interrupt me so I can end the sentence, but she doesn't. "I…just…I…just…was…wondering how…you were going to keep grilled cheese sandwiches from getting all…hard and, like…cold." Suddenly I want to seek out new phone calls and let Scotty bumble his way onto the line in my place.

"Trust me," she affirms. "If you believe in the sandwiches, they will be warm." After a few moments she snorts. "Heh, that was pretty mysterious, wasn't it! I keep building you up for the grilled cheese, if I let you down I'll never hear the end of it."

"So you're telling me there's a big payoff, then?"

"I give you my word. It'll come out of nowhere, I promise."

We talked for twenty minutes that night, about absolutely nothing. When she said good-bye and hung up I sat with the receiver in my hands until the service noises kicked in and I had to hang up too. That night I prayed for the first time in years, and I didn't stop until at least one-hundred fifty-five words into it out of principle alone.

CHAPTER 5

When I was eight years old I believed that I'd never been baptized. I thought my parents, who were infrequent churchgoers at best, had perpetrated this horrible act of carelessness on me without realizing how important it was, and now I was going to Hell because of my original sin. I didn't know what the original sin was, or why I had done it, but I knew it was there and it scared me to death. I spent a solid week reading up on the subject and learned about the ritual, and how I needed to be dunked in the river and cleansed of my sins. I would sit on the edge of the bathtub trying to figure out how I was going to do it, if I could do it, and if it would even be recognized as legit. After a few weeks the pressure got to me and I ran crying to my Grandmother, telling her about how full of sin I was and how I needed to be saved. At this moment she informed me that I'd already been baptized and that I just didn't remember it because I was a baby. I knelt in front of the First Assembly of God and asked Jesus Christ into my heart, and, for the first time in my young life, I didn't feel like a complete idiot.

That's one of the wonderful things about coming out of the water as a baby, though. All of your sins are washed away right there in the open, so if you commit any more everybody knows it. The sins are kept in neat bottles in the recesses of your mind for you to remember, to build upon, to regret. If you didn't regret the sin what's keeping you from committing it again? If I didn't regret stealing a colored pencil out of a package in a department store when I was eleven years old I'd have a room full of art supplies but no real understanding of what I believe, or why I believe it. This guy got his hands nailed to a big plank of wood so we could steal colored pencils and not be damned, that's not something to sit around silently bemoaning. That's something to sing about.

You don't know what it's like until you've seen the sun through the waters surface that one last time.

There are too many Southern Baptists who take the denomination for granted and make the few of us who are trying to keep our heads up in a world full of famine, war, and power ballads look like small-minded idiots. I spent three hours on Saturday night doing my laundry, picking the perfect colored jacket of my father's to match the only pair of dress pants I own, so I would look nice sitting there beside her. At least I hoped I'd be sitting beside her. Regardless, I'd be in the vicinity and trying to look nice in the vicinity of that kind of beauty is like shining a flashlight on the sun. I realized for the first time that I'd truly outgrown my father and needed to do my own shopping, which would be an intellectual exercise if nothing else. The first thing I saw as I pulled into the mall parking lot was the Red Sea of Humanity, lined up around the mall with cardboard signs telling me about how all the gay people were going to Hell. There was even a little girl with a pigtail like in Aranea's baby picture with a sign that read "AIDS: God's Punishment For Homosexuals!" I tried to push the image of her out of my mind as I browsed through the coats and replace it with all the wonderful times I'd had at church, all the singing, all the fried chicken lunches, all the stupid looking puppets. The images began to run together and I lost track of my thoughts. When I came to I realized that I had wandered dangerously close to the granny underwear section and had to make a break for it.

All I could see in the mirror were love handles, which are far less love and more handle, bulging and pouring out over my nine dollar belt. Of course a lot of this is imaginary, and I know it, but I see it anyway and it makes me want to spend Sunday morning services bathing in the holy white reflection of Saint John. The walls in department store dressing rooms are almost always white, with the little impersonal bench and reassuring metal hook your only savior from emptiness, nothingness, you and infinity. I wanted to stick my finger down my throat and decorate the walls so there'd be something to look at, but I didn't want to mess up my sharp new threads. I chose a black jacket to match my hair, and a gray tie with little crosshatches on it to match my pants.

I wanted to show off the purchase for my mother. She's always telling me about how nice I look when I dress up and there aren't many opportunities outside of the funerals. For the first Saturday night I could think of they weren't home though, and the only person there to see my fashion explosion was my cat, named Cat, squatted behind a potted plant. I looked all around, just in case my parents were "taking a nap," but they were gone, and there was a twenty dollar bill resting on an open notebook on the coffee table. "Get yourself something to eat, will be back later, love Mom."

I could never get into the Crawford dorm without one of the keys, so I have to sit on the bench outside by the ashtrays and wait for someone who lives there to come in or go out. It gives me a moment to connect with nature; namely, trying to keep the squirrels from digging their way into my bag of sushi. I also get to read all of the handmade flyers littering the campus doorways.

"For Sale—Algebra textbooks! Never opened!"

"Roommate Needed, SBFNSBYOB!"

"Come see the hottest band on campus, Spaceman Spiff, this Friday at the freshman mixer!"

I get so interested in the thrilling presentations I almost miss the R. A. trying to sneak a case of Mexican beer into the dorm. In my suit I appear important, respect-worthy, and she makes sure to hold the door open for me.

Saturday night in the dorm is a magical place. Girls in expensive pajamas line the hallways to cry into portable phones. Visiting boys with buoyant curls of hair stuffed under baseball caps stand in huddles by each door, peering in with long necks in hand at designer jeans and simulated virgin orifices. The fraternity brothers have T-shirts with hilarious observations about beer screen printed onto them. I get more than a few looks from girls in animal print skipping down the stairs; little mutters of "oh my God," which is like the word "the" of the well-to-do college girl. They work it into every conversation, even when they're pumping gas. "Oh my God five dollars on pump five oh my God." I used to get offended, but then I realized that we were talking about completely different Gods.

Kirby Marie "Akiko" Takahata is sitting in the full lotus position with the denim waistline of her low-cut jeans brushing against Auburn's dorm room door. Dubbed "Kiki" for her ongoing contribution to the furthering of Asian stereotypes at school, the obnoxiously thin and genetically flawless twenty-two year old pre-med often spends her time reading up on proper Shinto and kanji in her spare time. Born to a suburban middle-class family with no deep appreciation of their heritage, Kiki was raised as a white girl in a field full of white girls. The seductive whisper of cultural individuality beckoned to her during her high school orientation, when a guidance counselor mastered the art of racial profiling and suggested that Kiki sign up for a karate class as an after school activity. Left alone with no ride home after her first practice class Kiki was forced to fend for herself for hours in a downtown strip-mall, becoming deeply acquainted with a Sashimi restaurant and a video store full of Japanese cartoons. Having been denied a dignified childhood in 1950's rural Japan, Kirby demanded that friends and family call her "Akiko." When I met her in Anthropology my second semester she was dressed in a full Asian school-girl outfit, looking like a sailor in knee socks, and within weeks we were creating film festivals. Her physical perfection and admiration of all-things I hold dear, including Godzilla movies and puroresu, meant immediately that I could never find her attractive, because dating her would be like dating me. Kiki's roommate, the aforementioned Alabamian, would sit on her bed eating Oreos and scoff at how she would never "read a movie." Over time Auburn moved closer and closer to the television, and once clothes began to uncover freckles and bare flesh Akiko migrated out into the hallway, where she has been, at least in my company, ever since. I squint and squat slightly to read the bold black print on the spine of her book.

Japanese For Busy People: A new, unique approach to effective daily communication in Japanese.

"Japanese For Busy People?" I ask in my best casual conversation voice, "You're the busiest Japanese person I know. Why're you reading that?"

"Oh, hi Brooks. Nice suit, did somebody die?" Kiki closes her book and glances forward. "You know, some Japanese people believe in reincarnation and some don't, so it's really up to the individual to decide whether Grandfather is now a cat or still in a jar on the mantle."

"Nobody's died in a week or two, so things are looking up." With my breath lost between personal disinterest and social brevity I let out a heavy sigh and cover my emotions neatly with a giant blanket. In this situation, a giant blanket covered in cherry blossoms. "You don't have to be Japanese to keep your loved ones in jars. My friend Chinese Gordon's mom kept her great uncle over the fireplace, and then one day someone knocked it off and the cat used it for a litter box, and hilarity ensued."

"You should make a movie about that, you'd make millions," she says, flashing teeth whiter than the skins of the people she's displaced combined.

"Will do," I laugh, "right after my first novel about the swat team that fights dinosaurs."

Kiki bends her knees and props herself against the wall, reaching up to play with one of the chopsticks holding her hair in a bun while she talks. "I don't know a lot of Japanese, so I'm brushing up before my family visits next weekend. I'm going to make Hamburger Helper for them and put a bunch of rice noodles in it. Culinary satire."

"Learned anything crucial conversation yet? All I ever learned from Spanish class was that Raquel es una abogado de Los Angeles."

"*Biru ga ii desu*," she says, pointing at her dorm room door over her shoulder with her thumb.

"What does that mean?"

"'I'd like some beer.' Auburn's been repeating it all night. I think she has brain damage. What does yours mean?"

"Rachel is a lawyer in Los Angeles."

"If you're ever hit by a car in a Hispanic district in Southern Cali you're saved," she groans.

"And if your wife leaves you and takes your Japanese dog and truck you'll be able to drown your sorrows without any cultural obstacles."

"Oh!" she exclaims, stomping her feet against the carpet. "Did you bring me the Origami book?" Before I can even slap my head and think of an excuse, a chopstick flies into the air and bounces off of my forehead. "You always forget to bring me the book. If I asked you to bring me a book about gross Anglo orgasms with my roommate you'd bring it when I asked."

"Why would I need a book to tell me about gross Anglo orgasms?" I say in my best hey-hey voice, accompanied by my thumb and index fingers as zinger guns.

"Oh you white devil you!" she responds, half-heartedly shooting me back with theoretically the same gesture. After a sigh she opens her book again. "Just bring it to me Tuesday after I get out of Karate class."

"I'll try to remember," I say, turning towards the flyer-laden door to begin my knocking. Moments later my back is pressed against the black metal support of Auburn's futon as she straddles my hips, lowering her mouth to my neck as the dimly lit Christmas lights strung haphazardly over our heads flicker on and off silently. Two young men like the ones I've seen in the doorways are seated, legs agape on the carpeted floor, playing video games. All I can see are the blue-tinted curves of their profile framing glazed, focused eyes. Empty bottles form little meaningless forts and trails between them. They concentrate on which play to choose next as Auburn wrinkles my only pair of dress pants with her thighs.

"Auburn?"

"Hm."

"Are you going to introduce me to your…to your friends, I guess?"

"They aren't my friends, I don't know who they are, they're just some guys," she says. "Your outfit. The suit. You look good."

"Heh, uh, well, thank you, you're wrinkling them, though. I just came by tonight to see if you liked the way I looked in these clothes, I don't wear them much, and I brought dinner and all," I say, holding up the brown paper bag with the untouched, expertly prepared Tokyo rolls inside. "Normally this is a good thing, but I don't know if I'll be able to iron them in the morning, I'm supposed to wear them to church, and…"

As soon as the word "church" falls out of my mouth her hip gyrations stop and her fingers loosen their grip. I can hear her holding her breath for a moment before she lets out a loud exhale, biting down so hard on my neck that my esophagus is punctured and we're both left blowing hot air.

"Okay, Brooks fun fact. You don't go to church anymore, correct?"

"I haven't gone recently, no."

"You stopped going to church when you were a kid, right? Your grand-mother and grandfather, right?" She purses her lips and looks me dead in the eye; at least I assume she does. The light from the Playstation football game backlights her until all I can see is the silhouette of her head, and the little spiky tufts of hair protruding all around it.

"I tell that story too much, don't I?"

"You told me once that religion was a crutch for the weak."

"Actually I think Jesse the Body Ventura said that."

"Whatever." Her breath smells like cheap tequila. I work at the grocery store. I know the difference between top shelf and store brand.

"I know," was my weak reply, "but tomorrow is different, I'm supposed to…"

"The one you're in love with. The little girl. The one with the big teeth." Her voice is dark like the room and surly like the smell.

"Well, I…"

"Brooks, you're a deluded little automaton." Her fingernails scratch against the stubble of my chin and her face falls directly against mine, so her lip ring grazes my mouth as she speaks. "Your love is misguided. It is merely desire. You're being straddled and you're thinking about church."

"Don't talk to me like that," I bark, grabbing her wrists and pushing her away from my face so that her back arches and her knees came raise up from the couch. "You don't have any right to judge my desires, especially when they aren't even desires. I told you how I felt, and it's not my fault that you can never deal with…"

Auburn shakes her hands free and leans across my chest, reaching over towards the ashtray on the edge of her bed. A muffled grunt from her throat alerts the attention of one of the men, the Miami Dolphins, who nods his head and hands her a joint. "Desire and love are the same thing, save that by desire we always signify the absence of the object; by love, most commonly the presence of it. You just want what you can't have." She takes a long toke and resumes her position of command. I sit there silently for a moment trying to match the quote with the random author.

"Thomas Hobbes," I utter, as the guy with his cap on backwards scores a touchdown on the guy in the wacky beer shirt. "You just quoted Thomas Hobbes. Why did you do that?"

"It's my namesake," she says, smoke billowing from the corner of her mouth. "I've always been a bit of a tiger."

She leans in and kisses me, and all I can taste is the disgusting reality that I won't be able to compensate for this anymore. Akiko once told me that it would take twenty-four percent oxygen in our atmosphere to catch the entire planet on fire. Since Lynchburg was magma and trilobites the atmosphere has steadied at twenty-one percent. In that blistering moment I want the elements under my command so I can express my extra three percent. I stand up violently and set her down on the balls of her feet. She stumbles backwards as I make my way through her door and out into the hallway. I can hear her yelling my name and I only stop my power walk when I meet Kiki coming out of the bathroom.

"Hey again" is all Akiko can say before she realizes that something abnormal is happening and jumps in front of me. She has a red bandanna wrapped around her head like a dew rag and an electric toothbrush sticking out of her mouth, which is admittedly very attractive in an unrealistic way that I have no interest whatsoever in experiencing at the moment. "Oh my God, what's wrong?"

"This whole thing. I just can't take it anymore. It doesn't make any sense, it never has. She's just...she's just not what I want. I don't know, she's just not what I want right now."

"That's a lot of exposition for someone to take on their way out of the bathroom." Kiki continues her electric brushing and communicates to me with simple words. "What do you want, anyway?"

"I don't know. I think I'm supposed to know by now."

"Well," she says, before her almond eyes spread open like blooming flowers. "Why is Auburn screaming your name down there? And..." she continues, pulling the toothbrush from her mouth, "why is she running out into the hallway in her underwear?"

I turn to see Auburn jogging out into the dormitory hallway in a black sports bra and glow-in-the-dark-star covered pajama bottoms. She stops a few feet from me and in the fluorescent light I can see the tiny beads of sweat, different from the ones I found so endearing, trickling down the sides of her face. Her normally dark eyes are fading into a lighter hue; her pink lips into soft shade of blue beneath the studded ring.

"Brooks, I'm sorry, I shouldn't have snapped at you like that. Henry…what was his name? Kiki, what was his name?" Kiki blinks her eyes and nods with no information to verify.

"Henry?" she asks. "The tall guy with the white boy dreads from figure drawing?"

"No," Auburn says, waving her hands around, swatting at the air a few particles from the tip of my nose. "The southern intellectual, the one from Mrs. Almeder's class."

"Oh, Henry Louis Mencken." Kiki glances at me and begins to brush ferociously, her eyes fixed on mine as Auburn continues.

"Henry Louis Mencken said that every normal man must be tempted at times to spit upon his hands, hoist the black flag and begin slitting throats. I didn't want you slitting throats out here without proper supervision." She begins to ramble and her words start coming out faster, running into one another and falling back into the same void she'd pulled them from. "You left the sushi, and I didn't get a chance to thank you for it, and those guys…" Her eyes dart around, looking for God knows what, and she presses her shoulder blades against the white plaster wall.

"Auburn, honey," Akiko begins as I take baby steps away from them. "You look like creeping death. You should have at least put on a shirt before you ran out into the hallway. Hacky-sack people can see you. That guy, at the end of the hall, he's got a beard like six feet long." Kiki laughs nervously but Auburn continues to slouch, randomly drooping her head and recoiling. "You should go lie down, call it a night." I have to agree. Lately I've been noticing more and more of Auburn's flaws, but she's always been generally accepted as being completely out of my league. On this particular night she looks like she doesn't know what sport we're playing.

"I'm…fine," is Auburn's affirmation, before she squats down against the wall and drops her chin down to touch her collarbone, exposing the sprouting red hairs on the back of her neck. I take a step forward and place my hand over them, to protect her from whoever may be watching. Slowly I kneel down beside her to watch her eyes, hidden beneath folded arms, dripping and developing a film. She tries to cover up how she is feeling, but the historical quotes just aren't coming easily. "Those...guys, the guys in the room, they...I just drank too much, I think, it's not..."

"All right," I sigh, knowing that the girl who talks my ear off even during the most intimate of moments not being able to form sentences means personal Armageddon. "I guess I'm here for the night. I wouldn't feel right leaving you like this. I'm sorry." I lean down and kiss the red hairs. "Do you know what we're supposed to do, even?" I ask Kiki. "I usually spend Saturday nights selling the alcohol, not really...catching it."

"Yeah," she nods. "I'll bike across the street and get what we need. Just make sure she's okay until I get back."

"I'll do my best." I lift Auburn to her feet and look into her eyes. They've begun to roll back into her head, but not so much that she can't look back at me and make me feel kind of bad for getting so mad at her. I can always put the sushi in her mini-fridge. I can hear Kiki shouting back at me from the stairwell.

"Try not to have a whole bunch of sex while I'm gone."

Auburn has begun to dribble little droplets of regurgitation out of the corner of her mouth, and wrapping her arms around me to keep from falling down. A bit of her spit up falls onto my tie.

"I think I'm fine with that."

Our first trip is to the third floor women's bathroom, which is a first for me. It's a lot like the second floor men's bathroom, only without urinals and the toilet paper is quilted. I make sure to stop and check out the suit in the mirror. It looks nice, except for the off-yellow spot on my otherwise gray tie, and I can't get my belly to look small enough to make it all look like it's supposed to. I helped Auburn into the big handicapped stall with the metal rails on the walls. Every time she vomits she begins to cry, which is often, and I wipe her forehead with a balled-up, damp wad of toilet paper. When I realize how crass this is I decide to go back to her room and look for a towel.

"I'll be right back," I assure her, "just...try to make it into the toilet. At least I don't have to hold your hair."

"Not all of us in the stall are professionals."

I shake my head as I walk back toward her room, trying to figure out how a girl with her head stuck in a toilet and probably suffering from alcohol poisoning could still be clever enough to get me like that. I push open her doorway and flip on the light switch, much to the dismay of the two nameless frat guys having a break on the futon.

"Hey, is that chick coming back? Auburn, or whatever?" He ends all of his sentences with question marks.

Beer baron chimes in with his opinion as well. "Right, so like, are you her boyfriend? Cause she was all over you." He tosses a piece of the sushi roll into his mouth and I do my best to ignore it.

I make my way over to her chest-of-drawers and pull open the second drawer from the top, where she keeps her socks and underwear, and find a dishrag.

"No, I'm not her boyfriend. We're just good friends." I look around at all the bottles lying on the ground and then back towards the gentlemen, one of whom is now up and rummaging through Akiko's DVD collection.

"You must be really good friends!" he laughs, resulting in an impromptu high-five.

"Yeah, I guess." I try to walk to the door before more conversation is conceived, aborted, and spat at me.

"Dude, she needs to hurry up and get back, we need more weed." The less invasive one switches roles as he stands up from the futon and begins opening and closing drawers. "I know she keeps it around here somewhere, they always keep it in a place like this," he educates.

"Dude, we don't need more weed," says his friend, fondling around in his pockets. I'm almost out of the door as he pulls out a Ziploc bag with a collection of white pills floating around at the bottom. "The world's first and only organic ecstasy experience!" I hear the sentence as I'm leaving with the rag and stop.

"You aren't going to…you weren't planning to give any of that to her, were you?" I ball the rag up in my hand and squeeze it until it turns into coal and then diamonds.

"Well yeah, that's why I brought it, huh. I mean, if you aren't her…"

Before he finishes the word my swing had already begun. I'd been in a few fights in high school that resulted in me holding my chubby arms up in front of my face and not hitting back so I wouldn't get suspended. My arms aren't chubby any more, and this isn't a fight. I hit him with straight knuckles just to the right of his exaggerated Roman nose. His head jerks back and he fell into Kiki's movie rack, knocking it over and spilling films they'd never hope to understand all over the floor. He falls backwards onto the palms of his hands and sits there on the ground holding his face, while his friend in the backwards cap offers a helpful "damn!" and a laugh. I shake my hand out and walk back to the bathroom to help my friend.

I find her lying with her cheek to the seat of the toilet. Her eyes are barely open and she isn't moving, but she is still throwing up and I can see it filtering up past her teeth and down her cheek into the toilet. Being a professional I know what I have to do, at least until Kiki gets back. I peer up over the stall and see a chubby girl in leopard-print pants checking for hickeys and bide my time, wiping the eye-shadow and the puke from Auburn's face until the girl is gone. When she finally leaves well enough alone I lift Auburn up into my arms and carry her like a hostile bride across the restroom and into a shower. I sit her down on the small bench, impersonal like the benches tend to be, and begin to remove my suit and tie. When I'm down to my boxer-briefs I begin to remove her clothes and turn on the shower.

Sometimes I wonder to myself if I'll ever see Aranea Cavatica's body the way I see Auburn's. Auburn has a soft stomach and freckled thighs. Her arms are tense and her back is knotted, as if her body is just too fragile for the feelings it contains. Her breasts are large and pierced and I wonder what kind of person she was before they were. I wonder if she just woke up one morning and started looking up all the great quotes from all the psychological madmen and hypocritical fathers of our country and put holes in her body. I wonder if I might've loved her, had she been the one who hugged me in the graveyard, and I wonder why I was using her to compensate, when I knew that I hated using myself. I wonder what I'd even do with Aranea if I had her.

Tonight I'll spend holding her here in the shower, her naked body doused and quivering beneath the icy chilled water and pressed against mine, until I know for sure that she will be okay. As I slick back her hair with my fingers she opens her eyes slowly and mumbles something almost incoherently into my ears.

"So you love her, huh?"

I don't answer because we both know, and what we have isn't going to be about that anymore. It wasn't ever about that. When she gets over her psychosomatic bullshit and I get over mine we'll know that we only made it through because of each other, and we'll never forget it. When I pull her head out from beneath that water I know that she is going to be different, because her sins are just there in the open for everybody to see. Maybe just for me.

CHAPTER 6

9:49 A.M. *Tick. Tick. Tick. Tick. Tick.*

I come to in a stupor and suddenly I'm driving, pedal to the floor, across town to church. I've got eleven minutes before services begin and at this frenzied pace my poor car is doing almost seventy. Approaching the John Lynch Bridge I look out across the James River and take in the skyline of the city over the glistening fog coming up from the water below. There are birds sitting on the rail of the bridge and I remember when my Mother told me they were "Santa's Birds." She said they'd watch me when I was being good and fly back to the North Pole to tell Santa, so he could get my Christmas presents ready for shipping. If I was bad, or generally disobedient in any way, they would report the malfeasance in the same manner and I'd be left with the modern equivalent of the lump of coal—blue jeans. I smile and remember the time my Dad told me that Santa would prefer cube steak and mashed potatoes over milk and cookies and in that moment my eyes see the two lumber trucks racing up the bridge.

Regaining my focus I notice the lack of force pressing back against my foot and despite my frantic pushing I can't make the car make the noises necessary for forward motion. The clutch falls into neutral and the tires, already low on air pressure, seem to move over the damp tar like ice and I'm there, and nowhere else. Nothing moves. There is no sound. The key, normally the master of the lesser car parts, is now a voiceless dictator, struggling to keep his empire from collapsing but ultimately taking his own life. One of the lumber trucks moves into my lane. The birds turn their heads without a word and fly off to the North Pole.

The truck's grill tears through the gas tank like a lion through a gazelle and spills the guts throughout the vehicles insides. Within seconds the car and myself, moving sideways across the bridge and inverting the skyline, are engulfed in flames. My eyes slowly rise to the top of my window and I can feel the hood of the car ripping open on the blistering street. My hands, cracked and melting to the bone, try to cover my eyes so I cannot see, but I can only see. A crack in the road catches me beneath my eyebrow and pulls me apart, and the last thing I see is the cracked visage of Aranea Cavatica through the fiery wrath with torn eyes. She reaches out to me adorned with giant wings, her feathers stretching out across the sky until they break from the wing and fall all around me. They are tipped with blood and I know that it hurt her to stretch them out so far. I want to touch her lurid skin set aglow by her invidious eyes but the green engulfs me and softly her fingertips vanish into the darkness.

I'm lying there in the street and Santa's birds return to the railing. I'm there, but I'm dead. Where are all of the things that made me move? It had to be something strong to keep my knees stiff and balanced. Do I know how to play the harp now, or have cartoons lied to me my entire life?

When I awaken I'm seated in the Old City Cemetery on Taylor Street, where my Grandparents and Curtis were buried, with my back to the first tombstone I ever cried in front of. The grass has changed. For some reason I remember what the grass looked like. It's a darker shade of green here and the sky has the off-white tint of a misty morning to offset the amber of the treetops. Across the hills I see a tiny girl with teeth too big for her mouth and hair down to her fingertips bumbling down the hill, trying to keep the slippery bottoms of her dress shoes from sliding down the curvature of slick grasses. I know who she is because I've loved her since she was this.

Before I can move I am on my feet racing out to her. She runs past Curtis' grave. Her fingertips grace the edge of his headstone and cause little flowers to spring up where her touch had been. Here Curtis has a headstone and a tomb; a statue of an angel and bouquets of flowers. At the Old City Cemetery where I'm not dead he has a placard and dirt. I keep slipping on the loose soil and falling to my knees only inches from an open grave, until I notice that all of the graves are empty. It's beautiful and breathtaking to see this place, this plot of land where a thousand families have lost what it took to make them move, neatly sliced open and emptied. In the distance I can still see her skipping along. Just before she exits through the rusted black gates she turns to me and raises two fingers. By the time I get where she stood she is gone, and I cannot see her through the bars. I try to pry them open to no avail.

After a few moments I can see a man walking towards me from the outside. He is dressed in green corduroy bell-bottom pants and a butterfly collared polyester shirt despite his apparent forty or fifty years of life, and he walks with a rhythmic stride. He has tightly curled hair framing a confused face, and stops a few inches from the other side of the gate to bend down and peer into my eyes.

"May I help you?" His voice sounds like he's talking into one of those big area fans that sit on the ground, and cracks somewhere in the middle. The look of confusion turns into a broad and hyperbolic smile.

I become disoriented and rest my forehead against the elaborate locking system holding the sides of the grate together. "I was just trying to catch up with the girl who just ran through here, she's…"

"Aranea Cavatica, of course, I know her. Why did you want to catch up with her?" His bushy eyebrows crumple his forehead into a grill of wrinkles. His words come in and out so softly that I miss every third of fourth word.

"I was just confused, because I haven't seen her like…she was a kid, and with the whole linear time thing we have going on I thought…"

"Yes, I know. She has not been like this for a long time. I know what it's like to be confused. Once I was excited about joining the glee club, but it interfered with football practice. When the guys on the team found out they gave me grief and I thought about quitting, until they found out that a lot of really tough NFL players like to sing. I was happy that we worked things out. The recurring childhood was her decision. It is impossible to sway the convictions of the impetuous young mind." He pauses and looks around. "That might make a really great bumper sticker."

"Well, can I go through or what? I can't seem to get it open…"

"Why would you want to do that? You should really think things through before you go waltzing through gates. Once I got the role of Benedict Arnold in my school play, and…aren't you missing the top half of your head?"

I haven't really thought about it, but I am. "I hadn't really thought about it, but yeah. I seem fine though."

"Yes," he says, sliding a pair of reading glasses up the bridge of his nose. Reaching into his deep pocket he pulls out a small notebook and begins to flip through the perforated pages. "Elwyn Brooks White, it says here that you spent last night with a naked girl in the shower, is that correct?"

"Uh…yeah," I utter, trying to figure out what's going on without the important lobes of my brain being intact.

"It appears that you've engaged in premarital sex with this girl as well. Is that accurate?" He looks up over the reading glasses and gives me the most disapproving employer look one can achieve outside of a job interview.

"Yes."

"And there have been others?"

"Yes."

"How many?"

"A few."

"How many?"

"…three, officially."

"Officially?" The man shuts his book angrily and throws it over his shoulder before pointing a thick finger at me between the bars. "What gives you the idea that you're good enough to be here, with her? Every attempt you've made towards forgiveness and redemption has been spoiled by your desire to rise above your teenage mediocrity. You're chasing after Aranea Cavatica when you don't even have half of your head working properly, and you smell like pot and girl dorm. Besides…if you did end up winning her over, what would you do with her?"

I couldn't argue. Looking behind him I can see Aranea as she was at Curtis's funeral, with the clunky black shoes and the big panda bear umbrella. She softly bites her bottom lip and raises two fingers just above her waist. When I look back the man in the ugly clothes is stomping away.

"Let those who fight in the cause of God who barter the life of this world for that which is to come; for whoever fights on God's path, whether he is killed or triumphs, we will give him a handsome reward." Suddenly he is gone, and only Aranea is there staring back at me.

"Stop pretending," she says. "You only have ten minutes left."

With my eyes half open and one hand repeatedly swatting the thigh of my wrinkled dress pants I try to maneuver Akiko's digital alarm clock so I can see the time without knocking everything over and waking her up. The images from my daydream begin to wash away with the ebb and flow of my passing thoughts and I find myself caught in a moment of lapsed time, where I'm standing and moving but not aware. Through the dorm window I can see the dust and bird refuse on the top of my car. I tilt my head to the side and stare. In my peripheral vision I can see Kiki sleeping there cuddled up like a child with the big stuffed panda she got from her great Aunt in Osaka. I begin to make an observation but suddenly the image of a panda bear umbrella hits me like a logging truck and blows the top of my head off. I struggle to focus my eyes on the red numbers without destroying the entire night stand.

9:50 A.M. *Tick. Tick. Tick. Tick. Tick.*

In seconds I'm hopping around on the ball of my foot, trying to fit the dress shoe around my wide arches without tumbling into the freestanding balsa wood closet. The futon is empty, and I try to think of a time when I was asleep long enough for her to leave without me noticing, but deduce nothing. Auburn has a morning habit that involves ritual grooming and make-up application that has withstood the rain, sleet, snow, and finals. She demands that the act isn't superficial, but merely a personal expression of what color she wants various parts of her face to be. I'm not sure where she's gone off to, but it's nice to assume that even a brush with deadly poisoning wouldn't send her mirrored world spinning from it's axis.

Out in the hallway I'm sprinting towards the elevator, trying to remember the precise directions necessary to make it to church in nine minutes. Lynchburg has over one-hundred churches in fifty square miles so random selection is out of the question. "So here's what you have to do," says Aranea in my mind. She continues to talk but I notice that the bridge of her nose in my mind has a really cute slope and the images of the empty graves and the cold, iron bars wash together and turn everything black. As the elevator doors slowly shut I catch a glimpse of Auburn Bryant walking out of the stairwell, in her pajamas and make-up free, clutching one of the paper bags from the school's bistro.

Maybe it's repressed memories or Pavlovian conditioning from my days as the fattest kid in P.E., but I have serious issues with running. I enjoy the athletic aspect and appreciate how it makes the flaccid parts of my person stiff, I just wish that I could do it without looking like a nimrod. My back stays straight and in place as my knees raise slightly and slam the heels of my feet into the surface, like I'm a stationary oil driller gone wild. I try to swing my arms to make the movement look more natural, but it's all vanity. Even now, ninety-some-odd pounds lighter, I stop after a few yards to collect myself and find my lungs out of breath. I think they're faking orgasm to get me to slow down.

I'm huffing and puffing as I'm leaving the school parking lot, making sure to stop at the front gate for a half-second to wave at Nancy, the seventy-six year old security guard who never remembers my name. She grins vacantly and waves back, reaffirming my desire to die a fiery death before I have that many stories to tell. Barreling down the driveway to the school through the admittedly pretty but completely cosmetic forest-like habitat I'm putting point A on top of point B and pressing them together in a clenched fist, hoping that my natural tightness will manifest the confusion into completely pretty but admittedly cosmetic logic.

I squeeze under yellow lights like a fat boy under a limbo stick but the laws of the land, especially the laws of the boring residential area between the school and the city, don't apply on an easy Sunday morning. I've got my hands at two and ten and my nose just inches from the steering wheel. The sign outside of the fast food restaurant says "May I Help You?" I hear the words in my head like they're being spoken through a fan and suddenly I'm not going so fast.

I can see the John Lynch Bridge up ahead in the distance. The stretch of concrete is named after the founder of the city. At age seventeen he started a ferry service across the James River. Fifty-five years later the city he gave up the ferry business, seeing as how he had a whole city named after him now, and built a big bridge instead. It's unusual given the weather but there's a dim fog rising up from the flow of the river. Images of tiny daisies sprouting on a tombstone flip by like a slideshow in front of my eyes. My hands slip to four and six and my car slows to twenty in a fifty-five. A mini-van following closely behind me makes an angry lane change and avoids hitting my bumper by inches before shouting me down with its horn. Meeeep. Meeeep. The sounds echo through the cracked interior of my poor 1978 hand-me-down Toyota but I can barely hear them, because I'm slowing to fifteen and then down to ten. The monolithic motorist, an older gentleman with painfully permed hair and a polyester shirt, stops to shoot me a disapproving look before speeding on across the bridge.

When the speedometer reaches zero I'm on a gravel curb a few dozen yards from the bridge, staring through my windshield at the warehouses in downtown Lynchburg. People are making their way across the bridge in their cars, passing by the same view they have to see every morning, probably bemoaning the fact that they've been called in on a Sunday or whatever. The side of my brain keeps pushing "only five minutes left!" over the skyline but it becomes translucent and I keep my eyes fixated on the streets, on the clouds, on the river.

I start thinking about the reasons why I kept visiting Auburn, and wondering when the undeniable power of faith stopped motivating me and the vagina started. The first time I had sex was an accident born from empathy and pain. She was a small, plump Christian girl who had a horrifying, black scabbed scar on her hip from where her stepfather had held her down on the bed and forced himself against the back of her throat. I started dating her the day after my high school graduation and learned to love her like a pet. It was my chance to play out all the romantic comedy situations I'd planned in the borders of my school notebooks to do for Aranea, like bringing her flowers when she was sick or planning a secret picnic in my car during a rainy winter day. Three months later, on the same bed she'd been held down on four years earlier, she gave me tiny scars with her fingernails trying to force me into her so she could erase the pain and replace it with something easily forgotten. When it was all over I was obligated and attached. When she met a really cute guy with wavy blonde hair at her church she gave me a plastic grocery bag full of dried, crumpled up roses and not a single tear. It was like my pet died. The things that made her stand up and move around had vanished. I cried for a whole year.

I replaced her with a new puppy, one with olive skin and magenta hair who had her own apartment with sponge-painted walls and a big red velvet couch. From her I learned that I was hiding in a shell and that my real personality was somewhere deep inside. She gave me a tarot reading and made nachos with little strips of steak in them. I sat Indian-style on her floor and watched all of her independent films as she regaled me with stories of clubs, stories of bisexuality, stories of whips and chains and things that I'd never known about outside of slavery and Bible stories. Her musings on Kegelcisors and loves lost at the all-girl school were drowned out by the cheesy MIDI of the Nintendo. Only the patented Kegelcisor® can cure incontinence while enhancing intimate pleasure! Doot doot doot doot. She rubbed my forehead with the back of her hands and told me about how horrible my ex-girlfriend was. I did find out that she was right, however; my real personality was hidden deep down inside and was taking that outer shell for granted. Once it was chipped away and broken I couldn't pray hard enough to have it back. She stained me, and when it was over neither of us cared. I started reading every religious tome I could find cover to cover, from the Holy Bible to the Holy Qu'ran, looking for the answer. She kept a paper grocery bag full of condoms in her closet. Seems like all of my relationships end up being about paper or plastic.

Even when Auburn Bryant and I found some common solace in each others' conversations I could only find one answer; I wish I could take it all back and just wait for Aranea Cavatica, even if I never spoke to her again. She was, and is, the basic representation of everything I wanted to be when I was twelve years old: attractive, intelligent, endearing, a good Christian. A great Christian, really. I wanted to dunk my head into the James River and wash away all the sin I'd inked into my skin. I wanted to spread my arms out and fall into one of those open graves so I wouldn't be here, so I wouldn't be too weak to tell Auburn that I couldn't be with her anymore. So I could just sit on the damp grass and watch Aranea through the gates.

The sun peaks out through the dark clouds and pours the prerequisite silver lining onto the shimmering but still kind of drab river. I awaken from my memories sitting there on the railing overlooking the passing water, swinging my legs as cars zipped past me on their way to the rest of their lives. No matter how long I sit here I won't think of anything but Aranea because she is the imperfect ideal. The thing I don't have and don't understand, because it's almost like she's what I want to be. She is the only one I can count on to hold the back of my neck and make sure I don't drown in the river. She can make the sins go away, and even if she can't she can smile at me and touch her scars to mine and make the sins hide away out of respect. Suddenly I don't want to get to know her anymore. I wanted to be with her, in a box at the end of her bed, just letting her be herself and letting me watch it. I smile, because I know there's no turning back now. I swing my legs around onto the road and begin the walk back to the car, which is when I see the logging truck careening onto the shoulder just before the bridge.

The explosion knocks me to the ground and can be seen as far away as the school, a few miles up the road.

10:11 A.M. *Tick. Tick. Tick. Tick. Tick.*

CHAPTER 7

As I bike into the church parking lot at around 12:20 my mind fills with Theo-sophical warnings. Theosophy teaches about God and the world based on mystical insight, following chiefly Brahman and Buddhist theories especially in regards to reincarnation and pantheistic evolution.

Once upon a time in a world filled with a thousand religions it was prophesied that a Christ child would appear to save humanity. C. W. Leadbeater and Annie Besant, leaders of Theosophy, wished with all their hearts that the Christ child would come to their group of believers and escort them into a wonderful new future of clarity and unmitigated prosperity. They even prepared their very own manger scene for this new savior and called it "The Order of the Star." The had shepherds come from afar, thousands of followers, and, I like to assume, some camels.

One day they found a silent and striking boy named Jiddu Krishnamurti and were certain they had found their diamond avatar in the rough of India. They trained him in the mysterious knowledge, language, and information he would need when he assumed the role of patriarch of the new future. He studied diligently and loved and respected his elders, the new family he'd found. Jiddu, however, was troubled by the predetermined cage in which he lived and fought day in and day out to fend off the doubts that come along with just being a regular boy.

Underneath a pepper tree in California, Krishnamurti had an overwhelming vision, one amazing apple, or a pepper I guess, that fell on his head and unveiled to him the secrets he'd been searching for. Besant and Leadbeater were overjoyed by this wonderful news and gathered the thousands of people who shared their wish to begin preparation for the new order's convocation.

All different kinds of minds, different races, men and women, were all preparing themselves for the reality of the event: that this, after all this time, was their new experience

Thousands of people arrived for his installation, eager with anticipation. Thousands wishing upon the Order of the Star. Their wishes came true, too, because Krishna opened up their minds and did something nobody would've expected, something completely and utterly new. He looked them in their eyes, proclaimed that, "Truth is a pathless land," and he walked away. The Order of the Star was disbanded. All the while the faithful waited, certain he was testing them, convinced he would someday reveal himself as the Avatar they had so yearned for and who would soon show them how to live. They wrote books and essays and told their children what to believe in.

Besant and Leadbeater were dead a few years later, without their miracle. Krishnamurti, saddened by their passing, went on with his life, holding discussions with people, including those who were searching for answers to the troubles of life. His purpose in these talks was to suggest that searching for the answers to the troubles was the whole problem; that we trap ourselves within the walls of our beliefs and creeds, and the emptiness goes on and on. He also called into question the act of ridding ones self of the search. "The moment you really see that the question, 'How can I change?' sets up an authority," he said, "you have finished with authority for ever." Jiddu grew to be a very old man and died without pulling off a latex mask to reveal himself as the great Messiah of the world. He never gave the world the sign they were looking for. His churches don't line the street and we don't preach of his loyalty on our money.

Besant and Leadbeater had wished for something completely new, and they had gotten it. The next big thing had passed them by because they were looking in the wrong direction. They were waiting for something static, something frozen, to be worshipped. Instead they were presented with something honest and pure, an ever-evolving sense of self. It was so startlingly different from what they expected that they had failed to recognize it. They kept staring back at black and white moving pictures of themselves in their minds, until there was a color television in every suburban home and their precious film began to crack and fade.

They were just like me, so inexpressibly afraid to fail that they'd rather just stay themselves and wish for something better, building little nativity scenes while they waited for the Messiah. Buddhists, Brahmans, Baptists. Theosophists. We're all waiting, really, and nobody knows when it's going to come, we only know that it will be here, so we keep our fingers crossed. The only problem is that we miss the point sometimes. And the greeting cards say "Be careful what you wish for. You just might get it!"

"You probably don't deserve this," says the atmospheric voice behind me as I'm leaning the bicycle against the fellowship hall walls, "but you're going to get it anyway." Glancing over my shoulder I see Aranea and a paper plate adorned with a grilled cheese sandwich and what appears to be potato salad-like. "What's that on your tie?" she asks.

"Oh, uh, I must've spilled something on it during breakfast. My mistake," I mumble, tucking the puke-stained and crusting end of my tie deep into the fold of my jacket. "I'm sorry I'm late, there were circumstances and…thank you for the food." The foreboding point of the sandwich is sliding into my throat before the grace hits her ears.

"Well, that's my good deed for the day I suppose." She folds her hands together behind her back and bends over slightly, peering at the Schwinn propped against the red brick of the adjacent wall. "I thought you had a car, actually. In fact I sat on the roof of it. I got my butt all wet. If you needed a ride I could've…"

"No," I interrupt, "I just…needed the exercise? Exercise. That's a horrible excuse. I've always wanted to train for the Tour De France and I thought to myself 'today's the day!' Yeah, that's better." The runt of the Cavatica sisters scrunches the bridge of her nose and lets out what passes for a sympathy laugh. When I get home I expect a letter from the Federal Government requesting the rights to that joke for future air raid assaults.

"Regardless, I'll give you a ride next time, just give me a call. It sucks that you got here so late, you missed a really great sermon, Paul, our youth leader, he gave a sermon about love that was just amazing." She lowers her head and smiles, fluttering her fingers along the fringe of her knee-length sun dress. "It's like, love is ultimate selflessness. It is the total sacrificing of one's self, even one's very life, for the good of another person. The person that they admire and respect more than anyone else on Earth. And when you can get that in your head, you begin to understand that love isn't needing someone, it's wanting someone. The true compliment is when somebody knows your faults, knows your secrets, and doesn't love you in spite of it, but loves you because of it. Because they want to,' he said."

As we walk along the fellowship hall wall we pass random teenagers and adults who have flashed into my memory before, people I passed in the hallway once or every day, people who asked about the price of reduced meat at the grocery store. Aranea stops to say hi to them or to hug them before we move on. The wall extends from the building and around the church yard, wrapping around the two buildings and parking lot, blocking off the steep hill which leads to the graveyard below. When we stop to sit we're staring out across the scattered trees that frame the cemetery, like guardians over the little gray buttons popping up from the soil. The sedentary position gives me a much appreciated chance to disembowel the potato salad with my plastic spork. Seems like old times. She continues to tell me about the words of the youth leader, her eyes lighting up and her hands inverting and expressing the importance of various words. The afternoon sun beating down on my dress clothes makes me want to strip to my unmentionables and get savage with the church food, but instead I keep my eyes sleepily open and my ears listening to every crevice of her vernacular.

"Wanting someone is love's emotion, right? But not its essence, of course—love is more than an emotion. Having massively dorky feelings for someone is easy. I had feelings for the guy on the TV show 'Teen Angel' and that only lasted like a season. So I had to move on," she laughs as she tries desperately not to replace the youth leaders words with her inappropriate but all out tangents. "Love is the commitment inspired by and resulting from that raw emotion, but it's an integral and often overlooked part in the completion of that love, and it is directly orchestrated by God as a metaphor for the love He has for His creation." I lower my eyes to my plate. "As He is the author of love, unrequited love can't exist. Two people must contribute to create it, and the resulting union, that commitment that seals it all, begins the triangle relationship. You know the triangle idea: that man and woman are on the bottom corners, and as they move upward towards God, they move closer to each other? It's not mine, I've borrowed it." I nod.

"Seems like something you feel pretty strongly about, then."

"Yeah, I feel strongly about love. Isn't that the most beauty pageant thing you've ever heard?" She snorts and flexes her toes so they stretch out as far from each other as possible.

"Hah, yeah, do you feel strongly about right and wrong as well?"

"If I had only one wish it would be to cover the world in little plush teddy bears clutching red hearts that say 'I Love You' on them in cursive. I'm a humanitarian if nothing else." We share a laugh as I toss the scrap of bread crust down the hill to the birds below, who thank me by flying away. "I wonder if that little cardinal is okay?" she softly asks herself, before she realizes that I'm listening and changes the subject. "So how are you going to make this up to me?"

"Make what up to you?" is my clever response. "Oh, yeah," I say as my brain passes toxic gas, "what did you have in mind?" When I'm lying alone at night I wonder if my guardian angel really is just standing there with flash cards telling me when the right moment comes to say something suave and I'm just too secular to see them. If I were any more suave I'd be shampoo.

"Well, there's a really great band playing tonight at evening services, I thought maybe you'd like to come. You look a little tired, though. Did you not sleep well last night?" She bites her bottom lip softly again and waits for my excuse, because she knows it's coming and is expecting a big one. As I open my mouth a giant sports utility vehicle honks it's mighty horn as friendly smiles and passionately waving Caucasian hands wish us well.

"Good-bye Nea! We'll see you next week!" proclaim the joyful duo, one with a full gray beard and the other with pearl earrings. Aranea smiles at them and returns their exclamation and happy gestures. I want a bolt of lightning to break from the clear blue sky and set the unnecessarily large monstrosity of an automobile ablaze for their flagrant use of such a ridiculous abbreviation of her name. As they drive away I read their bumper sticker. "WARNING! When the Rapture comes, this car will be unmanned!" Make that two lightning bolts.

"Uh, well," I begin, still squinting my eyes disdainfully at their successful trivialization of an entire book of the Bible, "I did have sort of a bad night last night, so maybe tonight isn't such a good idea. But I definitely will be here next week."

"Oh, okay," she nods. With a spork in one hand and a paper plate in the other I'm sitting a foot or so from my gravity and suddenly the banter ceases, our thrift store upholstery torn away, and we've suddenly been reduced to awkward boy and mysterious dream girl again. The grilled cheese sandwich isn't being made for me anymore. It's already in my stomach, and even if I professionally throw it back up it's never going to look like a grilled cheese sandwich anymore. I may as well put in my order for another sandwich.

"Actually, they're holding a film festival at the college I used to go to tomorrow from like five 'till midnight, lots of really great foreign films, Studio Ghibli stuff…I thought maybe you'd want to go too, it's free and all. I can give you a ride on my bike. We'd be super cool."

"Oh, man, how can I resist?" she laughs. "But isn't wrestling on tomorrow night?"

Yes. Yes, it is. "For you, I can miss wrestling." That might've been the biggest compliment I've ever given another human being. I am walking, breathing shampoo.

"Excellent, Aranea Cavatica, breaking down the walls of popular culture. I'd love to." She gives me a double thumbs up, which is so massively dorky that it causes me to skip over love's essence entirely.

"Great, so it's a date!" I say casually, and if the conversation is being video-taped the viewer can press the pause button and pin point the exact moment when God breaks his straight face and reveals to me that I'm on one of Heaven's sadistic hidden camera shows.

"Oh." She looks away from me briefly before looking back, then looking away again. "Oh."

"What? What's wrong?" Did I just stick my head into every rear end on the planet? My words become short and uncertain, like I'm sixteen years old again and I'm trying to work up the nerve to talk to the pretty girl in the cafeteria. "Did I…"

"No, no, it's okay. I just don't date." She speaks the words so solidly that they chisel themselves into the wall beneath us. Aranea begins to slowly swing her legs as she continues, and I listen while the tears begin to warm up in the bull-pen. "I realize this obsession with a word might sound anal. You've got to understand, though, 'date' has an awful lot of societal baggage attached to it; and if you're going on one, you can't help but take some of it with you."

"Wh…what do you mean?" I'm not even sixteen anymore. I'm pondering how cool I'm going to be when I'm sixteen. She turns to me and places her palms directly in front of me on the bricks, looking me directly in the eye as she begins the speech that, until now, I never realized she's probably given a few times before.

"Despite anything you'll hear to the contrary, a date always entails at least a little bit of commitment. Were that not the case, breaking one off wouldn't require an explanation. So dating is, essentially, commitment to a total stranger. There's no need to date somebody you already know; not when the purpose is to familiarize. Now when people say they 'don't date seriously,' that usually means they either hook up or hang out. But neither having sex nor playing video games actually constitutes a date. At least not by itself."

"Well, yeah, if playing video games constituted a date I'd be going steady with Super Dodge Ball." The angels give me a sympathy clap and a gold star for effort. She begins to process the statement and stops, which is probably for the best.

"It's hard to explain, I guess, I don't want to…"

"No," I interrupt, preferring to take all of my failure in at once. "Go ahead."

"You're sure?" She seems genuinely concerned, but by this point I'm working monosyllabically.

"Yeah."

"The end result of dating, most people hope, is a commitment to one person who you enjoy on both a friendly and romantic level. Sorta 'desire to hang-out plus desire to hookup equals material for marriage.' Friendship should be the priority, though—casual hanging out should lead to getting to know a person, which develops romantic interest in that person. Right?"

"I guess."

"The way I see it defined in the lives of others, a date cannot be casual, because it's essentially about finding somebody to marry and that's a pretty serious thing. Even if you're not the kind to literally hook up, it's the same basic self-centeredness of already having an agenda when you meet someone. So I define a date as the presence of two agendas. Two people going out, yeah, but with the understanding that it's more than a hangout or a hookup. That the evening has a filter of romantic potential on it. Society's commercialized ideals, your preconceived notions, whatever. Both of those really murder decent human relations. If you're not giving people the benefit of the doubt, you're probably labeling. If you're labeling, you're limiting. You see what I mean?"

My hands start shaking, but I nod. My mind starts focusing so sharply on each word she says that the smart part of my brain, the part that pushes me through religious studies and helps me rationalize my way through vocabulary tests, starts nitpicking and disagreeing, but the logic is Aranea's so the other half figures I'm just wrong.

"The dating mind is narrowly set because it sees another human being, from the very beginning, in a subjective light. So when some guy is out on an understood 'date' with a girl, he's most likely not trying to feel her out as much as feel her up. The meeting is a superficially cued examination, and he's holding her under a microscope smeared with his own fingerprints. Not on purpose, really. Maybe he's trying to fill the omnipresent void or whatever. Maybe he's searching for his 'other half,' though I can't imagine why anybody would want a fifty percent person. Whatever the case, as he narrows her down to fit an ideal-shaped mold, all of her possibilities, including that of her friendship, get squeezed out to make room for his illusions. I'd say that's a pretty crappy way of getting to know someone. Dating by this definition generates interest from the exterior, and replaces the intimacy with BS posturing. You just end up putting yourself into the equation every time you think about them."

Some kids walking by are singing "I'm in the Lord's Army" to themselves and I smile, which is the first time since inner ear surgery that I've smiled during such intense pain. Not only was my Providence-supplied social ammunition not enough to win the battle, it was shot down in the runway. And then the enemy paraded over it with elephants in clunky black shoes. Really big clunky black shoes.

"There's also none of this trite, 'check yes or no' stuff going on, where suddenly some binary appears and you have to either accept the person as a friend or shoot them down the furnace with the rest of the bad eggs. You simply don't feel that pressure if you get along with them exceptionally well, you'll naturally want to invest more into the relationship. You know? The weight will be evenly distributed. That's the difference between a pure friendship and a selfish one. One begins without bias and develops into significance; the other has significance sort-of awkwardly thrust upon it."

For a moment I forget what her hair looks like and I really want to know if there's a bathroom in the graveyard down there.

"So, I dunno. I'd like to think that relationships could be free of connotations. That girls and guys could just hang out without staring into a mirror the entire time. If girls would only stop looking into things too hard and guys would stop only looking into things which make them hard, the world would be a better place. When I meet a person, be it guy or girl, I want to look at them as human beings first, and I want to see the friendship as an opportunity to show them God's love. I know it sounds Sunday School, but I can't think of a better way to say it. So yeah. I don't date. I hang out. But now you know, that means much more than just clever semantics to me. And if God isn't lining me up for the nunnery, maybe one day He'll let me marry my best friend."

"The moment you really see that the question, 'How can I change?' sets up an authority," he said, *"you have finished with authority for ever."*

CHAPTER 8

"Actually, they're holding a film festival at the college I used to go to tomorrow from like five to midnight, lots of really great foreign films, Studio Ghibli stuff...I thought maybe you'd want to go too, it's free and all. I can give you a ride on my bike. We'd be super cool."

"Oh man, how can I resist?" she laughs. "But isn't wrestling on tomorrow night?" Yes. Yes, it is.

"For you, I can miss wrestling." For you I would miss a thousand wrestling shows. I would climb mountains and swim in deep oceans and clip the knees out from under every seventies soul compliment. I would survive. Love would keep us together. We would boogie oogie oogie till we just couldn't boogie no more. We would lie together on the beach and fake French each other as the waves rolled seaweed onto our backs.

"Excellent, Aranea Cavatica, breaking down the walls of popular culture. I'd love to." She stands up and adjusts her period ball room gown. Brushing her wavy hair back over her shoulder she glances at me. Her eyes tell me all I need to know, pushed together and supported by the wired undergarment of sexual attraction.

"Great, so it's a date!" I say casually, snapping my fingers.

The American wife stood at the window looking out. Outside right under their window a cat was crouched under one of the dripping green tables. The cat was trying to make herself so compact that she would not be dripped on.

"I'm going down and get that kitty," the American wife said.

"What cat?," her husband asked from the bed. "Do you mean this cat?" he grinned, pulling the fluffy feline up from beneath the bed by the loose skin of the cat's back. Brooks laughed the laugh of a nineteen fifties sitcom punch line as the animal playfully licked his cheek. "Also underneath the bed here I have a table with your own silver, candles, springtime, a hairbrush, and some new clothes." Aranea smiled so broadly that her head lost balance and tilted to the side.

"Oh you!" she exclaimed, rushing into her husbands waiting arms while a gathering of Italian hotel workers cheered and clapped from the doorway.

❧   ❧   ❧

I make my way over to her chest-of-drawers and pulled open the second drawer from the top, where she keeps her socks and underwear, and found a dish rag. "No, I'm not her boyfriend. We're just good friends." I look around at all the bottles lying on the ground and then back towards the gentlemen, one of whom is now up and rummaging through Akiko's DVD collection.

"You must be really good friends!" he laughs, resulting in an impromptu high-five.

"Yeah, I guess." I try to walk to the door before more conversation is conceived, aborted, and spat at me.

"Dude, she needs to hurry up and get back, we need more weed." The less invasive one switches roles as he stands up from the futon and begins opening and closing drawers. "I know she keeps it around here somewhere, they always keep it in a place like this," he educates.

"Dude, we don't need more weed," says his friend, fondling around in his pockets. I'm almost out of the door as he pulls out a Ziploc bag with a collection of white pills floating around at the bottom. "The world's first and only organic ecstasy experience!" I hear the sentence as I'm leaving with the rag and stop.

"You aren't going to…you weren't planning to give any of that to her, were you?" I ball the rag up in my hand and squeeze it until it turns into coal and then diamonds.

"Well yeah, that's why I brought it, huh. I mean, if you aren't her…"

Before he finished the word my swing had already begun. The crowbar sunk into his neck just below the mandible and ripped upwards, dislodging his jaw and sending a drift of cracked teeth and blood spraying against the dorm room window. I stood above him, gripping the length of metal so fiercely that my hands themselves began to bleed. Repeatedly I brought down the sharp curve into his face, rearranging his features as though I was God himself molding a lump of clay. Behind me I could hear his friend expressing various curses, each one sounding more distant as the door slammed and his footsteps raced towards the elevator.

Beneath my towering visage lay the expressed love of Picasso's life, the harsh realism and strung-up organs of Frida Kahlo at last revealing themselves to me outside of the body of this boy, this worthless boy who exchanged money for education for his magical job-giving pieces of paper. I had taken him somewhere he would never have ventured without me, to a blistering wonderland of art and imagination, a place where he was no longer a pair of khaki shorts and a baseball cap but a myriad of bright reds and haunting blacks; no longer an MTV demographic but a dazzling physical representation of rage and release; no longer a drinking buddy but an oil painted Prometheus, a still life oozing onto the carpet. I knelt before him and kissed his forehead. He had shown me true beauty that I could never have imagined.

Auburn sat propped backwards in a bean bag chair so that all I could see from my position on the futon were her shiny purple toenails reflecting the sunlight through the window.

"So if she won't go out on a date with you because you aren't some magical gift from God, why don't you use that against her?"

"Use that against her?" I say with my brow clenched almost against my bottom lip. "What do you want me to do, tell her that Jesus is standing behind her and then pants her when she turns around?"

"No, that might be misconstrued as a sexual assault. But I do have a friend in figure drawing who looks a lot like Jesus if you need a character actor."

"Auburn, you go to college. A solid two-thirds of the guys in your classes look like Jesus."

"Well, whatever. So what it boils down to is that you love her enough to drive yourself and those around you insane, but she won't reciprocate unless God herself gives the girl a sign, right?"

"Basically."

"God is a concept by which we measure our pain. I'll say it again," she says, before pausing. "God is a concept by which we measure our pain. If she doesn't believe in casual dating, if she doesn't believe in kissing, if she doesn't believe in strong hand holding, if she doesn't believe in romantic trial and error, then take the power into your own person to give her that sign from God that she's looking for. If you don't, dear friend, the dream is over." I sat silently for a minute staring at the <u>Tank Girl</u> poster on her wall before collecting my thoughts and wrapping them in iridescent paper.

"I don't know how to give her a sign from God. I'm not God. I'm not even Alec Baldwin with a God complex. I'm just me. All I can do is just trust that if I do enough good things for her, and if I can impress her enough with some things she's never seen before, that maybe she'll open up her eyes and see that I really do care about her, in a non-weird kind of way."

"Nobody cares about anything in a non-weird kind of way. Do you really think that if you stand outside her window holding a boom box over your head she'll fall in love with you? That doesn't work in the real world. In the real world your arms get tired and you get the cops called on you. This is not a romantic comedy. If nothing else it's a romantic tragedy. Romeo and Juliet isn't about love, it's about stupid teenagers. Shakespeare didn't fall in love with Gwyneth, he was a bald guy from the drama club in tights. Feel free to dramatize the past, but the present needs to stay the way it is intended for the Mercutios and the James Courts of the world. Nicely colored but generally uneventful."

"Oh, I've got it," Auburn commented, raising a finger high into the air. "You'll dig a big hole and hide in it, and then when she walks by you'll push a giant monolith up from the ground and she'll be forced to evolve into somebody who gives a damn."

"I've got it!" screamed Jiddu Krishnamurti, scrambling out of bed in the middle of the night and rushing to notes. Flipping through the loose leaves of paper and grasping for a pencil with his free hand, he felt as though he had just adjusted to the hot bubbling water in the Hindu hot tub of enlightenment. Happily he scratched down the answer to it all and threw it to the ground, dancing around his room like a child on some eastern hemisphere's holiday morning.

And the scratching on the paper read, "Love is all you need."

"Or how about this," said Auburn from the top bunk. "What if you put in some quality time with the rim of the toilet, and then suck in your gut for hours at a time while she walks around not noticing you? You can drive your-self deeper and deeper into personal madness. But I guess that's kind of a macabre message for God to be sending."

"She doesn't 'not notice me,' she notices me. She invited me to church with her…"

"You don't think she invites everybody she knows to church with her?"

"Well,…I had a dream sequence about heaven with her in it, and there was all this symbolism with gates and empty graves and introspection that…"

"You found symbolism in your relationship with her? Weren't you the guy who wrote his first college paper comparing the Axis Powers during World War II to the Muppet Babies? 'Nanny' represented the faceless world power of America that showed up whenever there was a problem. Gonzo and his big nose and funny voice represented Jews. Should I go on?"

"Well…no, please don't."

"Aw, I'm sorry sweetie, did I make you uncomfortable?" said Auburn with her bottom lip tracing the back of my neck. Her fingers walked across my bare chest, leaving crescent-shaped footprints that carried themselves during trial and suffering with the Lord nowhere to be found. "Why are you being so destructive about this anyway? She's just a girl. You're walking a fine line between art and cliché."

"I just don't know how to do it. I've never had to do it this way before." I could feel her corpulent soul pressed against my back as the dimly lit room's humidity rose in vaporous clouds. "When I was there in the graveyard the first time nothing made sense, it was like my world had broken and I was falling. But then she was there, and she hugged me for no reason, and she made me feel better for no reason, and I don't know why she was there or why she did it. There was something in that hug that kept me thinking about her and kept her in my life, even though she wasn't a part of it. She was always on the border, just walking around my life looking around, seeing what was there, seeing what she could help me with or fix. She sometimes did more by just walking past me than by ever talking to me." My voice lowered into strained whisper as each syllable had to tear away from my throat to break free. "My high school was all on one level, with the exception of the gym which was down a flight of stairs at the end of the hall. Behind the stairs was the art room, and every day before fifth period she would walk past me coming from art as I was going to gym, and it was like..." Moments passed as my body moved against hers, our blood making the bodies slick. "Every day gym class was hard for me, because the kids...the black kids in the class, they would single me out as the...as the fat kid, as the kid who wouldn't...or didn't...or couldn't fight back, and they'd hurt me. It wasn't just the Jehovah's Witness with the trapper keeper. I never told anyone but they would hurt me some way every day, hurt my mind or my body or my heart. And every day before gym class she would pass me, and it was like she was there letting me know that this was not all there was, and that it would be okay eventually. It was like...it was like God sent her there, concept or not, to let me know that the hurting would stop one day."

"Maybe it wasn't a message from God at all," she said. "Maybe it was just block scheduling."

"If I let my life go one-second thinking it wasn't a message from God I would probably go crazy. I'm probably already there. I keep thinking back to little moments in my life that didn't really matter and are done with and reliving them in my head. I just can't stop thinking about them. It's like I'm addicted to pills, I have to pop the same memory eight or nine times a day now to make it have the same emotional impact I think it should have. Maybe my mind is just warped."

My front teeth were pressed against the smooth inner curve of her pale thigh when she opened me up. "Maybe," she dissected with her little knife, "the problem is that you've convinced yourself that you're more than just casually warped, but are pained by the feeling that you're too average and white and middle class to actually be so, and therefore unable to articulate your feelings to anybody."

The muscles in my face constricted and heaved as I watched the tiniest unforced teardrop roll from my eyeball and fall that great and brief distance to the arc of her thigh. As it fell to the blanket I gathered myself naked and trembling like a wounded creature to one knee, sliding my face up her body, never denying or releasing the connection between my nose and her skin, before resting my head on the pale flesh of her stomach.

"Maybe," I think to myself, "the problem is that I keep fearing that the things I do for Aranea will never exceed the efforts of any other random soul who felt something cheap for her. Maybe if I felt something cheap for her she'd give herself to me and I could have her, and we would never mean anything, and I could pretend." My eyes closed and I could feel my body begin to jerk, and no matter how hard I pressed my face into the soft mound of her belly I could not prevent the remnants of withdrawn memories from squeezing themselves out to leave puddles of saline moisture around her navel.

"There, there," she said, laying her hands against the back of my head. "My cracked plate."

❦   ❦   ❦

THE REAL FACTS OF LIFE

By Pastor Christopher Daniels

In life, we must always consider the consequences of our actions. In Christianity, we must always consider the consequences of disobedience towards God. If we misuse our sexuality, what will be the consequence?

> "Be not deceived; God is not mocked: for whatsoever a man soweth, that shall he also reap" (Gal 6:7)

It is a common misconception that a girl's virginity is her own. While it is the choice of the girl how her virginity is lost (or rather, given away), her virginity is really a gift from God, given to her to care for. She has but one opportunity (as well as a responsibility) to give this gift to her husband. If she chooses unwisely, she cannot get it back And if a girl's virginity is given away prematurely, she ALWAYS feels used after this has happened. For she has given her gift to someone not chosen by God for her, and she has violated His will.

Today, the value of virginity is lessened by the media, it is sacrificed to the pagan god of "entertainment." Though most girls do undoubtedly prize their gift, they are faced with many seemingly good reasons to give into temptation. Some girls feel that giving away their virginity will make them "fit in." Some give it away because they think it will bring them "love," or to retain the supposed "love" of their boyfriend. Regardless of the reason, it is selfishness, it violates God, and it is a decision that cannot be taken back.

Young men also have a priceless gift, and when they give into their impure feelings before marriage, they too have lost an innocence that cannot be retrieved. Sexual gratification is momentary, but not worthwhile. This is a fact for young men as well as young girls. He too will find the consequence in mocking God.

ALL sexual activity occurring before marriage is selfish, prideful and degrading to God. To run too quickly into this holy and beautiful act is nothing short of profane, and it is most assuredly in violation of God.

Engagement, despite the claims of some, is not an excuse for giving away this mysterious gift. Despite the vow of commitment shown by a couple engaged to be married, their reasons for acting in violation of God are just as selfish, and still nothing more than giving into temptation. The Bible states that sex is to occur *only in marriage*. And it is only God who can unite a man and woman in holy matrimony. A commitment between two people does not make them married, not without permission of church and state, who are God's tools for unification.

Despite what may seem like a copious amount of reasons to give away one's virginity, there need be only one reason to refrain until marriage. That reason is the word of our God. Something else to consider is this: not all engaged couples marry. What would be the consequence if, after engaging in pre-marital sex, a couple did not marry and later the man or woman decided to marry another? Their marriage bed would most assuredly be affected by the young man or girl's previous undermining of God. Again, God will not be mocked.

Any sin leaves scars. Scars that remain for years to come, if not for the rest of one's life. The same is true of premarital sexual intercourse. It too causes scars. Sometimes in the heat of a moment, it is not easy to think ahead of that moment, to think of the consequences, of the scars. But it is impossible to act against God concerning such a remarkable and profound act and not leave a scar. Even many years into a marriage, the scar left by pre-marital immorality can still affect your beloved husband or wife. I have seen couples in counseling who took part in these illicit relations before marriage with each other. I see in them judgment, guilt, blame, and a trauma within their conscience. I hope that they now realize that we reap what we sow. Sin leaves scars.

Though the cut of sin may heal, the scar does not disappear. It stays with us until we move into our next life. I would like every young man and woman to think about this scars, scars to ourselves and those we cherish, before they enter into an act that violates the will of God. The play isn't called Romeo and Juliet and Mercutio.

"Hey Auburn," I asked, watching her wrestle around with her dog in the front yard of her Alabama home. Out of the corner of my eye I can see her mother and father standing together on their front porch laughing. Auburn's hair is long and red, and she is happy. "Why do you speak in quotations all the time, anyway? How do you even know so many quotations?"

"I'm a twenty-three year old woman. Nobody is going to listen to me no matter how much I say. I'll never write like Toni Morrison. I'll never paint like Mary Cassatt. I'll never sing like Etta James." She stretches out in the grass and looks back at me. "What I can do, however, is combine their thoughts and talents in such a way to better express myself. I like to think I feel things that are too strong for me to understand. But I know somebody out there has felt it too, and has struggled with it long enough to make some sense out of it. I'll try not to duel with things I can't defeat." She raises her arms above her head and frames a cloud with her hands as her father turns and walks into the house.

"Ouch," she says, scratching through her bleached hair with one hand and staring at the dripping blood on the end of a finger on the other. "Tybalt, you bit me. Bad dog!"

The dog and the house and the perfect family fades away and she's herself again, raising up from my chest and wiping away the tears on her stomach with some random sock. She reaches over and grabs the telephone as I lower myself back onto the futon.

"So," she says, "wanna order some food? I think the bistro is still open."

"Did you ever stop to think that your play is really just Romeo and Mercutio and Mercutio?"

"Did you ever stop to think that maybe nobody's writing a play about you?"

"Did you ever stop to think that nobody's thinking about you?"

"Did you ever stop to think?"

"Do you ever stop?"

When I finally decide to flip the light switch the sight of blood covering the floor and glistening white porcelain shocks me and I have to catch myself against the vanity to keep from falling. My white T-shirt is dyed in chaotic splatters. I try to grab it but my fingers are doused in the same blood and I cannot keep myself from staining it further. The various lobes of my brain try working together in this stressful time to figure out why I chose to wear a white shirt for an event like this, and after a few moments they decide that I subconsciously wanted this scene in the movie to look visually fantastic. The audience would gasp and be taken aback, thinking I'd taken a razor blade to my wrists or to my throat in a final act of desperation. They would murmur to their boyfriends or wives or elitist message board dwellers that the cinematography was amazing even if the plot had become predictable and melodramatic. The rambling tangents swirl down the drain as my eyes roll back in my head and I fall to my knees again.

I didn't intend for it to happen this way. I just wanted the standard release. I wanted the food out of me so I could express the self-pity to myself in a way that even incognizant parts of my body like the lining of my stomach would put their arms around me and offer me solace from the inside. Instead of solace, internal bleeding was offered and here I am now with my hands and my mouth covered in sticky, warm circulatory refuse. The palm of my hand loses its grip on the rim and I lose my grip on reality somewhere between the forward fall and my forehead colliding with the edge. Images flash through my mind of my creative writing teacher kicking trash cans across the room.

"Aranea Cavatica's arms are so long that her elbows rest comfortably at her waist. Her neck is long, her eyes are big and green, and her upper lip is the same size as her bottom one. There is an unbearable earnestness to her beauty, and it bothers me."

"The ability of Coach Brown to keep the Lady Bees' spirits high is a testament to her weird habit of standing around in the girls locker room staring! Also, the soccer coach has put in a request that prettier, more single girls try out for the J. V. team this year!"

Somewhere near the fourth second before I hit the ground I wonder what Melissa VanOverloop is doing lately and I think about a Hemingway short story I read in freshman composition, and Aranea. I wonder if I should've hit the fraternity brother in Auburn's room that night, or if I should've hit him again, and again, and again. I wonder if I should have killed him.

Somewhere near the third second before I hit the ground I think about what a bad movie Tank Girl was, and if a sign from God is really all I need to create to hold Aranea in my arms. For a few of the moments in this second I think about how funny it would be if I stood on Aranea's roof one afternoon, and how I could write "miracle" on a thousand pieces of confetti and throw them into her yard when she walks out. Then I think about the clean up job and realize that it's all fun and games until somebody loses their sanity.

Somewhere near the second second before I hit the ground I think about how great the Plastic Ono Band album was, and I wonder what Krishna would think of the film <u>Roman Holiday</u>, and how the best part is that they don't stay together in the end. I wish my life had that level of poetic reverence. I remember crying little streams into Auburn's belly button.

Somewhere near the first second before I hit the ground I try to think of a good quote for this occasion and if I will ever stop, or if I will ever stop thinking, or if there are any plays written about this sort of thing. I wonder what the title would be.

Somewhere near the zero second before I hit the ground I think about how I should have flipped the switch before I started falling, and of Aranea, and of Aranea, and Aranea.

OCTOBER

CHAPTER 9

For an instant all I can hear are the heels of black boots centralizing the orange and yellow leaves beneath them and breaking them like hammer strikes to the bottoms of stained glass windows. All that is left behind are shattered blades hanging from sun-drained veins. The boots press on down to spread splinters of color along the ashen sidewalks lining the upward and downward trails tracing the hills to her house. Every tenth step is marked with a fallen piece of sharply cut construction paper bearing the word "miraculum." The rectangles are arranged by color and stacked inside the limpid plastic trash bag bouncing against the shoulder of the traveler with each stride. There are hundreds of slips of miraculum and so many hills.

The project started more as a vision than as a desperate cry for attention and the creative proprietor stands by that vision, despite the underlying obviousness of it all. The actions, or, more specifically, the plan, have not been completely mapped out but there is an inherent hope that Providence or a moderately strong wind would give wings to the good intentions and pave these sidewalks with them.

There is an intersection at the top of the final hill before the journey's end where the side of her duplex is only obscured by a few trees, and in these increasingly chilled afternoons the trees have shed their skins and the view is clear. The confident soul would look back at the night's work and smile, counting on that moment when the music swells and the flower petals fall around the boy and the girl like rain. The confident soul would sit down, Indian style, in the middle of the street to stare down at her lawn and imagine the coming events; the big eyes, the scrunched noses, the dancing and the hugs that swing around. The soul with one more street to go and butterflies holding bags of vomit in his stomach tries not to slip on the loose leaves on the sidewalk.

The plan is like a giant painting of a big-legged Victorian woman hanging in a museum. The little boys on field trips scamper in to collect themselves in to huddles and snicker at her nipples and the way she looks like she has Down Syndrome; like some child's beautiful doll filled with water. The strokes are technically sufficient. The image captures a feeling between its thighs and thrusts deeper than the lines and shades suggest. The use of positive and negative space is profoundly vocal. It was created by someone who worked vigorously day and night against their own doubts and against their own convictions as a necromantic gift to the world. When the little boys think about it later all they will remember is how funny it was that you could see her boob.

I am hanging here in the center of the street now, motionless, waiting and watching for the little boys to leave so I can be appreciated. There is a smell of damp grass in the air, sounds of rakes penetrating and raping the leafy lawns, beams of sunlight catching bicycle spokes and spinning into oblivion. The colors flash before me as they die, remarking on the subtlety of a life gone unnoticed. They rise to Heaven or fall to Hell as I watch without a word or a movement of my eye as the wind picks up and the happy screams of children echo and fade behind my mind.

On the way down my legs cross and suddenly Whitestone Drive is my kindergarten class and the glistening pavement is the purple rug where we began each class. The fold of her living room curtain is visible just above a row of bushes. Wind begins to slip into my ear and spin before it breaks free from the curvature of the cartilage and rejoins the school of motion whistling and pooling around me. The sounds form into my teacher's words. She was a dark-skinned lady with a broad smile and dangling gold earrings. When she spoke to me it was never an order or a lesson. The little boy with the bowl haircut and chubby cheeks sat at a desk in the rear of the class drawing wrestlers in notebooks while the other children struggled to form a capital R between the green lines on their tan worksheets. They were so slow, so dense and normal, and I could feel nothing but frustration towards them. Each day a contest would be held for a folder that when scratched smelled of watermelon and each day the folder found it's way to my desk. It felt so important to smell the watermelon, or the grape, or the strawberry. The thought of her earrings spinning makes me lose my train of thought and suddenly I remember that I cannot recall her name, or what she ever taught me. The words in my ears are gone before I can recognize them and life goes on.

Each house along her street is filled with one of the people who learned at the same time as everyone else and understood when everyone else understood. They have moved on with their folder-less lives and are comfortable the way things are, living upwards of five hundred and as few as three feet away from a girl they could never hope to appreciate. Why won't they stop being so pedestrian and just learn things? A swell of jealous hatred bubbles up from within my ribcage to singe my heart. At once my hands want to pierce their windows, my fingers to wrap around their throats, my knuckles to bleed for them and for myself. My arms want to dig deep into the street itself and tear it to pieces, to render the soil barren and to burn the leaves. The muscles in my throat yearn to scream her name into their faces. The ducts in my eyes want to show them the kinds of tears they should be crying for her. Every part of me jumps at the chance for patriotism but the reality is that the parts are all alone here in the middle of the street and can't even work up the nerve to walk on down the hill.

Above the houses the sound of thunder staggers behind a commuter plane making its way overhead. My eyes ease their way down as a tiny girl emerges from one of the front doors. She is not an especially pretty girl and her hair is caught in loose pig tails that were probably intended to be beautiful before boredom set in and she wouldn't sit still. Clutched between her fingers is a small black baby doll that is not especially pretty either. The girl's knees have miniature scars decorating them and the doll has a pink outfit with booties. As the girl trots down steps taller than her legs she swings the plastic baby around and around until the outer fibers of material begin to pull free and the brown skin smacks against her fleshy olive arm. Happily the little girl raises her arm into the air and sends the smiling faux-infant sailing back up the steps and onto the porch. Between outbursts of laughter the girl with scarred knees turns to me and pauses. Her eyes meet mine. We have nothing immediately in common and she waves to me. My fingers raise and return the gesture but she has already turned around to make her way back up the steps. There are good reasons why the street is in one piece and why the leaves are still damp. Aranea is not the street and the street is not Aranea. One day the fat kid might fall in love with the olive skinned girl with memories of torn flesh around her knees, and no amount of unrequited emotion should come between the boy and his harmless fantasies.

Finding it difficult to deal with such a display of rampant humanity my body expands and stretches back onto the asphalt. The airplane passes my nose and escapes my sight. Looking into a cloudy sky my mind wanders back to its last flight, the early morning flight where the sky looked like pumpkin pie and the clouds looked like blue cotton candy, and how nice it would've been to fall from the plane into them. They seemed like the moon walk at the fair. I felt like my body could go bouncing along them falling as I try to stand, tumbling over onto my head and laughing until Mom makes me stop. A deep sigh fills my lungs and the beauty of that moment caresses me. In this moment of relaxation a small black projectile is noticed, until seconds later when a shot rings out and fills the street with violent noise.

The image instantly brands itself to me though I can confess to have only seen it in passing. Some living things, ants for example, have terminal velocities that are not fatal, and can survive falls from heights that might be fatal for humans. Regardless of what crazy Gods and bush-men may say, a Coca-Cola bottle even partially filled will not rest comfortably upon impact. From the porch where the little girl stood it must've looked spectacular, a missile colliding with the pavement and spreading before popping like a balloon. In my memories moments after the sound I recall the silence of the fall and impact more than the severity of the consequence. Some twenty feet behind my skull it landed, twenty-one feet, and as the red and white label whipped by me on some shard of shrapnel meant for the stars my eyes blur and focus on the Dodge Durango swerving to avoid the blast.

Being Indian-style in a situation like this is counterproductive even if you're an actual Indian, because it means you only have a few moments before the pungent odor of premium unleaded and the chalkboardian squeal of the snow tires in autumn begin to crush bone. My knees bend like a folding chair as my body heaves itself off toward the sidewalk and my eyes are fixed on the little girls steps, so I only hear the sport and utility of the vehicle tearing through my hefty plastic trash bag. Fractions of seconds later my leg stops moving. In a moment like this one begins to contemplate life as a vegetable. Even if one gets to be one of the more delicious vegetables like corn it's not worth it, because you can't run anymore and you can't dance anymore even if you never ran or danced in the first place. Suddenly I start wishing I'd danced more, or ran places instead of driving, and right before my nervous system shuts down I look back to see that the tire just ran across my shoelaces. The shoe is a goner. More fractions deduce their way from the situation and my functions begin to work again just as I lay the side of my forehead against the pavement and close my eyes. The palms of my hands are still gripping the curb as a tornado of perfectly cut "miraculum" swirl in the winds above me.

The drivers eyelids snap open to squeeze his sockets and his heart begins to race as he questions whether or not he has ended my life, and giving him a basic amount of empathy I cannot find fault in this. From the ground the tires appear to be bending and spinning and the silver metal body shakes and threatens to break apart, like a child's tree house filled with too many children. My heart pushes past the lungs and peers out desperately from between my ribs as gravity shoots the car down the hill like a pinball trigger and into her front lawn. In my mind I can see drops of urine trickling down the man's thigh and onto his expensive upholstery. There are instant thoughts of the man collapsed and crying against the opened door of his SUV as the police collect the bodies; images of her windows cracked and her curtains unfolded and decayed; Polaroids still gray and undeveloped of her fragmented lips smiling as they close her inside the box forever.

I lay there on the ground for what seems like minutes trying to make my words form and soar, but nothing. No sound. No children laughing. No bottles of soda from Heaven falling to Earth. No scraping together of clouds. Nothing.

A chill overcomes me as the leaves raise from their tombs and race past me down the hill. The next sound I can hear is the plastic trash bag getting trapped on my ankle. It reminds me of how potato chips sound in your head as you eat them and like the leaves on the soles of my shoes. The wind has picked up and the tornado has dispersed like Santa's birds waiting on the power lines to see what happens next. Through the storm of green and blue construction paper she appears, standing in her open doorway. She is so far away but her warmth rests beside me on the street. Her eyes are closed but the green shines through until I cannot tell where her eyes begin and the miraculum ends.

Once again the volume is unbearable as the Durango locks it's brakes and hits the curb at a seventy degree angle. Sixty-seven. My eyes refuse to leave Aranea Cavatica as she smiles peacefully, surrounded by arrows of mud and dust powering up from beneath the wheels and onto her white doorway. She only moves to guard her face with her right hand, she does not blink. The front bumper buries itself as the car strikes Aranea's stone birdbath, causing the family of Cardinals sitting atop it to ascend toward the rooftop. The white pillar falls parallel to the ground and plows the soil before wedging itself between the concrete bullfrog used to house her spare key and the steps of the small porch connecting the two sides of the duplex. All at once the forward motion stops and the birdbath flares upward from behind, leaving the Dodge propped up like a space shuttle; like some beautiful avant-garde isosceles triangle. Aranea stands still until the noise stops. She leans to the right to see the driver battling his air bag in the front seat. She leans to the left to see a plastic bag swoop by and hook itself on the passenger mirror. She leans forward and draws a heart in the mud on the front bumper.

My feet are creating footsteps but it feels like the wind is holding me up and pushing me forward. The driver of the Durango, a man in his late fifties who is probably in his thirties, is standing beside the geometry now, brandishing dollar bills with one hand and cursing into his cell phone with the other. His words are so loud but they don't matter, and I can't hear or understand them. The doors of the houses lining the street are opening now and little girls with dolls are hobbling down steps bigger than their legs. People who learned to read when they were six or seven or four or one are wandering down driveways, stretching their necks up and tilting their heads back just a bit to see what made the noises, never once suspecting a plastic bottle and a bag full of paper. Crazy drunk drivers, they think, reckless teenagers, potholes in the roads. That lousy Governor. They raise their hands above their heads and talk to God in their own ways and I try not to fall to my knees.

It takes me too long to reach the bottom of the hill, because when I'm finally there I can't remember why I didn't stay at the top. The people from the houses have congregated along the curb to stare at the steady stream of motor oil dripping from beneath the engine of the 5.9-litre Tower of Pisa. Baby birds have drifted down from the rooftop to inspect the bird bath, now cracked and barely suspending the interrupted disaster. Murmurs of property damage and insurance companies fade into the air but nobody listens, and from between the upholstered bodies of the neighborhood my eyes meet hers, and I know she is here and not in the box.

Her smile turns into a frown and back into a smile when she reaches me, standing about six feet away, five feet and six inches. My body is hunched over, my arm clutching my already bruised insides until I look like I'm trying to keep my intestines from spilling onto the pavement. She looks down at my feet, then tilts her head just inches to the side, smiling so that the bottom of her upper row of teeth is visible. Aranea's eyes squint and focus directly into mine. Her pupils look like puddles reflecting the dark greens of a forest canopy against the milky pure white of a rain-fallen morning sky. Her cheeks are flushed a washed-out red, either from the beautiful realization of a near-death experience or maybe just aesthetic necessity.

Forcing a smile that comes as naturally as opening my eyes I raise my right arm to show her the patchwork of lacerations, now black from the dirt and oil on the street. The vein in my wrist is throbbing and the teardrops of blood tracing the corridors of my wounds look like a frothed stream winding it's way through the rocks. She quickly turns her head to the side to avoid directly smiling at my pain and raises her right hand. The scars on her palm have been splintered, and rivulets of blood are slowly making their way down to her wrist. I turn my head in the opposite direction to avoid directly smiling at her pain. After a moment we manage to look directly at one another again.

I take a few steps toward her and whisper, "I…made you a present." At the top of the hill there is a dark brown stain from the descent and fiery death of a Coca-Cola bottle. The entire neighborhood is talking to each other and laughing or frowning, and the children are screaming as they ride their bikes in circles to mimic the crash. There are a hundred pieces of paper spinning around us decorated with imperfect calligraphy and an SUV spiked like a flag in the center of her yard. My arm stretches out across the distance that seems like a thousand centimeters and raises with a tiny piece of folded paper between my index and middle fingers.

Unable to speak she takes the paper from me and unfolds it slowly. Inside, in perfect calligraphy, read the words: "I'm sorry." Her body jerks and her lungs let out a heavy breath. She begins a motion to hug me, but before she moves I lean forward and wrap my arms tightly around my waist, resting my cheek against her shoulder and not saying a word. Looking to the side I can see her hands just floating there in the air an inch from my shoulders. She lets out a snort and breaks into laughter, wrapping her arms around my neck and squeezing until my cheeks turn red.

Down the street, perched on the hood of the Dodge Durango, is a full-grown Cardinal clutching a green piece of construction paper in his beak that reads "miraculum."

CHAPTER 10

"Aranea? Why do you have big metal cheeseburgers in your back yard?"

"I wanted the little fry guy with the spring sticking out of his butt but I couldn't get it shipped. I thought the cheeseburger labyrinth was the way to go." Aranea squats and leans to peek through the arched opening and into the dirt-floored dome of the hollowed meat and cheese. "I have to come out here every few days to make sure no stray animals or needy children have wandered in and gotten lost."

"You always knew you were dealing with needy children when they couldn't navigate the burgers." Looking down I'm surprised to see slight streaks of black beneath the messed brown ringlets. I've noticed the difference in shades of white on the enamel of her teeth but I never noticed black beneath it all. "It's good to know that we've got a local chapter of the Ronald McDonald House in our neighborhood."

"And more importantly," she smiles back, "countless smiles have been shared, lives have been touched, and connections have been made."

In the time passing here after the fiery death of the concrete frog I have been listening to the tow truck fail to find the appropriate angle to remove a sports utility vehicle from a front porch. I have smelled gasoline and the earthy scent associated with dispersing masses. Aranea is drawing small hearts in the dirt. I can see the ridged contours of her chest as she breaths in and out, and I think about how delicate she felt between my arms. The realization sets in that I actually held here there for a moment, and though it was inconsequent and birthed from the realization that we were both so amazingly alive that I want it to happen again and again, to be there when she needs me to hold on, because I'm always holding on. Blades of grass around the dirt mounds are swaying back and forth and I can hear them rustling together. I reach out with my hand to touch her shoulder, but when her head begins to move my arm recoils and I'm left standing off balance, about to fall over like a goon into the cheeseburger. She glances over at my feet and grins, and I notice how the skin of her face is pulled tightly over her skull. I wonder if she worries about the angles in her wrists like I would, or if she's as comfortable in her skin as I want to be. In my own.

"Here," she says, standing up and grabbing me by my wrists. "Here," she continues and all at once I'm a deer and she's eight million headlights. Her head nods softly as she whispers, "I've got something peachy to show you."

There are four statues on her old seventies floor model television. Four blocks to be precise, each with a wooden cat striking a cute pose amongst springs and flowers. Each has it's own letter: M, E, O, and W.

"Aren't they great?" she says, her lips stretching out like a caricature to put every tooth she has on display. "I found them in the trash can outside of art class, you know, the big one near the band room? I don't know if you were ever in the band, but yeah, anyway, I found them and there were three of them, the M, the E, and the W. I felt bad for them and thought they deserved a more complete onomatopoeia."

With the initial shock of being in the Cavatica Household in a recessive stage I begin to notice the way her living room looks like an attic, with cardboard boxes stacked in corners and rays of light from the afternoon sky plowing through her heavy curtains to expose the snowflakes of dust hovering in the air. Strangely it feels as though the environment has expanded from the couch and the pictures and the grilled cheese promises. Two copies of every yearbook she's in are stacked on her bookcase, along with all of the books I can remember from school. Great Expectations. The Odyssey. Wuthering Heights. Ethan Frome. To Kill a Mockingbird. The smart part of my brain, the part that rewrites Hemingway and tells me to jump out of the way when cars are barreling down on me, wants me to sit her down and explain to her that anybody who puts, Ethan Frome in the same bookcase as, To Kill a Mockingbird should be put on a sled and slid headfirst into a tree. Then again the bookcase is Aranea's, so the other half of my brain tells me to go out and buy a copy of Ethan Frome.

"Where did you get the 'O' cat?"

Quickly she turns to me and bows, bringing her right arm across her stomach and extending her left arm into the air behind her. "I made it myself. I had to do a lot of research before beginning, since you know how much we learn about actual creative effort in Brookville High School art classes." An image of Mr. Thrasher throwing chairs across the room and threatening to punch us in the face for gluing Tony Moon's feet to the ground comes to mind.

"Hah, yeah, you know it's aesthetically life altering when you're in an art class called 'art.' I spent more time doing work for the pot-heads around me than I did for myself. I must've drawn fifty grim reapers one year."

"Melissa VanOverloop was the one drawing the grim reapers in my class." I turn my head away at the sound of the name but smile because it wasn't really so bad. "Only the grim reapers had these giant eyes and cat ears, and sailor suits. And sometimes they were on horses," she continued. "It was weird for the sake of being weird. Like German expressionist film. She really had a lot to offer." All I can do is shake my head as I pick up a ceramic cardinal from the bookshelf, examine it indeterminately, and place it back.

"She moved to California over the summer to sleep with a guy she met online."

"Oh," she murmurs, her eyebrows lowering and arching against one another. "Really?"

"Yeah."

"Oh. How unfortunate. That's nothing like German expressionist film at all."

"I don't know, unless she was in a chat room with Dr. Caligari. But she did reappropriate an alienated universe by transforming it into a private, personal vision. Maybe she knows what she's doing after all."

"But aren't we all doing that?"

"What, chatting with Dr. Caligari?" She tilts her head to the side and laughs as I turn to her, bugging my eyes out and wiggling my fingers. "I must know everything. I must penetrate the heart of his secret! I must become Caligari! LOL."

"That would be a really revealing age-sex-location check." Outside I can hear what appears to be the tow truck finally pulling away. Aranea trots to the window and pulls back the heavy curtain to glance out into the yard, dispersing a cloud of dust and a bouquet of light into the room. "My yard looks like the fertile crescent."

As she stares at the muddy ditches carved through the grass I watch her ribs push out a deep sigh from beneath the sheer ivory cotton jersey hanging like a cobweb from her shoulders. I can almost hear her toes wreathing within the spurts of shag. Her eyelids begin to close but only fall to half-mast, leaving just a bow of green. The light is slowly turning from white to orange. Behind her, hanging on the wall, is a framed and autographed picture of a construction worker. "Can't get enough of your love, baby! Best wishes, Barry White."

"That was a Mesopotamia joke, by the way."

"The 'cradle of civilization,' I got it. I was just waiting for the follow-up ziggurat joke." Walking to the window I can see deep gashes in the Earth, tire tracks filled with greasy clumps of grass and rock. Aranea scratches her elbow and stares off into the increasingly pink sunset as I lean across her to get a better view. She smells like feathers and baby powder. "But hey, look on the bright side. With these irrigation ditches you'll finally be able to successfully establish a permanent civilization."

"Yeah, the city-state of Cavatica. When my code of law is enacted your bad joke will be penalized by a bad joke of my own." Her laugh makes me feel like Gilgamesh. "I think Hammurabi's Code goes in that category of things we remember despite the fact that we've never been forced to recall them. Eli Whitney is in that category as well. If you listened to the public school system you'd be convinced that humanity peaked at the invention of the cotton gin."

"What I never understood was why in seventh grade they started teaching you about Mesopotamia, right there at the beginning, and then by the end of the year you were at World War II. Then, instead of picking up in the forties they go back to Mesopotamia again the next year. When U.S. History finally comes around in the tenth grade you can't help but think of Calvin Coolidge as a Priest-King."

"The patron saint of presidential alliteration, perhaps?"

"I dunno, 'presidential alliteration' makes it sound too P-E, like he had to start eleven words in one sentence with the letter 'B.' I would think he'd be closer to the Secretary of Literary Device."

"But Brooks, wouldn't it be better to back this banal bantering with a better base than Calvin Coolidge?" She takes a step back and raises her hand into the air for a high five. "Oh yeah, baby, nine words, that qualifies me for the 'participant alliteration' award!" As she high-fives me she jumps an inch or so, eleven centimeters, kicking one of her legs back and shouting "woo."

I turn away from her immediately and fix my gaze on the atmospheric color wheel of the Virginia afternoon sky so she won't see me smile. The conversation has been filled with smiles, but not a smile like mine. My smile is the smile of vindication, similar to a child who has been told he will not be getting a video game all year unwrapping "The Legend of Zelda" on Christmas morning. Like Annie Besant finding Krishna in the dirt. Aranea's "woo" lets me know that my efforts are not in vain and that someone up there, Jesus or Cornelius or somebody, has a warehouse full of signs that are ready to go as soon as they can get Heaven's Department of Transportation to send workers out and put them up. I know that she is worth it, or at least that the effort is worth it, regardless of what "it" ends up being. Such is my experience with "woo," which is not as extensive as some dream sequences would have you believe.

"So do you think there's a parody shuttle run?" she asks.

"Maybe if they made an astronaut do it. But I think that might be the irony shuttle run."

A few moments of silence slip by while she walks across the living room and into the kitchen. Her feet make sticky sounds on the linoleum. Outside, caught up in the trees, I can see slips of blue construction paper clinging to branches, trying not to get spirited away into the darkness of an imminent night sky. The house seems empty when she is in the other room, and it gives me time to think about the things I've said. Suddenly I'm looking for the bathroom, trying desperately to think of an excuse to muffle the sound of the purge of emotions and personal sorrow that come with the realization that even puke won't come out when you've got your feet in your mouth. The lining of my stomach begins to stretch. I can't breathe and I want to take back all the things I said about grim reapers and German expressionism. I want them replaced with love poems and compliments, a simple "you look great today," or a verbose "your eyes remind me of something incredibly green!" Maybe a tree, but less brown. Perhaps a pear, but not the yellow ones. Of all the times to forget what is green in the world.

"Mmmph!" The strained noise comes from the kitchen, and I turn to see Aranea hanging from both hands in the doorway, an apple clutched in her mouth. She dangles there for a moment, kicking her feet, before dropping. In mild displeasure she smirks and shakes her head, pulling the apple from her teeth and pointing a finger at me. "With all this talk about physical fitness I thought I could manage a few pull-ups, but I don't think I have it in me." She puts her hand against the doorway and laughs. "You know, one night I wanted to climb up to the roof to watch the stars and eat finger sandwiches, but I couldn't pull myself up. It was depressing. I had to eat twice as many finger sandwiches as a result, and I have no idea what the stars looked like."

"It must be miserable going through life with so many finger sandwiches at your disposal," I return, making my way past the couch and toward her. "You must weigh…" is all I get out before my insides suddenly become engulfed in flames and I drop to my knees. The feeling is like someone reaching up from below and pulling down on my stomach, trying to rip it from my body. Aranea stands there motionless for a moment before dropping the apple and kneeling down beside me. The apple rolls a few inches from my nose, and I can see her tooth prints.

"Oh my gosh, what's the matter, what did you do, what did I do?" She touches my shoulder but draws back, then touches my arm and draws back again. "I'm so sorry, did you want an apple? You can have mine." With her fingers she pushes the apple toward my mouth, laughing under her breath.

"No," I manage, "you're fine. I just..." This portion of the conversation is filled with argh-like exclamations and gurgling noises that remind me of those old men who blow their noses at the table in restaurants, and after each noise I want to apologize but can't muster up the strength to get the words out, so they turn into more gurgles. When I stop worrying about it and take a few moments to breathe, I can continue. "I've just been having...some...some problems lately with my stomach, and I guess diving for my life wasn't the best way to...go about..."

"Ooh," she interrupts. "I wasn't aware that you were diving for your life. If I'd known you were in such a bad way I wouldn't have let you stand around waxing seventh-grade-world-historical with me. Why have you had stomach problems?"

"I just," is intelligently repeated before I stammer on for a few seconds about how sorry I am to be kneeling here in the middle of her floor. I can feel the warmth of blood on the back of my tongue but force it down. I don't want her to see the bad sides of me, even when the bad side is the inside. "I've just had some problems with, my stomach, and..."

"Do you mean stomach problems like medical problems, or stomach problems like personal problems?" I look over to see her eyes wide open and staring, and suddenly she's a deer and I'm maybe two headlights.

"What do you mean...what do you mean by personal problems?"

"Is your stomach worried about finding a date for the spring social? You know what I mean by personal problems." I don't say anything because I can't say anything, for even though the blood has been pushed down the realization that somebody would know, even if she doesn't, is the scariest thing I can imagine. In a world full of billions of people I would take anyone else. A fitness guru, a family member, a guidance counselor, someone pointless to tell me they know. Or for my mother to touch my moist fingers and know without saying it. Even if it is said I don't want her to know, because she shouldn't know, because she deserves to not know. Instead of thinking up a clever excuse or blaming the dive from an oncoming demise I just kneel there in silence, hammering in nail after unnecessary nail.

"Brooks, what are…Brooks, do you…"

My silence answers twenty questions before the first question has been asked. I can hear a sad "oh" nestled in the back of her throat as my breath becomes heavy and pallid. There are tears in the corners of my mouth despite my position, and I think that the tears themselves chose to stick to my face and ride it out instead of falling and letting Aranea know they were there. I want to tell her about how I defy the stereotypes, about how I don't spend all day shirtless in front of a mirror like some narcissistic teen lamenting my love handles. I didn't get into perfect shape and still let my mind tell me I'm fat. The feeling only comes sometimes, like when I'm in the shower and my arms are crossed, and I think about how when I was thirteen a Garfield comic strip introduced me to the idea of not being able to see my feet, something I'd never even thought about before the accompanying fat joke hit the presses. I think about how the chunky old substitute teacher I worked with at the grocery store once told me that I was never going to get rid of my chubby cheeks because "it's hereditary," and how I wanted to ask her if her giant ass was hereditary. The yellow liquid sprinkled with red swishes around in my stomach and I can feel it, and this causes me to gag and lurch forward.

"Brooks, stop it for a second and listen to me," she says, grabbing me by the wrist. Aranea places my hand over her chest, and I can feel the ridges of her rib cage and the beat of her heart, and before she even says anything it is amazing, because for the first time I know that her heart really beats. I've spent most of my life listening to her heartbeat without any idea how it sounds. It feels like a mouse held in cupped hands.

"Can you feel that?" she asks.

Smiling I return, "You aren't going to pull one of those Tarzan 'apes-and-people-aren't-different-because-we-have-the-same-heart' speeches are you, because as much as I appreciate the touching gesture I don't know if being called a monkey is exactly what I…"

"Can you feel that?" she says, cutting me off in mid-ramble.

"Yes."

"My heart hasn't beaten regularly in three years. One day I woke up on the kitchen floor staring up at a refrigerator magnet, and all of a sudden my landlord is standing over me and I'm in a hospital with little tubes running up in my nose. I don't know if you've ever had tubes in your nose but it's harsh."

"I…I can imagine, but…"

"No, stop making jokes for a second and listen to me. I was dehydrated and malnourished because I didn't freaking eat anything for a week. And that wasn't the first week I did that. Look at my arm," she says, pushing the sleeve of her shirt up and holding her bicep out across my eyes. "You want to know why I can't do any pull-ups? Because I don't eat enough and don't have any muscles. I haven't seen the stars since I started living here and I end up with a plate of finger sandwiches that nobody's going to eat, and I do it to myself."

My eyes blink again and again as I try to understand what she's saying, which is hard even though she's blatantly stating it. The idea of Aranea Cavatica having the same problem as mine makes me want to throw the problem to the ground and back away, hands open, because suddenly I don't feel like I deserve to have the problem. The other ninety nine percent of my brain just feels bad for her. I want to fill her with a thousand pastries, hug her and tell her that she's an ignorant fool for thinking she wasn't thousands of bakeries better than the rest of us. The sympathy cowers in the corner behind the synapses and I just kneel there, waiting for her to throw me out of her house for almost regurgitating on her shag carpet.

"What I'm trying to say is that I'm in no place to tell you to stop doing it, because I've gone through the same thing. My body doesn't work now and my bones would break if a bird landed on my shoulder." She scoots over on her knees so she can face me, lowering her forehead to a parallel mark a few inches from my face. Seven inches. Looking up I can see her eyes looking up at me, and suddenly the background becomes green and the skin stretched across her skull feels warm and comforting. "And ever since I've been completely insane."

"I know, it's just my subconscious causing me to inflict wounds on myself. Suddenly I feel like I've become incredibly symbolic," I mutter, closing my eyes.

"Epic poetry blah blah," she laughs, continuing to rest her skull against mine gently.

"In a helpless kind of way it's like we're soul mates. Soul mates via horrifying eating disorders."

She smiles. "Is there any other kind?"

"I guess that explains the giant cheeseburgers in your backyard, at least."

"And more importantly," she says, "countless smiles have been shared, lives have been touched, and connections have been made."

CHAPTER 11

When I was young my beliefs were fresh and I knew that Jesus had died for my sins. I was so happy just being there, with my fat head and my mushroom hair. My mother loved me and my father loved me. My grandparents loved me. My family made black iron pans full of biscuits and white ceramic boat-shaped things full of gravy or green beans, and they always had glass lids that collected beads of moisture on the inside. Afternoons could be spent picking the solid embryo of fruits from the briar bush in my grandmothers front yard, throwing them over the row of hedges into the streets, watching them hit and roll. We tried to get them all the way down the street but they always rolled into the gravel a few dozen yards down.

Somewhere along the way the beads of moisture began to drip down into the green beans, and one day I showed up and they'd cut the briar bush down. The image of round fruits discarded in the muddy brown grasses will stay with me long after my idealism has died. Things were so great without any consequence. A thousand clichés of childhood raise their hands and read the answers from the textbook, and I'm struck with the realization that what I have loved and felt is nothing new. A hundred grandmothers died on the day mine died. A dozen little girls hugged a handful of little boys and made them feel better in the same way that she did for me, and though I've never seen her body and I've never felt her lips against mine I know that some of those boys have seen the bodies and have touched the lips and will feel a thousand more things that I can't even think of. What reality has done to my heart in these years since I carried boxes and dropped them into holes is not what should be expected of any child. We are all individual fingerprints that all look the same under the light, and for some reason I can't see reality in all of it's beauty, nor can I see how reality is anything natural or exactly what happens to everybody else. Death and disappointment aren't normal. They're just mean. I thank God for the good wrestling matches and the chocolate chip cookies and wait for something else.

Sometimes when the light isn't as bright I decide that I would give every breath that resonates in my scarred and weakened lungs to have something that makes me optimistic again. Not the optimism that is felt when lottery ticket gray matter is pierced and discarded by a quarter. The optimism that tells you that your father is a good man. Not the optimism that says, "Oh man I'm totally gonna score on my first date!" The optimism that tells you that God exists even if he doesn't live in the clouds and will kiss you on the forehead when you've got nothing else. The optimism shared by cheerleaders and reality show contestants can be purchased in cans and easy-squeeze tubes at the supermarket. It can be picked from trees and pulled from the soil. The feelings that I want I can never shake someone by the shoulders and demand, because I felt them before they had a name. Sometimes I feel like I will spend the rest of my life flipping through books of photographs, looking in the backgrounds for flashes of light and imperfections that made those moments so much better than the rest.

My living disease is that I will never be able to express the way I feel. The child has been carried in my womb for years and I can't fit the gestation into a rhyme scheme. I am crippled with the realization that I can't write a few paragraphs, hand it to someone I don't know, and expect them to feel the same way. I can't tell a stranger how bad it is that people won't just treat people the way they're supposed to. I can't tell a person checking out in the grocery store that I've met the most wonderful girl and how she smiled and did a twirl when I gave her a dozen roses. I'm too afraid of normalcy. This causes me to take longer looks at myself in the mirror. I used to sit up in the middle of the night with my teeth pressed into the windowsill listening for the trumpet to sound, and how horrible it was going to be that I hadn't done anything good enough for Jesus to point his finger down at me and say "come with me." Sometimes I would sit in the bathtub trying to hold my breath as long as I could to take my mind off the fact that a kid at school had told me that we were going to be blown up by nuclear weapons when I should've been building tree-houses and catching fireflies. It warped me into something beyond normal, something better than normal. Normal doesn't have a conscience. Normal doesn't feel bad when they feel a girl's heart beat out of time. I embrace what makes me different, and suddenly I'm afraid to tell anyone about the things I love or am afraid of. I don't want them to know I'm so pleasantly different, because someone who is exceptionally different will shrug me to the side, call me melodramatic, tell me that I need to do what they have done before I look any closer at life. "How can you write a book," they say. "Have you ever been homeless? Have you ever been beaten by your husband?" This simultaneously fills me with unmitigated rage and depression, because I know they can't possibly think about the same things I do and am afraid that they do and aren't bothered by it.

No moment goes by casually. I can't erase the image of the hole in Curtis's head. I can't scratch away the thought of the bones in Aranea's ribcage, and how the skin felt gripped and pulled like a trampoline because she does what I do backwards. I can't just walk up to Auburn and apologize to her for using her, because I have been using her. I could never love her. I don't love her. I love an image, I love a collection of feathers in the shape of my own theistic isolation. I love Aranea Cavatica because she was there when my innocence was first removed from me, and her arms wrapped around me to keep my heart from bleeding onto the damp grass. I run to Auburn because I am too weak to treat her the way she should be treated, because I have a disease that won't allow me to make her think of me in a way I can't control. Now I press my teeth to the windowsill and listen for the phone to ring, waiting for her to scream these things to me, call me pathetic, call me a whore, call me a shell of some twisted idea that I could never be. She would point her finger at me and say "come with me," and the scariest thing I can imagine is that her opinion of me wouldn't change.

I hate how I've treated her, and how I rationalize that it is okay because she isn't hurt. When I was a child and could speak at eight months old and read at two years, twenty-one months, my home schooling was in preparation for what I was going to face in elementary school. When I was in elementary school, in the back of class by myself, the worksheets and the books were to prepare me for the gifted classes that I would be taking; classes that would shape me into a middle school student. By the eighth grade I could do six classes of homework without even reading the directions, and all I could do was stare down at where my feet should be and wonder why they weren't there, and why I'd done this to myself. High school was Aranea Cavatica and nothing more, not even Curtis or Chinese Gordon. It passed by day after day to prepare me for college and I dismissed my Winnie Cooper as the television dream girl I'd picked for myself, the one we all pick for ourselves that is too good to be true, the one who moves away or dates the hated rival. College was preparation to graduate college, to move on to graduate school and onto a high paying job that would prepare me for a family, and for grandchildren. The family would prepare me for old age, and old age would prepare me for Heaven. Nobody stopped to think that I was a little fat kid and running that fast is impossible, and that the muscles in my legs would give out and I would fall, like we all fall, like all normal people fall.

When I fell it was into Auburn Bryant, a girl who wasn't there because she was preparing for anything, who wasn't the girl on the notebooks with hearts around her name, who would never start a family with me. I wanted to wait for Aranea and my orchestrated movie ending, I wanted to wake up on Saturday mornings and roll over to see the ringlets in the back of her head. I wanted to touch her belly button on the day we found out she was pregnant and laugh about how big she was going to get, and we would both smile and fall back into a hammock and on and on. Auburn was not just there. She was not a mistake. She was something that I could release myself into, someone who would take and take and not worry about how much I could give. Auburn pressed herself against me and softly offered a way to make the moments wander by aimlessly, and the idea that someone would accept me into that felt warmer than her kisses. Her breasts rest against her chest when she lies beneath me and nothing is threatening, the air isn't remarkable and the way her hair falls doesn't lick metaphors from the tip of my tongue. Times with her make me feel comfortably alone. My abdomen becomes tense from motion and my wrists begin to burn from supporting my weight on the dorm room floor, and it makes me cry sometimes. She can feel the drops of water fall onto her and sometimes she puts her fingers behind my head. She whispers things to me that I can't remember. I bury my face in her neck and cry when we lie there as one, and I am alone.

No hip music network will call me a hero for all the work I put into educating children about my disease. I can't hand out a pamphlet with facts and myths about being twenty-two and a boy and white, without a heritage to be proud of or a song for anyone to remember. I could join the army and fight for causes. I could get medals and have a parade. I can open up the Holy Bible and read what it tells me to do. But just like the policemen who aren't pulling babies out of wells I perform a thankless job, filling out the holes that remarkable people leave in the fabric of our species. Like the firemen who weren't there when the planes hit the buildings my job is reflected by people who have done what I do and who have said what I will say before me, better than me. Someone has already built the cathedrals and painted The Starry Night. Someone has already written <u>Charlotte's Web</u>. Someone has already given birth to Martin Luther King and Gandhi and Jesus Christ. I can't even give birth. And I know that somewhere an amazing painting that would change someone's life has been tossed away by an ignorant art teacher. I know that a book that could mean enough to a little boy to let him know that the world was going to be okay despite the hardships and the doubt and the death will get an animated sequel when a movie studio needs money. I know that the next Van Gogh was put on Ritalin and doesn't like to draw pretty pictures anymore. I know that maybe the next Dr. King was aborted, and that a thousand James Ear Rays should've been.

That's when I realize that people know who James Earl Ray was. People know who Sirhan Sirhan was. People know who Tomas de Torquemada was. Pol Pot. Idi Amin. Stalin. There are six new movies about Hitler every year. It goes deeper than that, down to insignificant people like JonBenet Ramsey, O.J. Simpson, the kid who got caned in Singapore. Members of boy bands. The guy who played A.C. Slater on "Saved by the Bell." Somebody who stood in the background in an episode of "Saved by the Bell." People who once watched "Saved by the Bell" and then shot somebody at a McDonalds. There will be more people at the funeral of a figure skater who paid someone to hit another figure skater in the leg with a blunt metal object than were at my grandmother's funeral. The drying puddles of compassion still collected at the bottom of my heart tell me that there are reasons why this makes sense, reasons that I should not and would not understand. The Lord created child murderers and porn stars in the same way he created my grandmother and I, and he loves us all. I want to sit him down with tears in my eyes and ask him how he can love us all equally. I want to know why he won't love the ones who are trying their best to love him despite themselves and the world he put them in just a little bit more. I want to know why he put me here so late in the scheme that I can never love him in a way that hasn't been done. I want to know why he takes us, and where he puts us, and why he keeps trying and trying when he's gotten a few of us right.

In turn I use Aranea in the same way I use Auburn. I use Auburn for instant gratification, the suggestion that in another collection of roads traveled I could walk up to a girl who takes pride in her self and win her over with the good qualities that I have. The assurance that a mind and a heart can overcome the parasitic fat of the belly. I would say, "come here often?" and she would say, "here's my hotel key" and we would be just like the people on sexy television. I could never star in sexy television with Aranea. Aranea is the only person I have ever met that is exactly how I think she should be. Her faith in the only begotten son is strong throughout the obstacles she faces, be they physical or mental, acute or obtuse, easily digested or hot on the way back up. She still goes to church. She has a Bible that sits on her coffee table that she consults when there is a problem. She is pure in all of the ways that I am not and hope to be. In the simplest terms her existence and the way she exists gives me the evidence I need to regain my faith, because she gives me something good to believe in.

I want to love her in the way that I am told to love her. I don't want to think about her above or beneath me. I want to think of her beside me. Her hand in mine. Her eyes in mine. Suddenly the terror inside me jumps out from around the corner and I think about how lame it is of somebody to put a girl on a pedestal like that. The thought that I could objectify her in a way that defeats the entire purpose of seeing her as a reason for faith casts me down in depression, for after all this time the problem lies in my ability to love, and her ability to sin. Her sin is individuality. Her sin is her strange ability not to lamb in and lion out of my life like the teachers and friends. She stays. She is there when I need her, even when she is not around. If I can believe in her then I can believe in God, but without the strong belief in God she will never allow me to believe in her. Therefore, her many sins have been forgiven—for she loved much. But he who has been forgiven little loves little. My forgiveness is in the fact that I shout the obvious. Love never fails. It remains even when the tangible fades away. It is a butterfly that sits in your hand when you try to let it go. Love is knowing that when you breathe in you're going to breathe out again. To love you must have complete confidence. When you begin to question your relationship it is the single moment when you prove to yourself that it doesn't exist.

Aranea has complete confidence in God. God is love. When I begin to question my relationship with Him it is the single moment when I prove to myself that He doesn't exist. Without Him she cannot have confidence. Without Him, she cannot love. Auburn's notebook says, "Brooks notes that when he contemplates on the certainty of his existence, he knows the truth of his existence clearly and distinctly. He proposes a general rule: everything he perceives clearly and distinctly is true."

Instantly the answer becomes clear. To be the kind of person who deserves the quieter moments of Aranea Cavatica's time I would need to remember the things my grandmother taught me about faithfulness, meekness, patience, and forgiveness. It's easy to remember those things, she had paper cutouts of different kinds of fruit with each virtue written on it. Meekness was grapes. She would stick each fruit to the blue felt board and tell me about how they are the qualities that go to make up the character of God himself, and therefore of Christ, and therefore of their spirit. The fruit of the spirit. As long as I stay the way I am I could never be dependably faithful, or long-suffering, or even good. Standing back up again is the only way to get where I'm going. I fall and blood pours from me. I cannot stop vomiting. I fall and Auburn is there to envelop me with her warmth. I cannot stop. I cannot stop. I cannot stop. I cannot stop.

But wait, suddenly the cue card is held right-side up and I learn that Aranea would never accept my attempts at recalling Christianity because it is for her, and not for Him. She forgives me for my sins and prays for me, but I can never believe it in the way she believes it. I am too normal to hear God speak to me. I am too melodramatic to love her as a best friend. Lynchburg is full of Christian schools. Christian schools are full of girls who turn down Christian boys who ask them on dates. Christian boys place their sheltered and depraved visions of normal onto girls who don't deserve it. They place the visions on girls who do. They exist in a circle where boy meets girl and both meet God, and neither is as good as God. So they try and try to be as good as God and the ones who succeed buy sports utility vehicles and lead happy lives. The ones who are not as good as God, the ones who can't convince themselves that they are doing the right thing, keep trying. The colleges don't allow R-rated movies. The restaurants are owned by Jerry Falwell. Meanwhile, caught up in all of this circling and worshipping is me, and all I want to do is be allowed to love the girl I choose. The writing on the wall says "you aren't Christian enough for the Christians" and no amount of marching around it causes it to fall. It haunts me. It rapes me when I sleep. It reaches a skeletal, icy hand into me and pulls my innocence until the tendons snap.

The fruit of the spirit. The fruit of the looms. One or the other.

So what I'm left with underneath it all is the feeling that I'm a work in progress that he started and left for somebody else, and that person, not being God, didn't know what to do with me. There are beautiful brush strokes covered in pencil ashes, solid lines broken into a spray of color faded by exposure. I don't hate God for leaving me under care because they did the best they could, and that since he knows everything and we've been planned since the flood that it was what was meant to be, and what I do with my life is what was meant to be done.

Where I was raised God hasn't really "left" at all. He is everywhere. He is on television screens and in wallets and on little folded pieces of paper that they hand you when you're ringing up their groceries. He is in hearts that do good and hearts that do evil. He tells us to be patient with each other because he's not finished with us yet, and blames the gays and the abortionists and the ACLU for the buildings full of innocent lives that were broken and stricken to the ground. He is in my Grandmother. She is in the ground. He is in the ground. He is in Aranea. She is in my heart. He is in my heart. He was there before she was, and they talk and play games and reassure each other. It makes me smile because there is nobody else, no human or concept that I want to love more than Him. Then I blame myself for feeling like a battered wife. It's all my fault. He did it because he loved me. It makes so much sense to me now.

When I was young my beliefs were fresh and I knew that Jesus had died for my sins. A thousand religious philosophers throughout time raise their hands and laugh in humorously exaggerated accents that they rationalized why God existed centuries ago, and how they are the ones who defined him and his glories for us. Without them we wouldn't know what a sign from God looked like. We wouldn't know how to make one. I wouldn't know how to make one.

There was a moment when her forehead touched mine and I wanted to tell her about how she helped me remember God. I wanted to tell her how sorry I was that she had to ever know what a hospital looked or smelled like. I wanted to tell her that if I live to be a thousand years old, in a house with a thousand monkeys and a thousand typewriters, that works of Shakespeare and banana-related refuse aside I would not begin to understand why she didn't see in her what I did, and why she would look at herself and not be instantly filled with the satisfaction of flawed perfection. I wanted to ask her to sit around with me reading books and doing nothing, so that later we could talk about what we read, or learn new words in the dictionary. I wanted to show her that no matter when the sign came or what it looked like that I was forever pinned to this loop around her life, since no part of my brain would imagine that she would be pinned to mine.

Then there was the moment when I leaned in to kiss her and she pulled away like a smacked puppy that couldn't understand why it was being punished. As her what-are-you-doings fell from her lips I felt my insides burning and knew that in the same way the she never did I deserved and deserve it, because without it I could not define myself. The fruit never just rolls down the road. It hits a bump you can't even see if you get right up on it and rolls off into the gravel. So now I sit with my teeth pressed against the windowsill, thanking God for the Sunday School classes and the beautiful paintings and wait for something else. No moment goes by casually.

No moment goes by casually.
No moment.

CHAPTER 12

"It says so right in the Bible, God burned down Sodom and turned the land into salt and crap because it was a town full of guys going at each other. It says in Romans that they're all worthy of death. Like, gay people are worthy of death because they let their bodies burn in lust for each other, which is gross by the way. But yeah, like, he destroyed the cities as an example for anybody in our time who would do that. I don't understand why a dude would find another dude attractive anyway." Scotty shrugs his shoulders and mops the same little circle of floor over and over.

Scotty's friend Simon is the wastebasket receiving Scotty's balled-up pieces of notebook paper. Simon towers over Scotty, filling out his hooded sweatshirt with pale, thick pounds. The flames on the elbows likely mirror his inner fire. The skulls on the chest likely mirror his inner skull.

"And you don't think it's weird in the least that God would burn an entire city that no doubt also had a bunch of women, a bunch of kids, and probably some guys who weren't 'going after strange flesh' in it just to make an example, because he didn't like that they were sodomizing each other?" Simon asks. "You know that not everybody in Sodom was a sodomite. There has to be some irony that the Bible is missing, some guy in Sodom who was raging against the stereotype and ran a flower shop, who stayed at home and drank ale while his wife cooked him dinner. Some real Biblical asshole who deserved to be killed probably, but got killed because of what somebody else did. Like God is one of those tough cops on TV who get all distressed over the bystanders they kill, and then the next week they do the same thing."

"Ironic? Like, fly in chardonnay ironic? Like the song?" Simon throws his head back in laughter as he smacks Scotty on the shoulder with the back of his hand. Scotty grips the handle of the mop and begins to scream the lyrics at the top of his lungs. "It's like ray-ee-aaaaain! Hah hah!" I've had a long-standing belief that people who randomly burst into song should be herded off into special camps so I return to decorating my register with showers of purple cleaning solution. I imagine this would be what it looks like when the Grimace sneezes.

Tonight like so many other nights features Brooks the Customer Service Representative pulling a Dante and picking up the graveyard shift for someone who's sudden illness caused them to make other plans. If my post-teenage musings on religious conviction and love are to be victims of the predictability status-quo there is no feeling I feel more commonly than dissatisfaction at my menial task obligations. The people here are not the people you see in the day-time; they are the disenfranchised children of the sunlight, people who fill their days to the rim so that a minute spent purchasing buy-one-get-one-free Fritos and bologna overflows the cup. Scotty sings the ironic refrain and misses the lyrics in his own moment, swirling over that same spot on the reflecting pool that used to be our dirty floor. In my mind I can see St. Peter holding up a big cue card with "Brooks Works Graveyard" written on it, pointing at it, and smiling.

"Hey Scotty, if you're finished with the floor you can go ahead and go, I'm good by myself."

"Yeah, aight." Scotty leans the mop handle against the security system and takes off for the chip aisle and, subsequently, the time clock.

With the exception of the extra dollar and fifty cents per hour the proudest aspect of the eleven to seven shift is the solitude. The colors of the grocery store are beautiful when you're allowed eight hours to take them in, like a record that sits in the collection for months until the thoughtless words of a father renders it personally significant. Red boxes and green bottles, blue birthday candles, yellow paper surrounding white flour. The cereal aisle can provide solace itself; a thousand shades and smiling faces wrapping a lonely mind in warm sensory relief from the white walls and black night. Tigers in necker-chiefs and silly rabbits seek only to please on the most basic taste levels while a Greek chorus of girls on hair dye boxes beam with approval from the parallel shelves.

As Simon browses the menthol cigarettes two teenagers rush by, a girl with a minuscule roll of baby fat folding over the abrasive navy edge of designer jeans, a boy with solitary black hairs leaping across expanses of upper lip. Her hair is scorched blonde and his hat is on backwards. They giggle to themselves and avoid eye contact, walking waist to waist, before disappearing through the deli and into the dog food aisle. Scotty passes them on his way back from chips and takes a moment to do an exaggerated double take at the faint impression of butt crack peeking up from above the girl's pants. He shakes his head as he walks towards me and I know he's going to stuff my last few minutes of populated conversation into her most impersonal orifice. Scotty stops about ten paces before my register and pulls a sealed plastic bag from his pocket.

"Swear to God, why is it that all the prettiest girls go out with the ugliest guys? That guy's a complete drug dealer or something, that's gotta be it." He peels back the plastic lid from his cylinder of chips and dumps as many chips into the bag as possible.

Simon springs to life and responds, "Whatever, man, you deal and you don't have a hot chick."

"Dude!," Scotty yells, hitting Simon in the elbow with a well placed throw of the now-empty canister. "I totally don't deal drugs, all right? Damn dog, you gotta go yelling stuff like that out in front of everybody. Just because I got friends with hook ups and sometimes I make a phone call or two for somebody doesn't mean I'm all, like, funding international terrorism."

"I dunno," I laugh to myself. "I think your argument loses credibility when you remain as ugly as you are without a hot chick."

"What did you say?" Scotty blurts as Simon clutches his sides, laughing, and leans against the fiberglass cigarette case. "What did you say?" He stomps the ten stomps to register seven and looks me confidently in the eye. Scotty's thug life scowl quickly turns to a relaxed expression of pleasantness when he realizes the six inches and forty pounds he's giving up, though I'm sure the scowl was never actually there at all. "Hah, right, right." He pats me on the shoulder before leaning down and grabbing my register microphone. "Peace out," echoes over the cereal aisle and through the reds and greens and blues.

Soon they are both gone and I am left with the snapshots of inadequacy that show up every night, and the misfits of efficiency that are paid to stock shelves. The stock boys usually only speak to me when it's time for their three a.m. lunch break and they need someone to ring up their beenie weenies. Otherwise they wheel cardboard boxes into the middle of all the aisles and then play football in the parking lot until the sun rises.

The regulars are books with no pages. Judging the person by their cover is the only option, but as people they are rarely judged. One man supports himself by pressing his fleshy bulk into the handle of his shopping cart. He is regularly sunburned and his facial hair holds secretions of saliva and crumbs of bread. His time of arrival is anywhere between one o'clock and one-fifteen, when the night manager changes the stickers on the meat. At a discounted rate due to health regulations, the meat is minutes old at one-o-seven. The man arrives like a vulture that procrastinated and had to find the carcass through hearsay. Any conversation with the man will bring up his most interesting life facts, like the time he lived in South Africa, and how he's a diamond miner. Each syllable is followed by a deep breath. He pays one dollar for a seven dollar piece of meat. He pays in quarters.

At two o'clock the lesbians usually show up, which is notable not because of their sexual preference but for their freakish level of contrast. The blonde has to lean down when she enters. The snaps on the side of her workout pants reach pectoral level on me. The brunette has to stand on the tips of her toes to see over the register. They hold hands and shop like any normal couple, as images of the blonde carrying the brunette around on her hip like a child floods into my brain. I imagine the brunette in a baby carrier, sleeping peacefully on the blondes shoulder as she shops for formula. They buy granola bars and happily make their way outside to their car, which is full of many clowns.

Then there is La Marcheuse, the Walker, a Protestant recluse named Henri broken by a hard life. She buys one sugar wafer when she arrives with the change in her pocket and continues browsing, usually stopping in the women's bathroom to lay on the floor and sleep. She may have been beautiful as a child, her eyes might've been green but have faded to a urine-tinted gray, with torn shards of scratched brown hair collecting in the oily spots on her forehead. She smiles with decay but decency so I don't follow procedure and allow her to sleep as long as she'd like, in the handicapped stall that is never used by guests or the all-male stocking staff during the shift. Henri leaves without incident or a thank you in the mornings, but it is okay, because her sin is thin and easily forgiven.

"Cashier to the back, please, cashier to the back, please."

The bowels of the store are operated in ways that I cannot and should not understand. From what I understand the bulk of the nights events on nights like tonight, when the wind is fluid and shards of rain fall and cut like glass, is basketball. The basket is supplied by a crate stacked onto several other crates. The ball is supplied by our toy display, which holds dozens of plastic balls baring images of childhood favorites like Cinderella. Watching high school drop outs imitate Magic Johnson with pull-up jumpers is an indescribable event, but watching them do with an oversized pink and purple bouncy ball borders on a religious experience. When I push open the doors the crates are toppled and discarded about the floor, and the desecration of the expectation causes me to fear the worst. The confluence of snickering stockers cements the fear.

"Brooks Brooks Brooks come here come here!" my night manager urges in a whispered scream. He motions for me as two (the sounds from a bathroom in the middle of the night) and two (the teenagers I saw earlier) meet each other and discover the wonders of cohesion.

"Nah, that's okay, I'm not really interested in what's going on in there," I say, shaking away his offer with my head and hands.

"Naw man," he persists, "they're…" He stops and lowers his voice even further, speaking from one side of his mouth and darting his eyes back and forth. "They're doin' it in the bathroom man, you gotta do something about it."

"I have to do something about it?"

"Yeah you gotta do something about it, you're the only person in the front, that's your job."

"How is that my job?" I demand, already subconsciously accepting the graphic responsibility about to ejaculate all over my good night. I interrupt his next sentence with the old classic, "Ugh, whatever," and push my way through. Just before pushing the bathroom door open I stop, and all of the background noise falls to a hush. All I can hear are the sounds of my fingertips touching and spreading on the door, and I think how the air rushing through my nose sounds like the ocean. My ear lowers and rests against the veneer and at once I'm inside a shell, hearing the water slide up the beach and gurgle with a dying fizz in a pocket of sand. This is, of course, assuming that the ocean in question is full of people having sex.

Then, silence. My eyes have time to pull back and focus on the sexually offensive "woman in a dress" logo on the women's bathroom before my fingertips lose connection and the door swings open. When scorched blonde, busy looking back over her shoulder and laughing, turns to see me inches from her face she perks and recoils, her eyelids snapping back against her frontal lobe, no doubt knocking loose some repressed emotion and ruining her spatial orientation. Now when she thinks about the bittersweet ending to <u>Pretty Woman</u> she'll see my face and scream.

"Oh my God, what are you doing, what are you, some kind of pervert, oh my God!" she says, smacking me in the face with a quick twitch of the wrist. This causes the offensive line behind me to disperse, covering their mouths with their hands, saying things like "Oh!" and "Aw!" Her boyfriend knits f-words and s-words into a quilt of prepubescent revelry as he shoves me, more accurately pushing me so that one of my shoulders moves. He grabs the girl by the wrist and pulls her away, and as the seeds of red begin to bloom across my cheeks I wonder only for a moment about the brown and purple marks that she will find there in the morning.

The night manager has a broad smile on his face and repeats, "Did she slap you? She slapped you. Did you slap you? She slapped you," until I swat him away. "Did you see what they were doing in there? What were they doing, did you see what they were doing in there?" He trots past me and into the bathroom, taking two steps in before turning, smacking his forehead, and groaning, "Aw, man, sick!"

"What?" I ask, completely and utterly not wanting to know.

"Dude, you gotta clean that up, man."

"Dude I've got to clean what up?"

"That," he says, pointing back into the women's bathroom.

Wandering back into the post-coital wasteland my heart sinks, reaching up with trembling arteries to signal for help but eventually being dragged under by the current of sticky, white observation. The baby changing station has been stained and used for the act of not changing babies but making them. The musky odor of private sweat lingers and will eventually gather in the mildew tracing the tiles along the floor. The toilet seat is propped up and a series of dirty black footprints line the rim. The mirror is foggy. The water in the sink is still running. And there in the corner, stuffed behind the radiator, is a bra. The Food Lion women's bathroom is where the bad people go when they die.

I mired in this for a few moments with various weapons. Big balled up wads of cheap brown paper towels. A mop. A broom and dust pan. None of these lit the fire necessary deep on the inside required to clean up such a substance. In ancient times I would be instantly rewarded by God for such a show of allegiance to a cause, even if the cause was further employment and community normalcy. On my fourth attempt, a plastic bag wrapped around my mouth and nose and two plastic forks from the deli, I decide to simply forsake my maker and push the baby changing station back up to it's upright and locked position. Attractively enough the station sticks together now, even without the lock.

One of the downsides of introspection is that you realize things about yourself. If I were bipolar I could have an excuse for my valleys to be low and my peaks to be high, my brights to be bright and my darks dark. Since nobody made this journey into procreation with me I can think out loud about why my moments of enlightenment and genuine happiness are sandwiched between these slices of refuse If I were bipolar I could have people take care of me and make excuses for me. If I were bipolar I wouldn't be mentally dented enough to make that joke about the Eskimo that likes women and men whenever somebody says the word "bipolar." We all get what we deserve in the end.

When my hands are washed and my brow wiped the intercom scratches and I remember that there are probably half a dozen people wanting to buy one, and wanting to get one free. The voice that begins to sing through the microphone waves a hand in front of my eyes and starts pointing to itself a few words into the song.

"I…don't know how…to love…him. What to do…how to move…him."

I rush back down the aisles with a troop of curious stockers in tow to spot Auburn standing beside the register, crowing in her charming off-key monotone. She once told me about crouching in the corner of chorus class for three years until breaking out in a command performance of the "whoa whoa" amphibious background vocal in a stage show of, "The Little Mermaid" her senior year. The loose folds of velvet hang from her arms and the silver embroidery at the fringe of her black skirt is gently rocked back and forth by the wind rushing in through the automatic doors. Casual indifference that lives in her face is replaced by a glimpse of pretty sadness, which bends into polite happiness when she notices me seventy boxes of cake mix down the aisle. Auburn raises a brown bag stained black from grease and waves.

"Hey, who is that?" asks Randy, the stocker I can distinguish because of his handlebar mustache and constant odor of vapor rub.

"A friend of mine."

"A friend of yours? You liar," he responds, effecting my walk and causing it to end with an insulted glare. "She's too hot to be a friend of yours." Before I can think of something clever about his mother to counter, he leans back from his stack of aluminum trays and gives Auburn what I can only assume to be "the eye," so much so that he looks like he's trying to limbo under the cookie sheets. I stand in silence staring at the back of his baseball cap until he shrugs and mutters, "She could probably stand to lose about fifteen pounds, though." Shaking my head I make a mental list of all of the places to purchase crowbars in Lynchburg.

When I reach Auburn she gives me a smile, but I only notice it in passing because the brown bag resting on the register has painted a warmed outline around the radar. I press the inside of my lips stiffly against my teeth and sigh. Right now someone is dumping human waste all over the women's bathroom in a malicious attempt to frustrate my day. I keep cleaning and cleaning. If I wanted to do actual work I would've taken up something lucrative, like diamond mining.

"Excuse me," Auburn says, "I've been waiting here without service for almost forty seconds. I'm in a hurry, my preemie is starving at home and I need to use these food stamps to buy a steak bigger than your head."

I open up the bag as she talks and am hit with the odor of cheeseburgers, probably double cheeseburgers. The underside of a bright red order of fries is peeking out from beneath the yellow wrappers, lining the bottom of the bag like a French-fried birdcage.

"I don't know," I respond, "some of the people who come through at night are sad, I try not to let myself get jealous that they eat filet mignon and I eat from the dollar menu."

"Well, jeez," she says, digging through her purse. "I would've brought you Crown Sterling, but they didn't have a drive-through open 'till midnight."

"I didn't mean it like that, I just…" Auburn's thick midsection is laced and spilling from the edge of her corset top, and my eyes get lost in the constellation of freckles between her breasts and neck. I outline Orion and Taurus the bull as I try to think of something kind to say, some way to genuinely thank her for going out of her way for me, but my eyes just can't get honest enough to look at her. "Did you need…I mean, why are you…"

"Brooks." She leans down to look into my eyes and I turn away, the scent of seventy dollar perfume surfing into my nose on the breeze. "Brooks, I was just in town for a party and thought I would drop by and bring you food. I'm not doing the creepy stalker girlfriend thing. I'm not even your girlfriend, I have to get that one checked before I move on to stalking and creeping."

She has succeeded in kicking my attempt at graveyard shift poetry in the butt while it was bending over. Now it's stumbling forward into the aisles and knocking things over. If I could stick a microphone in my nose to record the sounds of my brain it would sound like "doot, doot, doot." My thought process is a hamster sleeping in the wheel.

"Hon, normally I find that brooding artist thing you do incredibly attractive, and you know this, but today is my own personal sad anniversary so there's no reason for you to get quiet and weird and ruin it for me."

"You've only got," I stop to look at the clock on the ticket paper, "eleven minutes before we stop selling alcohol."

"I…" Her sentence stops after a vowel and we stand there not making a sound. My eyes become focused on the back of her hand, being scratched by a sparkling purple nail decorated with lacerated cuticles. She wears many rings but none specific, and if she told you that she bought them all herself you would not dispute her. Auburn breathes heavily, exhales, "Whatever," then turns and walks away to the overly lit and frigid beer section. I can see patches of skin on her back turn into fractals of pink and they outline the faded black symbols etched there just above the velvet.

A roll of my eyes accompanies the genuine desire to apologize, which is a dichotomy only truly felt by disappointed idealists. Reality debases unexpected kindness. The heart, or at least the part of the brain that lets the "heart" get all the credit, debases purposeful rudeness. I lock my register and push the mop bucket through the candy and past the magazines until I can view Auburn from around the corner. She is standing, hands on hips, and from behind I picture her eyes darting to and fro, searching for something that she cannot name but wants. Some thing that businessmen and lonesome country singers find at the bottom of a bottle, the pedantic lake in which to drown disobedient, child-like sorrows.

"So, why is this a sad anniversary?" A few decorative noises are made with the mop, and if she somehow speaks mop she knows I'm sorry.

Without turning around she mumbles, "Nothing." Auburn turns to me without making eye contact as I slowly walk to a place beside her, and there is an orphaned arc of gray streaking a few inches down her cheek. The death and burial of this arc is still evident on her face, wiped away and now somewhere amongst the dirt and shimmering clarity of the grocery store floor. "What…should I get?" she asks.

"Uh, well, that depends on what kind of feeling you're going for. If you want to take out your work-related frustrations on your back-talking wife, you wanna go with this," I motion, pointing up. "If you want to run into a telephone pole on your way out of the parking lot you could try a sixer of this," I motion, pointing down. "Oh, and if you suddenly have the urge to have sex with your brother you can try one of these," I motion, pointing to the line of gallon-sized jugs of faux-moonshine lining the end-cap. She follows my finger and laughs her normal laugh, where you can't hear anything but she's smiling, and that's better than nothing.

"I guess if you like your debilitating disease on the go you can try one of those single servings of white zinfandel. Look at them, they're in tiny bottles. Like forties, but for midgets." She reaches across my chest to pull one of the tiny bottles from its cardboard domicile, decorated with pictures of palm trees set against a pink sunset.

"Hah, yeah, and look at this," are the only words that show up in the creation process of that humorous observation, because when I reach across her chest to show her the "Lynchburg lemonade" our elbows meet, and my skin meets hers, and for a second we forget about how disappointed we are in our ability to connect. I can't talk on the phone without feeling awkward, she can't type online without using perfect punctuation. For the longest time we've known that the only thing keeping us from being happy, normal people is the fact that we are too self aware, and too much like each other to do anything productive with our time.

"If we were Ghostbusters here we'd be in trouble," I say. At the grocery store there is an entire aisle of shampoo that I could be, but alas.

She laughs again, rubbing her cold nose against my bicep, and another shooting star of mascara falls over the tracks of the previous. "What?"

"Our arms are crossed. It's, like, you know," as my voice gets quieter and softer, like someone in my head is turning down the volume for my own good. "We're crossing the streams, and, uh, the Ghostbusters weren't supposed to do that, and..."

Auburn stretches her neck and kisses me. She tastes like expensive lipstick, color-guarded and water resistant and applied with precision. The ring around her lip has become frozen in the arctic conditions of the alcohol shelves, and when it touches the skin below my bottom lip the chill races to the tip of every nerve in my body. All at once it feels like someone pulling me into the darkness by the back of my neck. It's like the dream where you take a step and the step disappears, and you're falling for that one moment in subconscious time.

"You are such a fucking dork," she smiles, and I agree.

"So, why is this a sad anniversary?" I manage to ask. The mop is so far away. All I can hear is the buzz of the air conditioning and the instrumental versions of soul seventies hits on low volume over the intercom.

"You really want to know, do you?"

"I wouldn't have asked you if I didn't want to know."

"Yeah, but you didn't ask me when I was fishing for it." Auburn turns from me and crosses her arms.

"That's more of a fault in the obviousness of your fishing." As she walks back to the cash register I kneel and pull out a twelve pack of the fizzy, white, citrus ice malt-beverage that she always manages to have two of in her mini-fridge.

"My fishing is fine, thank you," she says, not looking back. "And I only need six, I want to be able to drink a majority of them before Kiki fails a math test and threatens to stab herself in the stomach." I kneel again and replace the twelve with the six.

"Does your sad anniversary have anything to do with fishing?"

"Yes. On this day last year I was forced to purchase Big Mouth Billy Bass. He hung there on the mantle, lifeless, and suddenly began to sing. I haven't been able to look myself in the mirror since that horrible day." She turns to me and uses her arms to elevate her into a sitting position on the end of my register. "Are you ever bothered by the fact that our entire generation is based around our individual knowledge of popular culture? I'm writing a paper for my sosch class discussing the theory that popularity is based on how little about popular culture one knows. Also, the irony in the act of a 'jock,'" she says, making annoying air quotes, "picking on a 'nerd.' The only difference in the culture is that predator fills his head with sports facts and prey fills his head with space-opera facts."

"So you're saying that a jock is like rain on your wedding day?"

"No," she protests, "there is nothing ironic in that entire song." I smile as I hit alcohol-item-$2.00 on my register.

"Perhaps the true irony of the song rests in the concept that nothing in the song is ironic?" Auburn sits there banging the heels of her boots into the front of the register line, leaving scuff prints that I decide to let the morning people deal with. Two dollars crumple together in my fist and find their way into the register. I place the six pack, condensation already forming on the long necks of the bottles, into a plastic bag, and then that bag into another, as the register tape turns to twelve and begins to print. "You're avoiding the question, though. You wouldn't have brought it up if you didn't want me to ask you about it."

"Well, yeah, I know." Her voice doesn't sound the same. Bang, bang, bang, bang. Auburn chooses to fill her moments of confusion with silence, instead of the mindless stammering that most people do, so it's difficult to know when she's finished talking and when she's ready to start again. I've found that it is always a moment after someone else begins to speak.

"You..."

"There was, a guy, a long time ago," she interrupts. "Why does every story begin like this? The world is filling up with emancipated females and my sad anniversary story starts with 'there was a guy a long time ago.' Ugh."

"It's okay," I mumble.

"Is it?" she asks. "If I start talking about this I run the risk of becoming a sympathetic character. I, don't want anybody to give me sympathy, because I don't like enough people to accept sympathy as genuine. I don't want some random person patting me on the back and telling me that they're sorry for something. That's the most disgusting thing I can imagine." Auburn looks back at me over her shoulder and makes a wild but pointless gesture with her hand. "It's so disingenuous. Like a germ that they're spreading. I would rather them just spit in my face."

Suddenly my register beeps. I look down and there is orange juice sitting on the radar, going "beep beep beep beep" and ringing itself up a dozen times. To the immediate right of the carton is a white girl with braids in her hair in a pullover sweatshirt and hundred and sixty-dollar sneakers. The bridge of her nose is bright red and shades of purple fall like drops of water across her cheek-bone. She speaks in a high falsetto lined with cigarette smoke, minty cigarette smoke that comes in green packages, green packages waving back and forth on plastic shelves behind her like blades of grass in some meadow she'll never see. I feel sorry for her for every second she's there until the words, "I got these orange juices, they're supposed to be buy one get one free, so make sure that they ring up like that cause I don't wanna pay for two of them," come out of her mouth. Pitying someone who doesn't deserve it feels like mistaking the fresh soda for the can that has been sitting there all night.

"Oh, and I've got these," the customer continues, placing blue fives and green tens down with a frown. I nod and slide the food stamps to the side, and before I can stuff the orange juices in paper or plastic she fills the space with a sixteen dollar package of marinated chicken breasts. Hopping down from the register Auburn raises her eyebrows and smiles. I store my ninety-nine cent cheeseburgers alongside my lunchables portion of beefaroni and displace what needs to be displaced. Thank you ma'am. We're open twenty-four hours. This week we have two for one conditioner. You are all the same. Rinse and repeat.

The customer leans over the radar to peruse the receipt. The burned twists of hair pulled up from her neck wobble and sway as she asks me question after question that I thought I'd answered by being a cognizant human being. She smells like bong water and dirty diapers. The mulatto baby in the cart is propped up haphazardly in a car seat. It smiles at me from beneath a ribbed headband and I wave back. Parents who put headbands on bald children should have their children taken away. Your child is as beautiful as a springtime rose and all, but the child is bald. He or she will grow hair. Hair holds bows and ribbons. Scalp holds nothing. It is a fact of life. Take the good, take the bad. Take them both if you have to.

"Did you see the headband on that baby?" Auburn asks me when mother and child are gone. "If I ever have a child, which I won't, I'm going to graft a handle to its head and carry it around like a briefcase."

"What happened?" Her eyes open wide and she looks to her left, then to her right.

"What happened with what? With the baby and the headband? Inbreeding?"

"No," I say, using my man voice. "With the guy, a long time ago."

"Brooks," she says softly, "You might not want me to talk about it here. You're at work, and I'm just sad. I shouldn't have come to you for this. How wrong it is for a woman to expect the man to build the world she wants, rather than to create it herself."

"Yes," I nod, "And we have art to save ourselves from the truth." I rest my elbows on the counter and my forehead on the balls of my thumbs.

"You countered Anais Nin with Nietzsche." Auburn raises herself onto the counter and stretches out, closing her eyes and folding her hands behind her head like she's resting in my menial task hammock. "I think that says something profound about our interpersonal relationship." I stare at her until she opens her eyes. "Okay, so…"

"The answer to all of your questions is yes, so tell me before your booze gets too warm." She remains motionless for a few moments before rolling back onto her butt and sighing.

"His name was…we were dating when I was, uh, a junior in high school. I was seventeen and he was twenty-four, he worked for my Mom and he was…basically he was…"

"He was what?"

"He…asked me to marry him on my seventeenth birthday, and of course I told him no. I heard later from one of his friends that I thought I wouldn't marry him because he didn't make enough money. It wasn't that at all, really," she says, shrugging her shoulders. Bang, bang, bang, bang. "I just, I was seventeen, you know? I didn't want to get married to anyone. I still don't want to get married to anyone. It's an empty gesture. It's the time when two people are under the influence of the most violent, most insane, most delusive, and most transient of passions. They are required to swear that they will remain in that excited, abnormal, and exhausting condition continuously until death do them part."

"Well, yeah, of course."

"The kind of marriage you make depends upon the kind of…"

"Auburn." Her name slices through the words. Auburn turns to me with her eyes strained, waiting for something to burst. "Don't quote anything. Just tell me." Suddenly her voice lowers and she speaks to me as she speaks when my face is buried in her neck.

"He, and a couple of his friends, went into business for themselves, they ran an auto body shop, and he would come over after work with these big," she says, holding her hands open in front of her face, "these big grease stains all over his hands, and he was always so happy to see me. He would give me these academic compliments, like 'you look pretty today,' and 'I love what you've done with your hair.'" She tugs at an awkward strand of stripped white hair. "My hair was red back then, and really long, and I hated it because it made me look like some kind of vacant southern stereotype. I said things like 'aww' and 'y'all' and it was predictable and monotonous. He kept telling me that he was saving up to buy me this big expensive piece of jewelry that would 'win me over,' like it was some contest to pamper me, like I was that shallow."

I make a point to walk around the register and crouch down in front of her as she continues. The corners of her mouth twitch when she isn't speaking, and I begin to notice the counter of her make-up, and how the light pink is bordered in streaks of red.

"So every time he would get work at the shop he'd put a few dollars into a savings account and spend the rest on boy things, like, like bows and arrows, and hunting equipment, and those hats with foam in the front and mesh in the back. Those really redneck hats that have brown leaves printed all over the front so that he wouldn't be spotted in the woods. He'd wear that, and also a bright blaze orange vest, so you could see him from the highway. I would skip sixth period every few days and drive over to his house, and he'd show me all the things he'd bought over the week. 'Check out these rims I picked out for the truck,' or, 'look at this Beretta 1200 I got at the gun show.' And," she begins to cry, "he had this, Super Nintendo that sat in the corner that he got for some Christmas like a decade ago, and I would sit in this bean bag chair in the floor of his apartment and play it while he showed me all of his new toys. Because, I mean, how interested is a girl going to be in a Beretta 1200 police shotgun, right?"

I lean up to see if there are any tissues left on my register, but I can't see them and can't think of anything else to do for her.

"It's scary," she whimpers, "he was telling me about a new shotgun he'd bought, and I was so bored, sitting on the bean bag playing that dodge ball game. He was talking, and I don't remember what he was saying, and then there was a noise, and I thought it was a transformer exploding outside, because we'd been having a rainstorm and lightning had done that, and…I covered my ears and they hurt, like it was inside my head, and when I turned around I saw something small on the floor, and I reached for it and when I touched it, it had blood on it. I think I thought his dog had killed something and dragged it in, but…but then I looked over to yell something nasty about the noise and he was, he was on his knees." Auburn lowers herself to the floor and crouches in front of me, her eyes submerged in a tide of sadness. She tries to cry but the sockets won't let the drops fall.

"He was on his knees, Brooks, and somebody had thrown red paint on the wall behind him. There was, smoke, and it was coming up from behind him and I thought maybe something was on fire, but before I could even finish that thought what had happened hit me, and I remember screaming something and no sound coming out. Like a dream when you're being chased and you scream, and your voice is gone. Like somebody turned the volume down, and there was this black, this black stuff on his back. He looked up at me Brooks, and he looked up and he asked me what happened." Her stomach flexes and she loses her balance, falling a few inches to her knees.

"You…" is all I have to offer.

"He was so busy talking and showing off that he wasn't paying attention and he…" The words become barely audible. "He shot himself in the stomach, and there was blood on the wall that stuck and drained down onto the carpet, but there were spots that were hot and stuck in these, these clumps, I guess. He started crying but there weren't tears, and his face turned so white that it looked pink underneath, like I was looking through his…through his face, and he started apologizing and I wouldn't let him. I wouldn't let him apologize to me because I was selfish and I thought he was stupid for hurting himself like that. Brooks, he was in pain and I just thought about myself. He had a hole, a big hole that went through his skin and his shirt, and I was thinking about how it affected me, and what it meant to me, and I started photographing these images in my mind, like they were mine."

Auburn grabs my wrists and they begin to change colors, but I can't even find a "you" to offer. She begins to speak in a whisper, the air in her lungs coming alive and forcing its way out through words, whether she makes them or not.

"Then he, he started to scream. It was animalistic, he wasn't himself anymore, somewhere between alive and…and not, and the screams were so scary Brooks, he screamed and started scratching at the floor. He was…" she lowers her head into my chest. "It looked like he was trying to pick himself up off the floor, not himself but the pieces of himself that he lost. He wrapped his hands around the barrel of the gun, and he kept forcing it up against his chest, and I tried to stop him. I tried to take it away from him but he put his hand on my ribcage and his fingers were so strong, it hurt me and I yelped. My noise was so pathetic, like I'd been kicked in the side for being a bad dog. He started screaming that he was sorry, screaming, 'I'm sorry,' like I was in the other room, screaming it into the floor, screaming it into the gun. He pushed me down onto my stomach and I heard the noise again, and I covered my ears again because they hurt, because it was in my head. There was no way it was real, but I could feel it in that space between my brain and my skull, like my head was filled with it, the noise, the echo, the stench. I just stayed on the ground and screamed, kicking my feet like, like a child."

I look over her shoulder to see a few of the stock boys standing at the end of the aisle, faces nondescript, staring at her, or me.

"I rolled over," she continued, "and he was lying next to me, as close as you are to me now, and his eyes were wide open. There was this red streak coming from behind his head that was dripping down onto his eye, and it was blood, and it was coming down like he was crying, like he was finally able to cry. I knew he had shot himself in the head to stop all the pain he was going through but it didn't make any difference. I stopped crying and started thinking about how strange it was that blood from the back of his head was draining down against the back of his eyes and mixing with the blood that poured around when he fell. It was death, not boy in a box death, not sad relative wish we had more time death, it was death itself just lying there, looking at me. His eyes wouldn't close, the whites of his eyes were turning pink and he wouldn't close his eyes, and I started biting my lip until it bled. I don't know why but I remember it, I remember bleeding with him, like it was helping him, like he needed me to do that for him." She buries her face in my neck and cries. "The people from downstairs were there then, standing over me, and I think they thought I was dead because they were talking about us together. They were talking and I started seeing black, like someone was dimming the lights until I couldn't see anything. The last thing I remember was blinking and feeling warmth running over my face, and looking back over my shoulder at them huddled over him, thinking he'd done it to himself for me."

"Nobody still thinks that, do they?" I ask. "You've told other people about this before?"

"A couple of people," she sniffs. "My mother. She was…fairly supportive. She put me into therapy a few weeks later. They gave me pills and told me over and over that it wasn't my fault, when I never said it was my fault anyway. The only difference between me and a madman is that I'm not a man." From our embrace between registers six and seven she pulls away and looks into my eyes, then at my mouth. "I've never told someone about it and expected them to genuinely care. Sometimes I'm afraid that the first person I open up to is going to have a worse story of their own ready to share, thinking that they're empathizing with me when they're really just trivializing it and making me feel common.

"I wouldn't want to trivialize what you've felt. I don't really know what to say, you…"

"Don't say anything then," she interrupts, guiding her index and middle fingers along my jawbone. Auburn leans in to kiss me again but when I feel her lips I pull away.

"Hey, what are you doing?"

She doesn't answer.

"What are you doing?"

She leans in to kiss me again.

"Auburn, what are you doing?"

"What?" she groans, finally, angrily. "I need to feel warm. I need to feel strong."

"I think there are better ways for you to do that, though," I say, standing up. Auburn remains on the ground, collapsed on her knees, her head lowered as drops of ashy gray shatter against the floor. "I'm here for you if you want to talk and all, but that's…that's not something I'd really be able to handle like that, I don't think I'm good enough to…"

"I can't believe you're doing this to me." Her voice is thick and cold.

"What can't you believe I'm doing? I'm just…"

"No," she says, wiping her face and standing. "You're not just. You're denying me when I need you. I do know how to love you. You aren't Jesus, you're Judas. I can best love you by not ever thinking that you'd do for someone what someone does for you."

"Wait a minute," I say, pressing my palms firmly into the counter, leaving impressions of sweat. "You can't just change the way you're feeling on the fly because I didn't want to take advantage of you, you can't…"

"You could never take advantage of me," she states flatly and without remorse. "Are you forgetting all of the times you came to my door, holding out your hand, looking for some spare change? Remember the time you wrecked your car a week before exams and they wouldn't let you take the make-up tests, and you lost your scholarship? I sat with you on the steps outside of Crawford dorm until the sun came up, listening to you cry." I try to interrupt her, but she continues, her words growing quicker and closer, growing from the ends of their predecessor. "What about the time your parents screwed up your student loan payments and you didn't have enough credit to get financial aid and go back to school? I just squatted there with my legs spread and let you work out all of your problems."

The muscles in my face stop working for a moment and my heart recoils from the blows, but deep inside I understand that she is upset, and that she doesn't really mean what she's saying, even if she does.

"Auburn…"

"What about the time your idiot friend killed himself and all your perfect little zealot could do was make conversation?"

The sunburned, bread-bearded diamond miner presses his belly against the shopping cart and muddles in from the wind and the cold, stopping for a moment to nod in my direction. My night manager is busy breaking down cardboard boxes to fit as many as possible into the compactor. The stock boys have all meandered into the aisles to face and block cans of peaches, bags of dog food, boxes of hair dye. Simon and Scotty are drinking nonalcoholic beer on the curb outside of the convenience store and pretending to be drunk. Randy is sitting on the bottom shelf of magazines, flipping through to a story about the history of the Winston Cup. Auburn Bryant is an emancipated female. Brooks is staring at his reflection in the metal on the counter. St. Peter is writing on the blank side of his sign with a magic marker. The buzz of the automatic door drowns out "Shake Your Booty." Same as it ever was.

"I'm sorry," I say to her. "I'm sorry that I don't love you."

"You're one of those people who would be enormously improved by death." Her face is however she wants it to be. I don't look. "Besides, nobody asked you to." And with that, she was gone.

"Cashier to the back, please, cashier to the back."

On my way to the bowels of the grocery store I begin to prepare for the remaining seven hours of my shift. The overweight man is searching for someone with the authority to give him a green flag on expired meat, and the more things change the more they make me want to clean up ejaculate. I manage to smile as I unwrap a cold double cheeseburger and begin singing softly to myself.

"*If you strip away the myth from the man, you will see where we all soon will be…*"

CHAPTER 13

Adam, the Hebrew word for "man" and more than just some guy named Adam, was created by God on the fourth day of time. The first upright humanoid stretched his muscles four billion years later. Somewhere between then and there we had cockroaches and horseshoe crabs crawling on Eve's discarded apple cores and Lucy the Human Fossil's Ethiopian hut or, later, her body. Then there was an ice age, and Stonehenge, Pyramids and Olympics. Jesus showed up, died, and then had a rock opera. Now sheep have clones and so do kittens, but the cockroaches and horseshoe crabs are exactly the same. We have evolved, the level of which varies depending on the religious inclinations of the species, but they have not. They are identical to their ancestors. I have not changed since I was twelve years old. The weight is gone, and facial hair pops up in patches when I don't have time to shave. My feet don't fit into anything below a size thirteen. Every night before bed I catch myself starting my prayers, before I shake my head and tell myself that I don't talk to God anymore.

With Him in my heart or with Him closed off in a book on the shelf I can't feel the difference, I plunge up through the valleys and down from the mountains, I soar above the clouds or touch the rocks at the bottom of the ocean. The clouds are always the same, the rocks are always the same; the mountains don't grow and the valleys never sink. The highs and the lows are vibrant and colored now but they are always the same. I can't make myself evolve out of this shell of adolescence. I can't grow out of the habit of existing just outside the perimeters of death, watching the blades of grass wither and die around me and my tuft of emerald lawn. When the skies are burned and the soil barren and no air is breathed in the world it will still be here, my resolve, my self-depreciation, my confusion. I am a cockroach. I guess that makes Auburn the horseshoe crab.

Aranea Cavatica is not there smiling at me as I push open the wrought iron gate that leads into Potter's Field. It is almost empty. There is a monument that says the City of Lynchburg decided in 1986 to use this field to bury their dead, but there are only two or three lines of graves here, and hardly any tombstones. All that remains are assembled stones, and metal placards sticking up from the ground. The Old City Cemetery in the aftermath of an early morning rainstorm drains and smudges like an oil painting, and from far away the tips of branches on dying trees begin to melt and mix into chocolate swirls of mud and chips of broken grass. My idiot friend is buried beneath a placard six graves from the tall trees in the center of the plot. Between the trees is a sign that reads "In Memoriam," as if we couldn't figure that out ourselves, above a list of names; tiny letters forming the names of the indigent. The names run together and totter into the crotch of the botany. What used to be my grandmother is two rows back, in the corner.

Virginia is how it should be at six-fifty in the morning, because nothing moves. The sky is a sheet of snow, the silver linings bending and disappearing in the folds of fabric and perfect ice. The trees don't sway and the grass never whistles. The streets are empty save for the occasional headlight, drifting through the darkness unimportantly like the last firefly of summer. More than just the people below me we are a city of the dead, sleeping with the confidence that if we die before we wake, someone will be there to take our souls. Like the founders of ancient cities hoping for their city of seven hills to be the fulcrum to the lever of Armageddon, we gather our nuts in the tree and wait for winter, when we will be enclosed with a wrought iron fence and our names will be added to the monument. Our great reward lies somewhere beyond this life, so if our lives become destructive, hurtful, narrow, it is not that big of a deal. We bury our loved ones, keep our fingers crossed, and eventually forget where their placard is.

To deny that we secretly revel in death is to ignore the obvious. Down the hill from the graves is a butterfly pond, overlooked by an immense but fragile willow tree. The limbs hang down morosely, lifeless, over muddy water. Sandbags placed in the shape of a heart stand in the center, a safeguard against the previous day's flooding. Butterflies are gathered in little graves along the edge of the water, soft bumps of brown sludge formed into monuments, twigs in the place of trees. They die so young. In the branches above hangs a wind chime, waiting patiently. To the left a steep hill rises, cutting off the horizon. At the top is a tree, with a swing. It is only there if you are looking for it, like the butter-flies. The ground is never level in the cemetery, and at any point the hills and pockets of water make me feel like I am at the bottom of some incredible sink. All I can do is keep my footing and not go down the drain, with Curtis, and with my grandmother, and with the Confederacy. They are buried all around. I feel like my feet will break through the mud and I will be lost beneath the sur-face with them.

"Hey," I say to the Curtis Dean Bunch placard, 1980–2002. The placard has been here for three weeks now, the body for a month. My throat considers a speech of some kind, one of those touching graveside chats that the lovable yet flawed protagonist gives when his girlfriend or war buddy dies. I thought about bringing three by five index cards to ensure that I hit all of the expos-itory points that Curtis would want to know about; things like Auburn thinking he was an idiot for killing himself, things like me thinking he is an idiot for being gone. For a while I was sure he'd want to know that his mother wanted to divide up his video game collection between Chinese and I, and how funny that is considering the last thing we ever did together was play "River City Ran-som" on the old Nintendo. Then I remember that Tasha giggled when her new boyfriend slapped her on the butt in the grocery store a few nights ago, and how Crystal was thinking about a new baby with husband number five. Instead of a speech I opt to sit Indian-style a foot, thirteen inches, from the placard and not force Curtis to remember himself. There is no easy way out for him in the afterlife. He can't shoot himself in Heaven and end up back here. Even if he could, I'm not selfish enough to want him to.

A drop of rain clips the tip of my nose and falls into my lap, and suddenly I'm awakened from my meditative daze. I raise my arms like the statue of Christ to feel for the rain, like we all do, but feel nothing. When my forearm raises to wipe the water from my nose I hear the sound of a dog barking through the line of trees across the street. The sun is rising behind the clouds now and they have the texture of cotton, like I could reach up with my fingers and move them from below. The dirt covering Curtis doesn't even look like a pile of dirt anymore. Grass has grown over the dirt and dried, before the water came down to make it brittle and soggy. My fingers slide beneath the grasses and I think about how it wasn't even that long ago that he did this to himself, and it was just a few days ago, a few weeks, a month, that we buried him. We buried him. They buried him. I carried him. The tenth grade philosophers and hit popular songwriters have been telling the truth all along, time does move on, even when it stands still. I don't even feel like I've had any time to mourn. I haven't convinced myself that it is okay to just sit with my back to the wall and cry without any specific reason. I haven't visited his mother like I promised or even come back to the grave before now, and it has suddenly been so long. Instantly so long.

"Oh my God," I murmur to myself, beneath the sound of a deep wind swirling from the butterfly pond and sweeping across the graveyard. The synapses in my brain fire off like bottle rockets but all at once, until nothing makes sense. In one part of my brain I'm thinking that maybe I should've paid more attention to those hit songs that were written in five minutes about love and teenage camaraderie. I wonder if I was the biggest goober on the planet for trying so hard, when the whole act revolves around not trying. Another part of my brain wants to go home and shoot myself through the heart, so that when I lay there dying my brain can look down in triumph, knowing that the bastard that had taken credit for my sadness for so long has finally gotten his. If I go home to do this I won't be able to find a gun, because my mom isn't a sociopath and my dad was never into hunting, so I'll have to swallow "too many pills." Then I remember that I don't have any pills, not taking into consideration the gel caps that cure my aching stuffy head and fever without putting me to sleep. If I over dose on Pink Basmati it will just give me the runs, and they don't write about famous artists who died from the trots in history books. All that would be left then is the slashing of wrists, or the throat. There is a wooden block full of steak knives on my kitchen counter at home, but whenever I try that I can never get up enough nerve to stick the point all the way into my skin. My hands start to shake and I think about how much pain I'll be in, and how much pain I'd be in if I didn't have the guts to lay there and die like a man. I can cover throwing up with food poisoning or an upset stomach, but no parent or friend is dumb enough to believe that you slipped in the shower and fell wrist first onto the razors. I tried sticking my head in the oven once, but it just made me fat. We don't even have a garage, so I can't sit in a running car and go to sleep. What would I hang myself on? Why would I hang myself? I can't manage to keep my curse-to-vocabulary ratio down to five dammits per sentence when I get a crick in my neck from sleeping on it wrong. Above most other things, though, suicides go to Hell. Above all else, I'd miss wrestling too much. So now I'm just sitting here waiting for the rain to start so I can go home and stop thinking. It's been a long night.

I didn't mean to come here this early, or at all. Third shift came to a close without ceremony at five fifty-eight, two minutes before schedule, twenty minutes earlier than usual. Management often finds it easier to keep an employee in the store overnight than have a higher paid employee arrive on time in the early morning. I've been borrowing my Mother's car, a Camry that was forged in the fires of Mount Fuji, a device of evil that consumes the driver. With red-tinted images of Auburn in my mind I could not hope to begin the journey to sleep, so a pilgrimage to the all-night gas station became my destiny. Instead of doing something productive like microwaving a chilly dog I did what I always do and marched straight to the bathroom.

Between long, piercing glances into the mirror I put quarters into the machine, which always helped me out when I was feeling self conscious and couldn't get up the nerve, even at twenty-two years of age and in the middle of the morning, to buy condoms with a straight face. The drive to school would take twenty-six minutes with no traffic, and our basic make-up taking anywhere from thirty minutes to two hours, so I put down a dollar ninety-nine for a big Mountain Dew and sucked it up. It would make neither she nor I feel better about ourselves or each other, but it would replace the images of her screaming on the floor with the normal, acceptable image of her screaming on the floor.

I even made the trip all the way to campus, adroitly avoiding the sharp supervision of the seventy-year old female security guard who watches the front gate and makes the visitors, and often inexplicably the students, sign in for security purposes. When I was a student she carried a loaded gun on her hip even when off-duty, which struck me as odd before the unexplained series of blown tires plagued campus security. After the terrorist attacks she began carrying not only a loaded gun, but a heavy purse. I avoided her by driving my car by slowly as she napped. The campus is beautiful even in the dark, with random dorm televisions highlighting the trees just outside the windows with flickering blue strokes. Streetlights line the sidewalks and light green benches with an amber glow. At the end of a mentally and physically tiring morning a place that used to be home starts to feel like a bed, and the moon even gets a comically exaggerated happy face that sings lullabies as cows do hurdles in orbit. When my mind becomes fatigued is when it becomes the most righteous, possibly because of my Sunday School training and those long nights spent at the windowsill waiting for the end of the world. As quickly and decisively as I arrived I made my exit, speeding over the speed bump loudly enough to wake the security guard and not taking even a moment to admire the fawns in nightcaps grazing by the roadside.

At six forty-five I drove into the Old City Cemetery and pulled off onto the side of the road across from the Station House Museum. My eyes have been closed for the last ten minutes. If I cry here and if I cry because of this it is not because of Curtis and not because of what happened. I'd be crying out of my own self-pity. I've done enough to myself already without having to make my emotions that basic. I don't even know if I could make myself feel something as simple as "pity," I would have to add layers to it; self-pity with a hint of remorse and a jealous undertone, maybe. If I allow myself to burst into dramatic tears and start clawing around in the mud I'm destined to be just like those beneath me. The scariest part is that if I do that I'm destined to be just like everyone else; a slave to my emotions, unable to complete the simplest task because of what it means to my heart. I want to rip his placard out of the ground and throw it over the fence, because it is he and people like him who have made it so difficult for me to let myself love appropriately, or ever really love at all. Because of him, because of this, this world, this constant situation of linear existence I am chained to the reality that everyone I let myself love goes away, and everyone who stays won't love me back.

The wind stops for a moment and Potter's Field is silent. With nothing to set fire to my senses I begin to dig with my fingers, nothing committed, just fingers scratching Earth. Without warning I feel a bright light and heat against my eyelids, enough to make my tears feel cold as they trip and fall down my cheek. The silence is faintly broken by the sound of a bird chirping, and when I open my eyes there is a cardinal standing on my best friend's footstones. The bird stands there like the only color in a black and white film, pecking at the grasses as the sun breaks through the curdled sky. Every few seconds the bird tilts its head to the side and hops, but never too far, for it stays on the stones and stares at me. Moments later the cardinal's calm cheep is matched by another, and in my peripheral vision I spot another standing a few feet to my left. My vision is abruptly drawn back to the original bird, who totters from his perch and flies a few inches from my face, before resting behind me. When I turn back another bird has taken his place. They surround me but do not observe me, each bird existing in each direction distinctively; quietly singing, quietly standing.

Instinctively I extend my legs and rock back onto my hands. The chirping becomes synchronized and I begin to ask myself rapid-fire questions, is this a dream sequence, did I fall asleep in the middle of a cemetery, or did I wander into a horror movie? Before I can answer or even finish the innumerable questions the birds stop, all at once. No movements, no sounds. They stand and look. Then, as if pulled by strings, they leap from their stances and fly up, up high into the tree branches. Any other season the leaves would've shielded them from view, but here and now they are naked and exposed, state birds in peril amongst the barking holes in the evergreens. Silence. Then, footsteps.

I look down and to the left to see her spreading a red and white checkered blanket over the muddy spot. With the corners of my mouth looking like drainage ditches, curved downward and lined with water, I don't allow myself to look at her. I don't notice anything new about her hair, or what she is wearing, or what she smells like. Her voice sounds like it always does. For a moment my heart jumps as I fear that I would become desensitized to her like I've become to everything else, but then I remember how tired I am and just nod. She sits down, Indian-style, on the blanket a few inches from my elbow.

"Where did you come from?"

"*The sky. Illinois.*"

"No, I meant, where did you come from? It's seven in the morning. I didn't hear your car pull up."

"*I know what you meant. I was dropping off my dad actually. Herman Horatio Honda is parked up by Kid's Haven Memorial. I was on the swing and then I felt a raindrop, and then I saw you down here. I thought I'd say hey.*"

"Hey."

"*Hey.*"

. . . .

"*You look tired.*"

"I am tired. I worked graveyard last night."

"*That's funny. My dad works graveyard. Only during the day.*"

"I bet he doesn't have to put up with people having sex in the bathrooms, or customers complaining about buy-one-get-one-free at five o'clock in the morning like I'm supposed to know what to do or care."

"*No, you're right. His customers mostly just lie there.*"

"I'm sorry, I didn't mean to be insensitive about your dad. It's been a long night."

"*I think that's funny. Nights are always the same kind of long. I just try to sleep through them. Like bad movies.*"

"Yeah."

"*People were having sex in your bathroom?*"

"No, not my bathroom. The grocery store bathroom."

"*People were having sex in the grocery store bathroom? That's disgusting. How does that even work?*"

"Aranea, when a man and a woman love each other, sometimes they…"

"No, I…I know how, I know how that works, I meant in the bathroom, in the grocery store."

"The baby changing station, and balance, I guess. I've never done it."

"Well I'd hope not! People should have some respect for themselves. They should at least buy something first."

"My manager made me go in and stop them, thankfully they were zipping up and shipping out by then. The girl actually slapped me on the way out, it was a nice touch."

"It doesn't sound like a nice kind of touch. Are you okay?"

"Yeah, I'm six-two and two-hundred pounds. Unless she's hitting me with a board with a nail in it or something I should be fine. I didn't want to crumble to the ground in a pool of blood in front of my co-workers."

"Ooh, you could've done it in exaggerated slow motion, like in…like in the movies. Jeez, I'm sorry, I shouldn't keep bringing up movies. I'm tired too, I wasn't expecting one of our conversations at this time of day, at the cemetery."

"One of our conversations?"

"You know, the snappy banter, referencing the past, that kind of thing. I always feel like I have to keep up with you."

"You…you don't have to do that, I'm just rambling off the top of my head most of the time. If I ever put any serious thought into what I said I could quote poetry, or Shakespeare, and I could walk around with a notepad writing these profound observations on life instead of making jokes about your cheeseburgers."

"Wow, was that a euphemism?"

"You'll see me dig up one of these people and ballroom dance with them before you'll hear me use a euphemism, especially to you."

"But that's what I mean, you remembered what we'd talked about before, I don't know anybody else who does that."

"It's just what I remember the most."

"You remember conversations with me the most?"

"I find myself doing five things at once to forget them, sometimes."

. . . .

"You look tired, too."

"I am tired. It's not every day that I have to wake up this early and play chauffeur. I didn't get to wear the little bowtie or anything, I just put on pajama pants

and a big wool hat that looks like some old lady's table cloth and now I'm thrust into context."

"The hat is cute. I have the urge to knit you."

"I could take that as a euphemism, but you said you wouldn't use those around me, so now it's basically you telling me that you want to stab me. I'm not sure how comfortable I am with that."

"Okay, that was a euphemism. But you have to forgive me, I'm about two paragraphs of verbose description away from passing out and drooling on the placard. I'm somewhere between reality and goofy surrealist art. Did you see those creepy birds a minute ago?"

"They're still up in the trees. They flew up there when I opened the gate. Maybe they thought you were dead, and were pretending to be vultures?"

"I think it says something that vultures would pick me out of a field full of dead people."

"If I were a vulture I would pick you out of a field of dead people."

"Was that a euphemism?"

"I don't even know what a euphemism is. I just made the word up."

"Good."

. . . .

"So what are your plans for the rest of the day?"

"I thought I'd hang out here and see if there were any furniture sales going on. Maybe I could find a bed at reduced price."

"See, you're doing it again."

"Doing what again?"

"You're referencing past conversations, tying everything together. Now I've got to think of a way to sneak the tiger driver into the dialogue. So, now that we're here in the graveyard all crouched down in the mud and corpses, what do you think about Japanese masked men?"

"Hey, you're the one who asked about the tiger driver, not me. I'm the one who got dropped on his head."

"I know. I'm sorry to bring that up, here."

"I don't think he minds. I gave all of my wrestling tapes to his Mom, I figured she needed better memories of him."

"I don't understand her."

"You don't understand her? Do you even know her?"

"The bruises on her face. I don't understand them."

"You're asking me explain domestic abuse to you? Aranea, when a man and a woman love each other, sometimes they…"

"No, Brooks, I'm not joking. Her son had…you know, a few days earlier, and she had bruises on her face. The thought that she clings to something that causes her so much pain is not what bothers me. What makes me sad is that in the worst time of her life, and logically her life pretty much settled on the bottom in that week, she still took the punches, and she didn't…she didn't do anything about it, you know?"

"I know. I won't kid you and say that Curtis never put bruises there himself."

"Oh, Brooks, I'm so sorry. I know how much you hate it when I say something so obvious and I know that nobody has ever sprang back into happiness moments after empathy, but to know that he and she went through that, and that she still goes through that, makes me sad on the inside, in places I can't reach. Places I've never seen. Places that don't belong in me."

"I don't hate it when you say anything, really."

"I can sit here and put my fingers on my cheeks, and on my nose, and I could never imagine loving someone who did that to me. Unrequited love doesn't exist, since it is impossible to go adamantly enough into a relationship with God and devote your life, the life that you've set aside for Him and His blessings, to someone who doesn't feel exactly the same way. If, if someone I gave my heart to would…"

"I really don't want to talk about someone punching you. I'm sorry if that borders on overprotective masculine posturing, and there is no connotation whatsoever attached to anything I'm talking about here, but if somebody did that, if somebody, to you, I would…I don't know."

"I know. Thank you."

"Yeah, no problem."

"I would do the same for you, you know. I've got big rings, I know I don't have a lot of force behind my punches, but I've seen a lot of karate movies, so if they attacked you one at a time I think I could hold them off."

"So what you're saying is that if ninjas someday randomly attack me, black ninjas, that you'll be there to protect me?"

"Soul mates via martial arts combat. It'll be just like the movies."

"And if I try to kiss you then you'll turn on me?"

"You're darn right I will. I'll pierce you with poison darts. I won't let you die, I mean, I'll travel to the mountains or whatever to get the antidote for you, but I'll let you writhe there in pain long enough to learn your lesson."

"Yeah, I'm sorry about that."

"It's okay. Did you eat last night?"

"I had a cheeseburger. A double cheeseburger, at about twelve thirty."

"Did you keep it down?"

"No. Did you eat last night?"

"No."

"Did you eat yesterday?"

"I had a fun-sized candy bar when I woke up. And you know that is bad for you, don't you? What it does to your teeth?"

"I am well aware. But they don't make mirrors in fun-sizes."

"They do, actually, at fairs. They have mirrors that make your head look like a pineapple, and mirrors that make your torso look like a big snake."

"My head already kind of looks like a pineapple. And your torso is as thick as a snake. So I guess we should go trick or treating and just be happy fat people."

"Don't you think it's more satisfying to be a moderately sized person who obsesses about being overweight, rather than an actual overweight person who doesn't care? At least this way we know we're trying really hard. If I was a happy fat person I wouldn't have anything keeping me up at night."

"You'd have heartburn."

"I don't know if fat jokes are the best way to make ourselves feel better. Hooray for us, we're outcasts!"

"I think it's okay to make a joke about one's own genre. What else do I have, making white people jokes? White people are so stupid. Have you ever noticed that they don't know how to dance?"

"Yeah, and what's the deal with airline food?"

"Besides, I can't feel bad about myself when I know that you feel the same kind of bad about yourself. The world just loses like six layers when I think that you feel fat, or less than average, or not completely better than everybody else. The rest of us are the vast recesses of space and you're the ball of gas that makes the light. That's what bothers me, that I finally find somebody who manages to care about me in a tangible way she has to be the most beautiful girl I've ever seen, and I have to go and be a boy about it."

"Did you just call me a ball of gas? That was almost charming. Maybe I'm just tired."

"That has to be it."

"Thank you for the compliment, though, I don't deserve it. You have this way with words, where you sneak in like seven adjectives that are just perfect and

thoughtfully placed, and I don't want you wasting your valuable exposition time describing the way my hair looks."

"I would never do that."

. . . .

"So what are your plans for the rest of the day?"

"Napping is first and foremost, I plan to make an event of it. I'm laying my pillows on the bed like Lincoln logs and sleeping like a zoo animal, maybe blowing up some balloons to make the hibernation festive."

"How long do you plan to hibernate?"

"Until feeding time, when they bring in the carcasses. I, of course, will not eat any of the carcasses, since that would render my simile inaccurate, and the last thing we need at this point in the conversation is illogical literary device."

"Yeah, I tend to rank illogical literary device just ahead of creepy birds and random black ninja attack."

"Right. Oh, and then at seven I'm meeting my youth group at the fellowship hall to plan our Halloween party. We do it every year, we have live music and bobbing for things, and then we have little kids running around in costumes and you have to give them candy, or else the whole purpose is defeated."

"I understand the custom. When I was fourteen I dressed up as Renee Descartes for Halloween. I went around proclaiming the existence of the one true Christian God to all the houses on my street."

"How did that work out for you?"

"Most people thought I was a musketeer."

"I'm sure God appreciated the witnessing. You'll come to the party, right? We usually have it a few days before actual Halloween, to avoid the holiday rush. We don't want anyone in the congregation getting trampled in the store by some crazy mother looking for Snickers at the last minute."

"Yeah, don't you hate how commercial the holiday has become? It used to be a celebration of the dead, and now look at it."

"We try not to tell the kids what the holiday is actually about. Anything that brings people together in the spirit of gluttony and bad fashion can't be all bad. They draw faces on the pumpkins in magic marker and tell ghost stories, and there is punch and such. It's a happy time of year. Everything is orange."

"I thought it was going to rain. Why hasn't it rained yet?"

"So you'll come to the party?"

"If the punch is orange I'll come to the party."

"Of course the punch is orange. Think of it this way, it's a good way to meet a lot of good people in the church outside of the sermons and the dress clothes. I know that you're going through some hard times right now, and maybe all that talk about the afterlife and where we go, and what we do, maybe you should wait a little while for that."

"It's hard not to think about death when it's all around us."

"Then why not celebrate it? We'll make you feel better by dressing up like skeletons and dancing around like idiots."

"There won't be any weirdness between us? There won't be any questions, or expectations, or…"

"Brooks, they're skeletons. If you can't see skeletons in black and white you're hopeless."

"That was a bad joke."

"I know."

"Time for sleep?"

"Agreed. You'll let me know how the furniture sale goes?"

"Absolutely. You'll keep me informed on the hibernation?"

"I'll have my keeper call your keeper."

"Goodnight."

"Good morning?"

"Good morning."

"Goodnight."

The birds are gone by the time I stagger to the Camry and fall into the front seat, check my safety belt three times, and shut the door. I don't even have to cut on the windshield wipers until I'm well past Kid's Haven Memorial and drifting my way down Fourth Street. The rain continues into the afternoon, but all I can feel is peaceful sleep as my mother complains about the muddy boots left sitting in the doorway.

CHAPTER 14

While I sleep a ship begins to enter my harbor through the canal of my brain stem. The ship holds a small crew with ample vacation clothing and a new sign from God, translated to me by the Hebrew fellow who works for minimum wage bringing ice and sandwiches to the cerebral cruiseline platinum plus members. I scribble down the idea onto a yellow sheet of notebook paper, fold it neatly, and slide it out through the ear. That way the idea will be there on the pillow when I wake up.

I don't have a dream-catcher hanging over my bed so many of the dreams escape and dissipate in the pools of saliva collected as adhesive between my cheek and pillow. There is no dream journal to record the images in, so I can only hope that my brain isn't petty enough to establish class distinction between idea passengers and idea personnel. This metaphor is completed by the mention of the "stream of consciousness," which remains the most alert stream in the head, despite the randomness of the current. I'm awakened by the passing thought that my layered and complex metaphor may actually be a pun, which would classify me less accurately as literati and more-so as simple and a tool. Bad puns are the fulcrum to my clever.

Places that should hold memory are filled with wrestling factoids, so many times I only remember a dream weeks later. By then I can't remember if I lived through something fantastic or just imagined it. This works both ways. When I wake up I am on my stomach staring at my hand, my left hand palm down with sheets peeled back to reveal bare mattress. The taut texture of the under-structure reminds me of Aranea's ribs, and in my pulse I can feel her heart beating again, continuously but out of cadence, clumsily, timidly. With her heart beating inside of me I feel tender and favored. An unremarkable sigh ushers in this morning like any other, as she is not here and I am clinging to a past that doesn't let me decide. To my left, on a figurative piece of paper, is a sign from God.

A beautifully crafted stained glass angel in pink opalescent glass with brass halo, wings and accents. A multifaceted clear jewel is used for her head. She is 9" tall and approximately 4" wide. A must have for the angel collector or for that someone special.

It has been sitting in a white box on the lilac kitchen counter for three hours. The wings have a silver tint when held beneath a lamp. In sunlight the pink catches fire and lights up from within. I've taken time to look at it in every kind of light. She looks as if she was crafted by the finest hands in Europe, in the underground cavernous workshop of a recluse consumed by and lost in his art. I paid sixteen dollars for it at the mall. It came wrapped in crumpled paper. On the average she is taken out and molested every six to eleven minutes, based on the information collected from the green digital microwave clock. When I began to sweat I shined her with it. When I began to cry I cried upon her. I wanted to bleed for her, but no logical way was presented.

Whump.

I am standing in the half bath adjacent to the kitchen when the whump occurs. What it must be like to be a whump, to be so consequential at all times. A glass that falls from the edge of a table crashes, a car hitting a deer splatters; these happen and are done, they plant seeds of discomfort and are forgotten. Whumps are bodies falling. Life exiting the body. Goodbyes whispered in wet spots on walls. Bloody stumps left quivering on the ground by Newton's Laws of Motion.

The long, thin shades hanging in a row like teeth across the sliding glass doors are gently swaying, and the rays of afternoon sunshine are marred only by the drifting rectangles and the brown smudges in a circle on the outside. Pushing the shades apart the stains look like gravy, like dabs of paint dropped from far above, lonely remnants of life squeezed from the bottom of the tube onto the cracked, cloudless canvas. On the cement patio a few inches from a plastic chair overgrown with ropes of tainted yellow weeds is a bird. Not a cardinal, just a bird. A brown bird. The kind that gather in parking lots and disperse with motion. It is pacific and hushed. The head is turned around and the beak lines the spine, and the wind pushes up feathers from the down. Blades of grass swing up from the dead Earth.

"Oh." I stare at the dish rack for a few seconds, trying desperately to come up with some plan of action. There is a hand towel draped over the handle to the stove; a white towel with red lining and baseball players catching pop flies. Aranea is named after a natural miracle. I'm named after my father's favorite third baseman. I wipe my hands instinctively but once the boys of summer are in my grasp I swing open the microwave door and cast them into the radioactive heat of the stadium, a crashing closure and beep sealing them off from their Fall Classic for eternity. Racing up to my room and managing not to trip on any of the stairs I dive awkwardly for the closet, my lungs squeezing and pushing out dilapidated air. A pair of seventy dollar L.A. Lights that have not been worn since the sixth grade are withdrawn from their peaceful resting place beneath stacks of comic books and left to discover themselves once again in the center of the floor. Within moments the remains of the melted snowmen are poured into the shoebox to line the edges, the soft nylon forming warm snowcaps along the sharp edges of cardboard. I even make sure to include a few balls of cotton, in case the bird needs to rest it's head for a moment, or shake out the cobwebs that come with wiping out like that. When my impromptu architecture has finished I push open the sliding glass door and kneel down to present the bird with his new habitat from humanity, but the bird is dead. The bird was dead before I even started. I kneel for a moment, then place the box to the immediate left of the bird and make my way back into the kitchen.

With the breath falling back into my lungs as drops of sighs I grab the white box from the kitchen counter and begin on my way. In the center of the living room I stop, look around at the wood panels on the couch and the pictures on the walls, thinking about my steps and how I would go about retracing them to find the car keys. The steps won't come and it's like they never happened. My breath is held and my hands are hardly moving. Looking down I can see the bones on the inside of my hands wielding the skin draped across them, someone underneath my palm setting up a tent for a furniture sale, or a funeral. The breath begins to come now in puffs, and, with eyes darting, I notice the way my black nylon pant legs hang down over the backs of my shoes, and that I'm stepping on the ends. Then I think about the nylon in the dish cloth. Suddenly I rush back across the kitchen and awkwardly slide the door open in a hurry, only to find my keys lying on the inside of the shoebox, the lid tipped down carelessly along the grass. In a motion I snatch the keys and deposit them in my pocket. I make sure to scoop the bird up into the box, replace the lid, and utter a placid, "sorry" before I leave.

I take the long way around to Aranea's house this time, around the stores and up through the woods, to avoid any out of control vehicles or falling objects. The streets in the wooded rural areas of Lynchburg all eventually lead to the same place, and are mostly off-shoots of the few major roads that make up the neighborhoods. Some are curves that wind and slither through apartment complexes on their way back to the mainland; some are abbreviated arteries plowing powerfully down hills and passing away into dead ends. The houses are all nicer than where I live, even when you go far out to where no-one lives. There are black driveways with basketball hoops set up atop black poles, white kids in white t-shirts heaving their bodies and falling with grand laughter and laceration. Aranea lives at the bottom of her street, so to get there from behind I have to park along the side of the road and walk over the twig-covered knolls that divide the housing developments. When I get there today the sunset is still an hour or half away so I think that I might sit in the car until the nature is more vividly important. Ultimately I remember that a twig is still a twig even when tinged orange, and that it is the events under the sky and not the sky itself that define me. The day is a field of blue, and the night is just a collection of dead stars.

The long way leads me across the line of wealth and to the chain-link fence surrounding her backyard. The rottweiler/beagle that lives with identity problems and in the apartment next to Aranea is bounding in and out of her big metal cheeseburgers, kicking up dirt and covering up the hearts that decorate the soil and foliage. The dog notices me and wants to bark, but refrains. As I walk along the fence it keeps it's eyes locked on me, before walking away from the cheeseburgers and toward Aranea's back patio, where a bowl of food and a bowl of water are placed at the edge of the concrete. On the neighboring patio are the remnants of a twenty-four pack of Corona and a brown potted plant. I make my way around unannounced.

The white box swings at the bottom of a plastic grocery bag when I walk, but I maintain a sufficient distance between ground and angel. Peering around the corner to make sure I'm not interrupting any random fifty-six degree barbecue I see a thin, middle-aged man fiddling with a roll of scotch tape. The man is wearing a brown suit, the kind that you see in seventies sitcoms and his hair is combed over to cover up no obvious bald-spot, like someone has lathered peppered black paint over his scalp. He meanders with a yellow piece of paper for a moment before pressing it to Aranea's door with his palm and adhering it with a crinkled triangle of tape. He adjusts his thick glasses with his index finger and thumb, squinting through the layer of Plexiglas at his work.

The moment the man turns to return to his roomy mid-sized Sedan the operation falls apart, the tape coming loose and the paper sailing softly to the ground, face down. He continues on his way, stopping every few seconds to fumble around in his jacket pockets.

I don't want to be nosy, but the paper has fallen face down and during my reconnaissance mission I happen to read many of the lines, written in poor cursive in red ink on yellow paper.

&

Aranea—

Didn't see you at church this week, stopped by about the rent. Will give call later. We missed you at services!

Stanley

As I try to make the tape stick to the door again I shrug my shoulders and reason that if Aranea isn't here I could give her the angel another time, sometime more appropriately beautiful or meaningful, instead of two pointless days after keeping her awake and out of services in a graveyard on a Sunday morning. I hadn't even thought about what day it was until the next day, when wrestling was on. The best part is that I have a back-up plan; to make good with Auburn and smooth things over, all-the-while delivering Chinese take-out, the severance package of the deities, and finally getting the origami book to Kiki, instead of letting it sit in my car for another three weeks. Thanks to bad timing and a visit from the landlord I'm relieved of my honest and thought-provoking emotional duties, until I hear the exaggerated, "psst!" from the sky behind me.

Initially all I see are fingertips gripped over the gutter. After a moment Aranea peeks her head down as well, her chestnut hair falling down like party favors from behind her ears, until she looks like a comet shooting up from the ground. Her necklaces are victims of gravity and slide up her neck until the silver pewter cross is resting on her chin, just above the goofy grin of a girl on a roof swooping down to surprise her unsuspecting houseguest.

"Boo!" she shouts, just before snorting happily and letting out a vociferous laugh. "Sorry to…drop in on you like this!"

"You haven't really dropped. You're just hanging, really." I look up to see her fingers shaking, and leaves sliding down the roof to fall onto her still flawed Autumn yard. "Be careful."

"Hey," she says, waving a hand quickly and then reaffirming her grip on the gutter.

"Hey," I return.

"You know, I should've thought this through before I actually ended up on the roof."

"Yeah, I was wondering about that too. Couldn't you have just not answered the door?" I pull the note from her door and fold it into halves, and then into halves again. "The guy didn't look menacing, I'm sure you could've worked things out."

"What you don't know is that when you turn your back he breaks out the nunchucks." Aranea pushes herself back onto the roof by wiggling her hips, in what I can only describe as an incredibly cute and bizarre activity. I appreciate that she continues a splay quip even when faced with her own mortality, if she ever is. "Usually my Dad gives me the money to pay him when I see him at church, but with my Dad getting called in to work on a Sunday morning and me being so tired, I just said to fudge with it."

"He mentions that in the note."

"Me saying 'to fudge with it?'"

"No, about not seeing you at church." I move out into her yard to see her, and make a conscious effort to neither create new nor step into existing holes. "Is your dad at work now?"

"As far as I know," she says, stretching out onto her back. "Come on up, the view is unbelievable. You can see all the way across the street."

I look back over my shoulder to see the duplex across the circle. One side has their door cracked open and a hibachi fired up on the paved porch, smoke rising and parading into the nose of the shirtless emissary of Virginia culture crouched in the doorway.

"Okay," I say.

Somehow I managed to get up the ladder without stopping once to imagine the wrestling moves I could do with/off of it. Aranea's roof is made up of faux-slate shingling to give the appearance of permanent and fireproof roofing without any of the pesky costs or benefits. From this height I can see treetops looming above the peak of the roofline, and assorted balls covered in dirt and decorating the roofing imperfections; tennis, base, rubber. Also, just as promised, the view allows the full spectrum of construction for the home across the street.

"You know what the best part is?" she asks. "From here you can't tell that he's shirtless."

"I think I might sit here for the rest of my life." I stagger hazardously across the roof and onto a comfortable spot a few feet, two feet and an inch, away from Aranea. Sitting down Indian-style on a slope above the ground is a new process for me, and in learning the ropes almost ended with me sitting on the handcrafted opalescent glass angel. The sign from God would end up like crushed leaves, a dead bird buried under a cardboard lid, no hope, no breath, no point. Something else to rot in the yard. "I brought you a present, here you go," I say, handing her the plastic bag.

"Groceries?" she asks, smiling.

"Yes, groceries. I brought you two-for-one evaporated milk."

"For all of my fudging needs!" she shouts, laughing. Her laugh echoes upward and shakes the clouds. "Wait," she interrupts, looking down into the bag. Aranea raises her eyes to mine. "You didn't actually get me a present, did you? Brooks."

"What?" I ask, wondering why I didn't have my answer to this prepared ahead of time.

"You actually got me a present."

"Well yeah, that's the crucial part of giving you a present." She closes her eyes and lowers her head slightly, resting a corner of the white box against the sun-warmed black shingling. Aranea opens her mouth but closes it, and repeats this gesture several times. My words draw swords and battle for the right to leap from my mouth and save me, but they all end up stabbed and dead. "Lovely day for a picnic."

"And me without my finger sandwiches. Again." She shrugs her shoulders and sighs, pulling the white box from the bag. "Why did you get me a present?"

"I came across it and thought about you. I woke up Sunday afternoon and I couldn't find five things to do at once, so I started thinking about you…our conversation, and I thought I would do something nice for you, since you always manage to do something nice for me."

"I haven't gotten you any presents, though. I don't know what you…"

"The graveyard thing."

"The other day? I was there and I saw you, it would've been inconsiderate of me to drive by and pretend you weren't there. I wouldn't…"

"Not that graveyard thing. The…the other thing."

Her eyes slide toward the lower-right of her face, and her lips quiver for a crisp moment before her words are formed. "…what do you mean?" Silence fills the space between us and all we can hear is the sound of the shirtless man wandering onto his porch, poking at the hot dogs on his hibachi, and returning to the mild warmth of his indoors. Red birds chirp and hop along barren branches a dozen feet away.

"You were…you are…like a can of soda," I say. Suddenly the roof and sky disappear. The birds are gone, the treetops vanish, and nothing exists outside of myself. Even Aranea is not there; only the shadows surrounding her, drawing a faint image of her in the blinding whiteness of historically memorable horrible things to say. From the corner of the room Jesus shakes his head, gestures towards me with his hand, and mutters, "you're on your own, buddy."

"What?"

"You were like a half-full can of soda to me, then. There are so many times in life when people are just empty, empty cans on the floor, on shelves, in the trash. They have made their mild impressions felt and have moved on. You enjoyed them while they were there, but nothing really stayed with you, besides maybe bubbles in your stomach to remember them by. My first girlfriend was like that, one of the girls who describes every boy they date as the love of their life, just throwing the word around like it was just some noun she could say. When she was gone I felt bad, the bubbles made my stomach hurt, but after a while I didn't even remember why it hurt so badly. The memories displaced and all I could remember was how she made me feel, and what I thought, and what I did for her, or what she did for me. I never thought about what she thought, or what she felt anymore. It kept happening to me, I kept trying and failing, hoping every time that I could find what I needed from them, hoping that they would give me something more than the bubbles. I needed somebody who I could think about when they weren't there. I wanted someone to be more than I expected, more than I could just assume. You were there for me in the graveyard when my Grandfather died, and you were there in the graveyard for me when my Grandmother died. Every time I was faced with this monolithic, evolved fact of life you were there in the crossfire with me, and I didn't know why, and you didn't make me ask you why. You just did something nice, for no reason, and it made me happy. Then…then Curtis died, and…have you ever had that moment where you've gotten sidetracked and your head hurts, and your eyes hurt, and you're just having a bad time…and then you see an empty soda can, but when you reach for it to throw it away it is still half full…and it's still cold…and it's, it's just the simplest, happiest pleasure you can imagine. Something you didn't ask for, or expect. Just…just a gift, from somewhere else, that let you forget long enough to remember. Just knowing that you'll be half-full when I reach for you helps me believe in something better, it gives me something to believe in. I forget that He's there and when I reach for Him he's still got at least something left. You're more than just the bubbles. And I don't know why."

"I thought you were going to compare me to gas again," she says, with a streak of water streaming down the bridge of her nose. "Brooks," she says again, as if to verify me. Aranea moves onto her knees and crawls over to me, before wrapping her arms around my shoulders and hugging me timidly but compassionately. "I can't think of anything to say to that. Thank you, just, thank you so much."

"The gas thing was pretty clever I thought. I thought I was the one who was supposed to reference past conversations." She doesn't release the hug and I wonder which one of the stupid words I said earned me the right to be so temporarily blissed-the-fudge-out. She even cleanses my inner monologue.

"You just referenced the fact that you referenced previous conversations because of a previous conversation we had about referencing previous conversations." Aranea laughs and lowers her arms to her side, resting her weight on the tops of her hands. "I think our friendship just took a turn for the hyper-ironic."

"We should re-enact the whole thing using hand-puppets," I say, pinching the tips of my fingers against the makeshift jaw of my thumb. "We'll make it through together, okay?" my hand says.

"Okay," says Aranea's hand. "So, what did you get me?" says the rest of her. She reaches back to grab the box, and I can see the contour of her hipbone poking out from just above the belt-loop on her jeans. For a moment I want to take the angel back and exchange it for sixteen dollars in cheeseburgers, but not being well-versed with her side of the eating disorder spectrum I wouldn't want to assume that she would ever eat them. The gift is for her, not for myself. I can only eat five dollars in cheeseburgers.

"Oh, gosh. Oh, oh." Aranea's eyes light up and the skies turn green, and my heart begins to beat like a Samba drum. As her fingers slide through the crumpled white paper to caress the angel I think of the tears I cried, the sweat I perspired, and the copious amounts of blood I was never confident or stupid enough to shed. The angel rises from the box, and, in her hands, begins to glow again from the inside, the pink radiating against the cloudless sky and lighting her face. "Oh Brooks, it's so…" Her fingers grip the base and it snaps, sending the circular stand falling to the rooftop and rolling into the gutter. The angel herself falls into Aranea's lap. "…broken. I know there has to be some symbolism in that." My heart actually stops here, and I am legally dead for the next ten to fifteen minutes.

"Brooks, oh my gosh, Brooks I'm so sorry, it was beautiful, I didn't mean to…" and it continues, until I nod silently and assure her that I know she did not intend to smash the handcrafted opalescent glass angel to violent death with a hammer.

"Brooks, I think I have some superglue in the house, I can fix it, no problem. Oh, I feel so bad," she says, taking a second to finally wipe the evaporating tear from her nose. "I'll make it up to you, I promise. I'll make it up to you right now."

"You don't have to make it up to me, I know you didn't do it on purpose, it's fine."

"Don't be so chivalrous, I know you probably spent a lot of money on that, and even though I didn't ask you for it or anything I know that it meant a lot, and I so appreciate it, I just…" In the middle of her sentence her voice changes from a hushed remorse to a peppy cheer. "I know! Do you mind if we stay up here for a while?"

"Were you planning on coming down before I got here?"

"Probably, but I'm comfortable now, so no. If you go down into the house and grab some sandwich stuff out of the fridge, I know I've got a loaf of bread sitting on top and I've got turkey and cheese and other stuff, we can sit here and make sandwiches and wait for the stars to come out, and it'll be nice. I can show you where I fell from. It's the big white one."

"The moon?"

"No, the other one."

"The other moon?"

"The other star, doofus!" she says, smacking me in the shoulder. "Anyway, I think a sunset picnic would be fun. We can tell sunset ghost stories."

"Poltergeists who only come out when it's breezy and nice out?"

"Oh, and I have books! We can read, and relax. When you go down for sandwiches look in the hallway closet, I've got big pillows and a blanket with panda bears on it." Aranea stretches her arms into the air and kicks up her feet. "We can spread it out so we don't wake up with shingles."

"I wasn't sure about the space travel and the ghost stories, but I would only be cheating myself by turning down your offer of a panda bear blanket." My mind races back around to where it began. "Wait, did you just make a roofing joke?"

"I did," she snickers.

When I'm on the ground, with images of a senton bomb from the top of the ladder dancing through my head, Aranea begins to crawl down the roof. She reaches for the glass base, lodged between a tennis ball and something else gross in the gutter.

"Don't forget the books!" she shouts.

"I won't," I assure her. "I've actually got a few books in my car, if you want me to go get them."

"Sure," she grunts. As I walk around to the backyard I'm left with the image of Aranea throwing long-lost tennis balls from the rooftop out into the street. One ball even bounces beneath the genitalia-like monster vehicle parked ten or eleven feet from the area's only active grill. Shirtless takes a moment to lean out into the cold to reap the reward for his adventure into the wilderness, but his inability to sense the motion of the balls draws him back into his home, wiener in hand.

At the bottom of the slope I slam the car door shut and punch the frame as hard as I can, screaming concentrated curses into the passenger window. My rage is superficial but I feel the need to express it, to validate its reason to be here. The first sign from God lead to property damage. The second sign from God is leading to sandwiches. I don't care about sixteen dollars. If Aranea wanted me to I would light sixteen dollars on fire and use it to cook grilled cheese sandwiches on the hibachi. It was broken before I could even get the speech out. I'm allowed to ramble about soda and bubbles as the head professor from the Retard Academy of Arts and Sciences, but the minute I step into something meaningful, the moment I open my eyes and harness my destiny, the shingles come loose and I fall into the trenches below. At the car I am furious at myself, I want to lay under the car and coax someone into running me over. On the hill my mind notices the orange twigs and I wonder if they've changed since I got here. When the dog is staring at me from the paunch of the cheeseburgers I am excited that Aranea has invited me onto her roof. Maybe that's why God has His way of nodding and letting my mind wander back to faith and reality.

"See, I can fix it," she says to me when I walk into the front yard, holding the angel in one hand and the base in her other. Aranea has leaves sticking to the tips of her hair, and dirt on her elbows. "The blanket and the pillows are in the hall closet, just go past the fish tank and it's right there."

I nod and push open her front door. The room has not changed since I was last here, and I can hear the bubbles and see the fluorescent blue light from the fish tank emanating from across the cardboard boxes and dusty furniture. As I approach it I notice that there are no fish in the fish tank, only a collection of fish tank novelties; a man in scuba holding the air pipe, a shack with a sign that reads "bait and tackle," a plastic penguin. The doors behind the aquarium are all shut and made of dark brown wood. And old ceiling fan is spinning and from television in the living room I can hear Linus, the sage, waiting for the Great Pumpkin.

"You'll be sorry if he comes!…Good grief, I said "if"! I meant WHEN! WHEN he comes!"

Not knowing the blueprint to Aranea's house I assume the hallway closet as the middle door and push it open. An eerie emptiness resounds as the door creaks open to reveal nothing; not a single thing. The room is empty, no boxes piled into the corners, no old mattresses, nothing. It is colder there, and without allowing myself to reason the void I slowly close the door. It's nothing. An extra room. The second door brings the gift of down pillows, and, beneath older, more monotone blankets, lie the panda bears. I gather it under my arm, and even the sight of the panda umbrella hanging on the inside of the hallway closet door cannot erase the curiosity. In a rush I push open the third door.

Silence. Emptiness.

Silence, then resolution. Then exposition. I don't even hear the words as they work themselves through in my head. Rising action, climax, words that don't exist in empty rooms, closed doors left behind for turkey and cheese and Wonder bread. And on the refrigerator, stuck with a magnet shaped like praying hands, is a green piece of paper stained with mud that reads "miraculum."

That's when I begin to understand.

That afternoon leading into dusk we sit on the panda bear blanket and talk to each other about our lives, not expecting anything from one another but harmlessness and company. I tell her about my trip to Kings Dominion when I was five years old, and the Smurfs stage show. They obviously weren't Smurfs—Smurfs were forest creatures the size of a toe, these were man-sized and somewhat furry, and they danced in circles and sang songs about their television show and line of toys. When the evil of the stage show was overcome the Smurfs, the Man-Smurfs, invited the children in the audience up on stage to dance, and even the parents. My Dad leaned down and asked me if I wanted to go, but I told him no, because I was too embarrassed to go up on stage and dance with everyone else. My Dad respected my decision and as the song hit the chorus the stage was filled with smiling kids and compliant adults, and the bleachers were completely empty. Only my Father and I were left in the entire amphitheater, two white dots sitting silently while the children and the parents and the Smurfs all smiled and sang and danced. By the end of the chorus it was too late for me to join in and instantly I began to feel the guilt that I'd never known, the obvious realization that I had missed out on an opportunity, I had let something pass me by because of my own doubt and reservation, and from beneath it began to devour me. I cried that night, the earliest memory I have of crying, and I cried the nights after. The park is different now and attractions come and go, and though Jesus may return to take me away or banish me to a lake of fire for the rest of eternity I will not be able to relish the golden streets or cry for the burning flesh, because I know I will never be able to take the love of myself back. Aranea cries a bit and holds my hand, and tells me that it was okay. It didn't matter, it was just an amusement park attraction. Like jumping dolphins and singing teenagers. I know. I've always known.

She tells me that like most things in life, making stuff is not an option—you do it because you have to. With motions from her hands and moisture on her lips she tells me that she knew when it was time to draw or write, or both, because her heart would flutter and she'd get that quivering mass of stomach nerves that people associate with falling in love. She would just be sitting in her room biting her fingernails and all of the sudden her synapses would start firing, her hands would sweat and her feet would twitch and she'd race downstairs to find her pencils. Then she'd race upstairs to find her eraser. People get inspired to create like this every day. Maybe it was a little weird to run as much as she did, but the rest if it was pretty normal. Aranea rests her head on a pillow six inches from mine and stares up at the stars, pointing out the second star in Orion's belt as a funny place for her to have fallen from. She tells me that after all, creating is what we were made to do. Like C.S. Lewis said: "There is only one creator and we merely mix the elements he gives us." God lends us utensils beautiful and good, and the challenge is to use them without screwing them up. To stay true to ourselves by arranging the truth in beauty that He has given us. There is nothing new under the sun, yet everything the light touches is an inspiration. I wonder if Aranea reading the phone book to me would fill me with these indescribable moments of content, but then I remember the empty rooms and recall that the phone book is just names on paper. Aranea has seen things the way I needed to, and has listened to God in a way I must have forgotten.

When the sandwiches are gone and the origami book has been read, when the tennis balls have been tossed into the darkness and the handcrafted opalescent glass angel has been placed neatly five feet away to prevent further damage, we lie there motionless. My eyes are heavy from the days and nights of thought and pain. Since the minute Curtis died I lost something simple, not the will to carry on or the ability to express emotion like the people in the movies lose, something else. I just couldn't make myself go to sleep without thinking. Like when I was a child I would stay awake thinking about where he was going. I wondered how I could feel safe in Heaven knowing that so many people I loved where in Hell, and trusted in the adage that the happiness in Heaven is so complete that I wouldn't even think about them. I wonder what could make me forget. I wonder why I would forget. The questions would spell themselves out in bold letters and sound themselves out into my ears when the room was dark and silent. I would daydream and be awakened by rumblings in my stomach, pictures of blood on the toilet seat, my mother's touches on my spit and bile-covered hands.

Maybe the sign from God Aranea is waiting for isn't something physical, or something emotional. Maybe the sign from God isn't a sign at all, not magic marker on cardboard held up when the camera pans to me. Maybe it's just the progression of time. Maybe the sign from God is her ability to help me feel tired and not have to think about living anymore. Maybe she just kept talking and talking until she put me to sleep. Maybe that is wonderful.

"Brooks," she says with her cheek resting on my shoulder. "You're still coming to the Halloween party, aren't you?"

"Yeah."

"Good, I was just checking."

The night air is biting but the problem is solved by multiple blankets, two over Aranea and two over myself. My nose feels like I tried to snort an ice-cream truck, but the feeling of Aranea burrowing her nose into my shoulder makes me feel heated and warmed from within, like an angel, and even though it doesn't help my nose it's enough to get me through the night. The night is warmer than it should be, and we're too tired to climb down, anyway.

"Brooks," she says from her frozen lips beneath the blanket. "You aren't going to try to kiss me at the Halloween party, are you?"

"Nah."

"Good, I was just checking."

There is a moment between consciousness and solitude when your mind slows to a stop and the passengers unhook their safety harnesses and disembark. It is in this specific flash of roaming knowledge that I realize why this has happened and the only things that can happen from here. The rooms in my brain empty as sleep overtakes me and Aranea is left standing there, surrounded by a brilliant light. Slowly, deliberately, she closes her eyes too, and the light switch turns itself off.

CHAPTER 15

A goose feather is floating just above my lips when I wake up. It is slender and white; firm and delicate on the tips, and when I open my mouth to inhale the feather floats down to my teeth. I exhale and it lifts into the air again, like I'm a hibernating bear in an old cartoon, snoozing away so peacefully that only a visual aid could properly convey the message. When the feather goes up high into the morning light it catches the sun in shadows, carving the infinite blue with a bound brevity just slightly enough to break my dreams and define my early morning reality. The rhythm is peaceful and soothing, like an animation cell on a rooftop layering my consciousness over hand-painted scenes of forests and sunrises. Rise and fall. Morning and night. Clouds and stars. Love, blindness, and acceptance. Then I realize that I'm peacefully blowing on a feather which ruins the rhythm, and an errant breath sends it sailing off the rooftop and into the dead trees a few feet away. I lie there blowing nothing for a moment, but it is empty, so I stop.

Aranea is gone but I am here beside the groove she left in the pile of blankets; warm and hollow, like a den, blue fabric lined with white feathers and the fragrance of a true Dogwood flower. I look at the lines folded across panda bear faces and wonder why I've put myself through this. I wonder why I torture myself for nothing. I wonder if it would feel different if I tortured myself for something.

"Hey," says Aranea from the top of her pedestal, an ivory monolith lined with diamonds and rose colored mirrors, hoisting up a hundred pounds of static evolution. "What would you even do with me if you got me?"

Aranea could leap off and fly whenever the whim passed through her brain but she stays, kisses or no kisses, sitting there, waiting for me to figure out a way to climb up and help her down. By now I can only remember four adjectives to describe her hair instead of seven, and even the four I come up with are just rephrased from a thesaurus.

"Do you like me because of the way I look? A physical love? Because that's all you ever seem to talk about." She scratches at the soapy border of her circle and little broken flecks of purity drift down onto my head, like dandruff. Aranea is not tall enough to be freakish, not short enough to go unnoticed. An anorexic albino baby with teeth slanted forward and hair fading to black. Would she look this way to me if she hadn't been the only one in my life there for me? Would her imperfections have been sanded down to a smooth surface, a mirrored glance to objectify us both? I shrug my shoulders and "no" is all I can respond with.

"Do you think I'm not one of the snotty, presumptuous Christians that you always complain about? The same ones who gave you the eye in youth group meetings and killed your love of God, and, subsequently, your love of self? When your Grandmother died you lost your heavy weight on the scale. They hang out with their friends and throw cigarettes at birds. What if I let you down? What if I burn down the churches and the cardinals?" After almost a decade of writing and rewriting the paragraphs to thank Aranea in the bland human ways I've come to understand she turned from me. She didn't just turn from me, she had a speech prepared, a speech she's given to people I've never met, people with the same ideas and the same neurosis. Aranea invited me to church, tells me about God, and assumed that I had a church of my own to go to every Sunday morning. I don't even remember the other days of the week church is held on now, all I can remember are ten commandments and fruits of the spirit and my grandmother, and her hands. So, Aranea is nice. She hugged me at a funeral. That's what people do at funerals. Grandfathers and Grandmothers die, that's what they're supposed to do. I tell myself that she could be a walking pamphlet, but somewhere below my heart in the gall bladder I remember that all of the things Aranea said wouldn't have meant so much to me if they weren't inside of me already. I shrug my shoulders and "no" is all I can respond with.

"If you did end up dating me we wouldn't have sex until we were married, you know that, right? And we wouldn't get married right away, that could take years. Do you remember how to be in a relationship without sex?" Aranea lowers her head into her lap. Her head disappears beneath a blurry mass of black curls. "The minute I found out about the others it would be over." Without reservation I open my forehead and look at the fantasies. I see Aranea sitting on a porch during a rainstorm. I see her shopping for books at the bookstore. I see her waiting patiently on the couch for the pasta-in-a-box I took hours to prepare. Last night I dreamed that she played a song for me on a hand-me-down acoustic guitar, and though her voice was rare and expressive she couldn't remember the chords in the proper order and had to keep starting over. I was caught in an endless loop of flawed moments and it was all so perfect.

"I've been through the same boring troubles as everyone else. I'm always depressed, which is hard to be in the face of so much blind optimism. When I think about you I mostly end up thinking about how you help me love parts of myself. So if I ended up with you I'd just be happy to have known you." I say this to an empty blanket, shrug my shoulders, and whisper "no" under my breath.

On the way down from the top of the ladder I can look into Aranea's back-yard, over the cheeseburgers, and see the dog sleeping on his back, with moths dancing around his nose like a candle flame. He sniffs and sneezes, and in the morning light the world is asleep, as if it has ever been really awake. I stop for a moment to ponder the unbearable lightness of being; the bountiful gifts of a humane God, the peaceful feelings of enlightenment wrapped around moments of basic personal happiness. Then I think that I could probably hit a guillotine leg drop on the dog from here, which would look awesome because I would clear the cheeseburgers. I close my eyes and wince for a solid thirty seconds, in case anybody wants to shoot me in the head while I'm up here.

Herman Horatio Honda has left port for the Napoleonic war and the yard holds a silent depth; a reserved foreboding deeper than the plate tectonics of the elongated depressions. Piles of leaves wait along the curb to be whisked away by winds. The hibachi across the street is motionless and ashy, absent of the uncontrolled fires that raged within only yesterday. Everything is different. Things don't look like they did last night. The stars can't light these things and make them look as grand and cinematic as they seem to me when I've opened my heart up to divine suggestion. The Bible doesn't spend twenty minutes talking about Job's eyes; it gets right to the point and tells you that even some-one flawlessly devoted to a cause can end up on the bad end of a theological bet. Job had God punish him with dead sons and boils on his privates, and through it all Job kept his faith and earned his spot in Heaven, right next to all the nameless people who had normal lives and put ten percent of their pay-checks in the plate at church. I have spent my whole life—not just a few years, not just Sundays—keeping the faith that if I just try to live as good of a life as possible that I will be rewarded with something, anything, to make the rest of my life happy. The yard is empty. The street is empty. The house is empty, and I am all alone.

There is an origami swan sitting on the welcome mat. Last night's reading revealed that origami is not merely the folding of paper; origami is math. The connection is multifaceted. The folded model is both a piece of art and a geometric figure. I hold the swan at eye level. The sun catches the blue lines and the red, and as the charm of notebook paper water fowl begins to wear off before the smirk even leaves my face I notice the extra weight, and that the bird holds a gift. This discovery is the number two. When you fold the traditional water bomb base, you have created a crease pattern with eight congruent right triangles. This makes unfolding easy. Hidden beneath a wing is a key. The key is the number two. I hold the key at eye level. Looking through the notch I can see Aranea's front door. Two plus two equals door. Origami is not merely the folding of paper. Origami is math.

The lights are not on in Aranea's living room because they are never on. Objects in the room are arranged strategically like an Egyptian tomb to reflect the light through the windows across mirrors and lampshades to illuminate the walls and hall. At night she has a desk lamp that clicks on when a metal string is pulled, and Aranea must operate her nocturnal activities around the small circle of light or navigate heavenward to the starlight. On her coffee table is a menagerie of folded paper animals—a rhino, a hippopotamus, a leopard. Upon closer inspection I notice something strange; the rhino is folded out of the page in the book that explains how to make an origami rhino. The hippo from the hippo page. The leopard from the leopard. In the center of the table, on a yellow, circular ceramic plate, is a chocolate cupcake with sprinkles, wrapped in yellow paper. A small, folded piece of paper is wedged into the icing. The room smells like Elmer's Glue and candy.

Written inside the paper fold, in perfect calligraphy, are the words *"Eat Me."*

I laugh to myself and think perversely about shrinkage. My stomach rumbles, and I cannot resist the urge to pull down the dressing and devour the cake from below; feeling the spongy cake against my front teeth, tasting the chocolate on the back of my tongue. With a mouth full of cupcake I glance down and notice a second note, hidden in the space that the treat formerly occupied.

"Don't Throw Me Up."

I peruse the walls as the sprinkles break and descend into darkness. The picture of Aranea as a child is there, as before. A picture of Aranea in knee-high socks leaning up to drink out of a bird bath. Aranea shirtless at a birthday party, at McDonald's, with a paper hat and mushroom hair that curls. Mushroom hair that makes me jealous. Aranea, maybe ten years old, on the Old City Cemetery swing. All in black and white. All in thick wooden frames. The only color photo is a four by six snapshot of Aranea kneeling over a pile of broken glass. She is frowning at the camera, the glare in her eyes red from the lens flare; the blood on her palm a darker hue of the same. The video game cartridges and the stories let me know that Curtis is holding the camera, and I see her momentarily through his eyes. She doesn't look the same. Her forehead is broad, like mine. Stepping back I see that the pictures on the wall are all of Aranea. Different moments of childhood captured in cracked black and white. Nobody is with her. At the birthday party she is alone, laughing in front of a Hamburglar birthday cake. There are no birds in the birdbath. Even now she is alone in Curtis' living room. Her father is nowhere to be seen. It makes more sense than it used to.

The rooms are still empty, as I knew they would be. I walk into the room closest to the closet and listen to my feet echoing on the hardwood floor. I am lost in the emptiness and confusion, like the moments when I am alone to confess myself before Aranea. The ceiling fan has a thick layer of dust on the tops of the blades. Looking out through the window I can see into the backyard. The dog is obscured by the cheeseburgers. I can see a line of dying and dead trees fencing in the area just past the chain links and I say a silent prayer that any errant logging trucks will have wrecked long before making their way down the twisting road to my mother's car. The leaves and the sharp branches are so nondescript and begin disappearing into each other like an Escher drawing. Southern writers always mention the humidity and oak trees bathed in Spanish moss, or they write about the Outer Banks. People go fishing and crabbing. "Folks" in the Deep South are so defined by racial tension and Confederate pride/ignorance that they can do nothing but speak in wacky phrases, like "ain't that a hoot'n'a holler!" or "what's in your craw." Southern people call their parents "pa" and "maw," and in movies there are always chain gangs lining the roadsides like Negro slaves. It's a shame that I'm painted so colorfully in literature and that nobody will ever take the time to stare out at the boring, regular trees and soak in our boring, regular culture, and realize that despite our history we go about our lives largely devoid of Southern stereotype, save the accents. In black and white a small city in Illinois is a small city in Virginia.

There is a pain between my shoulder blades that tightens and pulls when my arms move, and the warmth of the house helps to ease the chill on my nose and lips from the night. My eyelids are like a fat person tripping on his way to a buffet. I want to see what is here; to take in the curiosities, to place the jigsaw pieces together and glue them to a picture frame. I want to fill my plate with the surprises Aranea has left for me while she is away but the weight of my own excess pulls me to the ground. Clumsily I wander back into the living room and rest my spine against the wooden frame beneath the plaid cushions. I slip my wide feet out of wide shoes to nestle socked toes in the green shag. A thick comfort embraces me and I'm left, head titled back, sighing. The word "meow" atop the television is the last image I see before black. The last thing I think is that I shouldn't have eaten a cupcake before going to sleep.

The creepy feeling of waking up in a strange place is nowhere to be felt as a loud, piercing ring jars me out of sleep. Scrambling to my feet I follow my ears into the kitchen. I pass a microwave clock that reads three sixteen, and the warmth seeping through the windows verifies this. It felt like I was asleep for five seconds. This is the tails to the half-full can of soda's heads—reaching for a drink and finding a half-full can that has been sitting on the table for days. A mild inconvenience, but grounds for homicide. I pick up the phone and mumble hello. Across the room I see a bright blue sports drink sitting on the kitchen table, with an open note reading *drink me for x-treme thirst quenching.* I laugh to myself, feel bad that I ruined the rhythm of the theme, and barely pay attention to the voice on the other end of the phone.

"Uh, sorry, hello?"

"Yes, is this Mr…Cavah-ka-tee-uh?" The roaring voice sounds out her last name like a kindergartner with a learning disability.

"Cavatica. I mean, no, this isn't him. He. Can I take a message?" I swat my hand at the top of the microwave in search of a writing utensil and find a pink ink pen with a koosh pig pen top. Suddenly, I grow a vagina. The palm of my hand is ready to record, but in the middle of his sentence I remember the pieces of paper practically filling the floor of the house and dart my eyes about for a replacement.

"Yes sir, this is Officer Arable from the Campbell County Sheriff's Office calling in regard to the 1992 Honda Accord registered under the Mr. A. Cavatica name that was involved in a head-on collision this afternoon on the corner of Timberlake Road and Waterlick Road, the vehicle was unmanned and I'm calling to get information for…"

I try to listen to his words and absorb each one clearly but they collect against the dam and burst onto my face, drowning me in shock; sucking my face and hands dry of blood. I begin writing on the palm of my hand to get some of the pink back. The intersection is a ten minute drive from here, and given my tendency for melodrama and hyperbole, I can probably make it there on foot in thirty seconds.

"Um, thank you, I'll…make sure to tell him as…soon as…thank you." The officer nods, at least I assume he nods as Police officers do, and rambles off some legal information before wishing me a good day and hanging up. I leave the phone dangling from the wall mount and race toward the door, but before I'm even across the ditches I race back and hang the phone up properly. Even in times of horror I can't afford myself that level of dramatic purpose.

The afternoon is a dream. The phone call is the result of a cupcake ingested before a nap. After messing with my brain it will go straight to my thighs. I am a boy with a girl disease, I can be a boy with girlish insecurities. My feet aren't touching the ground. They dig into the soil and leave footprints but never touch. The car moves up the hills and through the trees like a ghost. When I stop at a red light I cannot remember starting the car, or driving this far. Children laugh and play on the sides of the road in my head, but not on the sides of the road. They are only in my head because I think they should be there, to provide chilling background detail. They should be there to give me something to look at, so I don't have to look at the image of blood dripping down my pedestal. Her pedestal. *Whatever.*

At 5th street I think about when Aranea first touched me and how I knew that she was real. I think about how I have trouble being with her without wanting to touch her. My brain raises dual fists and prepares to bust the skull of any part of my body that thinks my desire to touch her is as perverse as my passing shrinkage joke. The touch is not impure. The touch is something soft, a touch on the cheek, a touch on the back of her hand—something to make sure that she is really, physically there with me, and that she's not a figment of my imagination. Not the "multiple personality" twist in movies. Not her own evil twin. Nothing strange. Just there, with me. Just there.

At 4th street I wonder about Job, and how he thought that what was happening to him was unjust. He discovered that his interpretation of justice was wrong. Only the reader knows that God wanted to show the accuser that Job was faithful. Job was upset and he wanted to put God on trial. God came and said, "I created the world. Do you know this or this? I know everything. You know nothing." Job understands that he cannot make a judgment. He didn't have the right. God determines the meaning of what is just. Job realized that all he could do was have fear, because God is so much more than humanity that rewards and punishment don't apply. God is to be feared. God is love. Maybe love is to be feared. There is no fate in the Book of Job. You lead your own life.

At 3rd street I remember that whether you were holding him or throwing him, Tiger Mask would find a way to pull off a wrestling move on you, most of the time landing on his feet. The Japanese people would "ooh" and "aah" and so would the kids in America watching on tape, and the teenagers watching in their friend's basement on a dub of a dub, or anyone else. A grown Japanese man in with the head of a tiger and a cape. The music playing when he walked to the ring sang, "Tiger! Go Tiger!" Hardly any damage would be done because it would take so many moves to hit the Dynamite Kid, his British arch-rival; a compact and impactive wrestler who made the moves look real by actually doing them. They would fight on and on, barely hitting each other until it counted, because seeing Tiger land on his feet to stop all these moves was far more impressive than the attempted suplexes and body slams. There is an optimism in this that I find difficult to describe, and seeing Tom Billington and Satoru Sayama standing across the ring from each other fifteen years later, both tired and not as they were, helped me to understand that everything is okay in the end, and everything comes full circle. I think about wrestling here because that's generally just what I do.

At 2nd street the sights begin to overtake me. I speed up and quickly stop whenever the cars ahead of me move. A discarded pack of playing cards is open on the street and the wind sweeps the aces and hearts up into the air, twos and fours and Jacks hitting my windshield and disappearing over the roof of the car. On a porch a hundred yards away a cat has fallen headfirst into a potted plant. The cat kicks until it stands on its head, balancing in the dirt and mulch. As I drive by there is just a body floating in the air where a fern should be. I am lost in the image until the screams of men awaken me. Two men in blue coveralls leap to safety as the Camry crashes through it's own reflection in the center of the plate glass window trying to carried across the street. I instinctively duck my head behind the steering wheel to avoid whatever glass or body came crashing through my windshield, but when I look again I'm just speeding up and stopping quickly whenever the cars ahead of me move, because I'm scared, and harmlessly insane.

When I pass 1st street and realize that it's named "Timberlake Rd." I remember that the streets here aren't named with numbers. My hands begin to shake. Close-ups of Aranea's eyes flash, streams of blood eroding her cheekbones and dripping down like tears onto my floorboard. Joints in my fingers disappear and my fingers become tight ropes around the wheel. I have not made a sound since the phone call, and, upon recalling this, throw my opened mouth to the sky and let out a scream, a broad howl popping and spewing from the corked neck of my silent acceptance. I am exactly like everyone else in this town that I have ever met. I am absent from the control of any aspect of my life. I have parents to tell me what is going on with the family. I have friends who tell me what I should and shouldn't like. I have loved God my entire life and the only way I can show it is with fear. I know now through my scream that I am more afraid than I have ever been. I am afraid that my guardian angel is small, red pieces on the side of the road. I am afraid that there is no fate in Brooks. I've been afraid of leading my own life. I'm afraid to face the consequences of how I've lead it. I want to throw myself at the feet of a theological concept and beg for mercy, to let him know that his point is proven and that the accuser can stop his punishment. I don't do this because I am too proud, and because the only tangible feet I can throw myself before are the feet of men in suits with collection plates that are exactly like everyone else in town, exactly like me. They cannot forgive me because they cannot understand. Nobody can understand. Nobody can understand Him. Some of us stopped pretending we did years ago, and we've been sick to our stomachs ever since. I throw my head down onto the steering wheel and begin to pray. I don't count the words. I don't listen to my voice. I pray until my shoulders strain and my nose bleeds.

"God?" I ask. "Is there really anything I can say here that won't sound bad?" His response is silence. I've heard it before, so I know what he says in return. "Yeah, I'm sorry too."

"Hey," He says, or I say. "She's right there."

I look up and Aranea is kneeling beside a bed of purple and yellow wildflowers planted along the side of the road. As hastily as possible I swing the Camry against it's will into the closest parking lot I can find, the parking lot of a bakery. I afford myself a moderate amount of dramatic purpose by karate kicking the brake pedal and bounding from the driver side door, leaving a distant bong bong bong to ring with an open door and the key turned in the ignition. I dash across the westbound lanes, over the ditch of the grassy median, and across the eastbound lanes. The cars coming and going allow me space to uncomfortably run, which I am thankful for. My socked feet get muddy running in the damp grass.

When I get to Aranea I want to dramatically shout her name. I would shout, "Aranea! My God, you're okay!" and she would turn to me with tears in her eyes, and we would hug. Then we would quip to each other and laugh about the death of Herman Horatio and the crazy old lady who ran her off the road. In the rational moments during the drive over I thought of these things to say, but now it just doesn't seem to matter. Aranea is kneeling in front of the flowers in a blue sun dress, and from behind I can see a red stain leaking from within the dress down along the back of her thigh and pooling in the bend of her knee. I look at her hand as she timidly pulls a yellow flower up from the roots. Blood is dripping from the palm of her hand down the green of the torn stem. It drips quickly and rhythmically, like a faucet having been used and left incomplete and unattended. Her hair is black, the black when you close your eyes, like in my dream. I assume for a moment that we are still there and that this is no more real than her imperfect chords, so I extend my hand cautiously toward hers. The moment before it touches I think none of the thousand petty things that never mattered, and wrap my fingers around hers, and the flower. She feels the moist heat from my hand and turns to me with her eyes closed, rivulets of water left to dry on her cheeks and ears. Cars rush by and blow our hair east.

"I thought I would walk home," she softly speaks.

I keep telling myself that anything I say here would sound bad, and that of all the times in my life when a popular culture reference or pun would be inappropriate this is the most important one. I consider saying nothing at all, so I mutter inaudible syllables and the whoosh-whoosh-whoosh of passing cars fills in the blanks. The yellow of the flower looks like sunlight above our cold, fleshed Earth. My hands are turning white. I can feel her pulse as the fluid builds and drains onto the gravel and dust.

"I couldn't feel my blood anymore. It kept going away." Aranea pules faintly and pulls her hand from mine. Dropping the flower to the ground between us she points to her stomach. "It turned black." Bleached there into the fabric of her clothing is a rancid black and apple-red spot. The blood is sticking the dress to her abdomen. It smells like disease. I want to cry, but can't remember how. I can see the blood turning the blue into purple, and her heartbeat thumping to break free. "I thought it was supposed to be water."

Her voice begins to haunt me and I blink repeatedly until I notice myself blinking, and then have to control it consciously. "You don't have to walk home. I have a car."

"It turned black," she repeats.

"I know," I say under my breath. "I can see it. It's purple."

"No, Brooks" she cries out. Aranea tightly grips her hand over my wrist in a quick motion that leaves me surprised. She squeezes until the blood from her scar oozes out like toothpaste over my hand. She opens her eyes to look at me and the green has turned to black. Solid black. A desolate circle of darkness floating in a sea of water and white. I can't see my reflection. I can't see the pigment moving. "It turned black."

"Can you stand up?" is the first thing I say. On the inside I am terrified. I want to recoil in horror. I want to scream at her, to question her, to tear her facade to pieces and reveal her. A drop of rain falls onto my heart. It hits like snow and rests as a drop amidst the swiftly pumping blood.

"I thought it was supposed to be water, when you're opened there."

"Not for you."

"I feel so light. I feel empty. Like I'm pouring."

"Aranea," I say. "Stand up." I make an effort not to step on her feet as I stand up, but neither of us is wearing shoes, which is odd but fortunate. My arms feel strong as I reach around to her back and lift her from the flower bed. Raindrops begin to fall heavily now, splashing against my heart and cooling the burning engines. There is a peace that washes over and through me, flooding my body with moment after moment of peace. The feather blows up, the feather floats down. Aranea stumbles when she walks but I am there to support her.

"Here." She closes her eyes as I crouch with my back to her stomach and place her arms around my shoulders. I think about where we've come since she laced her fingers timidly to keep my heart from breaking my chest. Her heart is beating slowly and her nose and chin are buried into my shoulder as I place a hand behind each of her knees and lift her onto my back.

With Aranea holding on to me, because she is always there, holding on, I follow my path back to the bakery parking lot. We leave a trail of red drops on the dark tar and brown grasses. I walk slowly and feel her breath on my neck. It feels so different from what I'd imagined. When I was a child I imagined it would be like the wind itself, crashing in like a wave and carrying away whatever wasn't held to the ground. As she grew and I lost my ability to see her as a person I alternately thought of her breath as sensual and disciplinarian; during the moments of confidence I would picture her dancing with her cheek pressed against my chest, and in every other moment, which is almost every moment, I pictured her breath as a compassionate reminder that there are more important things in the world than unrequited love. To some people unrequited love can't even exist. So why worry? In some books there is no fate. If you torture yourself with things that you can't understand you're only left with fear. As I cross stretch my leg across the dip in the median a gust of wind gushes across and beneath us. Aranea's hair and dress raise and beat in the heavy breeze. Aranea opens her mouth and sighs.

"*Piggyback*," she whispers.
"Some pig," I laugh.

CHAPTER 16

In the afternoons on Tuesdays and Thursdays there is an old man who loves women, for the dank residue in the stupidity of men produces in him an attenuate but centered sickness. He is a Christian in name and in practice; namely, that when he goes to church he places an extra five dollars in collection as a token of gratitude to his savior and favorite author. He reads the Holy Bible extensively. He believes that when a woman is married she has accepted the headship of a man, her husband. Christ is the head of the household and the husband is the head of the wife, and that's the way it is, period. This theory troubled him, because to look upon the blistered, freckled skin of the girls in his Women's Studies course is to look upon one of God's simplest gifts to vindicated man; the reward of absence of solace. He takes in each fruit as a new experience, valuing equally coconut skin oiled skin and faded, hidden skins, olives and peaches. The desire to expunge these thoughts weigh heavily with him in each moment they fill his nose and eyes, sitting in organized rows with hair pulled loosely into ponytails and baggy gray college sweaters pushed up on thin forearms, pencil erasers waving to him from the silent classroom.

Never once has his faith wavered from the Lord and he is proud of his, and surrounds himself with the great Christian theologians of the region, through e-mails or handshakes. Their resolve and stalwart dedication makes his belief stronger, and even in the afternoons when he arrives home with papers tucked under his arms to a woman he has forgotten he begins to love her again, for a moment, out of appreciation. Her arms are wide and she speaks in a shrill monotone about her day as he sorts tests and searches his briefcase for any red pen that still holds ink. It is important to him that he displace his own fears with red lines through hanging participles. He corrects accurately but slowly.

He was given the name Solomon as a child, and this made him happy because of the immediate connection with wisdom and the Holy Spirit. Children outside of the church often abbreviated the name to a playful "Sol" or "Solly." Solomon would throw his baseball glove at them and shout out curses of damnation before he was even guiltless enough to say the word "hell." He would darn them to heck and they would laugh, riding away on their bikes, as Solomon did what Jesus would do and turned the other cheek, turning a cheek from the dissatisfactory sin of ignorance, the sin of mental complacency. He dismissed their lack of respect as merely another example of their inferiority, and became especially disgusted when he made discoveries involving puberty and biology.

Solomon felt ashamed that his body formed into external protrusions and hung from his body like an animal, but conversely felt empowered by the perfection of a woman's warm mound. Touching created a bridge from his faith to his world, and thoughts passed over like cars. There were times when he was only inches from skin and could examine it closely, and he took these times to soak in the beauty like a bath soap, to wash himself in the dirt of the act. The Tenth Commandment, the last commandment, assumedly the most important in chronology since saved for last: Thou shalt not covet thy neighbor's house, thou shalt not covet thy neighbor's wife, nor his manservant, nor his maidservant, nor his ox, nor his ass, nor any thing that is thy neighbor's. There could be no beauty in property, and with the act rendered insensitive he could not bring himself to indulge, to taste. Now, when nubile breasts form and rest across his desk beneath a question or a response he momentarily regrets his path and recedes into the cleansing waters of his baptism, beneath the surface where their pert and didactic voices are jumbled into muffled hums. They call him not Solomon nor Solly, but Mr. Anderson, and this disconnects him enough to get through another period.

Solomon's life began to lose focus until the second year of his collegiate education where, mired in the repetition of text in the Christian studies program, he came to know Delia. She begat him with wandering eyes; he became obsessed with her indifference to textbooks and causes, and admired the way she would stretch out on couches and paint images in the air, images she would later sketch into a diary as a memento of the moment and thought. Some days he would find himself staying in from classes to watch her tie blades of grass together in knots. Delia was broad-shouldered and narrow at the waist. She would read papers intended to promote increased awareness among both men and women of significant differences between the experiences of the sexes. She would sit quietly and wait for his critiques—for his red pen—but his fascination with the subject began to overtake him, and all of her words began to sound like poetry. Never before had he imagined that the differences between men and women could be analyzed like science and taught from a textbook, and almost immediately his Christian studies gave way to women's studies. Delia's indifference to college became more vivid when placed beside Solomon's zealous passion.

Delia bought a cat. She began to love Solomon for his faith and for his powerful hands. Two years later they were married, but his commitment to discovering the root of his nausea became stronger. Delia's indifference to college became Delia's indifference to love, and then to living. The marriage was consummated forty-nine days after the ceremony. Solomon remained still with his eyes tightly closed as she moved over him, the bridge of her nose buried in the center of his chest. He wanted to place his hands within her and spread her open to peer inside. He wanted to dissect her and explain her parts, and her movements, and her thoughts. Solomon knew nothing and Delia knew nothing else. Seven years later Delia was narrow-shouldered and broad at the waist, reading Solomon's papers on sex roles and sexuality, the white pages bound tightly beneath plastic covers, frigid. Solomon sat in their living room petting her cat with one hand and holding his Ph. D. in Women's Studies in the other, wondering where the program could lead him when the studies were complete. With no other option he began to teach what he had learned, whether he understood it or not, at the same level he started. Delia never reads his essays now, and only reads the Bible on Sundays.

There are so many books in Solomon's eight by ten office that many of the most important volumes multitask as wedges and desk support. Women Without Superstition: No Gods—No Masters sits atop a stack of papers about dead grandmothers. In his mailbox, mixed in with neon flyers for staff functions and college literary journals, is the copy of Reviving Ophelia he lends out to anyone who will read. Solomon pats his male students on their shoulders and tells them to try harder and put in extra hours of study. Female students are welcomed in to the office during office hours for any extra help. The male students know this and pass glances to each other beneath baseball cap brims to share the knowledge, and most of the time Solomon sees them and knows. This is why he feels the way he does. He knows that his role and predilection toward women and their studies singles him out as an object of ridicule. He sees the boys shake their backpacks with long strides away from the classroom and silently berates them for their lack of purpose and individuality. He does this because they stink of ignorant youth and because their opportunities to grow are too slow to pass them by. Solomon closes his door and tilts his forehead against the chalkboard.

Outside, through open windows, he hears students laughing with each other, boys to girls, about how Mr. Anderson wants to "talk to them," and he hears the girls go "eew" and "gross." He clenches his fists and breaks chalk into pieces. Only forty-one. Full head of hair. Blue eyes. Strong jawline. His navel looks like a goblet, his belly like a heap of wheat. The things they laugh about are forbidden; there is no reason for his heart to sink and his eyes to shift, but they do. The girls come to him for information and guidance and he gives this to them; he loves them like physical possessions, like objects to fill, like crystal bowls to stuff with candy. The boys degrade him. He sees them as sticky-fingered children unwrapping the candy and stuffing pieces into their mouths when he isn't looking. He turns to them and they smile, caramel between their teeth. He wants them to be dead, or saved.

Delia prepares asparagus and pasta salad at seven sharp. Solomon sits in a black leather chair in his office until six. He has coffee with co-workers in the cafeteria prior to the student herd for dinner, and he enjoys being able to talk at length. He defends Susan B. Anthony and disputes Natalie Angier. With gusto he states that a Christian has neither more nor less rights in their association than an atheist. When the platform becomes too narrow for people of all creeds and of no creeds, he himself shall not stand upon it. He smiles and flips a silver dollar on the rough tips of his thick fingers and smiles, for the conversation doesn't begin or end with his quote. What makes him different is that the Lord Jesus Christ resides in his heart. This elevates him.

He reads Helen H. Gardener analytically. He adores her for her soul and spirit but ignores her logic. "Of all human beings a woman should spurn the Bible first." This stays with him in the back of his throat, so he must preface each sentence with an uncouth cough. He wonders why God's greatest creations could view his love as hostile and disingenuous, and asks his wife when he arrives home at six fifteen. She shrugs her shoulders and begins to tell him about her day and about things she has seen on television. Solomon frowns and makes note in his day planner with a small red x that he made another attempt. This reassures him when he begins to doubt his marriage, and later the cross-hatches can be collected and arranged into some sort of rational tapestry. He can cover his face with the cloth. He can deny the things she says he has done wrong. The bible teaches that a father may sell his daughter for a slave, that he may sacrifice her purity to a mob, and that he may murder her, and still be a good father and a holy man. It teaches that a man may have any number of wives; that he may sell them, give them away, or swap them around, and still be a perfect gentleman, a good husband, a righteous man, and one of God's most intimate friends; and that is a pretty good position for a beginning. It teaches almost every infamy under the heavens for woman, and it does not recognize her as a self-directing, free human being. It classes her as property, just as it does a sheep: and it forbids her to think, talk, act, or exist, except under conditions and limits defined by some priest. The mistakes are not his to have been made under the eyes of God, and with the divinity being infallible the only fault available would fall with her. He feels sorry for her for this. He loves her, deeply.

Solomon devours new books like sushi rolls, ingesting them raw and whole immediately, only stopping to chew briefly, to avoid choking. This often leaves him hungry and with nothing new. He is forced to chew on whatever is lying around, just enough to create saliva and prevent his tongue from cracking and drying. With nothing to grade on Mondays, Wednesdays, and Fridays, he is forced into watching television. He tells himself that he is "forced" by his wife, her love of reality television and sassy sitcom housewives bombards him with a cavalcade of poor female role models. On channel two a woman with breast implants is eating a handful of maggots. A woman snaps her fingers and points at her jilted lesbian lover who recently had a threesome with their Mom. An in-control working mother refuses to let her bumbling husband go through with another one of his hair-brained schemes. Solomon begins to think that Delia does this to him on purpose to lower his opinion of other women, to help him think more highly of her by comparison. He thinks she is selfish and prays for her. She laughs at the double etendre.

He asks God every night to show the inner beauty in her that he has once seen and knows is still there, but God is silent to Solomon in much the same way that he is silent to us all, and Solomon takes this personally. He throws his Bible to the ground and curses himself for being born with feelings that deny the Lord's logic; that a woman is an object to be adored despite the constant onslaught of faults. Mary Mother of God did not have to eat maggots to gain admiration, but she had a son with a famous father. Mother Theresa did not have a threesome with her mother to rise toward sainthood, but she was sometimes so hard to look at. Solomon bends over to pick up his Bible instead of kneeling, and returns to the living room, television, and Delia as penance for his wickedness. If he were Catholic he would have something to say and something to do for forgiveness. As a Southern Baptist he keeps his fingers crossed and hopes he isn't set on fire.

The shows about teachers working out their problems make him alternately glad and remorseful. He identifies with the companionship, the feeling of duty, and the constant cups of coffee. He is confused by the life-calling to educate, by the hipness and diversity of students, and by the physical attractiveness of the teachers. On television the teachers have flowing blonde hair and pouting lips, blue eye shadow, tight pants. Solomon knows a woman who works in the school store who is attractive in pieces. She has deep lines branching from the corners of her eyes and skin like leather. He has long theorized that she was a porcelain doll in high school. A trophy. Sometimes he finds himself noticing how her gray pants are pulled up tightly around the back like a hammock, swinging her a few feet above the ground. She turns to him and rolls her eyes. Her personal levels of self-flattery insult him. He imagines her spraying frozen mist from a fire extinguisher onto a glacier. If there is a sin to be committed, as there surely will be given his humanity and God-given imperfection, he will save it for a more thrilling and taboo moment. Being with her would be like running face first into a wet blanket hanging along the clothesline in the back yard.

On Monday night Delia watches a television show about teachers dealing with real-life problems in an urban high school. The show deals with teen pregnancy, school shootings, drug abuse, racism, sexual harassment, rape, and spousal abuse. Solomon marvels at how these things all happened on the same day at the same school. His job is so nondescript. Once during a fraternity party a keg of non-alcoholic beer was hurled from a window onto the wind-shield of a car, but that has been far and away the most scandalous thing to happen. The students on television have such mighty emotions and open up to the staff regardless of the situation, as if the feelings could no longer be contained in their confused, pubescent bodies. Solomon thinks about the times when he began to care about student problems, and the meetings in his office after class that resulted in shrugged shoulders and "I don't knows," complimented by the occasional "whatever." Immediately he wants to be opened up to like his imaginary peers. He wants to be a secret confidant. He wants to nod wisely and tell the girl that he has been there before. This brings a smile to his face, the first smile in six weeks, and the skin of his cheeks feel rusty and stiff. Above all he wants to have her secret, and keep it. In his mind Solomon unwraps a piece of candy and holds it out, palm skyward, waiting for one of his pretty little girls to reach out and grasp it. To taste it. To want more.

"I would do anything to pass this class!" says the midriff-baring twenty-nine year old pop singing high school student.

"Anything?" slyly suggests the five-o'clock-shadowed educator, cleaning his glasses in a way to suggest that his lens represents her femininity and his short, stubby thumb represents something altogether unmentionable.

"The penis," mumbles Solomon. He then looks around the room to make sure that Delia has not wandered back in and heard him, because this would mean both shame and explanation. In the darkness the seed begins to grow, even before Solomon can gather his pillows and wallow into the motionless bedroom.

Over the next few days Professor Anderson begins to see his female students less as glass animals in a menagerie and more as objectives on a worksheet, ordered from I to XX. The girls on television begin by inquiring about their bad grades. They will do anything to pass this class. The girl will shape her lips like a zero and her lips will decorate thick red streaks with rivulets of moisture, as if to suggest that the square root of one-hundred forty-four is fellatio. The girl will rub her hand gingerly along the professor's leather patched elbows and tweed-laden shoulders. This indicates clearly to the viewer that she is suggesting intercourse or something even more dastardly; things that Solomon has never dared allow himself think even when surrounded by his wife. Things he saw in passing through finger-covered glances at adult publications as a teenager. The girls, mass-produced lolitas, are perky and defy gravity in curious places. They have hair that sticks straight up in the front and lies flat in the back. They snap gum and twirl split ends around index fingers. Solomon sees girls like this in his own classroom, but he would never allow himself the sin of indulging in the refuse of good-taste; rather, if he were the characters on television, which he is not, he would not simply erode his judgments beneath the sparkling stream of adolescent perspiration. These girls are listed from fifteen to twenty. Last resorts. One through five are not sins but challenges, aspirations, personal masculine verification. Their minds and bodies are not possessions to be broken and thrown away when the thrill is gone. They are possessions to be looked upon with awe. He looks upon them as such.

Weeks pass and Solomon scratches though blue names with red pen, crossing off potential devious suggestion for a variety of reasons. Kristy has a high grade point average, and puts effort and thought into each paper and homework assignment. Scratch. Katie is the daughter of the Dean of Admissions. Scratch. Jennifer has a black boyfriend who plays for the basketball team. Scratch. As the names are covered at the top and bottom of the list Solomon becomes obsessed with the creative process. He is like a sculptor, carving away the pieces of stone that don't resemble his societal cohesiveness. Professors in movies do this all the time. Professors on television date students. Professors he knows date students. It is all silent but spread out like gummy mayonnaise to cover the great wide open. In this Solomon discovers his fault. The victims, no, illicit participants on television, in film, and in the arms of his friends and enemies are teenage girls, naïve stereotypes of backwoods family structures; children of single mothers, children of working parents. The women Solomon teaches are women, studying what makes them what they are, outside of the ovaries. Twenty-two years old. Some of them graduate students. Twenty-three. Before he has gotten the chance to know them and lust for them they have passed their primes and moved on with their lives. They wear too much lipstick and date men with square jaws and stubble. Solomon has not had stubble since his twenty-second birthday, when Delia asked him to shave. He considers growing it all back, but is afraid that by the time the beard arrives in full his face will have passed it's prime and moved on with it's life.

On a Thursday afternoon Solomon is lecturing about the film <u>American Beauty</u>. The spectacular portrait of Lester Burnham's striving-for-perfection wife created by Annette Benning gives more insight into a contemporary upper middle class woman in deep trouble than many other films whose main focus is women. As he begins to dissect Lester's daughter Jane his eyes pan and scan the classroom. His vision fixates on the tormented visage of a young woman in the second row, fifth chair back. He sees her obliquely for two days in every week but has found her at this moment for the first time. She wears no make-up. Her eyes are hardened and brown but round and damp. Her cheeks are full like her breasts beneath a pull-over sweatshirt. The girl is soft to the touch from afar like a worn pillow. There is a clear, plastic, cylindrical retainer holding open a small hole beneath her pale pink bottom lip, and her hair is sunlight white beneath a university baseball hat. Her paper is covered in pencil drawings of abstract shapes and words, letters with shadow, shading, and cross-hatching. There are no notes. Solomon continues on with his eyes locked on her paper but she never looks up, never acknowledges him. Instantly he feels a heated understanding for her motion as she goes through it, and this causes his heart to swell with blood. She is flawed and real. She is a mistake. She is beautiful. The lecture wanders to conclusion as he checks his list for her name but finds only Jessica and Betty and Jo. When he is done, which he seems to never be even to himself, the children—the adults stuff their notepads into backpacks and nod their way through his door.

"Excuse me, uh, Auburn, Miss Bryant, if you could stay behind for just a moment I would appreciate it." The words are so introverted that she hardly hears him at all, but pulls away from her march to approach his desk, where he sits arranging papers that don't need arranging. She smiles politely and waits for further instructions.

"Yes, I wanted to talk to you about your performance in my classroom," he continues. "We're getting close to the mid-term of the semester and I noticed that you haven't maybe been trying as hard as you'd like to be."

"I have a C, don't I? We've only taken one test and I got a seventy-one on it." Her voice is obviously indifferent, and this fills him simultaneously with a sadness of his limp message of education and a blissful memory of Delia when she was narrow and of her own.

"Well, yes, that's average, but not something to strive toward. You're a bright young girl, Auburn, I'd like to see more of an initiative."

"My mother once told me that my initiative was invisible."

"The invisible and the nonexistent look very much alike." Solomon fondles around in his sleeves for his hidden trump cards, but is interrupted.

"Doctor Thomas S. Vernon." She rolls her eyes as she says this, as if she's been forced to evoke the name a dozen times before.

"Excuse me?"

"Vernon said that. The invisible and the nonexistent look very much alike. Professor emeritus of Philosophy." She scratches a spot of bleached hair behind her left ear. He notices a dragonfly tattoo around her wrist and in his mind begins to dismiss her through Leviticus. Suddenly he is confused by which flaws are liable for seduction and which are grounds for dismissal and gets lost in her mannerisms. "I have a big book in my room full of philosophical quotes."

"Very interesting. I tell you what. Bring it by my office this afternoon around six o'clock, we can talk more...personally about your initiative, and you can point out all of my quotes as I say them."

"Oh," she says, stammering. "I didn't mean any disrespect, I just remembered the quote from..."

"No disrespect taken," he assures. "But I would like you to stop by my office this afternoon. We can talk about initiative or whatever you'd like. I'm sure there are ways we can come up with to help you out before midterms, and for the rest of the semester. It's in our best interest to make things as easy as possible for everyone involved."

"Oh, well, sure, okay."

"Auburn, listen to me." Solomon stands and places the palm of his hand firmly on her shoulder. She looks at it for a moment and shifts her glance to his chin, nose, and eyes. "You are a beautiful and talented young woman. I've had my eye on you all semester. I see a lot of promise in your work and in you. I wouldn't be telling you this and asking you to stop by if I didn't want to put a lot of stock into you." Her eyes widen. "I don't think you'll need a lot of time to get where you're going. If things go well you won't have to be in my office very long at all. Do you understand?" She stands stiffly, smiling politely, waiting for further instructions.

"I think so," she mumbles. "I mean, if you think I can get a higher grade."

"I think you're a straight A student on the inside," he says, leaning in more closely. Nods and comfortless smiles are exchanged. Auburn lifts her bag from the ground and, lowering her head, walks slowly away and into the scattering masses. He looks through the window as she walks down the hill and across the paved sidewalks leading to her dorm. Solomon allows himself only a modicum of celebration, not sure how the professors react in situations like this without tertiary characters present. He balls up his list and sinks a long jump shot, just like in his college days, into the wastepaper basket. Solomon imagines that any color-by-numbers situation warrants a congratulatory handshake to one's self, and that the level of difficulty in any situation should never be taken into consideration. The Lord loves all of his children, the meek and the lame, the strong and the efficient. He remembers that Moses ordered the death of every woman who had slept with a man and the acquisition of any who had not, in the book of Numbers. Then he asks himself how the professors react when the situation reveals itself, since, due to television content regulations, many of the situations are suggested, or, at best, simulated. He sees this as an opportunity and a learning experience on top of being a reward for his years of dedication and service. The bird of human reverence is killed at the same time as the bird that can restore his love of Delia. This will humble him. This will make him cold, and clean again.

Solomon cancels his three fifteen class and the young people cheer. He tries not to take this as negative reflection on his teaching ability but as a positive reflection of youth. This erases a third of his distaste but the salty mildew of their disrespect lingers behind his teeth. He uses this extra time to tidy up his office; to return stacks of books to the library or bookshelf, to fluff and dust the cushions on his chairs, and to turn the images of Delia adorning his desk face down, before removing them completely and hiding them in a drawer. Solomon makes a cognizant motion to remove his wedding ring before six, but as he clutches bare skin remembers that he removed it years ago because it made holding a pen uncomfortable. He remembers Delia screaming, then crying, then screaming. It hurt his feelings that she would become so attached to a symbol and so detached from its meaning. He checks the lock on the door and makes sure that the blinds close properly. With a long arc of his arm he deposits the meaningless trappings of schoolwork and technology from his desktop, since the dimensions of the room do not provide the area necessary for comfortable, fold-out furniture like in many other offices. He decides that the chair or the desk will suffice, depending on the gestures initiated. At five the secretary leaves, and Professor Anderson makes sure to wave and offer her tidings of joy for the remainder of her day. This leaves him alone in a faculty building, alone like he has been many nights, alone with papers and just enough resolve to wait until dinnertime to drive home. Tonight Delia will entertain the asparagus alone, if she cooks at all.

At six Solomon is adjusting himself in his leather chair, imagining how she would like him to look as she walked through his door. He pictures her as she appeared earlier and with minty fresh breath, covered in sleepy sweat-clothes, dripping through her shell of afternoon fleece. He crosses one leg but deems the gesture too feminine; he tries an elbow on the table for a casual look but deems this too coarse. The digital clock changes from six-zero-zero to six-zero-one, and immediately Solomon begins to think the worst. She has seen through him. He did something wrong. The technique is flawed, it only works when taped before a live studio audience. Maybe he is not attractive enough. He feels attractive. Women he works with view him as an attractive man, despite his inability to judge the attractiveness of self. He doesn't find men attractive, so how can he judge himself? At six o'two he searches his desk for a class roll, to search for names for a back-up list. Before the red two turns to three he hears a knock on the door. He throws the clipboard under his desk with a jerk of the wrist and shouts, "Come in!" with a hint of self-doubt and a dash of puberty. The doorknob shakes. A voice from the other side shouts, "It's locked." Solomon shakes his head and bounds to his feet, racing with one stretched stride to the door and, in a smooth motion, unlocks it. He breathes heavily once, quickly, and pulls the door open, doing his best Head Caucasian In Charge. He is greeted by something distinctly non-Caucasian.

"Hey Professor Anderson," smiles Kirby, the Japanese girl from his three fifteen class. In his mind he instantly associates her with number four, crossed off because of her assumed disbelief in the powers of the one true Christian God.

He must admit that her sharp eyes and prominently displayed cheekbones are incredibly attractive, but in a way he is in no way prepared to deal with.

"Hello Miss Takahata, I wasn't expecting you at this time of day. You know that I canceled class today, I gave William next week's syllabus to hand out, you can get all of the information you need from him."

"Heh, no, I got one," she says, holding up a folded piece of neon-orange paper. "I didn't really have a question, I was just going out to dinner with my roommate Auburn in a bit and she told me she had a meeting with you at six. So, since my parents have paid twenty-eight thousand dollars for me to be in the neighborhood, I thought I'd drop by and say hi."

"Oh," he says, images of failure causing his sanity to fluctuate, images of success doing this even more so. "Is Miss Bryant with you?"

"Yeah, she's in the potty. She should be right out. I think she's doing some touch-ups. I was just going to wait out in the hallway until you guys were finished." Kirby nods and smiles.

"Oh," Solomon grunts, having no idea what she is saying. "I don't know how much time we'll need, you might not be comfortable sitting out in the hallway. It could take an hour, maybe more."

"That's not a problem. I sit in hallways for sport."

With not so much of a flush of the toilet the door to the women's rest room pulls back to reveal Auburn Bryant in a black button-up sweater, a knee-length black skirt, and boots that wind and strap high onto her shin. Her hair is crystalline and spiked into horns over pink ears decorated with silver rings. Her eyes are lined with a wide black, tapering into upward winged curves at the ducts. Her lips have transformed from pink to a lethal red. In place of the clear, plastic retainer is a silver spike. In the center of her bottom lip the red is a shade lighter, as though she has forgotten it intentionally, or out of haste. She stomps reservedly up the stairs and to Kirby's side, pausing for a moment on her way to wave at Solomon, her eyes focused on her shoes.

"Hi," she says.

"You're a little bit late, I was worried that you weren't going to come." Solomon looks back at his desk as he talks. "If you aren't serious about this…"

"I'm four minutes late," Auburn barks. "I mean, I'm not that late. I'm sorry." Kirby leans her weight into Auburn's shoulder. She begins to tug at the shoulder of Auburn's sweater.

"All right, you give me this and I'll hold it for you until you're done. I don't think you're going to catch a cold in Professor Anderson's office."

Auburn mutters, "I don't know what I'll catch in Professor Anderson's office," under her breath, but Solomon is busy arranging chairs and doesn't notice. Auburn moves her fingers around the buttons and slides the sweater down her arms.

"If you'll just come in and take a seat," he says, never intending to complete his sentence. Auburn takes a few steps in, waves sarcastically to her roommate attaining the full-lotus in the floor of the hall, and shuts the door. She runs her hands over her bare arms and looks for a chair. She glances at the floor and at the artificial plants on his windowsill, but when he turns to her once more their eyes meet, and she smiles timidly. For the first time he begins to take in her appearance, and begins to compare her side by side with the view from his hand on her shoulder earlier in the day.

"Oh," he says. "You look…" The breeze from the ceiling fan circulates down to the floor and blows the edge of her black gauze skirt. The skirt brushes against the skin on her knees and she wants to swat at it, to scratch it, but refrains. Her shoulders and arms are bare; where the sweater once covered is now snow-white flesh, augmented with a collection of speckled brown freckles. Thin black straps lay over thicker black bra straps to hold a thin black top against Auburn's opulent abdomen. He is drawn aback by her breasts, pouring up from the top, pressed together and elevated. This causes a pain in the pit of Solomon's stomach. He searches for words to finish his sentence. He glances over her artificial lips, her artificial eyes, her artificial body. He wants to throw a blanket over her and push her through his door, back into the obscurity, back into the masses she pretended to break free from. He wants to splash her and wipe away the falsehood. He wants her to cover her face and stop disappointing him, like the others. Like everyone. Instead of insulting her he rambles through his thought process without a sound. His face remains stoic.

"Thank you," she says, blushing. Auburn's rhomboids relax as she eases herself into the chair, crossing her arms solidly over her stomach. She breathes out as if exhaling cigarette smoke, and the low sizzle of her air between her teeth seeps into Solomon's ear like a mite. He shakes his hand a few inches from his ear, somewhat like shooing a fly, but the bothersome noise resonates until she makes her exasperated sighs vocal. "So, do we just…get it over with, or is there procedure involved, or what?"

Solomon, now Professor Anderson, blinks his eyes rapidly, changing the subject many times before settling on something non-confrontational and vague. "I don't usually see you like this." He glares down at the dragonfly, over her breasts, and to the tip of her labret spike. She smiles. He continues. "I want to ask you something very personal, and I want you to give me the most honest answer you can, all right?" Auburn nods as Solomon sits and takes her hand in his. Her childish grin of confidence is replaced by one of trepidation. Her bottom lip tremors, but ever so slightly. She knows that at any moment it will begin, and she will have gained effortless but stained acceptance. "I want to ask you about your drug problem," he states.

"Wait, what?" Auburn questions, pulling her hand away and placing it over the plush, dry skin of her chest. In two minutes she will be affronted and offended. Over the next one minute and fifty-nine seconds she will feel confusion, denial, and regret. The regret will fuel her hatred because it is not a regret for the situation but a regret for her heart. In an hour she will consider stabbing him, but she will be in the middle of a bowl of macaroni and cheese and will stab the bottom of the pot mercilessly with her plastic fork.

"I want to ask you about your drug problem. Lately I've noticed you dressing all in black, wearing a lot of make-up, piercing yourself. I realize the symptoms and I want to help you. I'm here for you." Solomon removes his glasses and fogs them for a cleaning, somewhat because of the smudges and somewhat because he only wants a fuzzy image of her to distance himself from the horrible things God allowed him to think as punishment.

"You've noticed me piercing myself? What, like in class?" Auburn looks around for a pencil to grab, but the sharpest object she can see is the stapler, and at the very best that would just hold her together.

"Why do you have a spike under your lips?" Solomon points his finger at her face, which she ignores. "It looks like a cry for help. I didn't want you to think that you were alone, Auburn. There are people at home and people at this university who care about you, and want you to make the best decisions for your life."

"I've had this since I was seventeen."

"All right, all right now, no need to get upset, that's not what I had in mind for this meeting. I just wanted to let you know that you don't have to pierce yourself, or, or, or draw on yourself to be more attractive to men. In fact, God says in Leviticus, "Ye shall not make any cuttings in your flesh for the dead, nor print any marks upon you." So all you're doing is making an object of yourself, putting yourself out for the men who can't control themselves and see beautiful young women like yourself as nothing but conquests, markings on their cave walls. You don't want a man lusting after you, Auburn. You want a man to lust after your heart and your, no, you don't want him to lust after you for anything. You want him to cherish you for your heart and for your soul. Getting tattoos and doing drugs only helps to disintegrate your mind. What you should really be experimenting with is…"

"Look, I'm really uncomfortable right now, can I just go? I'll work harder in class. I just…don't need. Don't need this." She searches the chair and ground for her sweater to cover up but remembers Kirby in the hallway, and opts to cover her chest with her hands. The corners of her eyes are welling up with water not from sadness but from anger.

"If you think it's best I won't keep you against your will, but I would like you to take something with you, something to read in case you feel alone and need companionship." Solomon opens his desk drawer and removes a folded piece of laminated paper from beneath the photo of his wife. The pamphlet reads "The Real Facts of Life!" in bold white letters beneath a royal blue, rainbow sky. "It's really quite fascinating literature, it provides an in-depth look into premarital sex and dating, and how putting God first just washes all your sins right away. This is for you," he says, leaning over his desk, pleasantly gesturing with the folded paper as Auburn stares at him, mouth agape, lips almost touching.

"It is the final proof of God's omnipotence that he need not exist in order to save me."

"I don't appreciate that, Auburn."

"I didn't say it."

"Peter De Vries said it."

"Bite me."

Solomon is shocked by her hateful lashing out and hardly registers a movement before she tips over the cafeteria chair and stomps toward the door. He reaches out an arm, hand open, trying to sway her back into the room, but without words or reason the gesture is empty. Auburn pushes the door with no result, and figures out with no lapse between thoughts that the door opens by pulling, and manages to pull off a smooth transition between right and wrong.

"What, you're done already? That's new," hazardously laughs Kirby, shaken from her lotus by the slamming doors. "What?" she asks. "What?" she asks again.

"Let's go," Auburn demands.

"What? What happened?"

"Nothing, let's go." Auburn grabs her sweater from Kiki's lap and balls it up between her own hands, resisting the urge to throw it down the stairs.

"What happened? Was it not good?"

"Kiki, shut the fuck up and let's go, okay?"

"Hey, if it only lasts that long maybe I should screw my B and go for the gold."

"Fine, whatever." Auburn turns and stomps off toward the stairs, taking quick, hard steps like a circumspect race horse, covering as much ground as possible in the least amount of time without running or making a scene. The heels of her boots resound and reverberate within the faculty hall walls. She was taught that the human brain was the crowning glory of evolution so far, but she thinks it's a very poor scheme for survival. She will remember where the quote comes from as the macaroni and cheese dissipates and she is stabbing into blackness. Kurt Vonnegut, Jr. The Columbia Dictionary of Quotations. She loses her own thoughts in the quotes sometimes, so at any time she may or may not fill her mind with her self.

"Auburn, hon, hold on," Kirby shouts, but the back of Auburn's elevated middle finger shouts back loudly until it vanishes past the doorway. "All right." Kirby gracefully rises to her feet, images of mozzarella sticks fading into the distance. She is alone now in the faculty hall. She doesn't enjoy being in the faculty hall when it is full of faculty. This is even worse. With no other option for explanation she turns to Professor Anderson's door.

Because the door is already ajar from random slamming she sees no reason to knock and pushes it open without turning the knob. Solomon is sitting with one elbow on the desk, staring down at papers, tapping this fingers against the moderate brown.

"Is everything okay?" she asks. Her professor raises his face without warning, waking from a long dream. After a moment he shakes his head from side to side.

"Everything is fine. A case of mistaken motivations. Miss Bryant assumed that by making herself more attractive to me that it would increase her grades."

"Oh. What did you want her for, then?" The question is filled with incredulity. Her words are acute.

"Come, sit down." Kirby complies. Solomon adjusts himself. "I'd like to ask you a very personal question, and I'd like for you to answer me in the most honest way you can, all right?"

"Of course."

"Does Auburn have a serious drug problem?"

"Oh, no, not at all."

"Have you been around her when or while she was experimenting with abused substances?"

"No. Wait, actually, yes. About a month ago a couple of Pi Kappa Phi guys came by the room with some herbal ecstasy, but Auburn's inamorato punched one of their lights out before she took any. Which is hilarious, because herbal ecstasy doesn't really do anything to you anyway. It's like gingko biloba. It gets you as high as ginseng."

"Her inamorato?" he asks.

"Her un-boyfriend," she replies. "Just say no to increased cognitive function." She says this with exaggerated hand motions and wide, expressive eyes. Solomon smiles against his better judgment. Kirby grazes back a long strand of straight black hair from her olive cheeks and mouths a laugh. He begins to look her over, noticing her clothes, her smells. Her T-shirt is red and tight, embroidered with peony flowers. Her jeans are worn and stretched white down the middle of her reedy thighs. She smells like chocolate, caramel and honey blended with sandalwood, patchouli and vanilla. She is like spotless glass surrounding a piece of candy. This is pleasing.

"So will you talk to Auburn and make sure that everything is understood, and that assumptions should not be passed along as fact? I would never do something to compromise student-professor trust and confidentiality."

"I'll see what I can do, she really did think that you were going to give her Dean's List grade if she had sex with you." Kirby nods again. Solomon is not expecting things to be stated so ignobly.

"Yes, well, that's not usually how it works." Kirby simpers.

"Would it work for me?"

Quietude extols the sounds of "yes" loudly. In his mind Solomon is trying desperately to collect and organize his notes. The manuscript is in a hundred pages blown out into the evening sky, like a miraculous tornado of symbolism, like nothing ever experienced before. Like nothing ever. As she walks to the door and lifts the latch on the lock Solomon begins to ponder how Hemingway would've described this moment, and wonders if this is truly a sign from the Lord Jesus Christ that his mission of faith is not a mirage but a crusade, something not to die but to live for. He feels sinful feelings throughout sinful areas of his body, but excuses these as means to an end. If the act were not substantially sinful it would be fantasy, for nothing. It is the Devil himself that gives these fluids fire. The stories and twirling images in Solomon's mind are cast down as delusions of youth. They are the fictitious scat of a Godless mind.

The blinds are pulled shut. Behind them the sky is turning purple and the streetlights along the campus sidewalks are turning on. Kirby's knees are squeezed between the outside of his legs and the arms of the chair. Looking around her waist to make sure that the door is closed and locked he can see the edge of her jeans forming a pocket of empty space above her lower back. He makes note of the color of the ridge of her spine and this stays with him like red text, in the recess of his thought process, in the spaces between his distastes for Auburn and for Delia. He can feel her hard abdomen forming against his through her clothing and this causes him to forget what he is thinking and react, a Pavlovian thrust of the hips and clenching of the hands. Their lips meet and he tastes again for the first time the sweet saliva and warm pressure. This invigorates him.

She begins to moan. Solomon bends her back in the chair and clamps his hand over her mouth. Women should remain silent in the churches. They are not allowed to speak, but must be in submission, as the Law says. If they want to inquire about something, they should ask their own husbands at home; for it is disgraceful for a woman to speak in the church. He wants to expose her. He pulls up her red, flowered shirt to tear at the flesh but finds a white under-shirt; cotton, translucent. Undeterred he begins to search her vaporous colors and contours, taking her between his teeth. He sits down under her shadow with great delight, and her fruit is sweet to his taste.

Her body falls back onto the desk, clear of the banal decorations of work and family. Solomon neglects the papers that were being browsed during his moment of doubt. Kirby's mercurial body spreads these papers along with her as she slides, bedding herself with them, framing herself with words and num-bers. Her skin looks dark and like a part of the wooden desk amidst the white rectangles. He takes shape as an impending occurrence above her. His stomach contracts. She begins to kick, laughing. Always laughing. The words around her grow darker and darker on the pages. Solomon would not notice them if he did not know them so well. Numbers appear around her navel. Tattoos draw-ing themselves as verses between her breasts. He turns her over and she gasps. He wants them to go away. He sees colons. He sees darkness against the white. The white fades and the words are all he sees.

> **EXODUS 33:16** "So shall we he separated, and all of Thy people, from all the people that are upon the face of the earth."

> **LEVITICUS 20:24** "I am the Lord thy God, which have separated you from other people."

The Bible, it says…

JOSHUA 23:12-13 "…if ye do in any wise go back and cleave unto the remnant of these nations, even these that remain among you, and shall make marriages with them, and go in unto them and they unto you: know for a certainty that they shall he *how does it go what am I thinking* snares and traps unto you, and scourges in your sides and thorns in your eyes, until ye perish off from this good land which the Lord your God has given you."

DEUTERONOMY 7:3 "NEITHER SHALT THOU MAKE MARRIAGES WITH THEM: thy daughter thou shalt not give unto his son, *nor his daughter shalt thou take unto thy* son."

Translated from Hebrew and Greek. No version. The words. The truth. The infallible truth.

JUDE 7 "*Even as Sodom and Gomorrah, and the cities about them in like manner,* giving, themselves over to fornication, and GOING AFTER STRANGE FLESH are set forth for an example, suffering the vengeance of eternal fire."

"Any man who believes in Hell and doesn't want to be there uses every moment of power he finds to persecute those who don't care where they end up," he mutters to himself, beneath the sounds of Kirby laughing, kicking, talking. "I'm sorry, I didn't think I would have this much faith. I'm sorry." She doesn't hear him, choosing to grab the corner of his desk and pull it, causing a loud scratching against the floor. He begins to question his translations. He wonders if his life would be easier if he accepted the King James version, trusted the pure and true Word of God as determined by someone else.

PSALM 144:11-12 "*Rid me and deliver me from the hand of strange chil-dren, whose mouth speaketh vanity, and their right hand is a right hand of falsehood: That OUR SONS may be as plants grown up in their youth, that OUR DAUGHTERS may he as the polished cornices of a palace.*"

Is that what it says?
"Kirby, stop it, I'm sorry."

Psalm 144:11-12 "*Rid me and deliver me from the hand of strange children, whose*

"Kirby, I said stop it, I'm sorry. I thought this would make things easier. I thought I could understand myself better if I could understand…"

"What?" she interrupts, looking back over her shoulder, her eyes squinted, lips red, hair dampening and sticking behind her ears.

"Don't look at me. I mean, I said, I thought you…"

"Are you talking?" she asks. Solomon suddenly realizes that his voice is hidden beneath the violently quivering emotions stabbed like arrows into his neck. He wants to throw her down. He wants to pull away. He does not want her anymore, not like this, not like this possession. She is no longer an object but a concept. If he cannot deconstruct her he is lost in a book of blank notes. If he cannot stop himself he is below sin. He is below redemption. He is already in Hell. The room is humid and he fears that his door will stay locked when he tries to leave.

"Don't pretend like this is shocking," she says, as he lowers himself back into the leather chair. "None of this is shocking. Are you afraid that somebody might find out that college isn't about books and learning? That went out with cross-dressing and homosexuality. That went out with the dinosaurs."

"I'm just afraid."

"I know," says Kirby, rolling over and sitting up, resting her weight on the palms of her hand and balls of her feet; crossing her legs on the edge of the desk to cover her openness. "But you're afraid for the wrong reasons. You're afraid of…what, of God?"

"Yes."

"Yeah, well, there you go." She smiles. "You won't be seeing me in class anymore this year, correct?"

"Of course not," he says, thinking of Delia.

"And Auburn gets an A for effort, right?"

He says nothing. Then, "Yes."

"Good." Kirby leans forward between her legs and kisses him passionately, but he tastes and feels nothing. He can only see the face of Christ. He can only see the face of his wife. He makes a conscious decision to purchase and wear a wedding ring, despite his own lack of comfort. He will buy three wedding rings and wear them all on the same finger. When she is finished she licks her lips and laughs. "I know why you're so sad about this all of a sudden."

"Because you…you aren't…"

"You know what the difference between white people and black people is?"

"What?"

"Black people drive like this," she says, leaning back naked on the desk, holding her right arm out, rolling her fist in an arc from left to right. "White people drive like this," she says, leaning forward into Solomon's lap, holding both hands tightly closed in front of his face.

"But you're…Japanese."

"Yeah, you've got no idea how I drive." Kirby hops down from the desk, grabbing her pink underwear from the bookshelf, hanging from the edge of Secret Keeper: The Delicate Power of Modesty. "To be a women's studies professor you sure don't know a lot about women. But…" she pauses. "I guess that might've been the whole point so, forget I said anything."

Solomon does not watch her dress, and locks the door behind her when she is gone. He talks to God now in the way that a scorned child talks to a just-arrived-home father. He thanks all the people listening who are not God that man and God need no moderator to communicate; no angels, no cryptic scripture, no operator. Man can speak and God can listen. God can speak and man can only hope to hear. The saddest thing is that they hear incorrectly, like a kiddy game of telephone, and "Thou Shalt Not" comes out as "purple monkey trashcan." Men never do things so playfully and fully as they do when religiously motivated.

Tonight he sits in his office, in the dark, his Bible only lit by the sidewalk light outside of his window. The black print words run together into a blur and the red words are hardly visible at all, but he looks at them as the hours pass in the hopes that something, anything, will make sense. He has lived forty-one years believing that everyone but God was his equal or below, and that everyone was just waiting to die. Now he realizes that he is the one waiting to die. Nobody else seems to care. Perhaps the fault lies in that he is the only one who feels this way. Perhaps the fault lies in his human imperfection, and this is all written as a testament to his faith in the Book of Life. Perhaps he'll just go to Hell.

Delia covers a plate of vegetables with a paper towel and puts it in the microwave for him.

In the morning Solomon wakes up with his face sticking to an essay, something unimportant with no Bible verses written on it. He forms it into a ball and throws it into the trashcan, opting now to simply drop the ball into the basket instead of sinking a three pointer. He touches his face to feel the stubble that ornament all tortured souls. He feels nothing but smooth skin. During the night he was only to sleep for collections of minutes. Whenever his eyes close he sees images of Delia on their wedding day, the day when he showed up late to the service by fifteen minutes to put the finishing touches on a gender studies paper. He sees Delia sitting by herself in the kitchen while he watches television, touching her stomach, looking through magazines. He knows what she wants but is not augmented to give her this. He wants to learn ways to tell her he loves her, but cannot think of a way that seems equally meaningful and important. Then he sees Kirby, her mongrel skin hitting his thighs. His thighs begin to itch and he scratches them through his dress pants. He wants to leave. He wants to die, but cementing this would negate his previous years of work.

Professor Anderson grades his papers ritualistically until noon, when the faculty heads out to lunch and he can creep away unannounced. He passes Auburn's dorm. The urge to buzz her room and apologize overcomes him but he stops before he even turns in that direction. Talking to her again will not make things better. Talking to her ever again will only end in drama, and trauma, and sadness of self. He has been forsaken and hung on his own cross. Solomon has nailed the nails and Solly has placed a crown of thorns around his head. Now he just has to hang for days and wait for his blood to drain. When he gets to the parking lot and opens the door of his sports utility vehicle, Professor Anderson realizes that he has been comparing himself to Jesus and breaks down. Students pass as he kneels in the parking lot and cries, asking Jesus to come back into his heart. Please.

"Is that Professor Anderson?"

"Dude, keep walking."

He navigates the streets with his eyes bleeding water—pink from the strain, red from the night. His body threatens to give out. He can't feel the gas or brake beneath his feet and pushes his feet down with his best judgment. The change in his ashtray looks like thousand pound weights, and everything chrome or plastic looks like solid steel. He feels like he is dragging the apparatus on his back, pressing forward with his feet, stomping, hoping to stop and start with God's will. He cries, constantly. He presses his head to the steering wheel. He turns the radio off and listens to the spinning of the wheels. The spinning of his mind.

Solomon does not know that he has been involved in a head-on collision until he is leaning out from his driver-side window, watching the front end of a torn-apart Honda turning over onto itself and bouncing through the median. The back end, barely visible through his passenger window, is embedded in the front entrance of a furniture store. The fence surrounding the store has been cracked and splintered. Beneath the gravel and grass are black tire tracks, along with a thousand pieces of glass and circular patterns of blood. There is a brown-haired girl impaled on one of the fence posts, coughing up red splotches onto the brown wood. Her screams are muffled by her mouths full of life. Solomon falls out through his window and tumbles onto the road, his shoulder and arm snapping on impact. He feels no pain. He sees the girl on the fence and wants to reach for her. His body keeps turning and he can't tell where the sky ends and the blood begins, but he tries, and the it all turns black.

Now in the tenth month the angel is sent by God to the city of Virginia named Lynchburg, to a betrothed man whose name is Solomon. And having come in, the angel says to him, **"Rejoice, highly favored one, the Lord is with you; blessed are you among men!"** But when he sees the angel he is troubled at her saying, and considers what manner of greeting this is. Then the angel says to him, **"Do not be afraid, for you…"** and then touches her own face and begins to stutter. Solomon comes to his feet and reaches out for her but the light is too bright and he is struck down to the ground. He tries to see but is blinded. The world of color, of whiteness and darkness and browns and olives, has turned to red and then to black. Solomon's mind is overtaken by a blizzard of snow and feathers. He is cold, then warm. His mind becomes relaxed and relieved. He sees only a sheet of white, with simple writing along the center.

> *What if I could speak all languages of humans and of angels?*
> *If I did not love others, I would be nothing more than a noisy gong or a clanging cymbal.*
>
> *What if I could prophesy and understand all secrets and all knowledge?*
> *And what if I had faith that moved mountains?*
>
> *I would be nothing, unless I loved others.*
> *What if I gave away all that I owed and let myself be burned alive?*
>
> *I would gain nothing, unless I loved others.*
> *Love is kind and patient, never jealous, boastful, proud, or rude.*
>
> *Love isn't selfish or quick tempered.*
> *It doesn't keep a record of wrongs that others do.*
>
> *Love rejoices in the truth, but not in evil.*
> *Love is always supportive, loyal, hopeful, and trusting.*
>
> *For now there are faith, hope, and love.*
> *But of these three, the greatest is love.*

"Oh." Solomon blinks his eyes. "But that's so cliché. But…yeah. Yes."

"You made it easy for me," the angel says. "All I had to do was find the one Bible verse that isn't about killing somebody or what you can and can't do. Some of this is really nice if you shut up and look for it."

"Is the girl okay? I didn't mean to…"

"She will be fine. Can you walk?"

"I can."

"Then you will be fine, too. Your wife is waiting for you at home. She saved the vegetables for you. And a dinner roll."

"She loves me, doesn't she?"

"Yes. Forever. Despite yourself."

"She's going to stab me when I walk through the door, isn't she?"

"Yes. With a large knife. Duck."

CHAPTER 17

Aranea C. Cavatica, age twenty, died on October 22nd at 3:44 P.M. She lay dead on the bed for six minutes before being resuscitated by doctors. Her wounds were treated and stitched tightly to keep her soul from sliding down the inside of her skin and onto the starched white bed sheets like thick, store-brand ketchup. Aranea was wheeled into a room full of skeletal shells passed by and brittle grandmothers. Tubes were stuck into her nostrils and wrists to monitor internal injuries. The lining of her intestines was torn like construction paper and folded into birds and giraffes in her abdomen. In the early morning of the 23rd she was moved into a room with an overweight, middle-aged woman who was hit in the top of her head by a falling bowling ball during a routine closet cleaning. Aranea breathes and talks, sneezes and moves her fingers. Every thirty minutes the blood shows through her bandages. At 3:44 P.M. she receives a tan plastic tray and uses a white fork from a cafeteria cutlery packet to pierce and divide green Jell-O like a well-done steak. I hate hospitals.

The walls and furniture are a slick white, and I imagine that if I fell from my chair I would glide across them like a slip-and-slide right through the door. I feel like I'm caught in the downward spiral of a toilet flush, trying to find a hold on the porcelain surface. Everything is so clean. The windowsills have been dusted. The clipboards are full of crisp, flawless paper. The bedpan is shined. The smell of Windex and bleach heavy-duty detergents are overpowered only slightly by the odor that has adhered itself to every separation of tile, behind every ceiling panel, hanging just outside of every window. Asleep. Cold. Deceased. Defunct. Departed. Exanimate. Extinct. Inanimate. Late. Lifeless. Spiritless. Unanimated. Like someone has held me down and pissed onto my face and soap won't make it go away, until I want to cut the skin from my skull and throw it to the ground. Aranea is watching the gelatin simulate a jiggle and I watch her black eyes try to focus and find color in the white world. She's lost somewhere between Heaven and herself and I'm in the tax-funded Crocodile Mile. I hate hospitals.

I've spent the better parts of the last day crouching in a brown cafeteria chair refurbished to look like a barker lounger waiting for her family and friends to show up. There are two copies of every high school yearbook in her living room. The inside covers are empty. I wish I could muse on the hip and fresh class difference comedy that goes on in movie high schools but I can't find the holes to thread, because the "nerds" never considered themselves nerds and we never made Prom-pacts to lose our virginity. The hallways didn't stop when Aranea walked through them. The music didn't welcome her with an acoustic guitar rift or a patchwork love song. There wasn't any music. We were in school. The only music that played in our social background was during the morning announcements, and that was just because the AV Club chipped in for a tape deck. I want to think of Aranea three-dimensionally, and picture her sitting on a bench after school gabbing with her racially diverse girlfriends about the day's events. I can't see her like that. I can barely see her at all. She existed in context to only me for so long. I feel like I never gave her a chance to exist outside of it. I want to wait awkwardly outside the room with my back to the wall, arms crossed and looking pensive while her loved ones gather around to hear the story. Nothing. The television isn't even on. I hear her plastic fork scraping the green flecks across the tray and I want something better for her than me, but in a few weeks I'll thank God for at least being given.

"If I told you that I hated hospitals, would I be giving in to cliché?"

"No," says Aranea, gently shaking her head, her eyes never leaving their grasp on the colored reflection. "You'd be the every-man. Everybody hates hospitals. If you could think of a more…" She stops in mid-sentence, trailing off into silence. "If you could think of a more creative way to say it you'd be…something of a scholar I suppose. A poet. Ode on a Cube of Jell-O."

"Hey," I say, glancing down at my shuffling feet. "Please don't feel like you have to entertain me with the banter today. You were impaled on a fence post. The doctor pulled out a five-inch splinter. He has it in a Ziploc bag paper clipped to your file. I would understand if you wanted the conversation to take a more reserved tone."

She slides the gelatin halves together until they are whole once again and finally looks at me. Her eyes trust themselves briefly before retreating back to the safety of closed lids, like children tucked in to bed, reaching out for the nightlight.

"Your dumb jokes make me feel better sometimes. Your eyes are red. I thought you could use one."

"My jokes make you feel better?"

"Sometimes." Her voice is human and humane.

"Wow, I had no idea." My voice is in cracks and incredulous. "The first conversation we ever had was about suicide and guardian angels. I made jokes about your hand wounds." I shake my head, remembering the events as played by silent movie stooges in my mind. "I put my foot in your face. You should've thrown me into a shallow grave."

"That wasn't the first time we talked."

"It wasn't?"

"No," she says, writing on the lunch tray with her index finger. Her hair is jet black and pulled into a tight, unflattering and normal pony tail. My brain searches for what she will recall as I am the Brooks/Aranea historian, but my thoughts get lost in the observation that all of the jets I've ever seen have been gray. "The first time I ever talked to you I told you that my butt was wet. I'm Omega on the Latin alphabet of coolness."

"Oh," I mutter, remembering seven adjectives I use to describe her hair when I replay that memory. As I speak I conjure up seven more. "Of course I remember that." When I get to thirteen I think "long" and just quit while the vocabulary is good. While the vocabulary is propitious.

"Do you remember the first thing I ever said to you?"

"I've tried to remember the first thing you said to me every day since twenty seconds after you said it."

"I told you that I fell out of the sky. I gave away the whole plot twist right there at the beginning."

"No, you said something before that." I look away from her and lock my eyes on the bedpan. I don't associate any of the lame things that people associate bedpans with and use it merely as an object to focus my thoughts on. My thoughts being focused on a bedpan is not an irony lost entirely on me. "You said something else. I was so sad that I lost it somewhere."

For the first time since the moment before rooftop slumber she smiles. The smile is open and real, and she makes sure to expose every tooth possible, regardless of what the condescending jock nurses might say. "I did. I didn't think you'd remember."

The seat loses any comfort context and becomes an extension of my lower body. I can't feel the tips of my fingers or the tips of my toes. This is because of anxiety. No, fear. When I look into her eyes and cannot see myself I become afraid that I may one day be forced to spend my fondest memories with myself, by myself. She is sitting evidence that miracles happen every day. This thought is so corny that I want to place a giant red "THE END" stamp over my face. I want to think of something epic to describe my relief but hold reverence for the fact that sometimes clichés do come true. "What did you say?"

"I told you that your Father wanted me to come over and talk to you."

"What?" My thought process isn't even in the bedpan at this point. "You know my Dad?"

"No," says Aranea, pointing to the ceiling. "Your Father. Capital F. You can't expect Voltaire out of a ten year old."

"Oh." A fish tank with no fish. Empty rooms. Empty graves. "Where's your father, Aranea?"

"He art in Heaven," she says, snorting. I can see the pain on her face. I feel for her wounds and for her loneliness. I am envious of her faith and her strength.

"No, your father. Lowercase f."

"Oh," she says, looking away. She looks at the floor, at the windowsill, at the curtains. All white. No color. Empty. Pure, but empty. There is nothing to distract her, and this adds to her pain. "He's at work. I mean, no. He's not at work. He's not coming. He's not..." Her dead eyes search for the pigment in mine. "Ever coming."

"Yeah, I know," says Brooks, the deductive theologian. "I didn't think he would. I figured out a lot of it. I didn't want to assume that I was wrong and leave you here by yourself. Why didn't you tell me? What happened to him?"

"Everyone I meet is lonely. They have the love of God in them. He's living in their hearts. He's right there inside of them, but they're lonely anyway. They want boyfriends and girlfriends. They want mothers and fathers. They want heritage and vindication. They want to feel like they matter. It's so easy, but they don't get it right. All they need is love but they don't get it right." The blood begins to appear in spirals across her bandages. The fold in her hospital gown covers most of it but I can see it and know when it comes. "Then one day I woke up and realized that I wasn't getting it right, either. I didn't know how to be lonely. The thought never occurred to me. But all of a sudden I felt it. It made me sad. I didn't want you to be sad."

"So he...he's never been there? At all?"

"It never occurred to me that I'd need another one." Aranea winces and touches her stomach. The pain of the touch reverberates through her body. It becomes too much, and she is left sitting on the bed with her hands inches from the blood, fingers moving, dry in the idea of how to make things better. "It's funny," she says. "The son of man is the son of God. The son of God is the son of man. Christ the son is the same as God the father. God the father is the same as Christ the son. It's so confusing to people who don't believe, but it makes such perfect sense to me. I just understand it."

"Aranea…"

"He's always been there for me, whether I could touch him or not. I can't see him anymore, but my heart won't stop believing that he's right here in front of me."

My father is a good man. He and I are different men in many respects. I am my mother's interpretation of him. We have the same vertical ridges beneath the skin of our foreheads, tracing down from our scalp to the peak of our eyebrows. He stretches his legs onto the couch and lies motionless with the remote control in his hands for hours watching baseball. Sometimes we argue about wrestling. He put that love into me when I was a child. When I think of my father I see him not as he approaches his mid-forties but as a twenty two year old like myself. He is my interpretation of him. I remember him as a child most in the moments when he would help me pull the mattress down from his bed and drop to his knees. He did this to give me a false sense of equality for wrestling matches. He was one-hundred ninety pounds and I was somewhere in the fifties. We would both strip down to our tighty-whities and t-shirts. My father would give me some token offense and sell each three year old forearm with a jerk of his head and a "whoom" sound effect. Then he would sit on my back and laugh as he grinded his knuckle into my temple. I would scream and cry but would never submit, and when the pain was gone I thought about how much I loved it. It was so innocent. He would only hurt me if I asked for it. I would ask for it a lot. He has hurt me a lot. My father is a good man, and I love him.

"Once when I was three I had a King of the Mountain match with my Dad, which was basically him pushing me off a mattress over and over. I kept trying to jump back on but he'd pie-face me, push me right off. He would always play the bad guy and whenever I'd temporarily give up he would turn to the crowd and taunt. The crowd was the chest-of-drawers." Aranea smiles. She rests her elbows on the lunch cart and rests her chin on her palms. "I saw that he had his back turned, but instead of just running up to him and getting pie-faced again

I decided for a more epic entrance. I climbed onto this recliner they had in their bedroom, all the way up to the top. When my Dad turned I spread my arms and leaped off. I felt like the Dynamite Kid. My father moved instinctively and I went sailing over him. I landed ear first on the corner of the dresser. It split me open from here to here," I say, motioning my fingers along the cartilage in my ear.

"Oh my gosh. That's terrible."

"Yeah, I had to go to the hospital for stitches, and I had some damage in my inner ear. He felt horrible. I remember him sitting on the mattress with his head in his hands. I remember it sideways because my Mom had my head turned sideways in the sink. The next time we wrestled he put a ban on the high risk moves, but he made up for it by dousing his forehead in ketchup. It was great. He was wearing the crimson mask from my knee drops and clotheslines. A few years later when he found out he had appendicitis I got scared and thought he was going to die, but then he told me that I'd caused it by giving him a flying elbow drop. He knew exactly how to make me feel better. I really love him."

"I can tell," she says, laughing.

"We haven't wrestled in years. He always tells me that he's too tired. He works too much. He doesn't really ask me about how I feel or what I think. He couldn't remember what year I was born in once. My Mom has to remind him about my birthday sometimes. It's really a shame, but I don't even...I don't even mind sometimes. I wouldn't doubt for a minute that he loves me, even if he's not there for me when I need him. So I know what you mean. Even when I see him lying on the couch complaining about his weight or going on about work I remember how many times he bounced around like an idiot to make my fake punches look real."

"We all have our battle scars." Aranea stares down at the cross on her palm, dotted with ointment. "Have you talked to any of the doctors?"

"Nope, I'm pretty much out of the loop. I'm not family or spouse so I'm on a need-to-know basis."

"That's probably for the best." Aranea shakes her head as if to shake away the cobwebs. When she does this her ponytail flaps from side to side, absorbing the white from the room in the tips during motion and fading back into black when the tips come to rest. "I feel so badly for the man who ran into me. He had to handle so much worse. I'm praying for him."

"I feel bad for him too if he has it worse than you. You died for six minutes yesterday." The color leaves my face. I sit across from her, our faces frozen. My lips are blue beneath the pink skin. She is fractured. The wind would spread her thin and scatter her. She would gradually vanish. She looks like an image erased from a chalkboard.

"I died for six minutes?"

"Yes."

"Huh."

"They didn't tell you?"

"I didn't notice." Aranea leans back onto a bed of pillows. Their insides fluff and conform as hers cling like idioms to the body language of her trembling skin. "Dying is so interesting. It surrounds you."

"Like a hole." Bones in my neck and knees make tapping sounds as I stand. I rub the palms of my hands against my eyes to spread the specific reds into an expansive field of pink across my nose and cheekbones. "Do you want me to check on him?"

"If you don't mind." Doctors and nurses begin to bustle and huddle about in the hallway. "You should get some sleep."

"I slept in increments."

"You should sleep in a bed."

"I don't want you to be by yourself." The nurses pass a clipboard around in a half-circle a few feet from her door. They glance down at the papers and speak quickly to themselves; hushed tones, simple words. Sometimes they open their eyes wide and stare in. "I don't want you to be by yourself."

"I know."

"I, uh," I say, reaching into my pocket. "I had a speech prepared in case you died again." Aranea smiles and her eyes shake.

"You had a what?"

"A speech. When people die in movies they either get held and the person screams 'noooooo' to the sky or they get a speech. I thought screaming would be inappropriate, since there are a lot of other people here that would be disturbed."

"Hah, so let's hear it."

"Okay. You have to pretend that I'm doing fake movie crying after each period." I unfold the piece of paper. It's a receipt for my Halloween costume. "Oh no, dude, don't be dead," I read in my finest monotone. "Why God, why would you take her away from me. Why. Take me instead, God, take me instead." Aranea laughs, pulls a pillow from behind her head, and clamps it down over her face. "And then I had some stuff about sports utility vehicles and gas prices but it's honestly too political for such a tender and honest moment."

"I don't wish suspense and drama on anyone," she says through the pillow, "but the next time a car is driving into me head on, feel free to heroically dive in front of it for me."

"Will do," I smile. "Where were you going, anyway?"

"I ordered a costume for the Halloween party, I was going to the post office to pick it up."

"Oh, all right." I turn the piece of paper around and hold it up for her to see. Then I remember that she's under a pillow and I feel a bit stupid. "I confess, I had no speech. This says 'hall costume, nineteen ninety-nine' and something about sales tax at the bottom. Not really the epic poetry you've come to expect from our friendship."

"I think expecting something normal from our friendship is impossible."

"So as long as we're being killed we're best friends?"

"I don't see why not. You're still coming to the Halloween party, aren't you?"

"Yeah. Just try not to die again, okay?"

"I don't know how long I have left, but I'll stay with you until you don't need me anymore."

"How long will that be?"

"Until the day I die. Which was yesterday."

The intensive care unit looks like a series of empty classrooms with chairs stacked in the corners and monuments of old computer systems. Lime green lines bounce across black screens. Numbers arrive and change. On television the doctors and nurses balance the stress of saving lives with their own sexy interpersonal relationships, but here the staff looks bored and occupied. The nurses stare down at papers as doctors sleep walk from bed to bed. The importance of their walk is lost on me. I am out of their highly-paid context. The walls are all curtains and the smell of death is incisive and taintless. Urine masked with cherry air freshener. I ask about yesterday's car accident. My hands are washed and my face awakened. I make a concerned effort to never look too closely at the beds I pass. I don't want to see the faces of the boys and women standing together, hugging, crying. I don't want to see injured hands cradled. I have never been in an intensive care unit to visit a person who didn't die. When Aranea was here I was told to wait outside. When Aranea was dead I was in the cafeteria. When Aranea was alive I was relieved. When I was relieved I was on my knees in the bathroom. Narrow is the gate and difficult is the way which leads to life, and there are few who find it.

I find S. Anderson's morbid cubicle. He is not a person. He is a mannequin. His face is wrapped tightly to conceal his face, and I can see the long tears marking his forearms. The sheets are pulled tightly to his midsection and although the monitors beep I cannot see him breathe. I want to knock on him. I want to know that he is hollow. I see imaginary flies buzzing around his face and am reminded of the fire bombings of Japan in World War II I'd seen in history books. Piles of bodies. Humorously decorated mummies doused in fake blood and stacked in holes. The lesson plans for history always begin with Mesopotamia and end with World War II. They've probably updated by now. To me life begins with a fertile crescent and ends with a hill of corpses. I am so afraid to look at him. I feel like I'm underneath him. I'm underneath them all. At the bottom of the hole.

I am so afraid to look at him. In him I see myself. I can prepare myself to die. The Bible tells me to follow ten commandments and to accept Jesus as my savior. This pre-orders my mansion in the kingdom of Heaven, where I will live blissfully for all eternity. My body, fat and cumbersome, is merely the vessel that carries my soul through redemption. The possessions I accumulate, big or small, are merely accouterments to make life bearable in the in-between. Cars. Books. Trophy wives. "You can't take it with you when you go!" We are, no, maybe we aren't, but I am a soul trapped in this same old sickly skin day after day. My possessions won't come with me when I go. I possess memories. I possess the essence of the people who inspire and shape me. I possess the love of God. I want to possess the love of self. When I die do I lose these? Do I lose my memories? Do I lose people and God? Do I lose myself? Do I lose my soul? God takes me and my life is erased. Me, what makes me "me," is wrapped in bandages and piled on top of the others who never got it right. Piled on top of everyone. I am so afraid to look at him.

I am afraid to look at myself. I am afraid to look at God and see him. To see God means that I can't see my Mom and Dad. If they don't believe what I believe and do what they are told they won't be with me. The Bible tells me that these things won't matter. I will be with God and I will be happy. God the father is the same as Christ the son. Christ the son is the same as God the father. God is love. God is in my heart. We're all one big collective. We're here to prepare for and worship him. Him, with a capital H. Father with a capital F. I spent my entire life and every second I can manage to make myself stand out in this desolate mind of humanity and my reward, my moment of enlightenment, is to be exactly like everyone else in the kingdom of Heaven. I am afraid to look at myself because I see God within me. I want to love myself, but I am afraid to look.

I don't want to die.

I don't want you to die.

I don't want her to die.

I don't want it.

I don't.

In the intensive care unit waiting room is a beautiful woman, beautiful in her commonality. Her shoulders are broad and I imagine that twenty years ago she would've taken my breath away, but now she sits solemnly unwrapping honey buns and unzipping plastic bags of celery sticks. Her nose is short and round. Her nostrils flare about her dried lips as she breaks a stick into pieces with her teeth. The woman's cheeks are blood red, like Aranea's palm. I sit in the sixteenth chair to her left, the closest to the door. She flips through the waist-high stack of country music weekly magazines. When she notices me she swallows green mush and reaches out to me without moving at all.

"Are you alone?" she asks. I nod. "I'm sorry, I don't want to be a nuisance."

"No, it's okay. I'm just…"

"Uh huh," she whimpers. "My husband was involved in a head-on collision yesterday, I've been waiting for two hours for the doctor to tell me how he is. The nurses walk past the door every few minutes and I light up, but when they pass I…I'm so uncomfortable here."

"One of the best parts about being alive is that we have a set of understood logics to fit our most uncomfortable situations. Feeling uncomfortable in a hospital just means that you aren't a sociopath."

"It smells like death."

"So I've heard."

"Oh, I'm so sorry, I shouldn't just assume that…you have someone in the ICU, I should've asked."

"The other half of the collision," I respond. "They moved her out of intensive care this morning, she's in a room upstairs. Just a puncture wound, nothing serious."

"Oh my, your…your sister?" she says, rising to her feet.

"No, I'm an only child."

"I'm sorry, I'm so sorry about her." Her empathy instantly makes everything daisies and waterslides. "I'm glad that she's going to be okay. I saw Solomon a few hours after the accident. His face was so torn up. I couldn't recognize him. He looked like a demon. I was afraid to look at him."

"I know how you feel."

"It's all my fault. It's all my fault," she repeats, again and again. The woman begins to fill me in on the expository information that she never assumes I want to know, but since I'm the only person without a white coat on she assumes that I should know. "I was so mad at him. His secretary called me and told me that she thought he might be having an affair, that he was acting suspicious and trying to make her leave early, and I got so upset, I just opened up my Bible and prayed for God to give me the answers. I never thought something so horrible could happen to me. It feels like something on the television."

"I hope things aren't so bad for you." I placate her but feel genuinely bad for her. A large part of the curse of having a heart is that even when the disinterest is genuine it is accompanied by sympathy, and, if disinterest is maintained, guilt. I feel bad for her because it feels better than feeling bad for myself.

"I don't want to lose my husband," she cries. "I love him. I want to be in Heaven with him. But I don't want him to be there yet."

"Oh." I feel the same way and feel relieved that I started believing in Heaven again before Aranea left for it.

"I'm so afraid that I don't now how to be a good enough Christian. I don't know what to have faith in and what to take literally." Her words become fast and mangled within one another. "My husband once told me that he was afraid he wouldn't go to Heaven because it was full. Revelation seven four says 'And I heard the number of them which were sealed: *and there were* sealed an hundred *and* forty *and* four thousand of all the tribes of the children of Israel.' He didn't know if it was supposed to be literal or not. He was afraid that if he died before Jesus came back he might have to spend eternity waiting outside of the doors, since a hundred and forty-four thousand Christians have already died. It's so confusing sometimes. I love him so much."

"Your husband, or God?"

"We talk about Him so much that it's hard to distinguish anymore. I love my husband and I love God, I love God and Solomon more than I would ever hope to love myself. It's the way love is supposed to be. We're all the same in God's eyes. He made us from his own image. He loves us and wants us to be happy, and I've been so happy…I don't know how to show it anymore but I've been so happy, I've been so happy for my entire life."

"Then what do you have to be afraid of?"

"Do you believe in God?"

"Right now or in general?"

"There shouldn't be a difference. Do you believe in God or not?"

"With everything I have, yes." This is the first time I have said this since yesterday, when I was driving to Aranea. When I said it then it was the first time in five years.

"And are you afraid to die?"

"Yes." I have never said this word to answer this question.

"I'm not. That's what I'm afraid of. Things are so wrong but I'm so happy. I'm forty years old and I'm ready to die. I've done everything I'm supposed to. I know that when I die I'm going to Heaven. Every day I find a way to worship. Every day. I don't know what else I'm supposed to do. I don't know why I'm still here. I'm ready and I have to wait…I have to wait for so long. I'm afraid that if I wait too long Solomon won't love me and things will change and I won't be ready. I want to die right now. What's wrong with me?"

"I don't think anything is wrong with you," I say, and mean it. "At least you know your damage. I've been so idealistic about religion and love that I forgot how to do the first and overcompensated on the second."

The American wife tilts her head to the side and smiles at me; a fat smile, her eyes disappearing behind fleshy cheeks. "God saved your girlfriend. He's looking out for you just like he's looking out for my Solomon."

"She's not my girlfriend, she's just…" I give a long pause here. I think that's for the best. "I'm almost…ashamed of myself for thinking of her in that way. She's so much more than a girlfriend."

"Oh, are you married? I didn't see a ring?" She smacks her thighs and laughs at this because she has made a side-splitting and hilarious observational funny. I ignore her and continue to exposit, because if I don't get it out now I'll stuff it back in. When I'm forced to recall it in a moment of true importance it will be displaced by wrestling factoids and I'll shout, "Satoru Sayama was born on November 24, 1957!"

"My grandfather died when I was twelve years old. My grandmother died when I was seventeen. My best friend from high school killed himself last month. My friends have all been surrounded by death. So many people just…kill themselves. That's just it. And I've never been able to handle it. I keep thinking that I should burst into tears and throw myself onto the nearest coffin but something inside of me keeps me from doing that, and I always thought it was her. Aranea, that's her name, it means spider web but it means so much more than that. She showed up to hug me at every funeral and I didn't even know who she was. I didn't see her between them. She came and went. She's so strange to look at. Looking at her is like an activity. You have to be skilled. The things she says to me aren't especially clever or cool. But she's always trying to…I don't know, entertain me. She tries hard to be my friend. And there is so much about her that I want to be. I want to know God like she does. She helps me do that a little more every day. The whole time I thought it was love. It is. It is love. Just not what I thought it was. I don't want her to love me in the way I thought I loved her. Then we'd be just like everyone else. I want to think that she might love me the way I think I do now. I just…really appreciate her. I'm afraid to let her drift out of my life again that I don't know what to do."

"You're afraid she's not going to be there when you open your eyes?"

"Maybe I'm afraid that she's only going to be there when I open my eyes."

"You're afraid of death."

"And afraid to lose a girl who only shows up alongside it. Maybe she's a sign that I need to stop worrying about when this is all going to end and start worrying about the little exposed parts of me. The soft, squishy parts. The ones that make it so hard to love and be loved."

"That's sweet. You're right. Maybe she's an angel."

"She says that all the time."

Women on the muted television are having soap opera difficulties as a man with a thick beard enters the room. His presence brings American wife to her feet once more. His hospital nametag reveals what his white overcoat and stethoscope may have not. He embodies "doctor" in each step. I am sure that he practices this at home when nobody is looking. The man looks at me through the black frame of his glasses and, noticing that I am not a woman, turns to the only other person in the room and introduces himself.

"Mrs. Anderson? Hello, I'm Dr. Dorian. If I could speak to you out in the hallway for a moment." His sentence never reaches a definitive question mark. The woman stares at him for a few seconds before taking the hint. She is almost out of the door before she realizes that her purse, bag of celery, and country music magazines are being left unattended. She jogs back across the room. She stuffs the vegetables into an open pocket in her purse, deposits the handbag deeply into her armpit, and wipes honey bun crumbs into the floor. S. Anderson's wife chooses to leave the country music magazines where they lay. Meanwhile, I sit perfectly still. I think this is for the best.

The room is completely silent now, save for the buzz of the fluorescent lights overhead. The two women on television are pointing at each other. They have hair that poofs up in the front. They are both wearing solid colors with shoulder pads. As they bicker silently the conversation from the hall spills into the room. Dr. Dorian speaks in intelligible mumbles. Voices through a wall.

His tone is pointed and relaxing, but broken by her sobs. The cries grow louder. She begins to scream "no." The word "no" is clear, even through the wall. "No." "No." Dr. Dorian's hum remains constant as she denies him. Her word devolves into soft vowels. Ah. Ah.

Ah. Ah.

Ah.

Ah. Ah. Ah.

I turn the volume up on the television so I can't hear her, and so she cannot hear me crying from inside the waiting room.

CHAPTER 18

Hanging on the first doorway I pass is a cardboard cut out in the shape of a pumpkin. A black cat wearing a witches hat is climbing precociously up through the top as individually wrapped pieces of candy fall to the side. The word "boo" is written with an exclamation point in bold black letters. I wonder why such a nice cat would've went through so much trouble to give me a scare. Then I wonder why the exterior decorator needed to overkill the gist. I mean, I get it. I'm supposed to be scared. I want to roll my eyes and dismiss this all as childish but it makes me happy. I have to check my goofy nostalgic memories for razor blades. Cheap decorations remind me of elementary school. Teachers would staple witch cauldron pin-ups to bulletin boards and hang class-crafted ghost crafts from the ceiling. This all reminds me of being so stupidly happy for a day of no real consequence. I could dress up like my favorite wrestler and not be any stranger than the pedestrian kid who dresses up like Dracula. I think the cardboard cut out is definitely overkill, but it makes me so happy that I want to skip through the meadows and ride my unicorn over the rainbow on the way home. I drive past these doors fronting houses on her street and wonder why I'm the boy with the girl hyperbole.

It feels like I'm inside my own brain for the first time since Spanish class. Estoy adentro de mi propio cerebro para la primera vez desde clase española. The first baby of the girl with flippy hair is getting ready to start kindergarten. Tasha Mills wears annoying pants that stop just below butt cleavage when she goes to the grocery store, but this doesn't bother me. Not anymore. I know where Curtis had his heart; I know why Curtis had his heart there. I miss him but I love him, and that's all I can do. I have visited his mother twice this week while Aranea recovers in the hospital. I brought her a plush owl and she gave me the football jersey that he used to wear when we wrestled. She cries when she sees me but the time between tears is becoming longer. She asks about the girl I was with at his funeral. I tell her that she used to be my dream girl in high school, and how divine intervention and a likeable amount of my own dumb luck have kept her in my life. Crystal smiles and asks me if she is my girlfriend. I shake my head and tell her that Aranea might be my best friend. I love her now in the way I was meant to, and with the merciful hands of God I will avoid further complications. The message was not subtle. I'm casually dense. Now I will look both ways before crossing the street. La vida continúa.

Aranea came home on a Wednesday and I moved all of the cardboard boxes into her empty rooms. Some nights when I drive to visit her I stop in a fast food parking lot and stare at the dollar value menu. When I was in high school I imagined taking Aranea out for steak dinners, where I would order expensive bottles of French wine and laugh to her over candlelight about scientific and humanistic rationalism. Now I know that she prefers the to-go salads that come tossed in plastic cups and the character-shaped cookies. I never bring her food because I know how uncomfortable it makes her. She always tries to have a candy bar or a cupcake around for my visits because she knows how uncomfortable it makes me feel to think that she doesn't eat. The bulimic boy gets force fed out of pity and the anorexic girl doesn't get any food. We live such wonderful, rational lives. We talk about cartoons over candlelight.

The front yard of her duplex is beginning to fill in nicely. The rains have washed loose soil into the trenches and left dusty, hardened mud after humid October afternoons. Aranea's neighbors have decorated with a laundry-stuffed scarecrow on their side of the porch and jack-o-lantern trash bags in the grass. The bags are usually only half-full, resulting in a muddy yard full of bean bag chairs. I want to climb to her roof and leap off onto them. I could drop a big elbow and send leaves everywhere. I choose not to do this because I'm wearing nice clothes. My Halloween costume is in a paper grocery bag in the backseat of my Mom's car. I agreed to give Aranea a ride to her youth group's own party to guarantee point A reaching point B without vehicular manslaughter. I chose to wear a dress shirt and tie in case the worst happens. S. Anderson is still wrapped in bandages in the intensive care unit. I still think about him. Dr. Dorian told Mrs. Anderson that the hospital could keep him alive artificially for two weeks. I still think about him and I have prayed a lot during the week, and plan to pray for the second week as it comes. I think about visiting him to peel back the gauze and know him. I am still afraid to see him but not to be him. I congratulate myself for making progress. I don't even want to piledrive the scarecrow.

I knock on her door and place bets on her costume. I pray that she doesn't dress in leopard-print clothes, paint whiskers on her face, and try to pass herself off as a "cat." Every trite girl does that for Halloween. She is walking around the base of the pedestal she once lived upon. She sits in the shade of it and picks flowers. She is not a figment of my imagination or an idealistic dream of self-worth. She is a human being. She is deeply flawed. This is no reason for her to let me down by picking a sub-standard Halloween costume. The left side of my brain says angel. The right side of my brain says hobo, or pirate.

She opens the door in blue jeans, a red t-shirt with the word "terrific" embroidered across the chest, and a tiger mask. Not a mask that looks like a tiger. A tiger mask. The Tiger Mask tiger mask. A yellow hood that covers all but her eyes and chin from the lips down, decorated with black tiger stripes, white fur along the cheek bones, and a red jewel in the center of the forehead. Aranea has her hair tied up and stuffed inside of the mask as well. This makes her head look huge atop her gaunt shoulders; her face adorned with a beautiful smile and cold, black eyes. In this mask I am willing to desert all of my character development and forego the rest of my cognizant life to wrap my arms around her ankles and live in a box at the foot of her bed, but I bite my tongue hard enough to turn the taste buds into diamonds and remain as developed as I'm ever going to be.

"Is that your costume?," she asks. "What are you supposed to be, a Mormon?"

"Yes, actually. My wife dressed up as a hobo, and my other wife is going as a pirate. I've got a great book I'd like for you to read." Aranea smiles and laughs lightly, tracing a design about her abdomen. I know that the heavy breaths hurt her on the inside. My bad comedy probably hurts her brain. Puns alone have left my cerebrum looking like cheese. Brain d'Amour cheese. "My costume is in the back seat. I was going to change when we got there."

"Do you like my costume?"

"I kind of want to give you the flying head butt."

"Is that another one of your euphemisms?"

"No, absolutely not. I'm so far from euphemism that my footsteps turn to fossils before euphemism shows up. Some things in life work best without connotation, even if it takes twenty-two years and six minutes to figure that out." With her back to me Aranea closes and locks her front door. She turns to me and, without raising her head or making eye contact, presses her masked forehead into the center of my chest. "I respect you enough to actually want to give you the flying head butt."

"You want to hit me in the face with your forehead and I feel strangely relieved. What a queer relationship." Aranea looks up at me. Poets feel insightful when they describe eyes as "pools" of anything, but her eyes look like empty concrete holes. The filters are still there and operational but the water is gone, every drop. It makes no sense to me how one could be drained of life but still move. She still feels and her heart still beats. It felt like she was leaving me while she was strapped to my back. I couldn't see myself in the whites of her eyes or the frozen onyx of her pupil. Without the green flecks to color myself with I began to grow on my own. My lessons in understanding are passionate but still infantile. I am a pathetic leaf sprouting up through the soil into a world that will probably bomb the hell out of me. I wanted to reach into Heaven but it was the journey to the top soil that was passing me by. I touch her cheek and she doesn't pull away. We have evolved this much. She knows that I feel this pain without saying a word. I know that she trusts me but can't understand why I've done so much wrong. She closes her eyes and hugs me for no reason beyond the knowledge that I will hug her back.

The drive to the church is silent. Aranea rides with her feet close together. We listen to the radio. There should be an appropriate song to mark this moment but we only find car commercials. At the third light I hit red, and look right to see Aranea with her head tilted against the headrest staring back at me from beneath the tiger mask. She is expressionless but smiles when I notice her. She turns her face from me and leans her forehead against the passenger side window. Her head rests there until her eyes glance up to see a solitary man piloting a car three times the size of mine. Aranea quickly looks forward to avoid eye contact and then looks at me. She raises her right index finger horizontally and drags it across her throat, crosses her eyes and sticks out her tongue. Surrounded on the street by sports utility vehicles we sit silently in the car with each other. When the light turns green we both laugh, and our moment is marked by the quiet mumbling about finance rates and credit qualifications at the end of the commercial.

The church parking lot is empty to accommodate the fractal swirls of children darting back and forth across the pavement. They hold "trick or treat!" bags decorated with witches and ghosts or plastic pumpkin pails with black handles. The smart children who value productivity over style carry pillow cases. I park my die-cast car between a Lexus and a Hummer on the side of the road. Minivans are parked in the grass. A traveler on a bike would have to lift his bicycle above his head and sidle carefully pass along the road. The decorations, lights, and candy are all orange as advertised. Gray clouds in the sky block out the last few half hours before sunset. The tips of my fingers are cold but my palms are warm. Aranea is instantly met by gatherings of well-wishers who make high pitched vowel exclamations like "oh" and "ee." They all ask the same things. "I'm so happy to see you! How is your stomach?" "I love your mask, what is it supposed to be?" "You look so cute robble robble robble." I squeeze Aranea's hand and tell her that I'm going to find a bathroom and change into my costume.

The fellowship hall is full of people who have only seen me in passing. Two pirates, two hobos, three girls with their faces painted like cats. One small child is dressed as a ninja. His mother has him by the wrist and looks away as he stomps and whines, so I question his stealth. People glance over their shoulders at me as I pass, possibly mistaking me for a Mormon but realistically because I am a casual stranger. I am a face counter-culture enough to be remembered but not nominal enough to recall. They smile and nod so I smile and nod. It is all very nice and reminds me of my own family get-togethers. My Aunts and Uncles with give me hugs and firm handshakes and ask me how I'm doing in school, so I have to tell them for the second straight year that I'm not in school anymore. They nod and smile so I nod and smile. They sit in circles to count their blessings. I usually sit outside on the steps. If I smoked I would be the black-sheep brooding-artist of the family, but I don't, so I'm usually just lonely. I pass the costumed masses in the fellowship hall and consider joining my family's circle at Christmas, if only briefly.

I am forced to look into the face of my father in the mirror. For years I have longed to break free from the plastic novelty handcuffs of my marginally tortured adolescence. Now the days of blemished misunderstandings are leaving my face, so I stay focused on the ones that remain almost obsessively. As I dip my fingers into the white makeup I turn my head forty-five degrees to the right and see the fading pink scar behind my ear. Nobody notices it unless I show it to them, which fits. It helps me to remember that my internal scars are just as cosmetic and fleeting as the external, and that remorse for dancing Smurfs hurts me only like a bad hair cut in the long run. Being afraid to die is being afraid to ever be scarred. Everyone tells me that it's just part of life, and that life goes on beyond it. It helps to think that the people I love have died in the last twenty years or so, so that if only one hundred forty-four thousand people get into Heaven we'll all be waiting outside of the doors together. I smear streaks across my cheeks and chin, turning the pale paper of my face into a blank sheet of white. I use six containers of white to cover my forehead. I should've gone as "hyperbole" for Halloween, but it would've been hard to get people to believe my costume. Dress clothes disappear beneath a long black robe and I slide a black hood down just far enough to cover my eyebrows. A plastic scythe is easily assembled even in a church bathroom. I grimly reap my way back out into the fellowship hall.

Cubes of ice are left to melt in a bowl of orange punch a few feet from the restroom so I carry them off to the land of the dead, my stomach. I look around for Aranea over the lid of the Dixie cup. Older people without costumes are seated at tables on the left side of the room, eating miniature ham biscuits off of paper plates. To the right, people are predictably bobbing for apples. If they dive deeply enough into the water to pull out an apple with their teeth they win an apple dipped in caramel. This week at the grocery store we are offering bags of apples for a dollar twenty-nine, buy one get one free. Nothing celebrates a pagan holiday of death like almost drowning for produce. Then again, I'd rather blindly suck water up my nose than visit my grocery store. I turn around to look for Aranea outside when the paper or plastic hand of irony (or an ironic lack of irony) meets me face to face.

"What's up? Wait...Brooks?" Simon punches me in the arm and smiles. He is wearing baggy jeans, steel-toed boots, and a faded heavy metal t-shirt. He continues, "Talk about the last person I expected to see here. What's up, man?" Before I can answer he turns around and motions across the room. "Scotty! Scotty, dude, come here!" He turns to face me again. "I didn't know you went to church. I don't ever see you unless you're at the grocery store. What're you doing here?"

"Well," I begin.

"Brooks!" Scotty interrupts. "The grim reaper! That's tight! I used to draw the grim reaper all the time, I've got a big pencil sketch of him riding a dragon on my art folder. What's up, man?" Scotty is dressed similarly to Simon, but with less upper body mass and more unkempt facial hair. He has a nu-metal beanie pulled down over his ears.

"I'm fine. I was..."

"I was going to invite you like, last week," Scotty nods. "But you called in twice."

Ignoring him and out of general curiosity I ask, "Why didn't you guys wear costumes?"

"We did wear costumes," Simon affirms. "We're dressed as serial killers!"

Scotty adds, "Yeah, they look just like everybody else!"

"With that logic aren't you also both dressed like child molesters?"

"Dude," Simon exclaims, noticeably punching Scotty a lot harder in the arm than he punched me. "Did you see Jenny Eyres? She's dressed like a harem girl."

"What's a harem girl?" the lesser of two indifferences asks.

"Like a belly dancer."

"Oh, sweet." My partner in commerce raises his hand to shake mine. "I'm gonna go check that out, good to see you man, take it easy."

"Yeah, you too." He shakes my hand with his fingers instead of his palm and this bothers me. As they walk away I hear Simon complain that he's, "going to just be a pirate" next year. Scotty retorts with, "butt pirate." I laugh, because this is tastefully perverse for a church party and because the greatest gift my Lord has ever given me is the desire to be better than I usually am.

The conversations around me are joyful and make me happy by proxy. I listen to the story of how a middle-aged lady in a mauve business suit couldn't afford to buy groceries for her family until a mysterious donation in the form of an envelope full of twenty dollar bills showed up in her mailbox. A blonde-haired little girl dressed as a princess with chubby legs pelts a boy dressed embarrassingly by his parents as a cowboy in the head with a foam ball. A painting of Jesus with his hands over the eyes of a blind man hangs over the entranceway. Christianity has bred war, hatred, bigotry, and suffering. It can never be dismissed as trite or unimportant. At the same time it is not unrealistically pure. I could never believe in something like that. It's like rooting for a hero with no flaws. The golden streets and Kingdom of Heaven aren't what I'm in this for anymore. I don't really need "rewards." To me, being a Christian is wanting to be more than you've ever been. God made us in his own image and even he didn't get us completely correct. If even the one perfect Christian doesn't always do the right thing it gives me hope that I can be more like him. He gives us so many dumb little details I couldn't help but give him love in return.

An elderly lady with chamomile skin is sitting in a chair by herself. Children are playing through her feet but she doesn't move to suit them. Her hair looks like cotton growing from stalks on her head. She sits with dark, spotted hands in her lap, waiting for someone, and I find myself standing before her before I can speak or breathe. The woman has her eyes closed and I can see her chest moving slowly beneath her floral-print church dress. Her presence is immobile and undefined in a room full of clowns and demons. Teeth chatter in her mouth. She begins to speak but refrains. I want to kneel but remain standing. I reach to her face with my white, powdered hand and leave a touch of bleached dust with my fingertips. Fingers tremble. Hers. Mine. I want to give her what she needs for completion but I am only a facsimile, a fractured boy in a costume. A black balloon brushes past her on an undefined wind. My body is cold. I feel like I'm lying in the open on a late Autumn night. My fingers are numb now. The fear wants to overtake me. She calls my name.

"Brooks!" I turn to see Aranea standing in the doorway, waving. As she walks closer she sees the punch bowl, points to it, and gives me a thumbs up. "Orange," she mouths. I turn to the woman in the chair and she is looking at me, stabbing me with sharp-fingered eyes.

"I have been afraid for her for many days," the woman says clearly. "I have been afraid that she would come for me. But her eyes are dead. Her hair is dead. I am not afraid. It is not me they are coming for."

"I thought she would have more time than this," I say quietly.

"Then you know what she is?" the teeth chatter.

"I didn't for the longest time." The woman opens her mouth to smile. Her teeth are distant but white; her gums omnipresent but a bloody red.

"Don't fall in love with yourself, boy. It's only a costume. It won't be long now. I can feel the breath leaving me. It won't be long now."

Behind me I can hear people staring. I didn't realize that so many of them knew. If it had just sank in one day and they accepted it. Aranea approaches me and places her palm across the face of her mask. The woman closes her eyes and lowers her head.

"This mask is starting to squeeze my head," Aranea laughs. "I don't know how that guy wrestled in it. Somebody hugs me and my ears turn purple." She rubs her ears with both hands and smiles at me, but sees my blank expression and matches it. "What's the matter?"

"I don't know. This just doesn't feel right."

"You're right," she nods. "I should've said 'why so grim?' That would've been a lot funnier."

"No, Aranea, I'm serious." The woman begins to smile again with her eyes closed, and a part of me, a sticky, sore part of my stomach, starts to churn. "I don't think it's a good idea for us to be here."

"Getting spooked by the decorations? I saw a ghost hanging up that said boo on it and…"

"Aranea…" says the woman from her darkness. Aranea kneels down before her and places her palms over the hands.

"Yes, ma'am?"

"I was so afraid of you."

Aranea's movements go from brisk to solid stone in an instant. She raises up and takes a step back, pressing her back against my chest to divide the reaper from the woman. Aranea reaches behind her head to untie the laces of her mask. The knuckles on her fingers graze my chin. Her hands are frantic but focused. She removes the mask and casts it to the floor. No movement is unnecessary.

"You don't have to be afraid of me," Aranea says. "I'm not here for you."

"I was wrong. I wasn't meant to fear you. I need to know if you will be here for me. I need to know if you will be here for me when they come."

"It's not so bad."

"You aren't here for me but I need you."

Aranea nods. "I know."

"I'm going to die," the woman cries.

Aranea nods. "I know."

"They're going to come for me," the woman cries.

Aranea nods. "I know."

"But they're coming for you first."

The room suddenly becomes as silent as a graveyard and I can hear the door to the fellowship hall swing open and come to an abrupt stop just a moment from the doorstop. With my hands on Aranea's shoulders I look back over my own to see five stunning teenage ivory figures with crystal blue eyes, tar black hair, and gracious smiles walking into the hall in single file. Where they walk, light follows. Their footsteps illuminate the shadows of the rooms. They are the same height. The have the same gait. One after another they enter the room as the crowd of people move to the walls. I can see Scotty, Simon, and a girl in a harem costume standing motionless. Aranea does not move her head but I can feel her body begin to shake. She presses her back even more firmly into my chest, and I can feel her shoulder blades moving beneath her shirt and skin. The only sound is a distant hymn that seems to ride on the wind. Even their footsteps are silent.

"But they're coming for you first."

"Brooks," Aranea whispers. "I need you to go. I need you to turn around and walk out of the back door and never look back."

"That would be lame," I whisper back. "I'm not going to leave you."

"Okay, good," she says. "I was lying anyway. I don't want you to go."

I turn to the door and Aranea turns with me, my hands on her shoulders and her hands around my fingers. The sisters are impossible to distinguish.

The first stands a foot away from Aranea. Each girl stands just behind and to the left of her predecessor, so that they look like mirror images of the same person. Only the first sister speaks. Artemis. I can't believe I remember their names. I remember them like ghosts. I look at them like ghosts. I can feel their warmth from where I stand. It rushes over us like a wave. When it surges the roots of Aranea's hair turn white. When it ebbs the darkness resumes.

Artemis says, "We've been looking for you," and never acknowledges my self or my eye contact.

"I know," Aranea sadly speaks. "I've always known."

"We would like to speak with you in the chapel. We would like to speak with you alone." Her voice sounds like she is speaking in a tunnel. The words are strong and loud but far away, and far apart. Each word is like a musical note. She sings to Aranea in prose. Drops of blood begin to run down my fingers. Aranea's fingers squeeze mine until her bones feel as thought they will break and fall to the floor in adhesive pieces.

"I didn't know how to make the black go away. It kept soaking in."

"You are forgiven, as the Lord commands it," Artemis states. "You are forgiven, as the Lord commands it," Ashley states. "You are forgiven, as the Lord commands it," Aeris states. "You are forgiven, as the Lord commands it," Adelle states. "You are forgiven, as the Lord commands it," Alexander states. "You won't be punished. Your tasks have been arranged. We would like to speak with you in the chapel. We would like to speak with you alone."

"Brooks," Aranea says, looking back at me. Her eyes have come to life and caught an emerald fire, burning me from the inside with happiness and lighting my face with a soft, conclusive glow.

"Hey," I say, taking her hand. The blood pours out like water down my forearm. "Don't be afraid." Aranea gives me a dispirited smile and mouths "thank you." I let go of her hand. She shakes some of the blood off onto the carpet and looks at the crimson cross in the center of her palm. Aranea looks down at my feet and laughs diffidently. With her sanguinary grasp she reaches down to grab her tiger mask. The girl I'd never talk to opens her mouth and can't find the right words. She hands me the mask, stained by her heart, and turns from me. The sisters lead her out through the fellowship hall doors in single-file.

I watch her until she exits, and keep watching for her even as the door shuts behind them. With the slam of the wooden hall door the mute on the room is removed, and conversations begin and end where they last found themselves. Scotty has pulled his beanie down sideways to impress the belly dancer. The ninja is stomping. The cowboy is throwing foam balls at the princess with chubby legs and the ice cubes in the orange Halloween punch are melted and gone away. I turn to scream at the woman with chamomile skin. She is sitting stagnantly with her eyes closed and her mouth agape. The white cotton of her hair has turned to black. The balloon is resting on the ground behind her. She is gone. Aranea couldn't save her. She is gone, and Aranea is gone.

"I was so afraid of you," I think to myself, and look back toward the door.

I am forced to look into the face of Brooks White in the mirror. The bathroom is the only place I know how to exist in. I can feel the tissue on the inside of my stomach become burned and tear. The green viscid fluid fills my throat. The green viscid fluid fills my head. Staring down at the little reflective puddle of water at the bottom of the toilet I can see her face. Not Aranea. Not the girl from Spanish class. I see my mother. I see my fathers with capital and lowercase F's.

I drive my finger into the back of my throat and I see myself. My reflection is there in the water. My small ears and big forehead. My chin. My eyes. I see what Aranea sees. If I am never free from this I will see this forever, and with all due respect to my bent psyche I don't need to purge to remember where I've been. I want to free myself from ceremonial defilement. Even during those days when I could not force myself to pray I lived my life on my knees. I will live there again, but I can have faith in myself for a day. If God knows me and God can hear me speak to him he knows what I'm going to say anyway, and this gives me enough time to grab my tiger mask and run my awkward run across the parking lot and into the church, leaving only a plastic scythe and an open stall door behind.

The church building is red brick and has white, crossed doors. Gravel from the parking lot is in my shoes. My lungs begin to heave. My tendons begin to stretch. The world moves in slow motion and I feel years older as I reach and push open the doors. The carpet is red and the walls are hospital white. Wooden Jesus is hanging on a cross above me. Dozens of red upholstered pews are fixed in rows leading to a pulpit laden with violets, dogwood flowers, and statues. Behind the pastor's lectern is a white angel statue that reaches up with open hands to the sky, to the hanging light fixtures. From across the room I can see the melancholy pulsation of angelic wings below the statue. The feathers are long and white but tipped with red. It drips onto the carpet and disappears into the color. As I approach them they take on the timid reservations of a dying bird; moving with no rhythm, looking worn and desperate for care. I can hear her crying. Aranea is crying red tears as she clutches to the base of the carving. Her shirt is torn and her wings are larger than her back or legs. They drip with blood from inside of her. She cries with the blood inside. I drop the mask and fall to my knees. Her sisters have left us here.

I crawl up the pulpit stairs and sit Indian style next to Aranea as she cries. I don't say anything dumb. I don't say anything at all. Beneath her ripped shirt I can see her bandages soaked with water. I try to wipe away the streams of blood on her face with the edge of my black robe, and this helps but leaves pink streams from green oceans down her white face. She rests her head on my knee as the pressure from her flapping wings mats my hair down onto my scalp.

After a few moments I ask, "How long can you stay?"

Aranea places her arms around me and buries her cheek into my chest. "You knew. You never told me that you knew." The grim reaper sits in the church pulpit silently holding the angel.

"What did they tell you?" She closes her eyes.

"The man who hit me. The man in the hospital. I have to take him."

"When does he leave?"

"In six days."

"I'm sorry," I say, brushing away a funereal strand stuck to her face.

"And when I go, I can't…"

"I know."

"Oh no, dude, don't be dead," she laughs. "I don't remember the rest."

"Why God, why would you take her away from me," I laugh along in monotone. "Why. Take me instead, God, take me instead."

"That's such a good speech. Thank you for writing it for me."

"It is not often that someone comes along who is a true friend and a good writer."

"I love that book."

"Me too."

Silence.

"One thing bothers me," I say, looking at the red watercolor covering the white stone angel.

"What?"

"I didn't think you were actually going to make the statues bleed."

"I know," she says, pressing her forehead into my heart as powerfully as her frail, dying body allows her. "Heh, ouch."

CHAPTER 19

"I fell out of the sky," she laughed. "I landed on a pile of grass and now my butt is wet."

"You're telling me that I get to go to Heaven." Solomon is sitting up in his intensive care unit hospital bed. His face is clean-shaven and his hair is combed to the side. His arms feel strong and his voice is deep and virile, like in the days when Delia looked at him with admiration. He was the king of his castle until walls were built up around him. The sores on his forearms are cleaned and have almost disappeared. His face feels firm. After this conversation is his going to don a jogging suit and do laps around the hospital. The angel of mercy is sitting Indian-style on the end of his bed. Her face is young and bright but strange looking; her ears masked by black rings of hair. The angels wings are stretched out into the room behind her, knocking over the waste basket and blowing about the tubes that hang meaninglessly from machines. "When do I leave?"

"In a few days," she says. "We have to make the proper arrangements and you have to actually die first. You're kept alive by machines. This one makes your lungs go up and down. This one regulates your oxygen intake. The one that looks like radar tells the doctors if your heart is beating or not." The angel smiles and raises two fingers. "It's actually really neat. You're like the bionic man."

"I'm so worried. I don't feel like I've done anything to earn a place in Heaven. I have so many questions. I never thought to organize them."

"There are way more than a hundred and forty-four thousand people in Heaven, Solomon, didn't you Revelation 7:9? There is a great magnitude of people there that nobody can count. Every nation, every color, all different kinds of babies and animals. I mean, all dogs go to Heaven, right? So that means there's like a billion dogs."

"A billion dogs?"

"Yeah, and as soon as you get there they give you harp lessons. Jesus gives you this little cloud to sit on and you play the harp all day. Heaven is a lot like Sunday service, only it will go on for ever and ever. Lots of sitting, lots of quiet time."

"Oh." Solomon turns his head and his hands search the bedside for his Bible and notes. He wouldn't be here without them. They could've fallen under the bed, or he could've left them at work. That would be stupid. He can never go back there. Not now. He is so ashamed. He wants to apologize and make things the way they were, when he was too afraid to be controversial and they were too notionless to stand out.

"Solomon, I'm just kidding around with you. Heaven is salvation, and salvation is what you make of it. As many or as few dogs as you'd like." Solomon shakes his head in disbelief.

"This is so hard for me to understand," he continues. "Why you've come to me now. I always imagined there would be so much more to dying than this."

"Well, the gist of this is that regardless of what you do and don't understand you'll be dead in a few days and you're going to Heaven, so you'd be doing yourself a favor by just relaxing here and trying to say goodbye to your wife before you're gone. She's going to be in Hell here on Earth without you."

"And what will you do when you return for me?"

The angel raises her eyebrows and scrunches her nose. "You walk into the light and then it's bliss forever. I was thinking about buying a flashlight and shining it on you from your doorway."

Solomon lowers his face to the pillow. He is bathed in light but can only see the commotion of heavenly wings knocking over the defibrillator from the corner of his eye. "If I can't tell her, does Delia know that I love her?"

"Yes. Of course she does."

"Then this is it? This is all there is?"

"This is it. This is all there is." The angel rises from her seat and kisses Solomon softly on the forehead. "God loves you, you stupid, stupid man."

"*I just never had the inclination to sing with them.*"

She told me that she hides her wings on the inside. I don't know how they fit, but I know that they were pierced when the fence post went through her. They kept the point from going straight through her spine and out of her back. The tips bleed when she exposes them. Doctors and nurses in the hospital talked amongst themselves and treated it like any physical abnormality, like elephantitis or a third nipple. Some went home to tell stories at dinner about the weird girl full of feathers at work. Others are not paid enough to blink their eyes. Aranea balances herself onto a step ladder and leans up to pull a thick book from the top shelf. I can see bandages peeking out from beneath her shirt and smile at the unbearable remarkableness of predetermined coincidence.

"You know, Heaven isn't really anything like these illustrations. For starters, we aren't all naked children." College girls in arm chairs across the bookstore look up from their beauty tip and hairstyle magazines to glare condescendingly at Aranea tottering on the ladder. Her hair is wrapped in braids around her hairline like a crown of leafy thorns. Her shoes are plat formed to a degree that she could balance a ladder on the ladder and be safer at the height. If she falls I am there to catch her. I don't blame the girls for looking at her that way. Her hair looks ridiculous and it took me years to learn how to look at her they way I should. "I should take this back with me."

"Haven't you heard that expression, you can't take it with you when you go? You can stand at any point in the continental United States, close your eyes, and point and you'll be pointing at a more original thought."

"Why wouldn't I be able to take it with me when I go?" Aranea smiles at me from four feet above. "I mean, I'm going to buy it. I don't want to just leave it sitting somewhere."

"I don't know, I was under the impression that you were too happy in Heaven to worry about having things."

"What fun would Heaven be without stuff? God made all of these things. He planted the ideas for all of the books and gave talent for all of the paintings and photographs. That'd be like writing a love poem just to ball it up and throw it in the trash."

"You're right. But we only know what we've been told."

"It's so sad that more people don't realize that these books and pictures are all love letters to the world. From the people who create them and the people who created the people. It's so basic and easy to understand that everyone second guesses it. Like there's got to be something more complicated behind it all.

I mean, when you sit down to paint a picture you don't scratch your chin and go 'hmm, I'm going to paint a masterpiece.' It's more like, 'hmm, let me paint a big bowl of fruit.' It just comes out 'masterpiece.'"

"You took the same art courses that I did. It was either 'hmm, let me paint a bowl of fruit,' or, 'dude, I'm totally going to draw a naked lady with a machine gun.'"

"That's why you put your trust in God's hands. He lets you know to paint the bananas instead of being a big walking banana."

"Hah, was that a euphemism?"

"Yes, yes it was."

"You know," I say, pulling a copy of <u>Charlotte's Web</u> off the shelf and dropping it into Aranea's shopping bag, "you can be pretty creepy sometimes."

She laughs and places the illustrations of Heaven back on the shelf. Aranea reaches under her shirt and gently slides her index and middle fingers into the top of the bandage. After a few moments she pulls out her fingers and a bloody, three-inch long feather. She holds it out and lets it drift gracelessly down into my outstretched and opened palms. "I know," she nods. "Hey, wait a second."

I ask, "What? Is everything okay?"

"Do they use ladders in wrestling?"

"Sometimes."

"This whole time you've been standing under me you've been thinking about what wrestling moves you could do to me, haven't you?"

"No. Not even once."

"Which one did you decide on?"

"The powerbomb."

"I've got turkey and cheese and other stuff, we can sit here and make sandwiches and wait for the stars to come out, and it'll be nice. I can show you where I fell from. It's the big white one."

Aranea has been sitting on her couch for fifty-five minutes, waiting for me to return from the kitchen with a bowl of instant pasta that takes six minutes to cook. In the last week she has died and come back to life in the time it would take a normal man to prepare such a simple delicacy, but these are no ordinary circumstances and I am no ordinary man. I am the iron chef confederate; my body trained with binging and purging and my skill enhanced by the no-stick frying pan.

"Okay," I say, walking into her living room in an apron and two oven mitts. "I made two sandwiches, one for me and one for you."

"Oh, Brooks," she says as I set the plates down onto the coffee table. "Grilled cheese sandwiches. This is the big pay-off for all we've been through."

"It came out of nowhere, just like you promised. You sent me in expecting common spicy noodles and instead you found culinary enlightenment."

"There won't be grilled cheese sandwiches like this in Heaven." Her mouth is full and volcanic cheese stings her bottom lip. The words are funny and mumbled but the sentiment is there and appreciated more than I can tell her with an empty mouth. The word "cheese" sounds like "chief." It makes me want to be a better chef.

"Here, you can have mine." I lift up from the table and slide the sandwich off onto her plate. "I'll have no sandwiches and you can have two."

"Ooh, opposites day," she says, squinting her eyes and snorting.

"Ooh, opposites day, hur hur," I say, opening my eyes wide and bucking out my teeth. Aranea throws herself against the back of the couch and laughs as loudly and for as long as she can, holding the remainder of the grilled cheese in both hands.

"If I were a vulture I would pick you out of a field of dead people."

Lying back on the rooftop Aranea Cavatica stares up at the bottom of the rain clouds and plans to leave after dark, to see the stars shine brightly as she ascends. She has been practicing in her backyard and can now carry two suit-cases though the air, with enough dexterity to look up for ten to fifteen seconds at a time. Before she goes she wants to fly with her face to the moon, because looking down will remind her of all the things she can't take with her when she goes—the things she can't lift. Metal cheeseburgers. The dogwood tree. She has taken pictures of them and adhered them behind plastic sheets in an album.

She flips through the black and white photographs of her childhood and the moments she chose to save here and there. The most special ones are removed from the album and taped to the outside of the suitcases. A picture from the Kid's Haven Memorial swing. The time she spent alone in church as a child staring up at the angel statue. The view from her hospital bed. Always alone.

The one she cherishes the most is scotch taped to the top of her big bag: She and Brooks on the roof with an arm draped over the others' shoulder, two fin-gers raised, with their lower bodies obscured by blankets and empty Ziploc bags. The night sky looms behind them in the photo, so even if Aranea loses her vision and gets lost in the black of night she can look over her shoulder and see the stars.

For God so loved the world, that he gave his only begotten son. His daugh-ters were all perfect and stayed in Heaven by his side. They weren't really his daughters in the way that Jesus was his son, but God chose to love them each the same, as he tries to do, according to the information we're given, for all of us. God has created so many things if you believe. Man. The Heavens and the Earth. Cotton candy. The sun. The rain. Clowns and ninjas. When you've writ-ten so much the words begin to run together, and sometimes you forget why you wrote something, or how you were feeling at the time, or what you origi-nally had in store. God created his smallest daughter. She was all wrong. Her eyes were green instead of blue, and her hair was solid white, no color at all. He could not remember why he created her but her curious flaws touched his heart. He loves her and misses her voice. He listens to her heart and longs for the day when she will keep him up at night playing songs on the harp, messing up notes and having to start over again. He named her after the spider's web. One day he dropped her. Lost her somewhere. He tries to speak to her but she doesn't know where to listen. He digs graves and waits for her, alone.

The storm is beginning to pick up now. Dark gray circles form in patterns across the shingles. Aranea listens to the thunder and feels the icy pricks on her cheeks. They help to wash away the blood she cries. She has come here tonight to say goodbye to her house and to herself. On the rooftop nobody can hear or see her if she collapses. Her fingers catch raindrops. Her life has been happy. Distantly she wonders what it would be like to spend the rest of it. She wonders about distrust and lack of faith. Her mind experiments in pieces with longing. Heaven is where she belongs and she will be happy there, but she will miss this life. She will miss life. Life was her Father's gift, for her loved her enough to want this for her. Aranea is secretly envious of the people who have babies, share kisses, dance into the night to music they can't understand. They are techno remakes of her favorite old songs. They are beautiful, because geniuses are people who finish things. When they are done she will see them again. She will be sitting in paradise while everyone else mires in these yard trenches. The rain forms a stream of force around her face as she mixes the red and green but never white.

Her body begins to absorb the acids and dust from these falling tears. Life is not her only gift. She was given the love of petty things to carry with her for not only these years, but for eternity. Aranea stands and reaches her arms up to the sky. Her wings unfold and lengthen into the droplets, breaking them, scattering them across the roof and onto the ground. The wind fills the wings and pushes her back but she remains balanced, her hands falling down over her face, the cross on her palm dried up and stitched. Her temptation to fly away, to soar somewhere distant over the salty waters is great. She could live on these memories, live in these things forever, or at least until they come for her again.

The runt of the Cavatica litter, the only Cavatica he ever created, throws herself to the rooftop and lets go. The blood squeezes from her sinuses and from pockets beneath her eyes and heats her face. The heat is too much to handle, like fire across the bridge of her nose. She screams and digs her fingernails into the roof. She slams closed fists down to crack the shingles. This is not what she wants. Her brain loses focus and the tears come heavier than the rain or the reality. She cries for the pain she has experienced in her life here. She cries for the fence post in her abdomen. She cries for her cross. She cries for all of the stupid things that Christians cry for, like poverty and hunger and agony. She cries for her knowledge and for the things she will never learn. She sobs for Brooks. For Brooks, she sobs.

"Hey," Brooks says, taking her hand. Her blood is all over him. She wants to wipe it off with her shirt. The shirt is red. You couldn't even see it. "Don't be afraid," he whispers.

She lies in a puddle of her blushed tears as the rain falls harder than before. It hurts her neck. The wings that will fly her to Heaven lay limp against her back, soaked in the downpour, too heavy for her to stand. As she blinks the water dribbling down from the top of her head turns from clear to a sickly, clouded black. The black water leaves dyed stains on the tip of her nose. With her hand she reaches to feel the source and feels a puddle of ink on her crown, and when she pulls away to look at her fingers they are ebony and sable. Frantically she runs her fingers through her hair. The nails catch themselves in a curl and it hurts when she pulls, but she doesn't feel the pain. Raven designs litter the red ooze beneath her. Just as she prepares to cry out she catches a glimpse of a pure, ivory strand of hair falling down between her eyes.

Aranea begins to cry again but the blood filters out into water. She begins to laugh. Her smile grows out for miles. The laugh can be heard in the houses up and down Whitestone Drive. The smile can be seen out as far as she can feel. Kicking her feet she rolls her heavy feathered appendages over and lies on her back, yelling and howling until the rain stops an hour later.

"I'm not qualified to write your biography or anything, but it looks like you've gotten all the bad stuff in your life out of the way early so it's nothing but daisies and waterslides from here on out."

When it is time to say goodbye we meet at the Old City Cemetery. Aranea stands two feet in front of me with a duffle bag thrown over her shoulder. Her body looks strong beneath a white tank top for the first time since I've known her. Where she walks she leaves a trail of feathers in the mud. The joints in her wings remind me of how many parts of Aranea that I'll never get to see. I won't get to see her grow old. I won't see her skin wrinkle or her lips splinter and peel with age. I'm so happy for her. She wears a broken piece of a handcrafted opalescent glass angel on a black string around her neck.

"I'm surprised that the birds didn't show up for this." I look down over the grave placards. She first hugged me a hundred feet from here.

"I'm not officially leaving until tomorrow morning at twelve forty five. They'll probably fly me out, as high as they can go." Aranea scratches her nose and sighs. "A wind is coming by in a few minutes to pick me up. I have to get ready. It's a long trip."

I ask, "Aren't you cold in that?"

"Yes," she laughs, "I'm freezing. But I need the shoulder room." She stretches her arms out to the sides and makes the wings flap. We stand in the dead silence for a few minutes, or moments, or days.

"Hey," I say, without even attempting the right words.

"Hey," she says, without a pause. She walks toward me with a smile but before she can hug me I lean down and wrap my arms around her waist. I lift her up from the ground and squeeze her as delicately as I can. With surprise she pushes her palms against my shoulders and yells. Her wings extend and raise up to block out the afternoon sun. When we are still she lowers to her elbows and scratches the back of my head with her fingernails. One last time she wraps her arms around my shoulders and hugs me here, because she is always here. She is always everywhere.

"Brooks," she whispers.

"I know," I whisper back. "I'll see you in a few?"

She opens her mouth wide and grins. A penetrating gust hits me from behind and pushes me a few steps forward, and I can feel her begin to rise. "In more than a few." Aranea nods and presses her forehead against mine as hard as she can. In this movement I can remember the grilled cheese and the wrestling, the speeches and the violence, the beginning and the end.

I open my hands and the wind takes her away, propelling her backwards over the cold, filled graves and into the sky. As she goes she opens her palms to me and waves with her middle and ring fingers. She mouths the word "good-bye," but I just raise my hand and smile to her. Aranea turns and rises into the sky. I turn from her and walk back through the Potter's Field gates.

When I have walked for a few dozen yards I stop and close my eyes. I turn and open them. The sky is empty and off-white. I stand there quietly for a moment before turning again and walking to my car, never giving myself another moment to look back.

Dear Aranea Six Years From Now,

Hi! How are you? I am doing great (but since your me you hopefully already know that!). If you have not changed your name by now I'm gonna time travel to the future and kick your butt!

This is a letter I have to write for class for a time capsule so that when I graduate I can remember what it is like to be 12. I do not think I will be much different than I am now so I made a list of things I hope to have done and here they are:

1) I hope you have moved out of Illinois and have moved somewhere wicked awesome like New York City or Paris or at least somewhere near a lot of waterslides because waterslides are really fun!!

2) I hope you are in school and learning about all kinds of neat things and that daddy has gotten a better job and doesn't have to keep moving around. If you read this tell him that one day he will win the lottery and not have to dig holes anymore! But I hope he has already.

3) I hope you have found somebody who takes care of you and is not mean to you, and who doesn't make fun of your teeth or your hair. I hope you are still eating a lot.

4) Do not give up! Your dreams will come true if you just believe in yourself and hang in there. The cat hanging from the branch would not lie to you even if that poster was made in the 70s like I have heard.

Keep God's love in your heart and a smile on your face and every-thing will be okay. You have a guardian angel looking out for you so do not mess it up. I do not know how much Jesus pays them so make it worth there time.

Yours till Niagara falls,
Aranea C. Cavatica

Epilogue—November

A thin man in sandals is standing with his fists raised in the Crawford dorm. He has a thin, dirty beard and long hair that greases together at the ends. He bounces on the balls of his feet. "I don't know what you think you're doing. There's no way you could ever take me down," he says.

"This isn't a matter of 'taking you down,'" asserts Kirby Takahata, locked in a tiger stance. Her full body weight, one hundred six pounds, is on the back leg, with the forward leg weightless and resting on the heel. The toe is pointed upwards in preparation for a hooking kick or sweep. Hands are held ready in the protecting hands form. Her nails are painted sparkly pink. She has practiced the tiger stance in this hallway for every minute of the three hours since inviting him here. "This is a matter of revenge!"

"I see you looking to me in class. You want answers from me." The man confidently laughs. "It was merely a coincidence. Just because they looked the same doesn't mean I copied you. It's just homework!"

"It was my philosophy homework," Kirby bellows. "It took me years to reach that kind of enlightenment!" With grace she moves from tiger stance to the bow stance. With her fingers she challenges her opponent to "bring it." Feeling insulting the man swings wildly with a left hook. Kirby blocks the forward motion by jabbing her right elbow into his wrist, then extending her arm into a palm strike to the elbow. He recoils, staggering back a few steps and clutching his arm.

"Jesus!," he shouts. "You're as strong as the guys in carpentry class." The gaijin Asian princess taunts him once more.

Noticing a flaw in her stance at the knee he shifts his weight forward and attempts a powerful front kick. Kirby takes a step back and uses her shin to shift the momentum of his strike to the floor. With a swift downward motion she snaps her heel down into the bones of his foot, causing him to scream out in pain. The sandal goes flying across the hallway.

"Augh," he cries. "You nailed me! Right in my foot! Augh!"

Kirby stands straight up and bows. "Do you apologize for copying my ideas?"

"Yes," he shouts, hobbling on one foot and barely able to massage the sore, red spot with his hands.

"Good."

He asks, "So, can we go out now?"

"Yeah, of course," she says. "Just let me grab my phone. You wimp." Kirby laughs and pushes open the door to her dorm room. She trots across the room, making sure to step over the video game controllers, and snatches the cellular phone from her cubby. She turns to her roommate and her roommate's boyfriend and asks, "Are you two all right?"

Auburn speaks through her frown, barely moving her lips when she talks. "We're fine." The orange roots beneath her bleached tips are getting longer. With a sudden zest she begins to violently slam her thumb into the X button, coming out of her seat to growl and throw the controller to the ground. "Dammit!" she yells.

"Yeah, okay, you look totally fine." Kirby rolls her eyes and strides back across the room and out through the door, shutting it save for a crack on her way through. Auburn runs her hands through her hair and drops back into her seat, throwing her head back against the black metal bar.

For the rest of the afternoon and well into the evening they sit together, Indian-style on the futon, empty pizza boxes between them, saying nothing.

Acknowledgments

my sincere gratitude goes to the following—

emily rowley, for her personal assistance in the creation and editing of the story. For staying up late to help. For being a great friend and a good writer.

curtis bunch, for nodding when I needed nods and for giving me his name so I wouldn't have to type the real one.

karla jean davis, for authoring the cover photo and for being my helen of troy, the friendship that launched a thousand late night writing attempts.

leslie gilkenson, for being a wonderful cover model despite the rain and car accidents.

steve rice, for contributing his time and skill to the final cover design.

my mother and father, for avoiding cliché by not molesting me and actually staying married.

mr woodford, my creative writing teacher who taught me to love the written word vicariously through mindy compher and her dazzling personality.

to the women and men who filled the voice of auburn: **plato, jesse ventura, thomas hobbes, henry louis mencken, andrew lloyd webber, hitler, salvador dali, anais nin, hh munroe,** and countless others. okay, I don't give any acknowledgments to hitler.

0-595-27850-7